Praise for *Walks Alone*

"Compelling and heartfelt, *Walks Alone* is an extraordinary novel of hope, forgiveness in the great American west as cultures collide and a way of life fades forever. Author Sandi Rog is to be commended for her deft handling of one of history's most heart-rending events, weaving a story of love and redemption in the midst of unimaginable tragedy and loss. An absolute treasure of history and heart!"

LAURA FRANTZ
author of *Courting Morrow Little* and *The Colonel's Lady*

"A beautifully haunting tale, *Walks Alone* 'stands alone' as a love story that blazes a breathless trail across cultures and causes. With skill, sensitivity and rich historical detail, Sandi Rog woos both heart and soul on this unforgettable journey to love, faith and the true meaning of home."

JULIE LESSMAN
award-winning author of The Daughters of Boston Series and Winds of Change Series

"From the moment I opened the book and read the first page, Sandi Rog's novel *Walks Alone* captured my heart. If you love a beautifully written story with characters you will remember long after the book is done, then do not miss this one!"

KATHLEEN Y'BARBO
best-selling author of *The Inconvenient Marriage of Charlotte Beck*

"In vivid, colorful tones, Rog brings a fading Cheyenne world to life, creating an Old West that is both familiar and unusual to lovers of historical romance. *Walks Alone* contrasts the abrasive reality of an ancient nation in its final hour with the tender passion of a warrior for his captive. It's an irresistible love story that, alongside the knowledge of what brought the noble Cheyenne to their knees, will live long in the reader's heart."

APRIL GARDNER
best-selling author of *Wounded Spirits*

"*Walks Alone* is a story that took me from the New York harbor to the mountains of Colorado, and I enjoyed every step of the way. Ms. Rog pens a tale full of emotion and conflict with characters so relatable I was sorry to see it come to an end. I will definitely be looking for more of her works. This is a story I'm happy to recommend!"

LYNNETTE BONNER
Author of *Rocky Mountain Oasis*, *High Desert Haven*, and *Fair Valley Refuge*

"In *Walks Alone*, Sandi Rog brings alive a love story between unforgettable characters and handles with sensitivity a difficult period in American history."

JANALYN VOIGT
author of *DawnSinger*

"*Walks Alone* is the first book I've read by Sandi Rog, but I'm sure it won't be the last. Anna is a hurting child, desperate to be loved, and from the first pages I wanted to see her find a home and someone to love her. White Eagle might have been an Indian, or a savage according to Anna, but he was a gentleman even when she lashed out at him, fighting for her freedom. I couldn't help but fall in love with him, and couldn't wait to see where this unlikely couple would end up. If you are looking for a historical romance where different cultures clash, with nonstop action and lots of twists and turns, then you'll want to read *Walks Alone*. You won't be able to put it down. Great book."

LAURA V. HILTON

author of The Amish of Seymour Series, Whitaker House

"Ms. Rog delivers in shining a light on the Cheyenne tribe in this masterpiece. If only the teachers taught history like this in school! The setting, not to mention the characters, both vividly portrayed in this story, will transport the reader back in time. *Walks Alone* is a beautiful tale of love, hardship, forgiveness, and hope, along with a dose of acceptance. No matter what we've done, or how far we've run, *Ma'heo'o*'s (God's) outstretched arms are always there, ready and willing to forgive us. Beautifully done."

DEBORAH K. ANDERSON

monthly columnist for *Christian Fiction Online Magazine*

"What an incredible, heart-felt novel! Rich with Native American culture, intrigue, and romance, *Walks Alone* held me captive to the end. So many desperate choices necessary for survival had to be made, but the things the hero and heroine feared most also made them stronger in the end. The variety of emotions they experienced and the developing love between them compelled me to read on, and more than that, they caused my eyes to well with tears a number of times. I felt the characters' pain and sensed their relief as their many trials made them stronger once they realized they were not alone, but that God was with them all along. *Walks Alone* contains a lot of realism and spiritual depth, which made me think more about my own faith. Most of all, this is a story of unconditional love and finding true freedom in Christ. He wants us to come to Him because we love Him, not because we were forced. This novel is a beautiful portrayal of God's love for us and shows us why He gives us the freedom to choose. I loved *Walks Alone* so much that it's making my favorite fiction list for 2012!"

MICHELLE SUTTON

author of over a dozen novels

SANDI ROG

This is a work of fiction. All characters and events portrayed in this novel are either fictitious or used fictitiously.

WALKS ALONE

WhiteFire Publishing
13607 Bedford Rd NE
Cumberland, MD 21502

ISBN: 978-0-9834556-5-3

To my sisters, Kelli and Charis

Dear Readers,

I'm originally from Colorado and recently moved back to the States after living in Holland for thirteen years. But it took moving to the other side of the world to discover the truth about my home state and what happened to the Cheyenne Native American tribe, along with the Arapaho and Lakota tribes and other Nations, on the morning of November 29, 1864. This incident is known today as the Sand Creek Massacre.

Most of the events in this story related to Colorado's shameful past are true and accurate according to history—the massacre and its details (e.g. the toddler on the banks of Sand Creek), the popular saying in Denver "nits make lice" (a saying that made it acceptable for soldiers to murder innocent children), and some of Anna's words and experiences when she's abducted (taken from other white women who were abducted).

Cheyenne Chief Laird Cometsevah (a.k.a. Whistling Eagle) has read *Walks Alone* to check it for accuracy and is touched that a part of his tribe's culture and history is being told. While the Sand Creek Massacre is a disturbing event, I hope to not only give the Cheyenne tribe a voice, but to shine light on the hearts of these people.

Although my main character, White Eagle (a.k.a. Jean-Marc) is fictional, you'll notice he comes strikingly close to resembling the real man George Bent (a.k.a. Beaver), half-breed son of William Bent, frontier tradesman. George Bent was educated in white schools, fought in the Civil War, was at Sand Creek during the massacre, and then became a Dog Soldier and fought in the Indian Wars. His father was a Christian and his mother was a Cheyenne native, and he struggled between their two beliefs. It's because of George Bent that we are able to know not only the historical accounts of the Cheyenne, but also their cultural practices.

Come with me now as you read a story of forgiveness and love, unleashed in a world of misunderstanding and hate.

Sincerely,

Sandi G. Rog

Prologue

November 29, 1864
Sand Creek, Colorado Territory

A drop of blood warmed his finger, and crimson stained the white snow as Jean-Marc bound three dead rabbits together. "Sorry to kill you, my friends, but Mother and Grandmother need to eat."

He tied the knot fast and rubbed his hand along the soft fur. The skins would make a good muff for Grandmother this winter. He'd seen many white women wear them; they looked warm, and his *heveškemo* deserved the best.

He picked up the rabbits and added them to the other two he'd already tied together.

Running Cloud trudged around a thick cottonwood with his latest kill, a prairie dog, hanging at his side. "The chief has trained you well." He nudged with his chin toward the game Jean-Marc caught. "He'll smile on your success."

"You didn't do so badly yourself." Jean-Marc gave an exaggerated wave toward the fowl and two rabbits dangling over his friend's back. They hadn't found any deer or antelope, but what they did find was better than nothing. Jean-Marc's father would soon arrive from Denver City with supplies. Until then, he had to find other means to survive.

Running Cloud stomped through the snow toward him. "Do you think Gray Feather will be impressed?"

Jean-Marc chuckled and slapped his shoulder. "Take them to her father's lodge and see." Of course, they both knew Running Cloud's current offering was meager compared to the young buffalo he'd delivered to their lodge just four moons ago.

"And which woman do you plan to impress?"

Jean-Marc smiled. "My mother."

Black Bear stepped high through a powdery snow bank, carrying game over his shoulder. Twenty winters out of his mother's womb and a seasoned warrior, he wore the clothes of a brave with his tanned leggings, knee-high moccasins and silver armbands over his fringed buckskin shirt.

If only Jean-Marc could wear the silver armbands of a warrior. That'd make him a hero, a man. But to reach such a lofty position of honor among his tribesmen was not to happen. Torn between the white man's world and that of his tribe, he could never bring himself to fight against his own, let alone kill another man. Still, pangs of jealousy twisted in his gut. How would he ever become a man among the tribe if he refused to fight?

Bow and quiver strapped to his back, Black Bear glanced up through the cottonwoods. "We should get back before the sun stands straight up in the sky." His eyes flickered toward Running Cloud. "And before our mother starts to worry." He strode past them.

"We've only been gone one sun." Running Cloud fell in step behind him. "She knows we're hunting."

Jean-Marc glanced at Running Cloud and suppressed a smile. He knew Black Bear was merely attempting to annoy his younger brother, and by the scowl on Running Cloud's face, it had worked.

"We're only three winters younger than you. Besides, we're bringing food." Running Cloud stomped through the snow. "She'll be pleased."

Jean-Marc jogged ahead and untied the large dog that pulled a small travois piled with game and thick buffalo robes. They dropped their latest kills on the stretcher. He tugged on the dog's ropes and urged the animal forward.

Bending down, Jean-Marc grabbed a fistful of snow. As he patted it firmly into a ball, he contemplated his target. Black Bear was quite the brave, but would he be able to avoid a hit from Jean-Marc? He whisked around, took aim, and tossed the snowball at Black Bear.

Black Bear stopped. He looked at his chest, and then his eyes narrowed at Jean-Marc. He gathered his own snowball and threw it.

Jean-Marc ducked, and the white mass sailed over his head, missing him. A smirk of satisfaction tugged his lips into a grin, and he laughed.

All three tossed snowballs at one other. Eventually, they tested their strength to see who could throw the farthest. Snowballs sailed over the travois as the dog plodded ahead of them, until their fingers went numb from the cold. Drying his hands on his leggings, Jean-Marc walked backwards. His moccasins stamped a trail on endless acres of untouched snow.

Heavy breathing broke the stillness as they trudged through the wooded valley. When they left the cottonwoods behind, a cold wind stung Jean-Marc's cheeks, carrying an unfamiliar scent on the air.

He stopped, taking in his surroundings. Patches of snow dotted the stark landscape, and white flakes drifted over the ground like a wave foaming at his feet. He held out his hand to catch the falling snow.

Not snow. Ashes.

Dread crawled up Jean-Marc's spine. He lifted his face to the sky. A dark cloud swelled over the horizon, casting a shadow across the land. The black mass reached into the blue sky like a hand choking out the sun. He stared at the strange horizon. The village wasn't in sight, but the smoke came from that direction.

Fire.

He sprinted toward his home.

Mother. Grandmother.

"What caused it?" Running Cloud shouted. "It's too cold!"

"It's soldiers!" Black Bear raced ahead of them.

The answer made Jean-Marc's feet move faster. He charged over thick patches of snow and dead bushes. Cold slithered into his lungs, stretching icy fingers across his chest. But he kept running.

Gunshots sounded in the distance. He tripped. The frozen dirt bit into his fingers and knees.

Running Cloud yanked him to his feet.

Again, he sprinted toward home. His chest heaved painfully from the cold, heaved with every intake of breath.

Heaved.

Gunshots exploded louder over the plains, forcing his legs to pick up their pace. Several tribesmen ran toward them.

"Turn back!" someone shouted, and screams carried through the air.

Others took cover with their children in half-dug trenches.

Jean-Marc scanned the desperate people, searching for his mother. He looked for the colorful leather that dangled from her dark braids. The silver ring shining against her hand. Her buckskin dress with the blue and green pattern along its fringed hem. He didn't see her among the people escaping.

Voices shouted and screamed.

Jean-Marc jogged ahead. Song Bird stumbled toward him, her clothes torn, her arms sagging in anguish.

"Where's my mother?" He grabbed her by the shoulders and shook her. "Where is she?"

"I don't know!" Song Bird wailed. "They killed Gray Feather." She crumpled in his arms. "My girl, my little girl!"

Running Cloud appeared next to them, his almond eyes round with shock. "Gray Feather? Gray Feather is dead?"

Jean Marc watched as Running Cloud's shock turned to rage, a rage that matched his own. How could the soldiers attack? They knew this was a peaceful camp.

Shots sounded through the air, and sand exploded nearby.

"Take cover!" Jean-Marc pushed Song Bird toward safety and raced for the village.

He had to help the innocent. He had to find his mother. This village was filled with women and children and very few braves.

He stumbled toward the bank. A black cloud cloaked hundreds of distant lodges. Their burning scent invaded his nostrils. He dropped behind a snowdrift and rolled between thick underbrush, trying to find a safe place to hide and catch his breath. Running Cloud joined him. The acrid smoke hung in the air, and shots cracked above their heads.

The cry of a young child rushed to Jean-Marc's ears. He crawled on his belly and peered over the snowdrift between the dead brush. A small child stumbled along the other side of the bank, crying for his mother.

Another shot fired. Sand and snow near the toddler's feet spattered up from the ground.

The baby screamed.

"Let me try," a white soldier said, coming up on his horse. He dismounted, knelt down and aimed his revolver at the toddler, then shot.

Shrubbery against the bank split apart behind the baby. His black hair clung to the tears on his cheeks as he continued to wail for his mother.

Jean-Marc watched the soldier. Nothing was real. He was in a dream, like when he'd try to run after the buffalo but his legs wouldn't go fast enough. He forced himself to move and pulled an arrow from his quiver. His numb hands set the arrow against his bow.

He pulled the bowstring so tight it cut into his fingers. The muscles in his arms hurt as he aimed at the soldier's blue coat.

He'd never killed a man before.

He released the string.

The arrow sliced through the air.

Chapter

New York

Almost there. Her new home.

Freedom and grand dreams awaited, and Anna glided to them on a cloud across the ocean. The *Vesta* cut through waves as salt water sprayed her cheeks. Seagulls called above the sails that billowed into the sky.

It'd been two long months since she'd heard or seen anything other than the same groaning ship, the same hard working bodies of officers and crew, and the same gray water stretching across the endless horizon.

She brushed a strand of hair from her eyes and held her cap in place. Gulls soared above the towering masts and dove between the taut ropes that shot up and down on all sides of the ship. This was so much better than being tucked away in the cabin that rocked and creaked monotonously below deck.

"Anna!"

She turned to her father's voice but saw only faces of other passengers.

"Anna van Stralen!" her father called again.

She spotted him on the other side of the deck. She ducked under a rope, dodged past a couple, and tucked herself under his arm.

"There is it, my little one. America!" Papa whispered hoarsely through wind that whipped his blond hair above his collar. He hugged her to his side and pointed across the water.

Anna gripped the ship's railing and gazed through frigid air where mist rose to reveal a shadow of land in the distance. The scents of grasses, fresh water streams, and rich earth seemed to carry up like a faint vapor above the salty sea. What would it be like to have her feet on dry land again? She tried to imagine the trees and flowers, the cobblestone streets and houses, wondering how much they'd resemble Holland.

"There was your mother born long ago."

"Why are you speaking English, Papa?"

"I told you, when on America we arrive we must speak English. So, now we begin." Anna giggled.

He squeezed her close. "It were many years since I've used these words. Too many," he added with a shake of his head. "For this day on we speak English. The language of your mother."

"*Ya*, Papa." Even though she'd studied English, the thought of not speaking Dutch seemed strange to her.

"You are smart girl. You receive good schooling here. I make sure of it."

Sails whipped in the wind above their heads, and she huddled close to her papa.

He coughed into his kerchief, his breath evaporating into the crisp air.

"Maybe we should go below deck, Papa? *De* wind blows strong." Her tongue stumbled in her mouth every time she tried to hiss a "th" sound past her teeth. She'd struggled with it since trying to learn the language, and she hoped now that she was in America and surrounded by English, she'd master it.

"No, we are staying here. I dream of this moment for long time. We live in Denver City. Near the beautiful Rocky Mountains." He sighed. "You never saw mountains like in Colorado Territory. We raise cattle. I plan it all."

Anna grinned. They'd had countless conversations about their plans. She hugged him tighter at the thought of finally nearing their dreams.

"The Lord bring us so far."

Anna nodded, knowing full well they were spoiled by God. He always looked out for them. And she had no doubt He'd make their dreams come true. Despite never knowing her mother, Anna didn't feel like anything was missing in her life. She had everything she needed. As her father said many times, God always looked out for them.

"Mr. van Stralen," Mariska's voice called from behind them in Dutch. Anna's nanny pulled her heavy cloak closed against the breeze. "Would you like me to take Anna below deck?"

"No, that's not will be necessary." He waved her away. "This is special moments with my daughter."

Anna nestled under his arm for warmth. Speaking the new language felt like a game. She giggled.

"It's a bad time in the East," another passenger bellowed in Dutch to his friends as they walked by. "The North and South are still at war."

Concern clenched Anna's heart as the word "war" sank into her mind, dashing dreams of a new, happy life. She vaguely remembered hearing about the war before they left Holland.

"Be not afraid, little one. We not worry about that. The Lord protect us. Besides, we be far away from the fighting and death. We go west. To American frontier. *Denver City.* That is where we belong." His sky-blue eyes gazed out over the sea. "That is where we belong."

———⊶≋≋≋⊷———

Three weeks later and still in New York, Anna sat alone in the quiet hall of their rented, furnished townhouse. The large clock thrummed half past the hour, and she worried that each passing moment was one moment closer to her father's death. Each tick of the clock like a drop of water from a leaky faucet: drip . . . drip . . . drip. Each droplet, a draining of life. If only the incessant sound would stop. Wringing her hands to keep them from covering her ears, she stared through the banister at the Christmas tree in the parlor below.

Red ribbons and white popcorn draped around its greenery. Earlier that day Mrs. Stone, her father's lawyer's wife, had come to help Anna and her nanny decorate its branches. An effort to cheer her spirits. But Anna felt anything but cheerful. This would be the worst Christmas ever.

"Let him live, God. Please, let him live." She folded her hands until her knuckles turned white. "You made all those people in the Bible better, so I know You can make Papa well too." Yes. That was it. Jesus healed so many. He would heal Papa.

She sighed with relief, and her gaze fell on a newspaper lying on a small table next to her chair. The Dutch name Wynkoop caught her eye. Hands still folded, she leaned closer. It was page one of the New York Tribune where a Major Wynkoop told about his encounters with Indians in Colorado Territory. Her interest piqued as she read the words. Though they were in English, she was pleased she understood most of them. It'd always been easier for her to read the language than to actually speak it.

She became caught up in the story as she read about Col. John M. Chivington, who led a surprise attack killing Cheyenne and Arapaho Indians. Hundreds of women and children had been murdered. She couldn't imagine anything more horrible.

Those poor people. How could anyone be so cruel? Her father had nothing but good to say about the Indians he'd met along the Arkansas River. They had treated him with kindness and let him stay in their tent-like homes. Why would anyone want to kill them?

Indians.

She'd come to a land where Indians roamed. What did they really look like? Her father talked about them, had even described them in his stories about his long-ago travels to the West. It fascinated her to read about Denver City where she and her father would begin a new future. They were so near to their dream, and yet so far.

No, he wouldn't die. He couldn't die! They had to go to Denver to fulfill their dream.

"You may see him now." The doctor's voice carried down the quiet hall from her father's room.

Anna slid off the chair, bringing the paper with her. Perhaps reading about the West would help boost his spirits and make him well again? She'd try anything at this point. They'd been in New York much longer than planned.

When she entered the room, she walked slowly to his bedside and kissed his cheek. "I bring something for you, Papa." She spoke in English, remembering their promise. She held up the paper for him and pointed at the familiar Dutch name.

"Wynkoop?" Her father coughed then slowly turned his weakened gaze toward her. "As much as I'd like to, I can't read this right now." To her surprise and worry, he spoke Dutch.

Anna placed the paper on the nightstand. "I understand, Papa. You can read it later."

She straightened, trying to ignore how he'd changed in appearance just since their arrival in New York, his cheekbones more prominent, his skin pale, and his eyes surrounded by dark circles.

"Little one, I don't know——" he paused as coughs racked through his body— "any other way to say this."

"Then don't say it." She shook her head and her throat tightened. "Please, don't say it, Papa. We're going to Denver City." She smiled even though tears burned her eyes. "You need to get better so we can go."

"I'm dying."

His words struck her like the *Vesta* plunging into the waves, only this time, the ship sank beneath them, and the cold water swallowed her and the ship whole. Not daring to breathe, for fear she might release a wail as she drown, she stared for a long time at the lacy curtains draped over the window. Beautiful dreams, all fading away with the sun. She swallowed hard, widening her eyes to keep from crying, but she felt the betrayal of a tear as it trickled down her cheek and onto her chin. Soon, like that tear, she would be alone.

"Papa, please don't die." It was a foolish request, but she couldn't help herself. She felt like she was falling and had nothing, no one to cling to, no one but him. She fell on his chest.

The bed shook as her father coughed.

Was he laughing? It'd be so like him. Her head shot up.

He smiled. "If I had a choice, I'd stay alive."

How could she be so selfish? She wiped her eyes. At her age she should have known better. Ten was quite old, after all, but right now, she felt like a baby—his baby, and he was leaving her.

She scooted closer, desperate to take in every word, clinging to him over the bedcovers.

He ran his finger down the bridge of her nose. "Don't cry anymore. You must be brave." He gulped in air. "You will live with your uncle Horace, your mother's brother, and he will take care of you. I've arranged for him to provide for your needs and your education." He turned his head and panted for breath then expelled a long wheeze.

His face turned bright red against his light blond hair while he coughed. He was so thin, and his skin so pale. He no longer looked young and full of life like that day on the ship's deck.

He cleared his throat. "Just do as your uncle says and be a good girl." He coughed. "It's a shame . . . he never married," his words came out in spurts, "then he would . . . have a wife to mother you."

"I don't need a mother, Papa. I just need you."

"You have to be strong." He wiped a tear from her cheek. "No more tears."

"Yes, Papa."

"I wish I could send you back to Amsterdam. But no one is left. It's just you and me."

Just you and me.

"Oh, Papa!" She wailed. How could he leave her alone? "Please don't give up. Jesus will heal you! He'll make you better."

"It's not the Lord's will." He fought off another attack.

She waited and watched him battle for breath, his blue eyes now watery pools of gray. His words made her heart, like the ship, sink even further. He wasn't just going away for a short time, he was going away forever. Her throat hurt as she fought back tears, trying to stop crying.

He looked into her eyes. "I'm sorry I couldn't get over this, little one." He wheezed. "Just know I'm proud of you. If only I had more time . . . more time to teach you." He coughed. "Remember, I may be leaving, but the Lord is always with you. You won't be alone."

"Yes, Papa." She hugged his chest again, trying to swallow the knot that formed in her throat.

She wouldn't cry.

The heavy tray quivered as Anna set it on the small table in the study. She felt his gaze on her, watching her every move. When she first met Uncle Horace, he reminded her of Mama. They had the same eyes. Even though she'd never met her mother, she recognized the similarities from photographs. She'd felt less troubled when she'd noticed the likenesses, but immediately learned that those outward similarities were all that existed.

Anna picked up the porcelain teapot and tipped it over a cup. The hot liquid gushed out from its weight. She caught the long spout with her hand, burning her fingers and filling the cup much closer to the brim than she'd intended.

Her gaze darted to her uncle, who thankfully grinned at the lovely Mrs. Craw, missing the slight blunder. She set the heavy teapot back on the tray next to the dishes, her hands trembling and her arms aching. With clammy fingers, she lifted the cup and saucer then held it out for Mrs. Craw.

"No. Sugar!"

Startled, Anna jerked to the sugar, sending the cup over the saucer and onto the hem of Mrs. Craw's gown. The dishes clattered on the table as she grabbed the tea towel to wipe off Mrs. Craw's dress.

"You horrid little creature!" Mrs. Craw slapped her, sending stings of pain across her cheek.

Anna put a hand to her face and turned to Uncle Horace who sat across from them. His eyes blazed, and a frown darkened his threatening face.

It had been two months since her arrival, and she still hadn't found a way to please him. She held her breath.

He stood from his chair and lunged toward her.

Anna raised her hand to block his swing, but he grabbed her arm, yanked her to her feet, dragged her out of the room and down the carpeted hallway. "You stupid child. I ought to throw you on the street for what you've done."

The stairs leading down to the entry hall appeared before her. She clung to his arm.

He pried her loose. "Get off me, you little terror!" He tore her hands free and threw her down.

She missed the first step then tumbled down the others. Her shin caught between the rails of the banister, and she jerked to a stop. Pain shot through her leg as she dangled from the rail halfway down the stairs.

Uncle Horace turned to Mrs. Craw as she came up behind him. Her large hoop skirt swung up far enough for Anna to see her bloomers. "My husband believes I'm taking a stroll in the park." Hands on hips, the woman glared at Anna. "How am I going to explain this tea stain?"

Anna's hands trembled as she leaned up to pull her leg free. Would Uncle Horace come after her again? She grasped the rails and climbed to her feet.

"I'll teach you a lesson you'll never forget." He marched down the stairs, black eyes blazing, and grabbed her by the hair.

She screamed and shuddered. "Papa!"

He dragged her through the hall. "Papa's not coming. He never loved you anyway." They passed the grand parlor, and he shoved her into the small bedroom behind the kitchen.

She tripped but caught herself on the bed.

"Gather your dresses. All of them."

With quivering hands, she opened the wardrobe and collected all her garments. There weren't many, since her uncle had only allowed one trunk of her belongings when she moved in.

"Take that off," he said, pointing to the dress she wore.

Anna hesitated.

"Now!"

She got out of her dress as quickly as she could. Heat crawled up her neck to her cheeks as he stood watching. Glimpsing herself in the mirror, she noticed how thin and naked she looked.

Carrying her dresses, ready to surrender to whatever punishment he chose to deal out, she came to the door in only her chemise.

"Come," he said.

Favoring her bruised leg and trying not to trip over the dresses, she hobbled behind him back up the stairs. It was difficult keeping up with his long strides.

When they returned to the study, Mrs. Craw stood glaring at her with thin lips turned up as if in smug satisfaction.

Uncle Horace snatched the dresses out of her arms.

One at a time, he tossed all her lovely gowns into the large fireplace. The flames exploded and then calmed as they melted away the beautiful silk and crinoline fabrics.

"Nay," Anna whispered as she sank to her knees. Her father had given her those dresses. They were all she had.

"There are maid's uniforms hanging in your wardrobe," her uncle said, beads of sweat covering his flushed forehead. "You will wear those."

"They don't fit me, sir," she whispered, thinking about the adult clothing that hung there.

"Wear them!" He clenched his teeth. "Now go." He pointed to the door. "I don't want to see your sniveling face again."

She limped down the stairs, shivering from the cold and trembling over her situation. Trapped. With nowhere to run. She stumbled past the parlor and into the kitchen, wishing to warm herself by the stove, but the fire had long gone out.

Dejected, she limped into her small room, which had formerly belonged to a maidservant, and closed the door behind her. Her father's portrait stood on the nightstand, the only sight of familiarity and joy. Trembling, she hugged it to herself then fell on the bed and wept.

"I miss you, Papa." Sobs choked her for a long time while her arm and leg throbbed in pain. She sniffed and wiped the tears from her cheeks. Shivering in her chemise, she pulled the covers around her for warmth.

Her father's handsome, serious face looked back at her from the photo. "I wish you were here." Loneliness swept over her in a thick wave of nausea. She stared at her father through blurred vision, trying to imagine what he might say, trying to hear his voice. *The Lord is with you. You're not alone.*

If that were true, Anna should be able to feel His presence. She tried to feel God. To feel His closeness. Nothing but the cold draft sighing beneath her door swept over her cheeks and made her shiver.

Why was He so far away?

Not daring to give in to her fear, she wiped her eyes and then scooted up on her elbow, but painful tingles shot through her arm, so she decided to sit up. She kissed her papa's portrait.

"Tell me a story, Papa. Tell me about the Indians, just like you used to do." She'd hoped to meet some Indians when they went to Denver City.

With that, an idea struck, and she slid off the bed. Underneath, still packed in her carpetbag, she found the book her father had read before his death. She kept it hidden from her uncle, for he had said it was shameful to read books. She brushed against the jewelry box and Bible that once belonged to her mother. She kept those hidden too.

Anna sighed at seeing the purse of paste jewelry Mariska had given to her. Uncle Horace had released her nanny as soon as they'd arrived, and since then, they'd lost contact. She had likely found work somewhere far away. If only Anna could go somewhere far away too.

She pushed the jewelry box and Bible back farther into the carpetbag and grabbed the book, *The Last of the Mohicans*. Though her father had read it, he refused to read it to her, saying she was too young.

She climbed back onto her small bed, picked up her father's picture, and laid the book on her lap. Tenderly, she brushed her fingers across his face. How she missed his blue eyes and warm laughter.

"I wish you were here so you could read to me." She loved losing herself in the sound of his voice, and right now, it was the only way she could escape her life. Hmm . . . she could simply read the story and imagine him reading it to her.

Drained by her tears, Anna hugged the photo. If only she could leave this place. She didn't know how, but she knew where—Denver City. That's where home was supposed to be. Perhaps God would find a way to take her there? He could take her away, far away from New York where nobody wanted her. She would be gone, no longer a burden to anyone.

Yes. He would rescue her.

Please save me, Lord. Take me away from here. Far away.

———❦———

May 1870

"It will never happen again," Anna whispered to herself in the looking glass. After six long years, her uncle had beaten her for the last time. She winced from the pain in her arm where he had punched her the day before. All because she had returned late from the market. He might be growing suspicious of her so-called visits to the marketplace. But the last sewing project had to be turned in, the money she'd earned was now stashed away, and after several letters of correspondence, a teaching job awaited her. Amazing how much one could accomplish on her daily visits to the market.

She turned and pulled her carpetbag out from under the bed.

At sixteen, she had fulfilled her promise to her father and completed her education. Had the tutor not been ordered by the judge to come to the house for her lessons, she would never have gotten any schooling. Her uncle had been set against it. But the school had been paid, and since she couldn't go to them, they came to her. Thank the good Lord for that.

Now was her chance to leave. Her uncle was away on business for the day, the other maid was gone, and the only one left in the house was the butler who never paid her any mind. She packed the few things she owned into her carpetbag and turned to the bureau.

She smoothed her hand over the surface of her mother's jewelry box—she'd have to leave it behind. Anna's mother had died giving birth to her. All she had left were her mother's gems, given to her at the time of her father's death, her mother's English Bible, a few pictures, and what little money she had managed to save these past years from sewing in secret. The jewels were sewn into her bodice. It had been a tedious task, but at least thieves wouldn't find them.

Anna stashed the fake jewelry her former nanny had given her into a small pouch, pulled the drawstring closed, and put it in her carpetbag. They might come in handy if she were to run into thieves. She'd heard too many stories about the dangers of traveling west. Grabbing her things, she hurried to the front hall.

One last look in the mirror revealed her blonde braids stylishly looped, and she pinned her hat neatly in place. Her traveling dress, the only one she had time to make, suited her. Its sage color set off her green eyes, and the bustle was slight so as to provide comfort for traveling.

As she pulled her cloak on over her shoulders, she noticed a gathering of dust along the small shelf below the mirror. She smiled to herself. Never again would she have to slave for her uncle and put up with his beatings. Let him find someone else to dust and clean his house.

Carpetbag in one hand, gloves in the other, Anna van Stralen stepped outside the front door. She strode down the walkway with her chin held high. The entire world was open to her. Freedom and dreams waited to be realized.

The great frontier, her new home—Denver City.

Chapter 2

The New York Grand Central Depot swarmed with people, and after a long wait, Anna's turn at the counter had finally come.

"One ticket to Denver City, please," Anna said to the man behind the window.

The man pointed to a map on the wall next to him. "The Transcontinental Railroad can only get you as far as Cheyenne, in Wyoming Territory. The rails to Denver City aren't completed yet." He raised an eyebrow as if to question what a young lady was doing traveling alone to the Western Territories.

"Isn't there a stagecoach from Cheyenne to Denver City?"

"Yes, but you'll have to buy your ticket there."

"That'll be fine." She had hoped the tracks from Cheyenne would have been completed by now.

"First class or second?"

"Second."

She swallowed hard. It would take close to one third of her savings to get there, but that's what part of the money was for, and she'd still have enough to buy some material for new dresses when she got to Denver City. All she had now was what she wore.

The less luggage the better. Besides, all she could have brought were maid's clothes, and she wanted no memories of her old, miserable life. She handed the man behind the window her cash.

"Your last change of trains will be in Chicago," the man said.

"Thank you." She accepted her change.

After wading through people, soot, and noise, Anna finally made it to the hotel car on the train where a porter set her carpetbag on the board above the sofa. She turned and sat.

Through the window the conductor blew his whistle. "Aaallll aaaboooard!"

Shortly thereafter, the train lurched forward, and her stomach lurched into her throat. Once the train left the station, it moved at an alarming pace. Houses, buildings, and trees whizzed by, and her knuckles turned white as she gripped the windowsill. She'd never experienced such high speed. But her fear lessened as nothing happened, and she began to feel strangely exhilarated, like a caged bird just released, flying towards freedom, towards home.

Anna thought of the photo of her papa—the only remembrance she had left—wrapped safely in her carpetbag. Thought of his face staring back at her. Thought of his smile when they'd first arrived in America, of the sparkle in his eyes, and knew they must be sparkling now.

"Our dream will finally come true," she whispered.

⸻

Several days later and long past Chicago, Anna sat in the dining car, watching the scenery unfold before her eyes. The landscape spread out for miles. Occasionally, she'd spot a small farm or a ranch, but most of the land was wide-open spaces with fields and rolling hills of yellow, brown, and green. She sipped her tea, noticing the empty plate before her. She hadn't eaten this well in a long time.

"May I join you?"

A young gentleman with a black handlebar mustache stood next to her table. He smiled, put his hands behind his back, and rocked on his feet. "There are no available tables in this car, and I see you are nearly finished."

"Oh yes, please, sit down," she said, ashamed she hadn't spoken sooner.

"Steven Kane." He tipped his hat.

Anna introduced herself, then stood and prepared to gulp down the rest of her tea.

"No need to rush. Take your time, enjoy your tea." The man sat across from her.

"Thank you." She settled back into her seat and tried to relax. She'd never shared a table with a man before.

"And what's your destination, if I may ask?"

"Denver City."

"That's where I'm going." The man's smile broadened. "So, you'll be taking the stage from Julesburg."

Puzzled, she shook her head. "No. I'll be taking the stagecoach from Cheyenne."

"Cheyenne? There's nothing in Cheyenne. Why would you go that route?" He chuckled, and then his brows rose in question. "Are you meeting someone?"

She took a sip from her tea. She didn't want him to know she wasn't meeting anyone, and yet, what if she were about to get off at the wrong stop?

"I was told in New York that I could take a coach from Cheyenne to Denver." She cleared her throat, trying not to sound too ignorant. "It's much closer, isn't it? I mean, closer than Julesburg is to Denver City." She recalled all her studies of the railroads, and where they were being built, and according to the map, Cheyenne was definitely closer to Denver.

"Hmm." Mr. Kane rubbed his chin. "I suppose you're right, it is closer. But you still have to go a ways on the train, and I know for a fact that the service from Julesburg is much faster. The stagecoach from Julesburg to Denver City has won competitions for its speed."

Mr. Kane cocked his head, and his gaze swept from her waist to her face. "You could get off with me. I can assure your safety. That is, if you're not meeting someone."

Anna forced a smile, shifting uncomfortably. "Thank you for your kind offer, Mr. Kane, but I'm meeting my fiancé." With that, she stood and bade him good day.

Her conscience bothered her dreadfully for having told such a blatant lie.

The Pacific Railroad took Anna to Cheyenne, Wyoming, and what a desolate place it was. She stood on the platform, and tumbleweeds followed behind the train's path as it moved out onto the flat horizon. It felt good to finally be outside in the fresh air, no longer tucked away in the train's cabin car, and that much closer to the new life awaiting her.

After days of travel, and still enthusiastic with her newfound freedom, she went to purchase a ticket bound for Colorado Territory. No passengers were on the platform. Actually, no other passengers had gotten off the train. She recalled the large number of people that had gotten off near Julesburg. Surely, if that was where she should have gone, the man in New York would have told her so.

Her boots echoed off the wooden planks, and she glanced outside the station where three covered wagons and travelers milled about. Good. She wasn't alone.

"One ticket to Denver City please," Anna said to the man behind the window. The mere thought that she had made it this far and was just a few days from her final destination made it difficult for her to stand still.

The man behind the window looked up with crossed eyes. She couldn't tell if he was looking at her or at the wall. "I'm afraid the stagecoach to Denver City has already left." He gnawed on a toothpick. "Won't be back for another two weeks."

"What about a train that will take me back to Julesburg?"

"Hmm, I'm not sure when it'll be coming through again. Could be a long while. There's been trouble on the tracks, so we're running a bit slow at the moment."

Her heart sank. That meant she would have to stay several nights. "Where's the nearest boarding house?"

He chuckled as if she'd asked something funny and flipped the toothpick in his mouth with his tongue. "I'm afraid there ain't no boarding house available, ma'am. But we have a hotel, just across the street here." He frowned and shook his head. "Mighty expensive though, especially for a whole two weeks' stay."

Anna resisted the urge to cringe. She didn't want to spend more money than she had to.

"I'm surprised you didn't get off near Julesburg. Their service to Denver City by stagecoach is much faster. Most people coming from the East get off there."

She bit her lip, remembering the gentleman on the train. Now what would she do?

"I'm sure those settlers," he said, pointing toward the wagons, "would let you camp with them."

Camp? She hadn't brought any provisions to go camping.

"Heck, they might even be headin' for Denver City. You'd get there a lot faster if you traveled with them."

Anna studied the travelers. She could save money if she did that. She counted three women and three men who were probably their husbands. She heard the cry of a baby. They were family people. Perhaps it wouldn't be such a bad idea to travel with them.

Besides, it could prove to be an exciting experience, an adventure.

"Why don't you go ask?" The man leaned on the counter, closing one eye so she knew without a doubt he was looking at her. He clenched the toothpick between his teeth. "Watch out for them snakes though. They'll crawl into your boots at night."

Snakes?

She'd sleep with her shoes on. "Thank you for your help."

"Much obliged, ma'am." He winked.

Anna grabbed her carpetbag and went toward the wagons hitched outside the station. She stepped off the wooden platform and onto the dusty road. There were a few buildings, and some homesteaders behind those, but none of them looked inviting. Even the new hotel looked empty and dusty. In fact, everything looked dusty—and hot.

She wiped the sweat from her brow and pulled her hat further over her head to block the sun. Tumbleweeds rolled at the base of the platform. No trees were in sight, and as far as she could see, there were nothing but hills and plains beyond the buildings. Quite a contrast from the bustling streets of New York City and the busy cobblestone avenues of Amsterdam.

She looked for the most inviting person she could find and chose the woman holding the baby. The slender woman's dress was dirty, and loose strands of dark hair fell from her bonnet. Anna felt overdressed as she neared the weary traveler.

The woman turned to face her. A bruise glared under her right eye, but she smiled, and Anna forced a grin. She knew what that sort of bruise felt like.

"Just a moment," the woman said as she handed the baby off to a plump woman behind her.

The plump lady took the child. "You're simply wonderful with children. It's a shame you don't have any of your own." She walked away.

The slender woman's smile faded as she brushed the dust off her skirt, almost as if she were brushing off the woman's comment. Three children whizzed between them.

"I'm Anna." She smiled, hoping to relieve the tension that rose from the plump woman's words.

"I'm Beth." The young woman's brown eyes and rosy cheeks lit up, and she would have been quite pretty had it not been for the bruise.

The woman's name turned over in Anna's mind. It ended with a dreadful "th," but she ought to be able to pronounce it just fine. She'd finally mastered the language over the last six years, but anytime she became nervous, her tongue fumbled a bit.

"I'm on my way to Denver City, and I was wondering if I may travel with your wagon train, if that's where you all are headed?"

"Yes, that's where we're going." Beth smiled but immediately sobered. "I'll have to ask my husband."

"I have a job waiting for me there." Anna hoped Beth's husband would see that she was responsible, a hard worker, and not someone looking for handouts.

"How nice." Beth walked over to a covered wagon and arranged some linen inside, focusing on her work. "So, you're not married then?"

Anna followed and set her carpetbag down to help. "No." Her uncle never wanted her to marry. He never allowed her to be seen by anyone, much less courted, and kept her shut up inside to wait on his every need.

"Are you traveling alone?"

"Yes," Anna said.

Beth took the newly folded linen from Anna and placed it inside the wagon.

"I've come all the way from New York by myself." Anna lifted her chin, hoping to show Beth that she'd done just fine on her own thus far.

"I would never have had the courage to travel so far by myself. You're a brave woman." The loose strands of Beth's raven hair brushed against her flushed cheeks in a slight breeze. She quickly tucked the curls back into her bonnet.

"What are your plans?" Anna asked.

Beth looked down at her feet then back up at Anna and smiled. "We're going to be cattle ranchers. As soon as we're settled, of course."

"Are you settling near Denver City?" If they settled nearby, perhaps they could become neighbors, friends.

"My husband hopes to—"

"Hopes to?" A man's voice growled from behind Anna. "I'm going to, woman." The man stepped in front of them. He glared at Anna. "Where's my pipe?"

Was he talking to her? She couldn't imagine why he'd think she knew where to find his pipe. She looked to Beth for help.

"You left it next to your rifle when you fell asleep." Beth pointed a trembling finger at the wagon. "I put it on the buckboard."

The man eyed Beth through narrowed slits beneath bushy eyebrows. "Next time, put it where I can find it." He looked at Anna and motioned with his chin toward her. "Who's this?"

The man's behavior was all too familiar. To think, poor Beth had married such a person. Likely, he was the one who gave her that black eye.

"This is Miss . . . Anna." Beth looked at her feet. "She would like to travel with us to Denver City."

"I've come all the way from New York, sir." Anna tried to sound as polite as possible even though sparks of anger ignited.

Looping his thumbs in his suspenders, he looked her up and down.

She shifted her stance, hoping he would take his filthy eyes off her.

"You got money?"

"Oh, Al—"

Al raised a backhand to his wife.

Beth cowered, and Anna winced.

He stopped his swing in midair. "Go fetch my pipe."

Beth backed away, and with downcast eyes, hurried around the wagon.

Towering over her, Al glowered at Anna.

She stepped back.

"Food costs money, lady, and if you're not willing to pay then you can wait here for your iron horse."

"The tracks aren't finished yet, so no train goes from here to Denver City."

"I knew that." He shifted his stance and shoved a fist deep in his pocket.

By the dumb look on his face, Anna doubted he knew much of anything. Still, she ought to explain why she was so desperate to travel with them. She dreaded being a burden, though she dreaded even more having to pay for two weeks stay in a hotel.

"I would have to take the stagecoach, and it won't be here for another fourteen days. I have a teaching job waiting for me."

He eyed her up and down as she explained herself.

"I have money," she said, thinking how relieved she was that she had put most of it in a small pouch and tied it around her waist where it could be hidden under her dress. "How much do you need?" She had already planned on paying for the stagecoach, which would have been around thirty dollars. She could afford to pay Al that amount.

His gaze raked over her. "One hundred dollars."

"Why, that's outrageous! That'd buy a horse!"

He grumbled. "The price is one hundred dollars or nothing.'"

Her face went hot with anger. She may as well stay over night in the hotel for that price, but how much would all those costs come to? She'd have to pay for the coach, the hotel, and food. She needed all the money she could spare in order to find lodging in Denver when she arrived. Not to mention extra funds for new dresses. And if she stayed, it would mean waiting another two weeks before she reached Denver City, whereas if she traveled with the wagon train, she could get there in just a few days. That alone might make the cost worth it.

That's when an idea struck. "Would you be willing to accept jewelry, sir?"

"What kind?"

"I have a small, valuable stone that might suit your interests, definitely worth your price." Really the stone was worth slightly less than one hundred dollars because it had a flaw in it that only a professional would notice. At least that's what she recalled her papa saying.

She considered giving him a piece of her fake jewelry, and those paste stones probably would have fooled the brainless brute, but she wouldn't have felt right about doing that. In all fairness, she ought to pay these people something for allowing her to travel with them.

"Let me see it," he said.

"If you'll excuse me, I will fetch it." She curtsied to the man, and went to the front of the wagon where Beth was preparing Al's pipe. "Is there a place a woman can have a bit of privacy?"

Beth pointed to a small privy not far from the train depot.

Anna turned in that direction, and at once, stopped in her tracks. Had she taken leave of her senses?

She made an about-face. Two other men were preparing their wagons and could escort her on this journey. Surely their rates wouldn't be as high.

"I've never met such cowardly men," Anna mumbled to herself as she trudged behind the wagons. Her negotiations with the men had been miserably unsuccessful. Beth had said the others refused to help her because they were frightened of Al. When Anna went around asking the other men what they might offer, Al had become angry.

It'd been impossible to search for the jewel in that dark privy, so the men allowed her to follow behind the wagon train as long as she gave her word to later produce the stone, plus she'd had to pay each of the other two families a small sum in advance. It had been foolish of her to ask the others for help. The costs had become outrageous, but because she used the stone, it was still cheaper than staying in the hotel for two weeks and on top of that, paying for the coach, clothes, and a boarding house in Denver City. And . . . she'd get to Denver that much sooner.

So now, several hours later, she trudged behind the three wagons. The sun's heat bore down on her head, and her hat didn't offer any protection from its hot rays. She should have gotten off near Julesburg. But she couldn't think of that right now, it would only make her more miserable. She squinted and glanced up into the blue sky. It took her breath away every time she looked at it. Never in her life had she seen so much sky in one place.

Her carpetbag grew heavy, so she changed hands. It was heavy there too, so she wrapped her arms around it and hugged it against her chest. She pressed her dry, chapped lips together, aching for something to drink. Dizziness swept over her, and her steps faltered.

Just as they neared some trees, one of the wagons jerked to a stop. The owner shouted, and the men jumped down to assess the damage. From their angry expressions, she concluded they'd be stuck there for a while. Thank goodness they were near some trees. She could hide herself and find the stone, then maybe someone would give her a drink.

Shade.

She needed shade. Her legs and arms weighed her down like heavy boulders as she walked in that direction. If only she could take off her cumbersome dress and feel the air against her hot skin. She came upon a slight hill that had been impossible to see because the land was the same light brown color all around, blending itself perfectly together. Just over the hill, she spotted a small river running between some trees.

Water.

Holding up her skirt, she stumbled along the hill among the trees and stepped down the incline toward the fast flowing river. Just the sound of its rushing made her heart skip. How refreshing and enticing. Its coolness called out to her. Grasshoppers leaped at every step and swing of her skirt, mosquitoes swarmed around her face, and the ground took on a life of its own, moving beneath her feet. The pounding in her head increased as she neared the bank. She dropped at the water's edge ready to dip her face and mouth under the current.

"Don't drink the water!" Beth shouted behind her. She came running down the steep embankment with a pitcher in hand. "This is safe to drink. I've heard horrible stories of people getting sick from open rivers like this one. You should always boil the water first."

With trembling fingers, Anna grabbed the pitcher. She hated being rude, but desperation took over as she gulped down its contents with eagerness. It poured down her chin and bodice.

"Not so fast, slow down. You'll make yourself sick."

Anna noticed her sunburned hands and wondered how awful her face must look. But the relief of the water took her mind off her appearance.

"I tried to bring you some sooner, but Al wouldn't let me." Beth crossed her arms, frowning and shaking her head. "He said he wanted his payment first."

Anna licked her lips, moistening them in order to make the chapped, dry feeling go away. She motioned around her. "This is as good a place as any for me to find that stone. No one can see me here."

"I'll help you. First, let me go warn the others to keep their distance. I'd hate for you to be undressed and one of them come traipsing over here." Beth hiked up her skirt and headed up the bank.

Anna opened her carpetbag and took out her buttonhook then one by one unbuttoned her dress. Once all the buttons were undone, she slipped out of the hot, thick mass of material and shook out of her bustle. She reached behind her hips and yanked on her corset stays, allowing more air to fill her lungs. What a relief to be out of that heavy garment. There was a benefit to wearing maid's clothes—they weren't nearly as cumbersome.

She gulped another drink from the water pitcher and stood in the open air in her chemise, looking around to make sure no one was watching. Tall grass, trees and thick bushes covered the other side of the bank. All was quiet except for the sounds of insects and the water rippling over rocks along the bank's bed, calling her to its refreshment.

Since she was already undressed, this would be a good time to cool off. She sat down, took off her boots and unhooked her stocking. With ease, she slid the stocking down her leg.

Chapter 3

"Let's take that one," Running Cloud whispered in Cheyenne to White Eagle as they watched the woman by the river.

White Eagle kept low behind the thick shrubs and tall grass. He stared at the woman whose skin was white like snow as she stretched out her leg and ran her fingers along its length to remove the second stocking.

When she stood, she placed her hands on her waist, emphasizing the flare of her hips beneath her thin, white dress. She tilted her head and removed her hat then worked to take down her hair. Long, yellow locks cascaded to one side, down her back and around her. It curtained her body all the way to her knees as she shook out the pins. She then ran her fingers through her mane, catching the sun's light.

Never had White Eagle seen so much yellow hair. He glanced at Running Cloud who crouched next to him. Beneath his paint, Running Cloud's eyes widened. Together they looked back at the woman.

Her hair was now pulled over one shoulder, and she glanced around as though she were looking for something, as though she'd lost something on the ground. Hands on hips, she stopped over her boots. For a long time she studied them, as though she expected them to walk off on their own.

Finally, she lifted the thin material of her skirt, kicked one boot over and quickly jumped away. When the boot didn't move—he assumed she expected it to move—she kicked the other one and jumped back again. Keeping her focus on the boots, she knelt down, reached out and picked them up. She then bent forward, holding them as far away from her as possible, and shook them out. Nothing came out of the boots, and she cautiously peered inside them as though she were looking for something but afraid of what she might find. Pursing her lips, she bound the boots together by their laces and hung them around her neck.

White Eagle and Running Cloud tossed a side-glance at each other. They shrugged.

She turned her back to them to unbind something from around her waist.

White Eagle held his breath as he crept forward to get a better look.

She tossed a small pouch on a nearby rock, turned, and stepped toward the river. When she came to the edge of the bank, she dipped her foot in the water and gasped. Slowly, she stepped into the river and moved in up to her knees. The water tugged on the white material of her dress, dragging it into the current. She then moved in up to her waist.

With hair cascading over her back, she closed her eyes, lifted her face to the sky and sighed. A slight breeze blew loose strands of hair away from the young woman's partially burnt face and arms. Her hair lit up like gold under the sun.

White Eagle hoped Running Cloud wouldn't notice his fascination with the young woman. Never had any woman affected him this way. She looked like a ghost, floating over the water.

She moved in deeper but stopped.

He stopped breathing.

She held her boots over her head and dipped herself in up to her neck, releasing another long sigh. The water washed around her, taking the ends of her dress with it, gently pulling the fabric and her hair into a milky-white wave. Obviously her arms grew weary as she continued to hold the boots above the water, so she balanced them on her head.

His lips tugged into a smile. He cast a side-glance at his friend and realized Running Cloud was watching him. White Eagle forced a frown.

Again, she looked around but didn't see them hidden in the nearby grass. She held the boots in the air high above the water's surface, dipped her head completely under, and sat on the riverbed.

"That white woman is strange." Running Cloud pinched his lips together as if he'd tasted something nasty.

"White women are all strange, and they're cowards. That one's afraid of her own boots."

"Hmm. She's not lazy like the others. How many other white women did you see walking? She was the only one not sitting beside her man on those boxes pulled by horses."

"I don't think she had a choice," White Eagle said.

"If you think she's such a coward, why don't we go down there and see her reaction? Even better, I'll hold her down and you can take her."

White Eagle glared at him. A feather danced from the braid over his friend's shoulder, and for the first time in all their years together, White Eagle wanted to drive his knuckles into his face. Despite the Indian wars and the number of soldiers he'd killed, White Eagle had never ravished a woman. So why would Running Cloud suggest he do such a thing now?

"I have another plan," White Eagle said, trying to make him forget the idea. "I'll go down to the bank. I bet she'll take one look at me and panic." There was something about this woman that drew him. The need to test her bravery was strong. Would she react like the other whites?

Running Cloud grunted, shaking his head.

"She will," White Eagle said. "All white women are the same. I'll go down there, and if she panics, you give me the saber you took off that soldier at Summit Springs."

"You can go down there, but that's not enough. Let's watch them for two suns. If she's a coward, I'll give you the saber. But if she acts with bravery, I get your breast plate."

Anna stayed under the water and faced upstream so that the current's force would pull the loose strands of hair away from her face. It reminded her of the times her father used to take her to the beach in Scheveningen and swimming in the canals in Holland. It'd been that long since she'd done anything enjoyable like this.

The coolness enveloped her as she floated over the riverbed. What an invigorating delight. Her body cried out for her to stay under as long as possible. She continued to hold her boots up out of the water when the shadow of a figure standing on the embankment caught her eye.

After coming up, she rubbed the water from her eyes.

Beth gasped. "Anna, what are you doing?"

"It feels wonderful! Why don't you join me?"

"Oh, I wouldn't dare. Al would tan my hide."

Anna rose and climbed out of the water's delicious pool, her pleasure short-lived. It wasn't fair for her to enjoy its refreshment if Beth couldn't join her.

"Oh, my." Beth's eyes widened as Anna stepped out of the water. "Pray that no one comes near the embankment. Forgive me for being so blunt, but I can see right through your chemise."

Anna gasped, and her gaze darted to the trees. Thankfully, she didn't see any peering eyes or unwelcome visitors. Letting her boots fall down around her neck, she grabbed her dress and plopped herself on a flat rock next to her new friend.

The two of them bent over the gown in search of the semi-precious stone. Anna dripped water on her dress, but she didn't care. It felt more than wonderful to be wet.

"I'm sorry Al wouldn't allow the others to help you," Beth whispered.

"You don't need to apologize. You're not responsible for his behavior. Besides, the others didn't seem interested in helping me anyway."

"They think you're rich." Beth glanced at her, and then looked quickly down at the dress. "I mean, with your nice clothes and all, and then because you're traveling alone, and when you mentioned the jewel, well, I guess they all got hungry for money."

"I'm certainly not rich, and I do owe you something for letting me travel with your wagon train. Food isn't free, I know." She glanced back down at the dress. "I've found it." She tore through the threads and out fell the small jewel.

She set the stone next to her money pouch and stood. Balancing one foot on a rock, she slipped her stockings over her damp leg and hooked them one by one to her garter. She then tied her money pouch back around her waist, pulled on her boots and reached for her corset.

"You're not going to put that on over your wet chemise, are you?"

Anna shrugged. "I can't very well wait for it to dry. Someone might come and find me this way." She rubbed her hand along the cotton. "It's dry in some places already." She pulled the clinging fabric away from her shoulder.

"In what places?"

Both of them laughed, but Anna wasn't about to wait for it to dry. It felt good anyway to have the moisture against her skin. Beth helped her slip back into her corset and started doing up the stays along her back.

How nice to have a new friend. Anna sensed Beth needed one as much as she did. She knew how helpless and alone Beth must feel. The woman was so beautiful, Anna couldn't understand why Al would be so cruel.

"I'm sorry Al hurts you," Anna whispered.

Birds twittered and a sparrow's singing danced on the air, contrasting with the sudden tension pulling between Anna and Beth. The silence stretched out with Beth's tugging as she tightened the last stay. Anna braced her legs to keep her balance. She was sorry she'd said anything. Nobody had ever talked to her about Uncle Horace's beatings, and she thought Beth might want to talk or know that someone cared. After the final jerk on the was tied, she turned to face Beth.

Tears streamed down Beth's cheeks as she handed Anna her bustle and skirt.

"I'm so sorry." Anna placed her hand on her chest, then lowered it again so she could attach the bustle and step into the skirt. "I shouldn't have said anything."

Beth gave her a shy smile. "I'm not hurt that you spoke about it. In fact, you're the only one who seems to have noticed. The others haven't said anything, probably because they feel it's not their business." She held out Anna's dress jacket and helped her in it. "Thank you."

After struggling into the well-fitted fabric, Anna grabbed her buttonhook.

"I try to find my strength in the Lord," Beth said.

Her words surprised Anna. She'd learned the hard way that the Lord didn't keep bad things from happening. How Beth could find strength in that, she didn't know. She finished the last button and tossed her buttonhook into her carpetbag.

"I'm unable to have children." Beth sniffed and wiped her eyes. "Now Al feels I've ruined his life. He'll never be able to have the son he's always wanted." She sighed. "That's all he used to talk about before we were married three years ago. He loved me back then. And now I don't have any family left."

"Oh, Beth, I'm so sorry." Anna stepped closer to give her a hug.

"Beth, woman!" Al's voice boomed from the top of the bank, causing both women to jump. "Why ain't you fixing my supper? Get your lazy self up here and get to work."

Beth gave Anna a weary smile and climbed up the embankment.

Al glared at Beth, and as she walked past him, he knocked her upside the head. He then scowled at Anna, his thumbs in his suspenders. "Where's my payment?"

Anna snatched it from the rock, climbed up the embankment, and handed Al the stone. It was the first time she saw him smile, and it was a wicked one at that.

She trudged back down to the river and drank from the pitcher until it was empty. When she knelt over and splashed water on her hot face, its coolness tempted her again. She pulled her hair over her shoulder and let it soak in the flowing current, watching as the water drew her long tresses downstream.

It had been a rough trip since Cheyenne, and they'd traveled nearly all day. Despite the scorching heat and the lack of water, it was worth it. She had gained a new friend.

Beth seemed to be a caring person, and Anna would hold her kindness close to her heart. She was thrilled with the thought of them possibly being neighbors. She'd never had a friend before, and maybe Anna could be the kind of friend to Beth she herself had needed all these years.

Twisting her hair, she wrung out the water. When she looked up, a wild man stood watching her on the other side of the river.

Her breath caught in her throat.

He stood with a self-assured stance, his legs braced apart and his hands at his sides. A tan breechcloth hung at his bare waist, and his beige, buckskin leggings with fringed flaps emphasized his height. Silver armbands clamped just above his elbows, and black hair with feathers brushed over his shoulders in the slight wind, sending loose strands over his face, half covered in a black mask of paint.

Her heart galloped in her chest. She swallowed hard and waited for him to move or speak. When he did nothing, she forced her gaze from him and turned to see if Al was still at the top of the embankment. He'd already left.

She looked back to the Indian.

He was gone.

Two days later, Anna trudged behind the wagons again. Despite payment, Al still wouldn't let her ride with any of the settlers.

After seeing the Indian, she hadn't been sure if she ought to tell the others. She didn't want to be responsible for frightening everyone, but in the end she finally did talk to one of the men—not Al.

They had searched high and low for this so-called Indian, only to conclude that she had a wild imagination. Incensed by the memory, she tightened her arms around her carpetbag. Why would she dream up such a thing?

He was just as real as any of them.

To think . . . she had finally seen a real Indian. Papa would have been thrilled. He probably would have tried to befriend the savage. She giggled at the thought.

The sun's heat bore down on her head as usual, and a tumbleweed brushed against the hem of her dress, mocking her with its spindly limbs and dry branches. Just like the desolate bush, she might blow away, far away over the brown hills of sandy terrain. Hopefully, Beth would soon be allowed to bring her some water.

Dust from the wagons assailed her. If only she could ride with Beth.

A snake scurried across her path, and Anna squealed as it disappeared into a hole.

Watch out for them snakes. They'll crawl into your boots at night.

Anna could still see the ticket agent in Cheyenne, gnawing on his toothpick and leaning on the counter as he said those words. She had slept with her boots on, and after three days of traveling with these settlers, her feet punished her.

Denver City was just hours away. Surely, a bit of discomfort was worth the trouble in light of that fact.

She kept a comfortable distance between her and the others, not wanting to be in the way. Why must she be a burden to these people too? Two wagons could have fit between her and the one she followed. The ground spun, while the sounds of locusts and other insects buzzed in her ears. Her legs felt heavy, and her feet ached.

Denver City. Almost there. Her new home.

Her head pounded with each step as she chanted the words. The ground spun. The sounds of locusts buzzed in her ears. Her mouth felt sticky and her head ached. If she didn't get water soon, she might faint. And if she fainted, would anyone notice? She'd never fainted before. What would it be like? She didn't want to know.

"Lord . . . please . . . I need water."

Short screams and shouts from all sides snapped Anna to attention. Around them swarmed a colorful parade of Indians.

"Arm yourselves!" Al shouted from his wagon. He aimed his rifle. An Indian fired, and Al's rifle dropped.

Beth's screams carried through the air.

None of the other men dared raise their rifles, and no more shots were fired. One man jumped from his wagon, his hands high above his head. Savages bounded onto the wagons, while three others held their weapons on the men. The women and children cried and screamed.

Two Indians galloped toward Anna.

Hugging her carpetbag, she tried to run, but her feet took root and held her to the ground.

Dust and two painted warriors surrounded her in a stunning array of colors. It brought to mind the tulip parades in Holland, with reds, yellows, and blues jumping out at her. The horses tossed their wild heads, and their manes danced with feathers. Paint circled their eyes, handprints waved on their chests, and flashes of lightning streaked across their flanks.

The Indians circled her, sunlight reflecting off their silver armbands. They looked her up and down. Not daring to turn, she felt the gazes of the savages burn into her back. Their torsos, other than a breastplate made of small tubing, were bare and painted. Quivers slung over their backs with rifles at their sides. Would they use their weapons on her?

The screams and cries of the settlers faded into the distance, replaced by the horses' snorts and the crunching of their hooves. She felt as if the entire world had vanished, and only she and the colorful intruders existed beneath the great big sky.

As they came around again, Anna's gaze moved daringly to one Indian's face. Half covered in a black mask of paint, he brought to mind the appearance of a bandit. Only this bandit would likely steal more than her paste jewelry. The mask had a thin, white stripe below it, accentuating the black that covered his eyes. Red stripes of paint slashed across his cheeks and chin as if a knife had taken its pleasure on his face. His bright eyes snagged her attention and held her captive in his fierce gaze.

The man she'd seen on the bank.

Unable to move, all she could do was hold her breath and wait for the Indians to do something, wait as her heart thundered in her chest. The screams of the settlers had diminished to cries. Thankfully, no gunshots had gone off. She didn't dare look toward the wagons. Fear paralyzed her.

Lord, please keep Beth safe.

The other Indian moved closer. Long, dark braids draped over his shoulders. Feathers protruded from his head like a fan. He circled her, and the pounding in her head beat faster every time he came a little closer. He held a stick with feathers, and when just a foot away, he jammed the stick into Anna's hair, painfully forcing it loose from its pins.

"Take down," he said.

Anna dropped her carpetbag. With quivering hands and eyes welling with tears, she untied her small hat and yanked on the pins. Would they scalp her? Hair cascaded over her shoulders and down her back to below her waist. For the first time in her life, shame swept through her for having so much hair. Vanity hoarded all these golden locks, her crown of glory. Greed for this treasure would now cause her demise.

"Running Cloud!" The Indian with the feathered stick straightened and put his fist to his chest. He pointed at Anna. "You! Walks Alone. Gift to White Eagle." He pointed to the bandit-looking Indian, the one called White Eagle.

The meaning of his words slammed into Anna. She'd never get home.

Running Cloud dropped his feathered stick and dismounted in front of her. Anna found the ability to move and turned to run. He seized her by the hair, jerking her to a stop. He yanked her around and grabbed her arms in a biting grip. She tried to twist away, pushing against his powerful limbs.

White Eagle dismounted and strode toward them. He was much taller and broader than the savage who held her in his clutches. By his scowl and the fierce look on his painted face, Anna knew she was doomed. White Eagle reached out—Anna screamed. But he grabbed Running Cloud's wrist.

Eyes wide with surprise, Running Cloud turned, releasing his hold on Anna. White Eagle jerked him back and shoved him to the ground. Running Cloud raised his hands, palms up as White Eagle towered over him.

Anna turned to run, but White Eagle caught her by the arm and swung her around. Screaming, she shoved, but he held her against him. His hair and feathers cascaded onto her shoulder, and his painted face came inches from hers, emphasizing his bandit-like mask, the white stripe beneath it, and the red slashes on his cheeks and chin. Leather and sage assailed her senses as his breath feathered against her cheek.

"Lord help me," she whispered, wishing she could faint. Perhaps she *did* want to know what it would feel like. Now seemed the perfect time to lose consciousness.

Heavy breathing blocked out the sounds around them. A dangling feather tickled her face. His fingers slid up onto her chin—her breath caught in her throat. They glided across her cheek and tenderly brushed his feather away.

Their gazes met. Behind dark lashes, warm blue-green eyes swept over her from his gentle, almost sympathetic gaze.

There was a man buried beneath that mask of war paint.

White Eagle released a long, slow hiss as his gaze swept over the woman's face and down his arm where her yellow hair wrapped around his dark skin and silver armband— a stark contrast.

Despite the fear evident in the pine-green depths of her eyes, he felt as if she could see inside of him, as if her gut knew she saw a man, not a savage.

From her nose to her chin, her face burned bright red from the sun, and her lips were cracked and dry. This woman needed water.

Her gaze darted to her carpetbag. "Please," she whispered.

He glanced down at the bag. Did it have weapons? He jerked it from the ground. To her obvious dismay, he tore it open. He found a book, *The Last of the Mohicans,* and photographs. Then nothing of significance, just fake jewelry and other feminine articles. But one item practically burned like fire in his hand—a Bible. He hadn't seen the white man's book since he left Denver six years ago. The one his father had. He shoved it back in. No weapons. He stuffed everything else in and handed it to her.

Relief reflected in her eyes as she hugged the bag.

White Eagle ambled to his horse, his stride uneasy.

Distant cries of women and children carried up from the wagons as the other braves rummaged through their belongings. If only that man hadn't raised his rifle, no one would have been killed. But had their roles been reversed, White Eagle might have done the same.

He grabbed his water skin and removed the stopper. He walked back to the woman and held it out to her.

She gaped at it.

He shook the water.

She looked at him then back at the skin. Lunging forward, she dropped her bag. After a moment's hesitation, she snatched the water skin. Water spilled down her chin and over her front. She choked.

"Slow down," he said in Cheyenne. "I mean, slow down," he said again, only this time in French. He shook his head and went back to his horse. "I can't talk," he mumbled in English.

Running Cloud rode up to him on his horse. White Eagle boldly met his gaze. He'd almost forgotten about tossing his friend to the ground. He'd never before laid a hand on Running Cloud, who was more like a brother than a friend.

"We're taking the woman," Running Cloud said in Cheyenne, motioning towards Walks Alone.

"No." White Eagle turned to his horse and straightened out the blanket. "I don't want her."

"You're refusing my gift?" Running Cloud's voice rose as he thumbed his chest. "You knock me down for her, and now you don't want her?" He turned to Walks Alone, eyes blazing. "Then I'll take her." Running Cloud moved toward the woman.

"No!" White Eagle grabbed the reins, ready to grab more than that if he had to. "I'll keep her." White Eagle never agreed with Running Cloud's ways of war, ravishing innocent women, and if he even laid a pinky on this one, he'd . . . what would he do? Kill his friend? The thought of him touching her made him so livid with rage, he just might. But at what cost? He'd lose his life to the other braves protecting their war chief, and then what would happen to the woman?

Was he actually contemplating murdering his friend? A friend who had been more like his brother? What had come over him? Sure, it was the Cheyenne way to kill a man who touched his woman, but this woman didn't even belong to him.

Running Cloud leaned over his saddle. "She's mine," he said slowly, laying emphasis on each word, "until you make her yours."

White Eagle's fists tightened on the reins at his suggestion. "I don't do that, and you know it." His words were like the low rumble of thunder before a storm.

Running Cloud arched a brow, a smirk on his lips. He then laughed. "You think that's what I meant?" He continued to laugh. "Then you're a fool."

The significance of his words poured over White Eagle like a heavy rainfall. He meant for him to take her as his wife. *A wife?* He didn't need a wife. He was ready to tear into Running Cloud for that, but he kept his hands to himself. He had to calm down. There'd been enough fighting between friends with Black Bear on the rampage. But how could Running Cloud force him to take this woman as his wife? He ran his hand down his face, trying to contain his fury.

Clenching his jaw, he shook his head in disbelief. At least the woman would remain unharmed. But did he have to make her his wife to keep her safe?

White Eagle marched to Walks Alone, seething with fury.

Spotted Owl galloped up to them, letting them know the other braves were ready to go. Running Cloud took off toward the wagons.

Now Walks Alone not only hugged her carpetbag but also his water skin. He took the water skin, grabbed the woman's dainty elbow, and led her to his horse.

She gasped as they neared the painted beast, and it wasn't until then that he realized just how large his horse must appear to a woman her size. "Get on the horse," White Eagle said in Cheyenne. He shook his head in frustration. English. He needed to speak English.

Realizing she wouldn't be able to mount without help, he lifted the stiff and proper young lady from the ground. Wide green eyes looked down on his face. The position reminded him of his father when he'd pick him up and playfully toss him in the water. And just as his father had done, White Eagle lifted her above his head. She weighed no more than a child, and despite his anger, a chuckle rumbled in his chest as the woman, stiff as a board, hugged the bag as if it might keep her from falling. Forcing the grin from his face, he set her on his horse. He then pried the carpetbag from her fingers and, as she protested, tossed it to Spotted Owl who looked none too happy about having to carry the lady's belongings—he already had a bag of sugar, and some of the white crystals stuck to the corners of his mouth.

"I'm not carrying this." Spotted Owl made ready to toss the bag on the ground.

White Eagle turned on him. "You will." He had a feeling that bag was all the woman owned, and he hated the thought of leaving her photographs to the elements. What he wouldn't give to have pictures of his own parents. Or was that truly the only reason he wished her to keep it? His hand still tingled from touching the white man's holy book.

Another scream carried from the wagons, but White Eagle pushed it out of his mind, unwilling to investigate. They should leave.

He mounted behind Walks Alone, and she straightened. Her feet dangled over one side of the horse, and he sensed she might jump off, so he wrapped his arm around her waist and clicked the reins. The horse galloped away from the settlers. Spotted Owl, Standing Elk, and the other four warriors joined him. To his surprise, Running Cloud galloped ahead with the dead man's wife in his saddle. White Eagle clenched his jaw. Now he had two women to protect rather than one.

Walks Alone grasped the horse's mane then his arm, but quickly released him as if he might bite. Then she grabbed the mane again.

"Be still. I won't let you fall," he said, finally in English, his accent strange and thick. How long had it been since he'd used this language? It was one thing to teach his friends how to speak English, but to think on his feet was more difficult.

The other braves rode beside them, and she leaned into him but immediately pulled away.

White Eagle sighed. The settlers were headed for Denver City, but now these two women were headed west.

Chapter 4

White Eagle held Walks Alone in his arms as she moved against his chest. She had fought sleep long enough and finally lost the battle.

He had never seen a woman more tempting and beautiful. Her long hair cascaded over his thigh. He ached to wrap it around his neck and take in its softness. Instead, he gently moved his fingers through her yellow mane, watching it shimmer against his dark skin.

He found it difficult to have the petite, shapely woman so near and not lose control of his senses. He shifted slightly in an attempt to put some distance between them.

She snuggled in closer.

A sigh escaped her full lips, the kind a man would want to kiss, drawing his attention to the slight upward curve of her nose. He fought the urge to run his forefinger along its freckled bridge, fearing she might awaken. Her thin brows, a tad darker than her hair, didn't arch quite as sharply now that she slept.

What was a woman like her doing alone in a land like this? She didn't wear a ring, and there was no indentation of one, showing no signs of having been married. Her clothing told him she didn't come from any of the Western Territories or States. Why had she been walking alone so far behind the other wagons? Was a relative awaiting her arrival in Denver City? He hoped not. If she didn't show, they might come looking for her.

"It'll be dark soon," Running Cloud said. "We'll camp tonight on Rocky Ridge. It'll be safe there."

White Eagle nodded, fearful of what Running Cloud intended to do with the woman on his horse.

After they had left the settlers, White Eagle, Running Cloud, and the rest of the braves had started off toward the west, but as soon as Walks Alone fell asleep, they had turned south, traveling along the hogbacks. The rolling hills looked like giant loaves of bread he recalled the whites serving at his father's table. Now they were just beyond the hogbacks west of Denver City and climbing into the Rocky Mountains.

"Black Bear will return to our village," Running Cloud said. "We need to be prepared."

White Eagle agreed, contemplating the dangers that lay ahead for both the women.

"I'm honored to have you at my side."

White Eagle didn't look at his friend. He knew Running Cloud was trying to pacify him for forcing the woman on him. He ignored him and continued to run Walks Alone's golden mane between his fingers.

"Because you saved my life at Sand Creek, I call you White Eagle and my brother, but maybe you prefer receiving Walks Alone over the gift of my blood." Running Cloud's brow rose. "I'm not as exciting to look at."

White Eagle grinned then forced a frown, remembering he was angry with him.

Running Cloud's expression became serious. "The Great Spirit of the Sun has touched your woman. The people of our village will accept her. I'll make sure they do," he said. "Song Bird will be pleased that you'll finally have a woman to share your blanket."

Now it was easy for White Eagle to be angry. He didn't want a wife. Sure, they'd been watching the settlers for a few days, and he'd enjoyed watching Walks Alone soaking in the river. Despite that, he'd never shown any intention of taking her.

"Now you can have what you saw," Running Cloud said.

White Eagle suspected the next several weeks were going to be very difficult on the Eastern-bred Walks Alone. But how much more difficult would they be on him? He had simply smiled when he laid eyes on her, and now she was in his arms.

"White men treat their women like dogs." Running Cloud motioned to Woman Of Sorrow's bruised eye.

The slender woman sat stiff in Running Cloud's saddle, not saying a word or daring to look to the side. Her hands trembled when she reached up to brush a loose strand of dark hair behind her ear.

"This time she'll have a better husband," Running Cloud said, his mouth set in a rigid line.

Woman Of Sorrow was pretty, and White Eagle understood why Running Cloud would want her. But as a wife? Did that mean he wouldn't ravish her? Running Cloud didn't understand that white women were not gifts to be taken or given away. Sure, it was common to steal women from enemy tribes and force them to marry, but this was different. White Eagle knew that anger still raged inside Running Cloud towards the white man. So, if he intended to marry her, why? He'd killed the woman's husband. Was it out of honor or duty that he took her? Maybe he was taking Woman Of Sorrow as his wife to benefit the tribe?

That was it. Running Cloud planned to marry her as a means of securing safety from the white man for his village. If the war chief were to take a white wife, there was a greater chance that the village wouldn't fall under attack. He recalled Running Cloud voicing those very words just days earlier when they'd spotted Walks Alone by the river. Yet, if news of her kidnapping got out, that could make the situation worse. Either way, he knew Running Cloud would abide by his word and treat the woman with respect as he would any other Cheyenne bride.

That was a relief, but for the first time ever, White Eagle regretted not becoming war chief when it was offered to him. Had White Eagle become war chief, Running Cloud would be beneath him, not the other way around, and both these women would be on their way to Denver City right now.

White Eagle glanced down at Walks Alone's face, half white, half red. A straight line stretched horizontally across one cheek, over her nose, and across the other cheek, dividing her face. The top, white as snow, the bottom red and sunburned.

"The Great Spirit of the Sun not only touches her hair, but touches her face," Running

Cloud said. "Maybe we should call her Stripe?"

"Then you may have the honor of telling the woman her new name."

Running Cloud chuckled.

Anna awoke to find herself on the warrior's horse and practically drooling on the man's chest. She pulled away, her hair matted against her cheek from sleep. Heat crept from her neck to her face as she loosened her hold on the Indian. How dreadful. She shouldn't have allowed herself to fall asleep on him like that. She had actually fallen asleep. In the midst of dangerous peril, she'd fallen asleep!

But she'd been so exhausted and weary from all that had happened, she shouldn't be too hard on herself for losing what self-control and dignity she had left. Now that her headache was gone and the air cooled, she felt refreshed, despite the fact that she was still held captive.

She looked for Beth and found her still sitting in front of Running Cloud. Beth sat straight, chin high, and brushed a loose strand of hair from her face with surprising calmness. Why could Anna not muster the same?

Evergreens surrounded them, and they were no longer on the plains. The scent of pine filled the air as the horses' hooves made their way over rocks and rugged terrain. Birds called to one another, and one swooped down close to the riders. The warriors wore solemn faces, seemingly unaware of the beauty surrounding them.

The recent events turned over in Anna's mind. Earlier, White Eagle had spoken in English. Would he understand her? She cleared her throat. "Did you kill Bet's husband?" she whispered, horrified at her poor pronunciation, nerves and fear having gotten the best of her.

"*Non*—no."

So, he didn't pull the trigger, but one of his friends certainly did. She wondered who. Why hadn't they killed the rest of the settlers? And why had they taken her and Beth?

The Indians reined in at the top of a ridge surrounded by large boulders, between which a lovely view of the open plains came into sight.

A shame she couldn't enjoy it.

White Eagle dismounted. He helped Anna down and set her in front of him, and it was then that she took in his large frame. She only came to his chest, and his broad shoulders hovered over her. She arched her head back to look up into the warrior's captivating eyes. They were like none she'd ever seen.

He stared down at her, his gaze tracing her features with no evidence of emotion. Unable to bear his unrelenting stare, she looked past him at the trees and turned sideways to rub the soreness from her neck and shoulder as a means of occupying herself.

"Do you ache as much as I do?" Beth came to stand by her as White Eagle led his horse away.

Anna nodded and tried to put some order to her hair, resisting the urge to rub her aching backside.

"We're blessed they didn't make us walk." Beth hugged herself. "Indian women usually have to walk, while the men ride the horses. And the length of time they made those poor horses gallop, they must be in a hurry."

"Of course they are. They just kidnapped two women."

Beth took Anna's trembling hand. That's when Anna noticed Beth's hands trembled as well. "The Lord is with us. We mustn't forget."

Anna nodded, but all she could think of was how often she'd prayed in the past, how often she'd trusted in the Lord. But He had never rescued her. And now look at the mess she was in. God always seemed to disappear when she needed Him most.

Time to change the subject. "What I don't understand is how I could have fallen asleep. It makes no sense at all." It had been easy to relax into White Eagle while the horse galloped. It made the ride smooth, rather that jostling her around when the horse trotted.

Pinching her lips together, Beth studied White Eagle. "I think it's because you know in your heart he won't hurt you."

"How can you say such a thing?"

"Just look at him. He watches you with a sympathetic eye."

Anna glanced over at White Eagle. He looked away, and she looked at the ground.

"He feels sorry for you," Beth whispered, continuing to study him. "I'm sure of it."

The man had just kidnapped her. How could he possibly feel sorry for her? Wishing she could make her hands stop shaking, she tried to brush her hair out of her face. She turned to look for her carpetbag when two Indians came near with two small bags. They opened the cloth sacks and dumped out several turtles at her and Beth's feet.

Anna jumped back, staring at the black and yellow shells.

"Food," one of the Indians said with a thick accent.

Anna didn't take her eyes off the turtles, waiting for scaly heads and arms to appear.

"They're prairie turtles. I think they expect us to prepare these to eat," Beth said.

Anna shivered. "Then maybe they can fetch us a rabbit or a chicken. I've never touched a turtle before. Let alone *eaten* one."

White Eagle set a circle of stones to prepare a fire. From his shoulder strap, he pulled off a small horn and took a sheath from its end.

Anna backed away from the turtles, but to her surprise, Beth picked two up in each hand. "Might as well get started." Beth motioned to her, still visibly trembling. "You just rest a while. I'll take care of it."

Anna couldn't let Beth do everything alone, so she stepped forward to pick up the remainder of the turtles. She could only manage one, despite its small size. The softness of its bottom shell made her arms weak. As she took slow, cautious steps to where White Eagle prepared the fire, she stared intently around the edges of the yellow and black shell of the reptile. What would she do if it poked its scaly head out? She should be brave like Beth. She lifted her chin, searching for the courage she lacked.

To her horror, head and arms popped out. She squealed, and the warriors around her grabbed their weapons. She jumped back and dropped the reptile, fluttering her hands before her and wiping them off on her skirt to rid herself of their feel.

As the warriors became aware that there was no actual danger, she froze in place and looked up at their dark faces, readying herself for whatever wrath they chose to inflict.

To her surprise, they laughed, but the warrior with spotted owl feathers who'd been the most startled grabbed her by the hair and shouted words she didn't understand. White Eagle stood and shouted at the man. He released her.

She ducked under the warrior's arm, scurried away, and slumped onto a large rock.

Running Cloud hadn't reacted to the commotion and stood in the background with arms folded, watching Beth.

"Help," the Indian with elk antlers as a weapon said to Anna and pointed at Beth.

How was it so many of them spoke English? She rose and took a cautious step toward Beth. She had to be strong. She had to be brave. Brave like Beth. But she froze when she saw Beth pulling on one of the scaly necks; it made her think of snakes, and her knees went weak.

"We'll roast them," White Eagle said to Beth. A small flame flickered as he made a fire from his horn.

All the Indians watched Anna.

"Make food," the one who'd grabbed her said in his thick accent, a deep frown pinching his face as he glared at her.

Anger stirred. It sparked helpful embers of courage. "I should be in Denver City right now, not here in the middle of nowhere preparing turtles for supper." With that, she turned and sat on the nearest rock, hugging her knees and trembling. Even if it meant her life, she couldn't bring herself to touch another turtle.

The men mumbled to one another, and she distinctively heard one say, "Lazy woman." They obviously weren't pleased with her outburst. She was a coward, and shame swept through her. What would they do to her now? Would they beat her, kill and scalp her? She hugged her knees tighter and glanced out over the golden plains. If only she were there right now.

White Eagle spoke in a firm tone in that unusual language of theirs, and the men fell silent.

However, a few Indians mumbled, motioning toward Beth and nodding their approval.

Anna wished the ground would swallow her whole.

Anna couldn't sleep. The thought of turtles and snakes crawling on her caused even the slightest rustle of wind against her skin to make her jump. Since she'd refused to eat, her stomach growled, and she shivered as she stared up at the stars. Their beauty took her breath away—they looked close enough to touch. Never had she seen anything so wondrous. God's creation never failed to amaze her. She reached up to the tiny diamonds, imagining she could take hold of one between her fingers.

Lord, where are you?

The blanket of stars stretched forth, and she pushed up on her elbow. Over the ridge, she saw the plains of Colorado Territory. Distant lights dotted the flat horizon.

A city.

The moon illuminated just enough light for her to see details of the sleeping bodies. The men formed a circle and surrounded her and Beth around the low flickering fire.

White Eagle leaned on his elbow, watching her. Her breath caught. The moonlight outlined his arm, emphasizing the muscle there, and his painted face never turned away from her. Surely he'd feel embarrassed and look away, or he planned on starting a conversation. So she waited for him to speak.

Crickets played their tunes around them. Quiet snores from some of the men cut into their music, and the snap of crackling flames filled the silence.

Perhaps she ought to say something to get him to stop staring. "Is that Denver City?" She pointed at the lights.

He nodded. Still staring.

"I ought to be there now," she murmured. The lights were like gold in a sea of black satin. Her golden city. She could actually see it. After all these years, she finally had it in her sights. Now all *she* could do was stare.

She licked her dry, chapped lips, and scratched her stiff cheeks and chin.

"Don't do that," White Eagle said, his thick, strange accent hanging on the night air. "Your *visage*." He shook his head. "Your face. It is red. You'll get blisters."

"I must look like a cooked lobster." She dreaded the thought of freckles coming out. How would that look to the board of education?

"The women at the village have good medicine. They will give you some for your face."

"We're going to your village?" She tried not to raise her voice, fearful that the others might awaken. "What are you going to do with us there?" Visions of the whole tribe of Indians attacking her flashed through her mind. Maybe reading Papa's novel hadn't been such a good idea after all.

"Woman Of Sorrow will become Running Cloud's wife."

The news hit her like a blast from a cannon ball. "They will be *married?*" Anna couldn't believe it. Would he actually marry someone he didn't know?

"*Oui*—yes."

"What if she doesn't want to marry him?"

White Eagle tossed a pine needle. "She will."

"But what if she won't?"

"Woman Of Sorrow belongs to him."

"Why?" Since she was his captive, she deserved some answers.

"Running Cloud killed her husband. He will care for her."

"So he's the one who murdered Al." Anna glanced over at where Running Cloud slept. He was a frightening man. She'd never forget him pulling her hair and grabbing her. And now her friend was doomed to become his wife. Poor Beth. She deserved better. She deserved a decent husband.

She deserved a decent name.

"Why must you call her Woman Of Sorrow? I happen to know she's a delightful young lady." She wasn't sad, despite reasons to be so. If Beth was going to be trapped in this life, the least they could do was give her a better name.

"She will be."

"Will be what?"

"Happy."

"How can you know that?" How could anyone be happy marrying someone they didn't know?

"Running Cloud will treat her well."

But who would want to live with savages? Then her thoughts turned to herself. "What will become of me?" Her voice quivered. It was a frightening question to ask, but she had to know.

"You will be my wife." The man's face darkened.

Anna's cheeks grew hot, and she tried to breathe. "But suppose I don't want to marry . . . an Indian?" She kept from saying "a savage," since it seemed more like a personal attack, and the last thing she wanted was to rile up a wild Indian. Would she be trapped with this man for the rest of her life?

"You'll marry me under Cheyenne law. It means nothing to the white man."

"Cheyenne law? But we'll be *married*," she said in a harsh whisper. "I don't want to marry . . . you. I don't even know you!" She stopped to catch her breath, looking around to make sure everyone was still asleep. Thoughts of escape raced through her mind. Then thoughts of getting lost, attacked by wild animals or snakes flooded over her. Running away wouldn't be a wise idea, she'd never find her way to Denver City. Or would she? From here she could see the lights. If she would just follow the lights, she could get out of these mountains on her own.

"I have to be in Denver. They're expecting me." She hoped the savage would find this an important enough reason to return her to civilization.

"Who's expecting you?"

She sighed, preparing herself to hear the famous speech of a woman traveling alone and the great dangers thereof. She had lost count of all the people who'd warned her on the train. Just then, her thoughts knocked her upside the head. Didn't someone warn her of Indians? And now here she sat a captive. She decided his speech would be a bit late in coming.

"The board of education," she finally said.

"Do you have family there?"

She stared past him into the lonely shadows of the forest. "I don't have any family."

"What are you doing here?"

She breathed deeply. "I came all the way from New York to work as a teacher. If you will please escort me to Denver City in the morning, I would be very grateful." She tried to sound dignified, self-assured, though in her heart she was terrified and begging. "I don't wish to marry you. You seem like a decent person, but I don't know you," she added, trying to soften the blow, as if she hadn't already been blunt about it. "Please, I have to go to Denver."

He sighed and lay back down. "You've been taken by Indians. You can't expect them to deliver you where you want to go."

"Don't you mean, 'kidnapped'?" She lay down, trembling as she stared at the stars. She should have gotten off the train near Julesburg. Had she done that, she wouldn't be lying here right now, conversing with a savage.

"The others in the wagons didn't care about you. So you weren't kidnapped. Just given as a peace offering."

She crossed her arms to ward off the chill. "All they cared about was saving their own scalps. I've never met such cowards in all my life." Her voice hitched as she said the words aloud, thinking of how afraid everyone was of Al and how none of them were willing to bring her water.

"Neither have I." The purr of his voice was close, sending a tingle down her neck. He covered her with buckskin, and then moved away. The warmth enveloped her.

"Tank—*th*ank you," she said, glad he was no longer near, but grateful for the warmth. A knot came to her throat. She tried not to cry, isolation and loneliness choking her.

That lonely feeling was all too familiar.

She had hoped to finally be happy, maybe even find an essence of her papa in Denver City. It seemed home would always be out of reach.

But it wasn't out of reach. She could actually *see* it. Hope was not lost. Not when she was so close.

The lights of the distant city called out to her, winked at her. Taunted her.

Tonight. This night.

Her one and only chance to escape.

Chapter 5

Anna lay staring at the stars for a long time. The warmth of the buckskin nearly made her fall asleep, but she threw it off in order to stay awake.

When heavy, even breathing came from White Eagle, and she was certain everyone else was asleep as their snores continued to break through the silence, she turned to Beth and poked her.

"Bet," she whispered close to her ear.

"What?" Beth rolled over, still half asleep. "What's wrong?"

"Get up. We're getting out of here. I'm taking us to Denver City."

"What?" Fear reflected in Beth's moonlit eyes.

"Shh . . . ." Anna put her fingers to her mouth and glanced around. No one stirred. "If we're going to escape, we have to go now. Denver is still in view, and who knows how deep in the mountains we'll be by tomorrow evening."

"I can't go." Beth rolled over to go back to sleep.

"What?" Anna shook her shoulder. "Wake up. We have to go. Running Cloud is going to force you to marry him."

Beth faced Anna. "I know. Maybe he will treat me better than Al did. Besides, I don't have work waiting for me. What would I do? I don't have any money. I have nothing." Her eyes glistened in the moonlight. "And what if they recapture us?" She grabbed Anna's hand. "I have a bad feeling about this."

"We can figure all that out on *de* way *the*re. Please Bet, this is our only chance. We have to go now." It seemed she'd forgotten how to speak all together, but in this moment of desperation, it no longer mattered.

"I just can't." Beth shook her head. "Running Cloud has been—well—kind to me. I don't fear him. Not like I feared Al. I don't know why, but I just don't."

"But he murdered your husband." The urgency in Anna's voice rose.

"Any future he has to offer me has to be better than anything Denver City could offer. I'd likely be forced to work as a saloon girl just to survive. I'd rather live with Indians than be forced into that kind of a life." She took in a long, deep breath. "We mustn't be afraid," she said as if not only convincing Anna, but herself. She patted Anna's hand. "Everything's going to be all right. God will take care of us." Beth lay back down as if all was right with the world.

Anna couldn't believe her ears. How could Beth act as if this dire situation didn't exist? It was beyond Anna's comprehension. It was foolish!

Besides, where was God when Anna was being beaten by her uncle? How did He take care of her then? The only way God would take care of them was if they *did* something about it.

Anna didn't have time to argue with her friend. If she were going to get away, she had to leave now. This was her only chance to escape. She hadn't planned on leaving Beth behind, but she couldn't force her to go without waking everybody. If Anna stayed, there would be absolutely no hope. But if she went now, there would at least be a ray of hope, small one though it might be. Once in Denver, she would notify the marshal of their kidnapping and he could rescue Beth. Yes, that's what she would do.

Quietly, she got to her feet, wrapped the buckskin over her shoulders, and picked up her carpetbag. She felt like a tree standing amidst the sleeping bodies. Surely someone would take notice of her, but nobody moved. Holding her breath, she lifted her skirt and stepped toward a slight opening between White Eagle and another Indian.

Fingers clamped around her ankle. She froze, fear prickling from her toes to her neck.

"Where are you going?" It was White Eagle's voice, thick from sleep.

"Um—I have to relieve myself." The lie came on its own, without a single thought. In fact, it came too easily. She'd have to deal with her conscience later.

"What's the bag for?"

"It's necessary that I, um . . . I need things . . . it's not proper to discuss."

He seized her arm, his fingers tangling in her hair, and pulled her down near his painted face. "What things?"

"Womanly things." She clenched her teeth. "Feminine things that men have no business knowing about."

He released her as though she'd bitten him.

If it hadn't been so dark he might have seen the flame in her cheeks. Her papa had been right. After telling one lie, the ones after that just grew bigger. But desperate times required desperate measures.

"Go. But don't take long." He eased back down.

And go she did.

Once she put plenty of distance between the Indians and herself, she bolted between the trees. A constant view of Denver City was in her sights as she made her way across the ridge. Soon she would come upon less rugged ground and be able to work her way down the side of the mountain—she hoped.

The sounds of her breathing echoed off the trees. She gripped the buckskin tightly against her chest, even though the cool night air didn't bother her now as she ran for her life. Her carpetbag felt heavy, and her feet carried her over fallen branches and pinecones. To her left, the small lights of Denver City, so far away, were still in view.

The moon lent just enough light to ensure she didn't run into trees, but the rest of the woods were nothing but black shadows. She forced her mind on Denver. Home was where she was headed, and nothing would stop her. Not fear, not her uncle . . . not even a band of wild Indians.

"I'll kill the woman," Running Cloud said in a furious whisper so the other braves wouldn't hear. The moon's light illuminated his angry face. "I'll pass her among the warriors. They'll humble her."

That thought sent a shock of white-hot anger through White Eagle's system, and right then and there he knew if anyone laid a hand on her, he'd kill him. "She's mine, and I'll bring her back."

"She's not yours until marriage. Until then, she belongs to *me*." Running Cloud thumbed his chest, challenging his friend. "This woman's life is of no value. She's defiant and not worthy of our tribe."

"She is worthy," White Eagle said. "She's shown bravery by running away, though her escape will be in vain. You said yourself, Walks Alone has been touched by the Spirit of the Sun." He used any argument he could come up with, whether he believed it or not. Anything to save her hide. "She's strong, and a valuable gift. I want to make my gratitude known. I'll find her, bring her back, and make her my wife."

Running Cloud studied him, and then his frown softened. "She is brave, or foolish. If you wish to claim your gift then go after her. By sunrise, we'll continue on to the village. If you're not at the village after two suns, I'll take back your gift, and she will be given to the warriors to do with as they please." He started to turn then stopped and pointed at White Eagle. "If you don't find her, I will. If she comes in contact with anyone, she could endanger our village with the knowledge she has of us."

Even if White Eagle tried to take her to Denver City, Running Cloud would follow through with his word, sooner or later. Walks Alone's defiance to his authority had ignited his anger all over again toward the white man. Thankfully, Woman Of Sorrow hadn't tried to escape, or there would have been no hope. When his heart was ruled by anger, Running Cloud's wrath could be as deadly as Black Bear's.

They had been chasing Black Bear, who was still on the rampage destroying any and all newcomers to the Western Territories. They had followed him from their secret village as far as the South Platte. This last confrontation with Black Bear had been the worst yet, and White Eagle had fought well, despite the fact that he constantly resisted killing his old friend.

Because of Running Cloud's withdrawal from the renegade parties, Black Bear blamed White Eagle. Now he and Running Cloud were considered enemies of Black Bear, even though Black Bear and Running Cloud were brothers.

White Eagle had obviously pleased Running Cloud, and that was why he originally offered Walks Alone to him as a gift. She likely would have been killed if she'd remained with the wagon train anyway. White Eagle had little doubt that Black Bear would return and raid the travelers.

Good thing he took Walks Alone. But now he had to save her from herself.

The lights of Denver City became distant between the trees. The woods grew dense, and Anna was forced to work her way toward the opposite direction of Denver. She came to a clearing where shadows lurked in all directions. An owl hooted, and then a chilling silence hung on the air.

No longer able to be guided by the distant lights of the city, she looked up at the stars to try and get her bearings. It was important that she continue in the right direction. But she had no idea how to follow the stars, and she feared she was lost already. Still, anything was better than being held captive. At least now she was free, and eventually she'd find her way.

She started in the direction she thought was correct. When she came to the center of a clearing, a twig cracked several feet behind her. The light hairs on her neck rose. Was it just a small animal foraging for food? Or was it a bear? Slowly, she turned to look.

A large shadow loomed halfway from the edge of the clearing to where she stood. She froze.

Nothing had been there before. She dropped her carpetbag, picked up her skirt and ran.

The animal's movements thumped behind her and came closer. Suddenly, she was taken about the waist. Her screams carried up through the trees, and she found herself aboard a horse.

"If you ever do that again, I'll kill you myself." Its rider held her close, whispering harshly in her ear.

White Eagle.

"Nay!" she shouted and struggled to break free, but he held her fast. She scratched his arms and kicked.

The horse jerked its head back and sidestepped.

White Eagle reined in and slid with her to the ground, causing her to land on all fours.

Anna got to her feet and bolted. She barely made it a few feet when he grabbed her arm and swung her around. Screaming, she kicked, and when her boot met his shin, he loosened his grasp just enough for her to get away. She ran, but again, he swung her around by the arm. This time her palm met his face, and he jerked back.

Growling, he seized her arms and held her in front of him. She twisted and turned, but it was useless.

Not saying a word, he waited.

She pulled and twisted her arms, but it did no good. Finally, out of breath and strength, she relented, her whole being trembling. "Let me go." She threw him a scowl, but even that failed when her hair fell over her eyes. "Let go of me."

"Is it your time?" he asked.

"What?"

"Answer me."

"I don't know what you mean."

"Are you bleeding?"

She gasped, mortified that he'd dare ask such a thing.

"Answer me, now!" His grip tightened on her arms, and he jerked her inches from his face.

"No!" Tears forced their way to the surface.

"Little liar," he rasped, lightening his hold. He shook his head and released a long breath. "They would have killed you if it were true." She wondered if she detected a hint of relief in his eyes or if it was just the moon's reflection casting an odd light on his painted face. He gestured toward her with his chin. "What's your name?"

She turned her face away, refusing to answer. He chuckled at her useless display of dignity.

Tingles began in her fingertips and carried up to where his hands gripped her.

"You're hurting me," she said. Another lie. Oh, how easily they came!

With that, he released her—palms up—and stepped back.

Anna lifted a trembling finger and pointed it at his painted chin. "I'm going to Denver, and you're not going to stop me!"

White Eagle smiled, his teeth glowing white in the moonlight, and then gallantly swept his arm aside. "Go."

Uncertain, Anna backed away. Surely he didn't mean it. But what if he did? She hiked up her skirt and bolted. She ran as fast as she could, just in case the man changed his mind.

With surprising agility, White Eagle ran beside her and then jumped in front of her. She dodged to the left, but he blocked her way. She backed up, not letting him out of her sight. There had to be a way around. They circled each other like two wild animals ready to pounce.

"Stop it," she said between clenched teeth.

White Eagle stepped closer. She drew in a sharp breath. He stepped toward her again, and she stepped back again, but something stopped her feet. She found herself trapped against a tree.

White Eagle leaned against the trunk, hand over her shoulder and amusement in his eyes. "You don't even know the way." He moved in closer, and Anna held her breath. "We should have named you Talks A Lot." Grinning, his fingertips brushed against her cheek as his eyes seemed to drink in her face, her hair. "Aren't you afraid?"

"If you were going to kill me," Anna whispered, trying to fight off the strange way he made her feel, "you would have done so by now." Then she added with a bite of sarcasm, "Besides, we're supposed to get *married*. Or have you forgotten?" With that she ducked under his arm and bolted.

Chuckling, he caught her about the waist and swung her around.

She fought him, only with less fervor since her limbs felt as heavy as trees. She twisted and kicked. "Take me home. I don't want to marry you!" A knot filled her throat, but she swallowed hard. She refused to cry in front of this savage.

He set her on her feet and turned her to face him, holding her wrist.

Her hair hung in disarray all around her body and in her face, blinding her. She brushed the strands aside so she could see. "Please," she said, breathless. "I want to go home."

"I'll take you there after we're married."

"What?"

"After we're married. I'll take you to Denver City." His accent was strange and thick, and yet his English wasn't broken like that of the other Indians. What made this man so different? "When you're there, you can live your life as you see fit. You can marry who you want. Forget this ever happened."

Even this savage didn't want her. "Why would you marry me then set me free?"

"I marry you out of duty to my friend. You are his captive. If you refuse to marry me, he'll take your life." The moonlight revealed the frown on his painted face.

She swallowed.

"Don't defy him." He yanked her close. "You could have lost your life tonight."

"Would he have found me?" Well, that was a stupid question. If White Eagle found her then Running Cloud surely would have. "Are you sure an Indian marriage doesn't mean anything to civilized people?"

"Yes."

"And after we are . . . married," the word made her heart sink, "you will take me home—to Denver City?"

"You have my word."

"But why? What difference does a wedding make to my freedom?"

"If we are married, you belong to me. You become my woman and don't belong to Running Cloud. Then I can do what I want with you."

His last words brought frightening images to her mind. "Nay!" She turned to run, but he jerked her back to him.

"I won't take your womanhood."

Shocked at his boldness of speech, she reached up to slap him, but he caught it. Now, he held both her wrists in his steel-like grip.

"How dare you speak of such tings—things. You have no right." Tears welled in her eyes, and she lost the battle of holding them back. She may have started this conversation, but he didn't have to be so blunt about it.

He sighed. "When we're married, I'll take you where you want to go."

She struggled against him.

"I give you my word." His voice was low, almost soothing.

Still she doubted, mortified at the conversation they were having. "How do I know you're not lying?"

Anger spread across his face and his lips curved downward. "I've given my word. That is enough."

Desperate to change the subject, she asked, "Wha—what about Bet? Will she be set free too?"

"No. She belongs to Running Cloud."

Her heart went out to her poor friend. Hadn't she suffered enough in this world? Anna determined again that, as soon as she was set free, she would tell the marshal about Beth so he could rescue her.

"I don't want to go wit you, but I can't fight you anymore." She had no choice, nor the physical stamina. She jerked her wrists out of his grasp and started toward her carpetbag but turned and pointed a trembling finger at him. "You had better be a man of your word," *and not touch me,* "and take me to Denver City when this is finished."

Chapter

That night, rather than return to camp, they traveled long and hard. The deeper they went into the mountains, the deeper Anna's heart sank. Her eyes grew heavy, and she felt sleep taking over, but she opened her eyes in haste. She wouldn't dare fall asleep this time.

Black shadows of the forest came alive. The thought of wild animals lurking in the darkness made her move instinctively closer to her captor. Branches stretched out, reaching for her as if they knew she'd try to escape, and those same wicked pines shadowed the moon and stars, the only part of the forest offering her comfort.

White Eagle hummed, his chest reverberating against her side. It made her feel less alone, and she hated the fact that it stilled her nerves. Sleep tugged on her lids, and the baritone melody lulled her against him like a soft wind swaying a leaf. She forced her eyes open. "Stop it," she whispered, her voice muffled by the darkness, but he continued to hum.

"*Bonne nuit, ma chérie.*" White Eagle's breath tickled her ear.

Her lids grew heavy. What'd he say? Gentle shadows faded in and out, until finally she gave in to the stillness, to the low rumbling of his chest, to the murmuring of his voice.

When she opened her eyes, the early morning light and birds singing in the trees greeted her. She was still on White Eagle's horse, and they must have traveled the entire night.

"Did you sleep well?" he asked.

She pushed away from his body. Its warmth, though still inviting, clung to her. At least now, he wore a shirt with fringes along the arms and seam. Still, she would rather suffer from a chill than be so close to the man.

"You never told me your name."

She straightened her skirt and turned her face away. He may have been able to keep her from getting home, but he couldn't force her to say her name, not even if he threatened her with snakes. Her taste of freedom had been short lived, and she was tired of being everyone's prisoner.

"You're not from New York. I could hear it last night. You had an accent. Where are you really from?"

"None of your business." Ashamed that proper pronunciation had failed her the night before, she was determined to speak better today, no matter how nervous she became.

"Let's rest here." He helped her dismount near a river and then pointed to a clump of bushes. "You can go there. And don't try to escape. If you take too long, I'll come after you."

Her face heated at the thought of him finding her in such a state. She hurried to take care of business as he led the painted beast to drink.

When Anna returned, all she saw were trees. Across the river was a solid rocky cliff, and just beyond that, another snow-capped mountain. How would she ever get home? Would this man keep his word, or was she headed for disaster?

The lightning streak along the horse's flank and white handprints dotting his body rippled over the horse's muscles as he drank. The detail intrigued her.

White Eagle appeared from the trees.

"Why do you paint your horse?" The words tumbled from her mouth without thought. Curiosity had gotten the best of her.

"My people believe lightning gives the horse speed. And each handprint represents one less enemy I have to deal with." His eyes flashed beneath his mask of paint as he trudged toward her.

So he was a murderer. If only she'd escaped last night when she had the chance. At least then the lights of Denver were near. How had she gotten herself into such a mess?

Julesburg.

Funny how she had mistrusted that gentleman who had spoken to her on the train. All he had done was look at her, and she'd run away. Now here she was held captive by a savage.

She plopped down on the ground. The bustle in her dress was losing its spring, as was she. She opened her carpetbag and carefully took out the pictures of her parents. Would they be disappointed in her? Maybe she should have stayed in New York.

No. She never should have had to endure Uncle Horace's abuse. She had found a way out and worked hard to take it. Besides, she had been Uncle Horace's captive long enough. But didn't she find herself in much the same circumstance?

She sensed White Eagle standing behind her.

"Who are they?"

"None of your business," she said.

He knelt down. The warmth of his nearness made her shiver. "Your parents?"

She didn't answer.

Walking around, he sat next to her and held out some dried meat. "It's elk."

Her stomach hurt after refusing to eat the night before. She didn't care what it was, as long as it wasn't turtle, so she took it from him.

"Thank you," she whispered. She really didn't want to show any form of thankfulness, but the habit of good behavior betrayed her feelings. She bit into the dried meat. Its rich flavor made her mouth water for more.

He moved onto his side, propping himself on his elbow, and took a bite of his jerky.

"May I see?" he said, gesturing toward the photographs.

Chin up, she held them out just far enough for him to see but refused to let go of the frames.

"Your mother?"

Anna nodded.

"She was beautiful. You look like her."

Her cheeks grew warm, but she dismissed the compliment. In hopes that she wouldn't try to escape again, he might be trying to win her over with his smooth words, just like Uncle Horace did with his woman-of-the-week. He'd con them with his pretty talk, and once he got what he wanted, he dismissed them.

Gently, she wrapped the frames back up and put them away in her carpetbag. She took out her mirror and brush, and nearly fainted when she caught a glimpse of her face. The lower half was red and chapped, while the top half was white. She'd never looked so awful. Freckles would definitely come out. She moaned.

"It's not so bad." He cleared his throat in a way that sounded like he stifled a chuckle. "Smear mud on your face. That'll protect your skin from the sun."

"I'd look awful."

"No worse than now."

She turned to give him a piece of her mind then noticed a hint of amusement playing in his eyes. Managing a "humph," she turned back to the mirror. Her hair was full of pine needles and burs. She picked out what burs she could and pulled the brush through its tangles. It was far too long. What a pain it was brushing through the snarls.

"Want me to help?"

"No." She jerked the brush through a knot. "Don't touch me."

He took a deep breath. "Fine." He continued to lie there, watching.

Turning her back to him, she pulled her hair over her shoulder and brushed through the strands. She felt his eyes burning through her. "Stop looking at me." She tossed the words over her shoulder.

"A beautiful woman can't expect a man not to look when he has the chance."

Her cheeks went hot. "Don't you have something to do? Shouldn't you go feed the horse or something?"

They both glanced at the horse. He was eating the grass between the trees.

"Well, just go away and leave me alone."

"You've missed a spot," he said, holding up a strand full of knots and burs.

"How dare you touch me." She snatched it from him.

"I touched you more last night." He chuckled. "This was nothing."

"That's because you were busy kidnapping me." She climbed to her feet, moving her skirt out from under her. "You have no right to laugh and act as though nothing is wrong. You're a kidnapper. I shouldn't be here right now. I should be in—"

"Denver City. I know." His eyes narrowed, and he acted as though he just tasted something nasty. "If I hear you say that name again, I'll gag you."

"You wouldn't dare."

He raised his brow. "I would."

"Why you . . . you—"

"You what?" He lifted a shoulder.

"Savage."

He frowned.

Good, her words had the effect she wanted. She marched toward the stream.

"We better get going."

"What? We hardly had time to rest." Her backside was killing her, and the last thing she wanted was to get back on that horse.

"We'll stay in the shade of the trees as much as possible. Don't want your burn to get worse. It means going the long way, so we don't have much time. But first, get rid of that wire from under your dress."

"What?"

"You heard me." He waved a hand. "Do it."

"Why?" She would be forced to buy a new bustle.

"It's in the way." He pointed to some nearby bushes. "Go."

She stomped over to the bushes, and with trembling hands she wiggled out of her bustle. "Lord, I don't know what You have in mind," she mumbled. "But please get me out of this. And soon." The hem of her skirt fell to the ground and dragged in the dirt. It would be ruined.

When she returned, he'd bound her carpetbag to the horse and mounted. He motioned for her to toss the bustle aside. She hesitated. The red stripes suddenly seemed darker across his cheeks and chin, and when his mouth turned downward, she dropped it at her feet. He could look awfully mean and threatening when he wanted to, especially his eyes behind that black mask of paint.

He swung her up on the horse in front of him, his large hand encasing her own. One would be enough to clamp itself around her neck and strangle her to death. When she came down, she gasped from the pain in her rump.

He took her about the waist and set her on his thigh. It did ease the ache, but she was uncomfortably close to the man.

Later in the day, when they stopped near a stream, Anna watched White Eagle pull free his bow and arrow. He leaped onto a protruding rock with ease. Without a sound, he armed his bow with a slender arrow and aimed it at the water.

He stood there like a statue, and Anna couldn't help but admire the beauty of his dark hair as it hung over his broad shoulders. The sunlight cast a blue sheen over the thick strands.

She crossed her arms and waited. Would he succeed in making a catch? His face was serious beneath the bandit-like mask of black paint, and she tried to imagine what he would look like without it. The hard curves and outlines of his exposed jaw were rather attractive. The wind caught the leather dangling in his hair. From his moccasins, to his leggings, to the feathers in his hair, he was like no man she'd ever met.

The arrow flew into the water faster than she could blink, and he jumped in after it. When he pulled it up, a large fish floundered on its end.

She shrugged and turned her back to him. So she was impressed—that didn't mean she had to show it.

After eating, they were off again. By nightfall she was exhausted but relieved that the sun hadn't been beating down on her like before. Her head, for once, didn't ache, and her backside wasn't nearly as sore.

After making camp for the night, they ate a rabbit White Eagle had shot. She didn't mind preparing rabbit; she'd done that a number of times for Uncle Horace.

The stars were bright, and a whisper of wind in the pines had a calming effect. The mountain air carried a peacefulness to it she'd never experienced before. In New York City the rumble of carriages over cobblestones and the laughter and talk of people always filled the streets. Here, all was quiet, tranquil, as though she were alone in the world, almost like a dream. But this dream was a nightmare, and she'd never be able to escape with wakefulness.

Soon, supper was over and darkness cloaked the trees. White Eagle added branches to the campfire. He heaped together pine needles and spread buckskin over them next to the fire. He then motioned for her to come.

The firelight danced in his eyes as she walked over to him. Slowly she knelt down on the soft skin, taking in the warmth of the flames.

"Get some rest," he said, his voice a soft murmur.

Exhausted, she curled up near the warm fire, surprised at the softness of the ground beneath her. She rested her head on her arm, thinking how much more comfortable this bed of pine needles was compared to the thin blanket she'd slept on next to the wagons.

White Eagle stretched out on the buckskin and lay down behind her.

She stiffened, trapped between him and the flames.

"Don't want you sneaking off again," he said, causing every nerve to stand on alert.

"And where would I go? I can't see Denver City anymore."

Burning pine, mingling with his musk and leather, filled her senses. Conscious of the length of his body so near hers, she stared for a long time into the flickering flames, afraid to move, afraid they might inadvertently touch. But eventually, her eyes grew heavy and the noise of nearby crickets lulled her to sleep.

Sometime in the night, a blood-curdling howl awakened her. She bolted upright.

She was alone.

The howl came again, echoing off the canyon walls, and several more howls joined in. The light hairs on her arms and neck stood on end. The fire had dimmed, and White Eagle was nowhere to be seen.

"Mr. Eagle?" she called, her voice small.

From out of nowhere, branches dropped onto the flames.

"Here," he said, his voice a welcoming comfort, and for the first time, she was glad to see him.

"What was *dat* . . . *that*?" she asked, still shivering with fear.

More howls came again, and she bit her lip to keep from crying out.

He knelt down behind her and wrapped his buckskin around her, enveloping her in his protection.

"You're safe," he whispered in her ear.

"What was it?" She clung to him.

"Coyotes."

She bristled. "Will they attack us?"

"Not if we stay close to the fire."

"I hope Bet is safe."

"Running Cloud will keep her safe."

"He would harm me." Anna rested her chin on her knees.

"She pleases him."

White Eagle tightened his arms around her; she didn't fight it. Warmth, safety, and calm radiated from him.

"So, Woman Of Sorrow has a name. What about you, Walks Alone?"

"Humph." She turned her nose in the air, not caring if she risked the comfort of his arms. He was her captor, and she wasn't about to give him what he wanted.

Thankfully, he continued to hold her.

After some time, he encouraged her to lie down. She gazed into the flames, wishing she was anywhere but lost in the dark Rocky Mountains of Colorado Territory. It was as if the wilderness had swallowed her whole. What she wouldn't give to be in civilization again.

She cautiously moved closer to him. His heavy arm draped over her waist, its calming strength warming her.

Chapter

The following day, White Eagle stopped near a river to rest. Anna got her carpetbag, took out her brush, and proceeded to get the tangles out of her hair. She had lost all of her hairpins, and her dress was torn and filthy.

She should be home by now. She could be taking a warm bath and eating a decent breakfast. Her bed would be soft and inviting, and there would be no coyotes terrifying her in the middle of the night and no threats of snakes crawling into her boots. Her feet ached, for she hadn't taken her boots off since the day she bathed in the river.

Why wouldn't God allow her to be free? Why did she always have to be trapped, someone's captive? She marched over to the nearby water and wet her brush. Why had God allowed this to happen? Why wouldn't He help her get home?

Her hair wasn't cooperating. "I'd chop you off if I had a pair of scissors in my hands," she said to the tangled mass as she brushed it over her shoulder.

"Here." White Eagle tossed her his dagger. It landed, point in the ground, at her feet.

"This is all your fault." She pointed her brush at him, not in the mood for his games.

"I didn't choose to come to the west. A woman, all alone." His jaw pulsed in agitation.

It was obvious the sleepless nights were finally taking their toll. If he hadn't kidnapped her, neither one of them would be having sleepless nights. She decided to play it smart and keep her mouth shut.

"What would your parents say? If they knew their daughter went all by herself to the Western Territories?" He spoke in his thick accent and glared at her, disapproval in his eyes.

"It's none of your business. You don't know what my life was like before this. Who are you to say anything at all? You are nothing but a wild savage who has nothing better to do with himself than to kidnap innocent women."

Anna stood and marched away from him between the trees and up the steep bank. Her loose tresses snagged in a tree branch. She jerked herself free then stomped away through the brush.

"You probably can't even read," she shouted over her shoulder. "Intelligence is something you certainly don't have." Except for the fact that he spoke English. "Some people just have a knack for picking up new languages. Even those who can't read— even savages!"

She swallowed back tears. Perhaps it was foolish of her to come so far on her own. Her papa would turn in his grave if he knew where she was right now. And yet she'd only been finishing what they had started so long ago. "What do you know of freedom, of journeying halfway across the world to make a new home?" she shouted over her shoulder. "You don't even know me!"

Her foot slipped out from under her, and she slid down the embankment. She screamed and hit bottom, landing with her ankle wedged between two rocks. Pain shot through her foot as she tried to balance herself on the other.

White Eagle rushed to her, sliding part of the way and sending dirt and pinecones down the slope, until he was next to her. He braced her around the waist and eased the weight off her foot.

"Are you hurt?"

"My ankle," was all she could say as tears welled in her eyes. A whimper burst from her lips. She wiped the tears from her face, but pain shot from her ankle, and she cried out again.

"Lean against me."

She held onto his shoulder as he eased her pained foot out of the crevice. He scooped her into his arms and carried her back up the hill.

Anger welled inside as her ankle throbbed. She thought her situation couldn't get any worse, until now.

"This is all your fault."

"I didn't push you over the embankment. Next time, quit talking and watch where you're going," he said, breathless.

They reached the top of the hill. "Put me down."

He obliged her.

She balanced on her good foot and leaned against a tree. "I have never met a more arrogant Indian in all my life!"

Crossing his arms, he raised a brow. "Have you ever met an Indian before this?"

Of course not, but she didn't dare voice her response. Instead, she put her nose in the air and turned to leave. Knife-like pain sliced through her ankle, and she fell to her knees, crying in renewed pain.

He seized her, swung her back up into his arms, and carried her to their camp.

She cried on his chest.

"What's your name?" he asked.

She sniffed and pursed her lips. "Anna. I want to go home. Please, just take me home." The only home she had was a place she'd never been to before, and likely she'd never get there. Loneliness and defeat came over her. She should have gotten off near Julesburg. That thought only made her cry harder.

"I'm such a fool," she said.

"You're not a fool."

He set her near the water's edge, crouched down next to her and reached for her boot.

"Please don't." She sniffed. "Snakes will crawl in it."

He paused and raised his brow. "Is that why you don't take off your boots?"

She nodded, tears streaming down her cheeks. She appreciated his sympathy, but she still wouldn't be in this mess if it weren't for him. "It's not proper to make me marry you." She wiped her tears with the back of her hand. "Why can't you take me to Denver City? Just tell Running Cloud that you don't want me."

He rested his hand on a rock and chuckled.

Did he find her circumstances so mirthful? She sniffed back her tears and straightened, trying to regain her dignity.

"You haven't taken your boots off all this time because of snakes?" He roared with laughter.

This wild Indian with hair and feathers hanging over his shoulders dared mock her. Wiping her eyes, she looked down at her boots. Her ankle throbbed in pain, her dress was in tatters, strands of hair clung to her cheeks and hung disheveled around her waist, and her face, stiff from sunburn, brought to mind her lobstered appearance.

His continued laughter regained her attention. His smile was stunningly attractive and his eyes were bright beneath the dark paint. She shook off the warm feelings that stirred in her and forced her mind upon the fact that he found her fear of snakes so hilarious. Maybe she was being silly? She certainly looked silly. His laughter was contagious. A smile tugged at her lips. She lay back against the embankment and giggled.

"Anna." He leaned over her, his face split with a grin. "That is your name, right?"

She nodded.

"We have to take off the boot. Your ankle will swell up, and you'll never get it off."

"Just don't let any snakes crawl into it."

"You have my word." He put his fist to his chest. "I will fight them off like the brave I am." A gleam of amusement flashed in his eyes. He knelt in front of her and took her foot in his hands. "Do you mind?"

"No." He loosened the boot, and she held her breath as he pulled it off.

"So that's why you danced with your boots in the water," he murmured, more to himself than to her.

"What?"

His gaze flickered to hers. "Nothing."

The meaning of his words slammed into her mind as if a boulder had just fallen from the sky. She yanked her skirt down to cover her toes.

"You saw me? That whole time you saw me!" Her voice quivered. She felt dizzy with the knowledge of all he might have seen. "Were you there when I . . . ?" She couldn't finish. Of course, he had been there and seen her wet chemise clinging to her body. Thank goodness she hadn't taken off all her clothes. Still, heat crept from her neck to her cheeks. How humiliating. How dreadful!

"Take off your stocking. I need to see your ankle," he said, looking serious about the task before him.

"I will not!"

"Why not? I've already seen everything."

Gritting her teeth, she said, "Face the other direction."

He blew out air and turned his back.

She inched her dress up to her thigh, all the while keeping her eyes on him to make sure he wasn't looking. Blushing at the thought of his watching her perform these very actions by the river, she unhooked her stocking and pulled it off her upheld leg. When finished, she quickly draped the dress back over her leg and ankle.

"You may turn around now."

He turned and knelt down before her. "Can you move your foot?"

With it still hidden under her skirt, she moved her foot. "Yes."

Shaking his head, he lifted the seam of her dress and firmly took hold of her ankle. Holding it in his palm, he rubbed and squeezed her heel and foot.

She winced from the pain.

"Move your toes."

She wiggled them.

"It's not broken." He slowly moved her ankle from side to side.

Tilting her head and hiding behind several strands of hair, she admired the way his dark skin contrasted against her own. She reprimanded herself, for she ought to be ashamed that her ankle was exposed.

"Keep it cool," he said, and dipped her foot in the water. "It'll keep the swelling down."

She held her ankle under the water. It ached from the cold but soon went numb.

White Eagle walked up the embankment and left her.

As he strode away, a turmoil of emotions dropped in her lap. She pulled her free leg up to her chest and rested her chin on one knee.

How could she ever look him in the eyes again after he'd seen her in her wet chemise? Her head popped up. How many others had seen her? Cheeks hot, she pressed her chin down hard against her knee. She wanted to weep all over again. So much for thinking she'd been smart by keeping her chemise on. One thing was certain—from now on, as long as she was in the wild, she would bathe fully clothed.

Hands lifted her hair off her back, and she turned. White Eagle draped the tresses over her shoulder.

"What are you doing?" She almost told him to stop, but his gentle touch had been a subtle comfort.

He handed her a flower. It had long purple petals with white shorter petals in its center. She turned the beautiful blossom over in her hand and held it to her nose.

"Thank you." Was this his way of apologizing?

He held out a small, rectangular piece of leather, took hold of his tomahawk and sat down next to her. After laying the leather over a rock, he pierced a small hole into each end. He then laid the tomahawk in the sun and pulled a short stick out of his belt. With his dagger, he carved one end into a point and smoothed out its edges.

As she watched him, her gaze traced up the fringed arm of his shirt, to the colorful, beaded leather that was bound to a lock of hair behind his ear. Feathers dangled and protruded from his head at different angles. Every part of him intrigued her. How did he make the feathers stay in place? They had to be tied in somehow. She leaned in for a closer look and found that some were indeed tied with a thin strap of leather. Fascinating. The slight wave of his hair as it lay against his back made her want to twirl her finger around its ends.

He looked in her direction.

She quickly glanced away. The buzz of insects swarmed around them, making for a nice distraction as she waved at them.

He finished with the stick and picked up the leather. He held his tomahawk just right so it would reflect the sun. He then laid the hot part of the small ax on the leather. After waiting a moment, he placed the tomahawk back in the sun and used his dagger to carve a design on the warm part of the skin. His strong hands moved the knife with grace and perfection, capturing the sun with his tomahawk, then warming the skin, and with the dagger, drawing thin lines of delicate flowers and lacy stems along its edges.

Stunned that a wild man could make such delicate, beautiful designs, she closed her gaping mouth to hide her fascination.

He turned and took her hair in one hand. He motioned for her to watch as he bunched the strands together and wrapped the leather rectangle around her tresses. He then pushed the carved stick through the holes. When he released her hair, it fell over one shoulder, bunched together in its new clasp.

She examined his craftsmanship and stared in wonder at the beautiful wrap that bound her hair. She glanced up in his blue-green eyes. How should she respond? "Thank you," she whispered.

He took the flower, his fingers brushing hers, and placed it in her hair. He then dragged up his knee, leaned on it, and gazed at her as if he were studying a painting he'd just completed.

Birds chirped nearby as he stared at her, and she looked away, watching the water in front of them while her cheeks flamed with heat.

His bright eyes seemed to peer right into her soul, and his face, even buried under all that paint, was so very handsome. She feared he might see by her expression that she found him attractive.

He shifted, and her gaze flickered to his leg, to the leather flap draped over his moccasin. He rested his elbows on his knees and peered out over the water. "Why were you walking alone? So far behind the wagons of the settlers?"

She brushed her fingers along her new hair clasp, admiring the beautiful pictures he had drawn.

"Beth offered me a ride, but Al—her husband—wouldn't allow it. The others wouldn't let me ride with them either."

"The heat could have killed you."

"They thought I was rich," she said with a slight laugh. She waved her hand at the mosquitoes, shaking her head.

"Rich or not, you could have died." He stood. "Keep your foot in the water." He marched back up the bank.

Well, she didn't die, obviously. Now she understood why the Indians called her Walks Alone. She had wondered why they had given her such a strange name. Of course, they had seen her walking behind the wagons. What didn't they see? And why didn't she see them? Then she remembered the invisible hills in the landscape. She recalled the hill that hid the river. The land had appeared flat and desolate, but apparently it hid many secrets—and savages.

White Eagle returned with three small turtle pouches in his hands and knelt beside her. "Close your eyes."

She closed her eyes. His face, so near her own, forced her lips into an uncontrollable grin.

"Be still," he said. His callused fingers gently lifted her chin.

She took a deep breath, trying to control the smile from her face. Why was she smiling when he had embarrassed her so? She was his captive, after all. Still, she felt like a child, giddy all over. She cleared her throat. After his making such a lovely clasp for her hair, she wondered what else he might do for her.

He smeared something on her cheeks. The ointment he applied brought cool relief to her hot face. He rubbed it on her nose and chin.

"May I have a new name?" she asked, keeping her eyes closed.

"You already have one. Walks Alone is a good name."

She frowned. "It's just not very pretty, that's all." What did it matter anyway? It's not like she planned on staying with the Indians.

"You can open your eyes now."

He crouched before her with a boyish grin. Why did he find her so amusing, and what brought on his pleasure this time?

She noticed white on her nose and bent down over the water to see what he'd done. To her horror, he had smeared war paint all over her face.

She looked up at him. "What have you done to me?"

"Now you'll be protected from the sun."

Chapter 8

Birds chirped in the trees, and White Eagle pushed a branch away from his head as he and Anna rode through beautiful woods. The sounds of the horse's hooves crunching pinecones hung in the quiet air. Aspen trees bore leaves the size of half-dollars that quaked in the slightest breeze, and their white bark made him think of an enchanted forest.

Anna's quiet gasps interrupted the silence as she gazed with parted lips at the beauty and wonder of their surroundings.

Despite White Eagle's lack of sleep, he hadn't felt this alive in years. Never had anyone been able to make him laugh the way this little woman could. He shook the thoughts from his head. Had he lost his mind? He was attracted to a white woman. A woman who knew nothing of his race. Yet her yellow hair brushing against his chest numbed all reservations.

It took all the will power he had to keep from touching her these past nights. But he had been a gentleman and kept his hands to himself. He almost felt sorry he'd given his word not to touch her. He felt certain he could seduce her, and then she'd come to him willingly, but to try anything would have been wrong. He had a much higher Authority to answer to than himself—as his father always used to remind him.

With that Bible in her carpetbag, he knew she was under that same Authority. It made him watch her more closely. Would she behave like the white men who thought Indians were subhuman and treat his fellow tribesmen with disdain? He understood why she treated him that way. But there was something about her that made him question if she'd be the same with others.

Being around her not only reminded him of his days with the white man, but it made his mind feel tired from speaking English. He had to think of every word, every sentence to get it right. Luckily, she talked a lot, so he didn't have to, and she brought to mind a number of words he'd forgotten. After spending these few days with her, he noticed his sentence length improving, and the language was starting to feel natural again.

"Look there." He pointed across a steep ravine to a high bluff. A ledge protruded from the bluff's edge with a gathering of branches. "An eagle's nest." He glanced down at her. Those forest-green eyes seemed to soak in all that he showed her. He longed to be in her mind, to know what she was thinking. He couldn't help but notice how captivated she became by everything she saw. It encouraged him to show her more, to impress her.

"Eagles mate for life," he said, studying her, wondering if she might make the connection to his name. "They never separate." If he married her, they would separate.

Her gaze fluttered in his direction, but she immediately glanced away and shifted in obvious discomfort.

He stifled a chuckle. It was easy to make her jittery, and he had fun teasing her. "If a human ever touches an eagle's eggs, the mother will abandon the nest." He eased the horse closer to the edge of the cliff.

An eagle flew through the deep ravine and landed on its high perch on the rocky bluff. Her gaze traced the bluff and lifted into the blue, cloudless sky then down into the ravine where a river roared at its base. It was as if she tried to take it all in, the sounds of birds, the river far below, and the wind blowing through the trees.

"A mother bear and her cubs." He motioned toward the river.

She bent and peered down at a bear stretching its paw into the water.

"She's teaching her cubs how to fish," he said, wondering if he'd ever have an opportunity to teach his own children how to fish. Would she be the mother of his children? If they married, he could have no other.

The cubs leaped playfully on the riverbank, not paying any attention to their mother.

"They're so precious. I'd love to hold one."

"No, you wouldn't." He almost chuckled, intrigued by her innocence and fondness for the cubs. "A mother bear is deadly."

White Eagle turned the horse away from the ravine, and they entered the woods once again. They wove between more trees and worked their way deep into the forest as he pushed branches away from her face. Soon they came to an opening between the trees and found themselves at the edge of a meadow.

Majestic mountains surrounded a beautiful pasture. Colorful flowers bloomed on every hill and in the distant valleys, and pine trees cascaded down the snowcapped mountainsides.

"If only I could fly," she said as they entered the clearing.

"Hold on." White Eagle urged his mount into a trot. He put his arm around her waist to hold her steady, a good excuse to touch her. He urged the horse into a gallop.

She relaxed into the movements of the animal.

The beast's strength and power surged through his legs, and the mountains towered above them on every side. He hoped to dispel all her fears of falling.

Her hair, bound in his clip, whipped behind her, and she laughed.

The fragrance of the air filled his lungs. "Soar on the wind," he said. They practically flew between the majestic landscape surrounding them. "Like this." He took her hands in his own, intertwining his fingers with her small ones.

As she leaned into him, he slowly held out her arms and rested his cheek against hers as the horse continued its pace.

"Soar on the wind," he said again.

"I'm free!"

He grasped her waist. "Imagine you're a bird, flying over the clouds," he said in her ear. "Nothing can stop you. You're flying towards freedom. No one can hold you back."

She tossed back her head, surrendering herself to him. A childlike trust beamed from her, and that cool exterior melted away. The beat of the horse's hooves pulsated through them both as if they were one.

The wind whipped through her hair, brushing its yellow strands against his cheek. He seized the locks in his fist and buried his face in her mane. Without her noticing, he wrapped the thick mass around his neck, satisfying at least one small ache he had from the first moment he laid eyes on her.

A hawk soared past them and swooped down, its wingspan magnificent. It caught a rabbit in its claws and flew to the other side of the clearing. As they neared the other end of the meadow, he slowed the horse to a canter then to a walk.

"That was wonderful!" she shouted, short of breath as if she'd been running. Laughing, she whirled around to look at him. Her hazel eyes sparkled and then fell on her yellow hair still wrapped around his neck and dangling over his chest. She covered her mouth. "Forgive me," she said as she started to pull the thick mane off his shoulder.

He snatched her wrist. "Leave it."

The pulse quickened in her neck as her gaze fluttered uncomfortably back toward the front of the horse.

That afternoon, Anna and White Eagle met up with Running Cloud and his warriors. Beth had a contented smile on her face and seemed as fascinated with the beautiful Rocky Mountains as Anna.

She turned to Anna, and her eyes widened.

Anna smiled, but wondered what had surprised her friend. Then Anna's cheeks went warm when she recalled that the Indians had seen her by the river. She tried to avoid their gazes to hide her embarrassment but couldn't help noticing their frowns.

Several of them said something to White Eagle. They raised their voices and gestured in her direction. He responded in turn. They argued with vehemence back and forth, raising the hairs on the back of her neck. She found security as his arm tightened around her waist. Finally, Running Cloud interrupted the flow of words, and everyone fell silent.

White Eagle moved away from the others.

"What was that all about?" she asked in a whisper, not wanting to attract the attention of the unhappy warriors.

"You wear war paint."

She had completely forgotten about her incredible appearance. Her face became so hot, she wondered if the paint might melt away. She wished it would.

After stopping at a stream to wash off the paint, they came to an open valley where tipis sprouted from a carpet of green. An Indian village surrounded an empty circle with a large opening toward the east, the direction from which they came. A small lake shimmered to the left of the village, horses grazed in the western field on a hill, and dogs roamed about.

"Part of the Cheyenne tribe." White Eagle motioned with his chin toward the village.

"Cheyenne," Anna said, trying to recall what she knew about the name. She had mainly thought of it as the town that would take her to Denver City, not as Indians.

Then it hit her. When she was ten and had just arrived from Holland, news about the Sand Creek Massacre had reached the East. A former minister and his men attacked an Indian village, despite the fact that a Union flag waved in the center as a sign for peace. The soldiers had shot and clubbed the Indian people, including children. When the news spread, the American people had been shocked.

That happened six years ago, but would these people want to avenge what happened to them on her and Beth today?

"Our people were forced to Indian Territory. We escaped into the mountains. We are plains Indians, but we live here, rather than move to lands forced on us where they attack our people after promising peace."

She recalled a section in her favorite book where the Indians—men, women and children—all lined up to kill one of their enemies. It was fiction, but she couldn't help but wonder how accurate it might have been.

"Will they want to kill me and Bet?"

"They'll learn to accept you. They'll respect the one who is to be my wife."

To hear him use the word "wife" made it more real. But he had said he would take her to Denver City and that Cheyenne law meant nothing to white people, so they wouldn't officially be married. Yet, wasn't he Cheyenne? Didn't his own laws mean anything to him?

As they neared the village, the children came to greet them first. Boys and girls alike had long black hair, either braided or streaming loose down their backs. They stared with wide brown eyes.

One boy with a small bow and arrow in his hand moved in for a closer look. Another girl had a doll tied to her back with a sash. She and a few other girls stepped near the boy, staring at Anna.

Soon, women and other men emerged from their tipis or stopped the work they were doing. Some of the men's chests were bare, while others wore fringed shirts. Some had buckskin leggings with flaps and fringe below the knee. Most of their gazes focused on her and Beth. They neither smiled nor frowned, sending a nervous tingle down her back.

White Eagle dismounted and lifted her as if she weighed nothing. When she glanced up at him, a warm, reassuring smile reflected in his eyes.

Once her feet touched the ground, she leaned against him—in part because of her sore ankle, but also in an effort to calm her trembling. He said they wouldn't harm her. She should trust him. And if they tried anything, he was sure to protect her.

White Eagle held Anna so close, her loose strands of hair tickled his chin. The children swarmed in around him, all eyes on Anna. Some tugged on White Eagle's arm, chattering and bursting with questions, but he ignored them as he watched Anna gaze at his people in wide-eyed awe, in the same manner the children gazed at her. She studied the loop earrings, the beaded silver necklaces and bracelets. Would she look down her nose at his people?

The children were especially curious about Anna's yellow hair.

"Go ahead, touch it," he finally said.

All at once, Little Fox, Runs With Wind, and the rest of the children reached their hands out and touched the ends of Anna's hair. They babbled to one another with excitement as they stared in wonder.

Anna giggled.

"Her hair feels normal, only kind of dry," Little Fox said, smoothing Anna's locks between his fingers.

"Does it glow at night like the moon?" Runs With Wind asked.

White Eagle shook his head, stifling a chuckle at the children's reaction to the unusual color. He had no doubt the adults wished to touch her hair as well, but only children could get away with such behavior.

"Are you going to scalp her? " Runs With Wind asked, jolting White Eagle from his pleasant thoughts.

"What is she saying?" Anna asked, obviously intrigued with the conversation they were having.

"She'd like a lock of your hair," White Eagle said, clearing his throat. Then he turned back to Runs With Wind and the other children. "She's going to be my *wife*."

"Oh," the children said, nodding and smiling in understanding.

Runs With Wind tugged on Anna's hair until she bent down to meet the little girl's face. She laid her hand on Anna's cheek.

"I'd be happy to give her a lock of my hair." Anna smiled and held the girl's hand on her face.

White Eagle's throat tightened. She didn't show any sign of arrogance. Even her fear of them didn't keep her from showing kindness to Runs With Wind.

White Eagle knelt and brushed his knuckles across the girl's cheek. "This is Runs With Wind," White Eagle said.

Runs With Wind looked up at her and grinned.

"Nice to meet you," Anna said.

Running Cloud called the people's attention. All the villagers grew quiet and listened. As he spoke and told the villagers of their engagement and to accept the two white women as their own, several glances were sent in Anna and Beth's direction. Uneasiness reflected from Anna's face, and the pulse quickened in her throat. He could only imagine how nervous she must be encountering an entire tribe of Indians.

When Running Cloud finished, the older children took the horses and led them away. Wanting to touch her and spare her ankle, White Eagle scooped Anna up into his arms and walked with her toward the lodges. A nervous giggle escaped her lips.

Children continued to swarm around her and Beth, touching both their dresses. A few women walked by, studying Anna and Beth.

"Even that small child's ears are pierced." Anna pointed at a baby held tight to one of the women's back with a blanket. The mother handed the little one something to eat and the baby grabbed the snack between his dimpled fingers and stuffed it into his mouth.

"They have no shame in showing their ankles, let alone half their legs," Anna said, observing the women in their buckskin dresses which came just below their knees.

White Eagle cast Anna a side-glance.

"I remember Papa's stories of Indians and their foreign dress, but to actually witness it in person is intriguing."

White Eagle tried to see his people through Anna's eyes. Some dresses were painted with elaborate designs, while most were plain, and the children dressed similar to the adults.

"Papa would be thrilled."

White Eagle stifled a chuckle as he watched Anna take it all in.

Then her words hit him. Her father had contact with Indians? Who was her father? A tinge of guilt swept over him. White Eagle would want to kill any man who tried to kidnap one of his daughters. If he ever had a daughter.

As they came closer to the lodges, Anna pointed at the tightly drawn skins pinned together at the top, each forming a tipi.

"What are they made of?" She glanced up at White Eagle, her arms still around his neck.

"We use buffalo skins for our lodges."

"You call them lodges? Fascinating. I always thought of a lodge as a wooden structure. Not as a tent."

White Eagle reached Song Bird's lodge. She waited outside for their arrival. "This is Song Bird," White Eagle said, introducing Anna to the older woman. "Running Cloud says you're to stay with her."

Again, he tried to see his people through Anna's eyes. Song Bird's leathery face bore no smile, but she nodded. Her graying hair fell in braids over her shoulders, and golden hoops adorned her ears.

"She sprained her ankle," he said to Song Bird, explaining why he was carrying Anna. He imagined most of his people thought she was lazy, but it was a nice excuse to be close to her. He motioned to Anna with his chin. "Yellow Leaf, our chief, is her husband," he said.

Song Bird turned and ducked into her lodge.

"When your ankle heals, remember when you go into someone's lodge, always walk to the left of the fire. Only men are to walk to the right. And never pass between the fire and someone sitting before it. The place of honor is to the left of the owner. He usually sits at the back of the lodge. Never take that place of honor unless it's offered to you. To the left of the door is where everyone sleeps."

"So much to remember," Anna mumbled.

He grinned as he eased past the flap.

Yellow Leaf sat at the far end.

Anna cast a trembling smile at him.

Yellow Leaf studied Anna and motioned for them to come closer. White Eagle couldn't help but notice how out of place Anna looked among his people, but as he set her down it occurred to him what a ray of sunshine she might be for the older couple. "You'll become a daughter to them and carry out the duties of a daughter."

"What duties?" Again, Anna's eyes widened.

"Song Bird will show you."

The lodge smelled of leather and burning wood. Inviting to the senses.

"I feel so overdressed," Anna mumbled, looking at Song Bird's clothes. The dress came up over one shoulder, exposing the other. A flap draped over the front with a fringe. Her braided hair hung over her shoulders. "Not to mention, hot." Anna fanned herself.

"Sit," Song Bird said.

"She speaks English?" Anna turned to White Eagle.

"A little," he said with the pride of a teacher.

That evening after White Eagle had retired to his own lodge, Anna sat before the fire with Song Bird and Yellow Leaf. The fire was small, just large enough to cook food. Feathers, quills, and cloth decorations hung from wooden stakes that formed the structure of the tipi, giving an unusual homey appearance.

Song Bird handed her a tin plate with meat. She recognized its smell as elk, and her mouth watered. The dried elk meat White Eagle had given her that first morning had been delicious.

Song Bird set a bowl of vegetables next to her. Yellow Leaf took an extra plate and bowl and held them up to the sky. He spoke a few words then placed the food on the ground next to the fire.

"We offer food to spirits," Song Bird said.

Anna nodded, pondering her words, then their meaning hit like a bolt of lightning. She didn't know what to say. She watched the plate, unsure what to expect. What did *they* expect? The food to disappear? Ghosts to arrive and join them for dinner?

During the rest of the meal—and while Anna's gaze darted to the offered food every so often—Song Bird and Yellow Leaf hardly spoke, and when they did, it was to each other in their own language.

Song Bird chuckled. "*Tsevestoemose*," she said as she nodded toward Anna then nudged her husband.

Anna suspected the conversation was about her. She simply smiled and wondered what the jesting might be about.

"White Eagle," Song Bird said, smiling. "You give him child. Make him husband and father. He be happy."

Anna's face went hot. Obviously, Song Bird knew nothing of her and White Eagle's arrangement.

When everyone was finished, Yellow Leaf closed his eyes, hummed, and sang a short song. Anna sat with her legs crossed and her elbows on her knees as she listened in wonder to the unusual sounds coming from his mouth. When he stopped, he became quiet, solemn.

"What was that all about?" she dared whisper to Song Bird as she helped gather the bowls and plates.

"After meal, it our custom to offer prayer of thanks."

That made sense, only Anna usually offered a prayer before a meal. But didn't Yellow Leaf offer food to the spirits, as in more than One Spirit?

Oh, dear. An outsider. That's what she was. And it weighed more heavily than their cultural differences. No longer was it just because they were Indian and she was white. What to do? She should say a prayer to thank God. She didn't want Him to think she was paying homage to any other god but Him. To be safe, she did just that.

As she expressed her gratefulness for the food—and begged Him to take her to Denver City—she gazed into the fire. It fought off the chill of the evening and warmed her cheeks. The sparks snapped when Song Bird pushed around the smoldering logs. The orange glow captivated her as it rose higher from Song Bird's care. Its hypnotic flame flickered before her eyes, the tiny sparks shooting up and dropping back down like falling stars.

Anna watched Song Bird, feeling as though she not only cared for the flame, but for Anna. It amazed her that this couple would take her into their home. They accepted her and treated her as one of their own. Why would they accept a perfect stranger, especially someone from a different culture? A culture that brought nothing but grief to their people. It touched Anna in a way she couldn't explain, and it frightened her.

She forced her mind on her mission. Denver City.

Anna's eyes widened from staring at the blaze, and her body grew heavy. The aches, pains, and weariness from her travels swept over her like a blanket. Her ankle throbbed, and she longed to lie down. She hadn't had one good night's rest since she got off the train in Cheyenne.

Song Bird, seeming to sense that she was exhausted, helped her to the sleeping side of the lodge. Several buffalo skins and blankets were laid out, forming a bed. Song Bird showed her the blankets she could use and began to help her out of her dress.

Anna wasn't about to undress with Yellow Leaf in the tipi. "Thank you for your help. I'll be just fine." She knelt on her bed and pulled the covers over her clothed body.

Song Bird frowned and shook her head.

Too tired to care what anybody thought of her strange sleeping habits, Anna closed her eyes, and like the flames of a candle slowly dying at the end of its wick, sleep claimed her.

Anna's eyes fluttered open. Strange singing and drumming came from outside. She blinked and remembered where she was. It was dark, so she must have slept for a couple of hours. Yellow Leaf wasn't to be seen, but Song Bird sat near, watching her.

"What's that noise?" Anna asked, her voice cracking.

"They celebrate return of Running Cloud and men."

"Running Cloud is also your chief?"

Song Bird shook her head. "He war chief. He protect tribe from white man. One chief." She raised a finger. "Yellow Leaf."

Yellow Leaf seemed so ordinary, just like the other Indian men. It was hard to imagine him as a chief. There was a quality of humbleness about him that seemed different from any white leader she'd ever met—not that she'd ever met any.

Song Bird's English was pretty good. Maybe Anna could pry some information out of her. "Who is White Eagle? What can you tell me about him?"

"White Eagle father die. He have much sadness." She held her fist to her chest for emphasis. "He have no family. You bring hope. Now he have family."

Her heart went out to the man with whom she'd spent the last few days. He must have lost his father in a battle with the white men. Sadness engulfed her; she knew what it was like to lose a father.

"His mother die at Big Sandy."

Anna's blood froze.

Song Bird referred to what happened at Sand Creek. Her own people had killed his mother? How could White Eagle be so decent to her? She was lucky he didn't scalp her the moment they met.

"White Eagle save Running Cloud life. He almost die. Now he called White Eagle."

"White Eagle was there at Sand Creek . . . er . . . Big Sandy?"

"Yes. Mother of White Eagle save Runs With Wind. White Eagle find her. Save her life."

How awful. Anna sat up and leaned in closer to Song Bird. Now she understood the special bond between White Eagle and the little girl who came to meet them upon their arrival. He and his mother saved her.

"Sun come up in sky." Song Bird lifted her hand in the air. "We hear white soldiers. Many Cheyenne chiefs and Arapaho chief Left Hand. Chief White Antelope come out of lodge. He shout, 'Stop!' in white man's tongue, but they not listen. He wear peace medal from Great White Father, Abraham Lincoln, and sing death song." Song Bird sang, "'Nothing live long, except earth and mountains.' White Antelope die in front of lodge.

"Our chief, Black Kettle, want peace with white man. He set up big flag in middle of village so white soldiers know. He call everyone to stand by him. But shots fire from soldiers' guns, and women run. Our braves stand to fight, and we hide children in nearby bushes, but white man come after us. White soldiers kill children in front of mothers' eyes. Cries come up from ground as mothers weep for children. Cries stop when mothers also die."

Song Bird rocked back and forth and hummed. She sang in a way Anna had never heard. It was similar to Yellow Leaf's song of prayer and to the celebration sounds coming from outside, only this was a droning, mournful sound.

"They kill my daughter," Song Bird said.

Anguish filled Anna's heart. Tears of guilt welled in her eyes, blurring her vision.

Song Bird continued to rock and sing.

"I'm so sorry," Anna whispered, nearly choking on her words.

Song Bird didn't seem to hear.

The following day, Anna sat outside the tipi with Song Bird and Runs With Wind, who smiled and chattered without stopping. Of course, Anna couldn't understand a word the little girl said, so she just nodded and smiled occasionally, and that seemed to please the child.

Since Anna's ankle still wasn't healed, Song Bird had her do light tasks such as grinding roots and berries. Together with Runs With Wind, they crushed berries in a wooden dish using the smooth end of a short stick. Runs With Wind showed her how to mash the berries until the seeds and pits were thoroughly crushed. She gazed at Runs With Wind's little brown hands as they worked with deliberation, contrasting with her own white, uncoordinated ones.

It made her think of White Eagle's hands. She hadn't seen him since they'd arrived. What was he doing? Would he come by Song Bird's tipi . . . um . . . lodge that day? She decided she'd use the words of the Cheyenne in reference to their homes.

Beth had been taken to stay in another lodge—where, Anna didn't know. And since she couldn't walk, she had no way of going to look for her. Besides, the thought of wandering around the village on her own was daunting. What if someone didn't like her because she was white? She certainly wouldn't blame them. Would the fact that she was White Eagle's fiancée really be enough to keep anyone from harming her? She prayed Beth was faring well.

Runs With Wind's small fingers then pressed the crushed fruit into a thin, triangular cake about an inch wide. The girl looked up at her and smiled, her dark braids dangling over her shoulders. She motioned for Anna to do the same, showing her how to flatten the pulp and shape it into a triangle. Once Anna's clumsy fingers could manage it, Runs With Wind continued with her own berries and sang a song. After singing the song one time through, she sang slowly and encouraged Anna to join in.

Anna mimicked the words of the little girl's song. The strange sounds made her tongue stumble in her mouth, and both she and Runs With Wind laughed.

One by one, and still singing, they laid the triangular cakes out on a cloth to dry in the sun.

"They look delicious." Anna fought the temptation to lick the remnants off her fingers.

"We store for winter," Song Bird said.

Song Bird turned a skinned pouch over a fire. To Anna's disgust, Song Bird had filled the pouch with blood then folded over the top and sealed it with sinew. She had spent a long time tapping the pouch with a stick and turning it over. She motioned for Anna to hand her a porcupine quill from the pile at her side. Anna handed one to her, and Song Bird used it to poke a small hole in the pouch. A tiny drop of blood dripped out, so she put it back over the fire.

"When we live on plains, we eat all parts of buffalo, blood too," Song Bird said.

Anna nodded, trying to hold back the nausea in her stomach and focusing on the berries that she felt would make a more satisfying meal.

Later, Song Bird poked the bag again. This time no blood trickled out. When she opened it, the blood looked like gelatin. If that's what Song Bird was serving for the evening meal, Anna would skip supper.

Chapter 9

Several days had passed before Anna could walk around freely on her ankle. That morning after she awoke, Yellow Leaf entered the lodge. She tightened the covers around her shoulders, since she was only wearing her chemise and Song Bird was nowhere to be seen.

The old chief looked at her, walked to the back of the lodge opposite the door, turned his back to her and sat down.

"Thank you, Mr. Leaf. You're very kind," she said as she quickly slipped into her dress.

"Yes, daughter."

She stopped what she was doing. He rarely spoke, and she was a bit taken back by the fact that he called her "daughter," not to mention that he spoke English.

"Gray Feather my *nâhtona*. Daughter, you same."

Anna had no idea that she stirred up memories of their daughter. Once dressed, she padded over to the old man and laid her hand on his shoulder, noticing the art book he held in his lap.

"I'm sorry." She expected the man to start humming and possibly ignore her as Song Bird had done several days before.

"Fault of white soldiers," he said.

This was the most, or really the only, conversation she'd ever had with Song Bird's husband.

"May I join you?" she asked, remembering the manners of the Cheyenne. Had she already been rude by coming to stand so close? She didn't know.

He motioned for her to sit down as he faced the fire, so she settled next to him.

"My father died when I was just a little girl." She stared ahead at the dying flames. "It seems I don't have a father, and you don't have a daughter." She cast a side-glance in Yellow Leaf's direction.

He also looked at her then down at his book, his wrinkled face remaining emotionless.

Hesitantly, she reached out and placed her hand over his. He turned his palm up, wrapped his leathery fingers around her hand and looked at her, a smile in his almond eyes.

He turned one of the book's pages and laid her hand over the drawing.

At the top of the page was the outline of a gray feather. Below that, a soldier on a horse aimed his rifle at a young girl. He handed her the book, and she stared in horror at the picture.

"Your daughter?"

Yellow Leaf nodded.

Tears burned her eyes. She squeezed his hand as she thought about the pain of his loss, so much like her own pain, but greater. A father never expects to lose a child. She pulled her carpetbag open and took out her photographs. She laid her father's photo over the art book as she unwrapped its frame.

Yellow Leaf looked at the picture. She traced her father's face with her fingers as she'd done so many times before then handed the frame to Yellow Leaf. "I came all this way to fulfill our dream."

"*Navese'e.*" A small voice came from the door of the lodge. She looked up and saw Runs With Wind.

The little girl motioned for her to come.

Anna turned to Yellow Leaf. She didn't want to go when she'd finally made such a deep connection with this intriguing man. She wanted to ask him more about his people, about the horrifying picture she saw. He didn't look at Runs With Wind, but said something to her in Cheyenne. She then stepped away from the door's flap.

"You come far for dream." Yellow Leaf handed her the photo. "Learn our people. Go with child. She teach you."

Anna looked toward the door and saw Runs With Wind's shadow. She held the art book up to Yellow Leaf. "May I?" One way to learn more about his people would be to learn more about their past.

He nodded.

"I'll be careful with it." She stood and pressed the book to her chest, leaving Yellow Leaf to hold her father's photo.

She ducked under the flap and met Runs With Wind who wore a dress with fringes at the seams of the arms and skirt. Her two raven braids draped over her shoulders, and Anna couldn't help but wonder how much Gray Feather might have dressed like Runs With Wind.

Children ran by, squealing. This would be Anna's first adventure away from Song Bird and Yellow Leaf's lodge, so despite her troubled thoughts, she'd try to make the day special.

They walked past more lodges as she looked through the book belonging to Yellow Leaf. Scenes depicted Indians chasing down herds of buffalo. Not one arrow was seen flying toward the buffalo as they fell to their death off a cliff. Fascinating, yet her thoughts kept traveling back to that one horrifying picture.

In other scenes arrows flew through the air like hornets towards enemy Indian tribes. Some of the fighters wore buffalo horns on their heads. One warrior carried a blanket or a robe over his arm during battle, while in another scene, a warrior wore a yellow shirt, standing out from his tribe members. In other pictures, braves had on war bonnets with feathers dangling down their backs. Every picture told its own story of a particular battle, of success and failure.

They walked near a baby bound to a board in a cloth sack. The board was perched up against the edge of a lodge. His mother busied herself crushing berries into a small bowl. The mother cast Anna a suspicious eye as Anna stopped to examine the baby. Anna smiled, but the woman didn't smile back and continued with her work.

Curiosity got the best of Anna as she looked over the baby. He didn't seem to be uncomfortable. In fact, he sat in what was almost like a bag that had been attached to two strong wooden poles. Green and red geometrical designs covering the white sack sparkled in the sunlight. Beautiful glass and brass beads were sewn in and around the outside. The baby cooed, and Anna let him grasp her finger. He shot her a toothless grin.

"Aren't you precious?" she said, but a horrible thought jolted through her mind when she wondered how many innocent babies like this one had been killed that day of the massacre. Another baby cried in the distance. She recalled Song Bird's words and imagined a little one just like this baby being snatched from his mother.

Someone tugged on her arm. Anna straightened to see the baby's mother. The woman's eyes narrowed, and as she spoke, she motioned for Anna to leave.

A child whizzed by, shouting and laughing, and brushed against Anna's skirt. Boys aimed tree branch rifles at one another. One boy ran back to her, quickly touched her hair, then ran away, hooting and hollering. The other boys praised him.

Runs With Wind grabbed her hand and pulled her away from the baby and his protective mother. "*Eevo'soo'e*," she said, motioning toward the boy. She then gestured toward others in the village as they went about their morning tasks, chattering to Anna as she walked.

Suddenly, Runs With Wind stopped. She grinned, and her eyes widened. "*Nenaasêstse!*" she said, tugging on Anna's arm to follow.

They came to a lodge with a white bird painted above the door flap. Runs With Wind pointed at the bird then pointed at Anna and smiled.

Anna then realized that the white bird represented White Eagle. This was his lodge. Runs With Wind kissed her own hand and held it up toward the white eagle. "*Namehoto*," she said, then covered her mouth and giggled.

"*Namehoto?*" Anna said, curious to know what the word meant, sensing its significance to the little girl in relation to White Eagle. She would ask Song Bird later. "*Namehoto*," she repeated to make sure she would remember the word.

Runs With Wind grabbed her hand again and pulled her to sit down. They sat not far from White Eagle's lodge, and Anna opened the book on her lap.

It'd been several days since she'd seen White Eagle, and she hoped he'd be in his lodge, but there didn't seem to be any movement or sounds coming from inside. Beth had managed to find Anna on their second day there, but she was busy taking care of her own chores for Running Cloud's family. Anna hoped to see her soon.

Runs With Wind stroked Anna's cheek and traced her jawline, her chin, and then her nose. Anna giggled. She did the same to Runs With Wind, and they both laughed. Runs With Wind then took Anna's hand and held it against her own dark one. She tapped Anna's skin then her own. She realized the little girl must have been interested in her pale color, so she rolled up her sleeve, allowing her to see more. She noticed how pale her arm looked against her hand and cringed, imagining freckles covering her face.

Placing their arms together, Anna brushed the girl's soft skin. Gold would show its true color and glow in contrast to Runs With Wind's brown tint, while against her own white skin, gold would become so pale. She found the child's color far more beautiful than her own.

"So different," Anna said. She intertwined their fingers, her long ones folding over Runs With Wind's small ones. "And yet, the same." What an imagination God had to have invented so many different types of people.

As Runs With Wind studied her white skin, Anna's gaze fell on the drawings in the book. She turned the page and saw drawings of a fallen village, likely that of Sand Creek. Beneath an American flag and a white one lay dead children, old men, and women. White soldiers were drawn, retreating in the background, carrying scalps and shooting guns and rifles in the air.

She turned the page. A child, no more than two, stood on the bank crying, while three soldiers aimed their rifles at him. Her fingers trembled as she traced the drawing. That poor baby. He must have been terrified. On the next page, the child lay dead.

Anna turned away from the book.

The cries of a child caught her attention. A toddler wearing nothing more than a breechcloth clung to his mother. Tears streamed down his cheeks, and his fingers were in his mouth as he choked on sobs. The mother scooped up the baby and soothed him.

Anna's gaze dropped back to the book. She ran her finger along the body of the dead child. That poor baby on the Sand Creek banks had no one. No mother to pick him up and kiss him, no one to hold him and comfort him and tell him everything would be all right.

Reminders of that terrible day seemed to be everywhere. Song Bird and Yellow Leaf's daughter had died that day, as did White Eagle's mother. How many others in this village had lost loved ones?

Runs With Wind tugged on her sleeve.

She glanced at the little girl and forced a smile, but tears blurred her vision. How could these people not want to kill her when her own people had been so cruel? No wonder that woman didn't want her near her baby.

Runs With Wind put her hands over the horrifying picture. The little girl said something. She then stood and scurried away, leaving Anna alone with the book.

A moment later, out of the corner of her eye, Anna noticed someone coming toward her. She stood and swiped away her tears. It was Runs With Wind, pulling a man along by the arm.

The man hurried to Anna and cupped her face in his hands. She jumped from his familiar touch, but when she saw the blue-green of his eyes, she realized it was White Eagle without his war paint. She was right in thinking his features would be handsome.

"What happened?" His thumbs moved over her cheeks. "Why are you crying? Did someone hurt you?"

She shook her head. It was dreadful to be seen crying in front of him. Her gaze darted to the picture in the book, seeing the baby lying dead on the bank. She couldn't speak, so she just pointed at the art.

White Eagle looked at the picture. His eyes darkened.

"Forgive me. It's just so awful." With trembling fingers she covered her lips. "And you were there." She stepped back. "You saw these horrible things with your own eyes.

Song Bird told me." She wiped her nose. "She told me about how your mother saved Runs With Wind. No wonder the child loves you so much. You're her savior."

"I didn't save anyone." He straightened.

Why was his tone defensive?

"But she wouldn't be alive if you hadn't found her. So, both you and your mother saved her. You're her hero."

Staring at her, he opened his mouth as though he might speak, but he didn't say anything. He then glanced at his hand, as though it disgusted him. She noticed his fingers tremble, but he shook them out.

"Forgive me." She waved, feeling foolish for carrying on like a child. "I'm so sorry for all the pain your people suffered."

"You're not to blame."

"So many horrible things have happened to you." She dried her cheeks. "Back in New York, all we read about are the raids and attacks that the Indians have made on settlers, but we don't hear enough about what the white people do to you. Now I understand why the Indians would want to attack us. We've brought you so much grief. So much sadness and pain is drawn everywhere in these pages."

"The massacre at Big Sandy is the worst thing that's ever happened to my people. It's a day we'll never forget." He sighed. "We put down in drawings our history as we remember it." He nodded toward the book. "Let me see."

She held it open for him, and he turned the page. "That's what the whites call 'The Battle of Beecher Island.' The Cheyenne, Sioux, and Arapahoe braves almost won. It's where we lost Roman Nose," he mumbled. "For nine days we trapped about fifty troops on the Island in the Arikaree River . . . ." He shook his head. "The soldiers were so desperate for food they ate their horses."

"How dreadful."

He flipped the page to another illustration of a battle and grunted. "That was at Summit Springs just last year. Lost that one too. Tall Bull died there, the last of the great Cheyenne war chiefs."

He closed the book and handed it to her. "Come," he said as he led her to the flap of his lodge.

"Wait here." He disappeared inside, and when he returned, he held another book in his hands. He stood next to her and opened its pages.

"This is my mother when she saved Runs With Wind." The drawing depicted her as a spirit hovering over the child with wings of protection. It made her think of an angel, but what would an Indian know of angels? His large callused hand swept over each page as he showed drawings of victorious battles, the blessings of the rain and of the sun.

He then pointed to a drawing representing their departure from the plains into the mountains. The mountains opened up to them like arms, welcoming them to come and take shelter in their wilderness.

White Eagle showed her the small depictions of life, and of love. Her gaze fell on his dark hands, the thickness of his artistic fingers and their hard angles. "Did you draw these pictures yourself?" she asked. They were different than the drawings in Yellow

Leaf's book. These lines were smooth and curved, and each picture displayed a certain realism, while those of Yellow Leaf's had sharper, straighter lines.

He nodded. "I'm surprised Yellow Leaf let you have this." He motioned toward the book she hugged to her chest. "Only a few men keep a ledger. It's valued by the whole tribe. It tells our history."

"Oh, my." She handed him Yellow Leaf's ledger, fearing she might be rebuked.

He tucked it under his arm. "How'd you get something so sacred?"

"It must have been a misunderstanding." Perhaps he hadn't realized she'd intended to leave with it?

"Look here," he said, holding his ledger out to her. It was a couple holding hands. His finger followed the scene to a newborn child held in the arms of his proud father then to a child, older and standing next to his father. White Eagle traced over other depictions of family life: a woman carrying a child on her back as Anna had already seen done here at the village, and a father teaching his son to shoot an arrow and to hunt the buffalo.

She thought of the loss of his father, wondering in which battle he'd died, and then the loss of his mother and how tragic that must have been. Was he lonely, especially since he spent so much time drawing other families and their lives together? To her knowledge he had no brothers or sisters, or any other family left in this world.

"I hope one day you'll have a family of your own," she said as she looked up at him.

He stopped and gazed down at her, studying her with those intense, blue-green eyes of his.

She swallowed hard. Perhaps she should have kept her mouth shut. Unspoken words passed between them, and she wasn't sure she wanted to know their meaning.

Runs With Wind tugged on her skirt. Anna dragged her eyes away from White Eagle to the little girl. Runs With Wind motioned for her to come.

Anna turned to follow, but looked back and saw that White Eagle remained behind. He stood there, legs braced apart in his buckskin leggings, still holding the open ledger.

Their eyes met again, and a warm wind kissed her cheek, deepening the spell between them.

Runs With Wind tugged on her arm.

Anna followed but kept glancing over her shoulder at him.

<hr>

A child ran by and bumped into White Eagle, causing him to tighten his grip on the ledger. But nothing at that moment could have diverted his gaze as he stared after Walks Alone, her words having stunned him into silence.

Her long, yellow braid draped over one shoulder, a bit frazzled in places, as though she'd forgotten to comb it. It made him smile. Her dress was a mass of wrinkles too—he'd love to see her in Cheyenne clothing. Maybe he'd talk to Song Bird about that.

Walks Alone stopped and looked as though she were thinking. She then turned and faced him.

He took a step toward her, sensing she needed to say something.

"*Namehoto*," she said, her hazel eyes fluttering up to his.

He felt like he'd been punched in the gut and was just able to suck in air.

"*Namehoto*." She shrugged. "What does that mean?"

How'd she learn that word? He could barely bring himself to speak.

Her brows crinkled. "Maybe I didn't say it right?"

"You said it right."

"What does it mean?" she asked, lifting her hands.

"It means, 'I love him.'"

Her eyes lit up, and she strode toward him. His first instinct was to step back, but that was silly. How could he allow himself to be intimidated by such a slip of a woman? He was a warrior, a former Dog Soldier. He held his ground as she stopped in front of him.

"Those were Runs With Wind's words. She loves you because you saved her life. God led you to her that day so she could be saved."

Unsure how to respond, he simply stared down at her. He could tell his silence made her uncomfortable, but what could he say when he could hardly breathe?

Her cheeks bloomed pink. "Um, well, I better go. Runs With Wind is waiting." She gave a slight curtsy then turned and hurried off.

He watched her go, holding up her skirt and taking Runs With Wind's hand. Her words turned over in his mind. He'd never seen himself as a hero of any kind since the massacre, especially not as Runs With Wind's rescuer. But had he not found her, she probably would have died that day. It never occurred to him. And why did God help him to rescue Runs With Wind and not his own mother?

When she was out of sight, he started for Yellow Leaf's lodge to return his ledger. He thought about her reaction to Yellow Leaf's book. She'd actually wept, shed tears for his people. That was a rare reaction for a white person.

Yellow Leaf wasn't at his lodge, and after a long search, White Eagle found him wandering around the village. When Yellow Leaf spotted him, White Eagle held up the ledger for him to see. Yellow Leaf saw the book and headed his way.

"I was looking for this," he said with obvious relief. "How did you find it?"

"Walks Alone showed it to me," White Eagle said.

"I was telling her to learn more about our tribe, and the next thing I knew she was leaving the lodge with my ledger."

"It was a misunderstanding."

Yellow Leaf nodded. "She's a strange girl."

From the glint in Yellow Leaf's eye, White Eagle could see that he was fond of her.

Yellow Leaf looked down at the ledger then at White Eagle. His face turned serious. "She showed you the book."

White Eagle's chest tightened.

"Come to my fire." Yellow Leaf turned.

White Eagle didn't want to go to his lodge. Why did he have to remember that day? Out of respect for the old man, he followed.

Yellow Leaf tied up the door so that no one would disturb them and motioned for White Eagle to sit at his left before the fire, the place of honor as Yellow Leaf's adopted son.

Yellow Leaf smoothed his fingers down the long stem of his pipe and held the bowl upright. From his pouch, he gathered tobacco mixed with dried leaves of the *sumach* and pressed them into the narrow bowl. After dipping a small twig into buffalo grease, he held it over the lodge's fire, and then placed the pipe stem into his mouth and cupped the bowl as he lit the tobacco, puffing and blowing from the side of his mouth, over and over again. Once lit, he held the pipe straight up and passed it to White Eagle.

White Eagle gently grasped the lower part of the pipe. He held it upright and was careful that it didn't touch anything since Yellow Leaf believed that would be unlucky.

He took a long drag. The smoke streamed down his throat into his lungs, easing the tightness in his chest. Cheyenne tobacco was so much lighter than the white man's. It went down smooth, like the caress of a feather.

When finished, White Eagle passed it back to Yellow Leaf who then pointed the pipe stem to the sky and said, "Spirit Above, smoke." He pointed the stem to the ground and said, "Earth, smoke." He then pointed the stem to his right, in front of him, to his left and then behind him, offering the smokes to the four cardinal spirits the Cheyenne believed dwelt in those quarters, and said, "Four cardinal points, smoke."

White Eagle waited. Yellow Leaf already knew that White Eagle only believed in the One Great Spirit, and though Yellow Leaf wasn't convinced that there was only one God, he respected White Eagle's beliefs.

Yellow Leaf then said a long prayer asking for help from the Creator.

White Eagle listened, knowing that as soon as he finished, it would be time to talk, time to remember. He looked at his hands. Useless for saving anyone. Useless for saving that child. He closed his eyes, and the memories cascaded through his mind. His chest had hurt from running, the cold had been in his lungs, contrary to the warmth in them now. He had stumbled to the bank with Running Cloud and Black Bear, where they had hid behind the brush to catch their breath.

And that's when it happened.

Jean-Marc heard the cry of a young child. Shots were being fired.

A white soldier dismounted, knelt down and aimed his revolver at the toddler, then shot. Shrubbery against the bank split apart behind the baby.

Jean-Marc took aim. He let the arrow fly. It went astray, unnoticed into the dead brush on the other side of the bank.

"I'll do it." Another soldier dismounted and aimed his rifle at the baby.

He fired.

The bullet ripped through the small child. He crumpled to the ground, and his crying ceased.

The baby's body lay still on the cold earth. Blood painted the snow beneath him and engraved the lifeless image into Jean-Marc's mind.

Shaking his head, he pushed it out of his thoughts. He didn't want to look at the blood. The child's dead body.

"What did you see?" Yellow Leaf's voice cut into White Eagle's memories, asking him what he was thinking.

White Eagle's chest tightened. "I saw the baby I failed to save."

Yellow Leaf nodded. "You still blame yourself. You were only seventeen winters. Just a boy."

"Yes," White Eagle said, looking at his murderous useless hands. "But it was that day I became a man."

Yellow Leaf remained silent for a long time then sighed. "You are an eagle who makes his nest on the ground, where animals of the forest trample on your home. You leave your nest scattered to be picked up by the wind and other birds." Yellow Leaf gestured toward the sky. "You refuse to build your nest in the trees or on high rocks where an eagle belongs. And you don't honor the name given to you by Running Cloud when you saved his life." Yellow Leaf lifted his hands. "You must look to *Ma'heo'o* for help."

"God has left me," White Eagle said, remembering all the wars he fought, only to be left with no satisfaction of vengeance, as though he were drowning in other men's blood. It wasn't enough. It was never enough to cover the blood of that innocent baby, his mother, grandmother, and his people. And now, after all that carnage, why would God want him?

"But I've seen you reading the white man's Holy Book."

"Walks Alone's Bible." White Eagle had stolen it out of Anna's carpetbag when he came to teach Song Bird English. He needed to return it before she noticed it was missing.

"Why does the white man put their God on paper? In a book that can be destroyed by rain and fire?" Yellow Leaf motioned outside. "My bible is the wind. The wind is always with us and can't be destroyed."

White Eagle took a long drag on the pipe. He then slowly exhaled and watched the smoke float into the air, until it exited the lodge and disappeared into the blue sky. "*Ma'heo'o*'s like the wind because He's everywhere. But with a breath He can destroy wind and rain."

Yellow Leaf's question made him realize that no matter where White Eagle turned, God was unchangeable and so were His words. It didn't matter whether or not they were on paper. He just wanted to find God elsewhere—anywhere but with the white man.

"Nothing can destroy *Ma'heo'o*'s words. His words are on paper because white men are fools." White Eagle handed the pipe back to Yellow Leaf and had an uneasy feeling. Was Anna a fool? She was white, but he couldn't lump her in with the whole. Maybe that's where he went wrong? He lumped every white person in with Chivington—the murderer of his people.

"All men can be foolish," Yellow Leaf said. "Both the red man and the white man." He then took a drag on his pipe. "Maybe the words written in that book are supposed to be written in the hearts and minds of man."

White Eagle thought about Yellow Leaf's familiar words. Wasn't there a passage of scripture that said that?

Yellow Leaf motioned toward White Eagle. "Your father believed the words in the white man's book, and he was not foolish. But you are like a leaf blowing in the wind. You are lost without *Ma'heo'o*. You need to go to Him so you can find peace."

The place to find Him was in His word, so White Eagle's attempts would not be in vain. But how long must he wait? When would God grant him that peace he desired? His fingers clutched his knees. Ever since that awful day, peace—God—had eluded him. He couldn't bring himself to tell Yellow Leaf about his dreams, about his nightmares. About how that day haunted him in the night. Oh, how he wished they were just dreams, that there was nothing real about them.

Whether he wanted it or not, the memory would forever invade his thoughts, invade his mind.

Chapter  10

Squealing laughter and painted children spilled over the hills just beyond the village. Anna held her skirt high and ran from the frolicking braves riding stick horses with leaves tied as feathers in their hair. Her own long braids danced over her shoulders as she waved the buffalo cloak high above her head.

The children had painted her nose black and made streaks of red and brown on her cheeks and forehead. Their little fingers on her face had sent her to giggling, and now she laughed out loud.

With the wind in her hair and kicking up her leafy tail behind her, she hadn't felt this alive, this free since she was a child in Holland. The village stood at the base of the hill, and to her right the lake glittered in the sun, and the children's mimic lodges dotted the landscape to her left. The Rocky Mountains protruded above the trees, showing off their caps of snow, and she breathed in the fresh mountain air as birds sang and soared overhead.

Small blunt arrows from the seasoned braves tickled her sides, so she spun around, holding the skin high, turning and turning it in the air. Finally, she dropped to her knees and collapsed in the thick grass, out of breath.

Little Fox, the leader of the braves, and other boys practically pounced on her, using their hands as tomahawks, pretending to make the final blow, bringing the hunt to an end. Some groped her hair and touched her skin, but she didn't mind, and their little hands felt like a dozen chipmunks running all over her.

She mocked the groans of a buffalo, and even though she'd never witnessed the death of such a beast, she felt certain she imitated its moans with realism. She then rolled over and played dead.

The boys picked up the cloak and placed it reverently on the two poles fixed together as a travois. They hooted and hollered as they carried the buffalo back to their miniature village.

Anna lay in the still grass and gazed into the blue sky. Something brushed against her cheek. She spotted a purple flower, plucked it and held it to her nose. The same kind of flower White Eagle had given her. The horses grazed nearby, and she imagined what it would be like if this place was her home, a home she'd never have to leave.

Trees bordered the other side of the village. Just the other day she'd wandered off with Runs With Wind beyond the trees and they'd spotted some elk grazing in nearby fields. This peace could only be found in God's creation. In fact, because He created it, she wondered just how much her surroundings were like Him, how much they reflected His character. Hmm. She'd never thought of that before. This was what made life good, worth living.

A small ache turned in her abdomen, jolting her from her thoughts.

Her time.

She sat up straight, completely unprepared for what was about to happen. If she were in civilization right now, she would have everything she needed, but she had no idea what an Indian woman would do. She'd better find out, and quickly.

She waved to Runs With Wind, who just happened to be praising Little Fox for his prized "buffalo." Anna called to her and motioned that she needed to go back to the village. She hurried in that direction and when Runs With Wind joined her, they held hands. Once they entered the village, she tucked her purple flower in the little girl's hair. She said Song Bird's name in Cheyenne and tried to ask where she might be found.

Runs With Wind took her hand and pulled her through the village. Small children played and ran past them. A little boy reached out and touched Anna's braid then another chased him away. They came to White Eagle's lodge and Runs With Wind pointed at the door.

Anna peered inside. The dim light emphasized her black nose. Unable to remove the paint, she reached to remove her leafy tail instead, but movement caught her eye, and she saw Song Bird repairing a moccasin. Anna ducked through the door, relieved to find her alone. Anna wasn't sure how to explain what she needed, so she did her best to be as clear as possible without being too explicit.

"My womanly cycle has come," Anna whispered, standing as close to Song Bird as possible so she wouldn't have to speak too loudly of the subject.

Song Bird looked up.

Anna placed her hand on her abdomen. "You know—what all women get once a moon? *It*'s about to start."

Song Bird's eyes widened. She looked around the lodge then her gaze settled on White Eagle's shield and war bonnet. Suddenly, she sprang to her feet and talked and jabbered so furiously that Anna couldn't follow what she was saying. Song Bird waved her hands, motioning for her to get out of the lodge.

Anna ducked and backed outside the door, while Song Bird continued her loud chatter. Other women came near, stood by and looked Anna up and down, making her more conscious of her painted face and tail. Song Bird shouted at them and motioned for them to come. They began unpinning White Eagle's lodge. When some older men joined in to help, Song Bird hurried to Anna's side and led her away from the crowd.

"What happened?" Anna asked.

"A woman who bleeds must never enter warrior's lodge. You put curse on White Eagle."

Anna glanced over her shoulder at all the people working to take down the lodge. Some shook their heads and others shouted at one another to help unpin the buffalo skin as quickly as possible. Heat scorched her cheeks. Of all the people to curse, she cursed the one who was her only ticket to Denver City. And now the entire village was aware of the curse. Worst of all, the entire village knew that this was her time of the month.

Song Bird led her to a lodge where several women were inside. Some stood over smoke, and the scent of sweet grass, juniper needles, and white sage filled the air. Song

Bird took Anna's hands in her own.

"You not be ashamed, daughter. This my fault. I not tell you."

Anna was so hot from mortification she wished for something to fan her cheeks. She couldn't speak, reeling with shock over the revelation she had just made to half the Cheyenne tribe. She could never face those people again. Even Runs With Wind had been standing nearby and witnessed her folly. What a nightmare. If only she could go home. Home to Denver City, where something so personal could remain just that— personal. She covered her face with her hands. White Eagle would find out.

God! Take me away from here!

What would they do to her?

"Will I be punished?" She choked out the words.

"No." Song Bird spoke in earnest, gripping Anna's hands. "I speak to White Eagle. You stay here for four suns."

"I have to stay here for four days? Why?" Not that she was eager to meet the whole tribe again.

"Yes, until you pure. Stand with other women over smoke. This makes you clean."

The room of the lodge began to spin. She wished she could run away. She wanted to wail. To wail and disappear completely from the face of the earth.

"I want to go home." She fell into Song Bird's arms, no longer able to keep her tears at bay.

Just then, several chattering women gathered at the door. They pointed their fingers at Anna and shouted. The only words she could understand were "curse on brave warrior," "dirty woman," and "pray the Great Spirit would spare his life."

"It hasn't even started yet," Anna said, hiding her face in Song Bird's shoulder. "Surely, there's no curse until it has actually started. Right?" Her words seemed to reverberate off the walls of the lodge. She'd never spoken so—so—unrefined.

Song Bird held her away and looked at her with a sad frown. She shook her head.

"Then no one is cursed," Anna said, hopeful. "All this worry and tearing down his lodge has been for nothing."

"We must make sure lodge is pure." Song Bird rubbed her hand along Anna's arm in an effort to soothe. "We not take lodge down. We only throw back covering. We burn sweet grass and juniper leaves. When done, covering can be thrown forward and pinned together. Until then, no shield owner may enter lodge."

Well, that information didn't make her feel any better.

Song Bird took her hands. "You stay away from medicine, sacred bundles, shields, and do not touch feathers tied in man's head." Her gaze was earnest as she explained the rules. "No man may come near you. They may not eat from dish or drink from pot used by you. If he does, he be wounded in next battle."

The women outside continued chattering just as vehemently as before.

Song Bird squeezed her hands. "Do not eat meat from boiled water. Meat must be roasted over coals. If camp moves, only ride mare."

With each second, the women's voices seemed to get louder and louder. More words of "White Eagle wounded in next battle" and "unclean woman" came to her ears, while at the same time, Song Bird rattled off the rules. Anna looked to the women then to Song Bird, their voices hammering her from both sides.

Stifling a wail, she yanked her hands from Song Bird, pushed through the women who had gathered at the door, and ran toward the lake.

When she could run no more and found she was alone, she stumbled toward a small boulder, dropped to her knees and buried her face in her arms.

"I want to go home. God, why won't You let me go home?" She wailed and wept as hard and loud as she wanted. Thankfully no one was around, but perhaps if her cries were heard, they would want to get rid of her and gladly send her away. Oh, how she wished she could crawl under the rock and never come out. "Where are You, God? Why are You always so far away?"

When Anna could cry no more, she turned to look out over the pretty lake, keeping her cheek on her arms, too weary to sit up. Despite her misery, she couldn't help but notice the blue sky and steep hills reflecting off the water, and the quiet rustle of wind in the nearby trees. As if God were whispering to her.

No more tears. You must be brave. She could hear her father's words. *Remember, I may be leaving, but the Lord is always with you. You won't be alone.*

Anna always wondered about that statement. She'd never felt more alone than during her uncle's beatings. Why hadn't God rescued her from him? If she wasn't alone, then where was He?

Wiping her nose, she decided to be strong for her father. She sniffed back her tears and dried her cheeks, noticing the smeared paint on her hands. She must be a dreadful sight.

Someone or something tugged on her braid. She whirled around.

White Eagle, with a sparkle in his eyes, knelt next to her. She hadn't even heard him or felt his presence.

"You." She straightened. The last person she wished to see. "What are you doing here? Leave me alone. Go away." She covered her mouth. "But don't go home." She thought her tears were spent, but she felt like crying all over again.

"I've already been home."

"Oh, how dreadful!" She buried her face in her arms again, not daring to look him in the eyes. "I've never been so humiliated! Song Bird never told me . . . . Now your people believe I've put a curse on you. Not only that, the entire village knows . . . and now you know." She wailed. "Go away! You're not even supposed to touch me."

White Eagle cleared his throat; it resembled a chuckle.

Her head shot up, and she noticed amusement in his eyes. "What are you laughing at? Is my situation so amusing to you?" She swiped her tears, noticing the paint again, and bristled. "I'll have you know, this is all your fault!"

"My fault?" White Eagle straightened in mock defense. "I didn't wander into a brave's lodge with—"

"Oh, don't say it!" She stood, mortified. She marched off toward the village, anything to get away from him. If anyone saw them together, she could get into trouble. The other women had already made their opinions loud and clear.

But he followed, and they walked in silence.

She recalled the night in the woods when she first tried to escape. The anger in his voice when he thought it was her time then. Now she understood his concern. He would have been cursed. But now the inevitable happened. In his mind, she'd cursed him anyway.

Finally, she mustered up the courage to speak. "Are you angry with me?" she asked, her voice sounding small.

"No." He sighed, as if realizing something. "Listen. The only reason I was angry before was for your own sake. If the other braves thought you might be in your time, they would have killed you."

Anna gasped and shuddered. The thought of being killed for such a thing was awful. Thank the Lord White Eagle wasn't like the other braves. But would he still be willing to take her to Denver City?

That's the question she really wanted to ask. Dare she? Dare she approach the subject at a time like this?

"What's wrong?" He sounded concerned and bent close to her. "I'm not going to hurt you, Anna."

His words took her by surprise. She shook her head. "I'm not worried about *t*— *that*."

"Then what is it?"

"I—well—will you still take me—I mean, after the Indian wedding—uh. You promised dat—*that*—" She was a babbling idiot. There was no way she could get the words out. Bringing up Denver meant bring up their impending marriage. What if he changed his mind? She'd be trapped with his people and their strange ways for the rest of her life.

The corner of his lip twitched and amusement flashed in his eyes. "You're nervous."

"Nervous?" She put a trembling hand to her chest. He'd promised to take her. Why wouldn't he now?

"I'll take you to that city." He cocked a brow. "On one condition."

"What condition?" She bristled. She thought the only condition was marriage.

He grinned, flashing white teeth, giving her the impression that he might be toying with her. "Repeat what I say, and I'll give you my word."

She swallowed. "What do I have to say?"

"Three thousand, three hundred. and thirty-three trees."

"What?"

"Say it."

"Why?" She fisted her hands at her sides. "Why do I have to say something so silly?"

He turned away from her as if he might leave. "You don't have to say it."

"Tree thousand, tree hundred, and thirty-tree trees."

"Again."

"*Nay*—no!"

He shrugged and walked away.

"Tree tousand, tree hundred and tirty-tree trees." Wishing the ground would swallow her whole, she crossed her arms. "There I said it. Now, give me your word."

Grinning, he faced her. "I'll take you there." Humor danced in his eyes. "You must have forgotten that night in the woods. I'd already given you my word."

Her mouth dropped open and she wanted to stomp her foot, but watching the humor in his eyes and seeing her silly self reflected there, she couldn't help but smile. "Tank—*Th*ank you."

He stepped closer and looked down at her, his warm gaze and raven hair making her head swim. But her head stopped swimming when he lifted her tail of leaves.

She gasped.

Ignoring her tail, she tried to bring her mind back to the issue at hand. "I'm sorry if you believe I put a curse on you."

"Pray the Great Spirit will have mercy." He sounded sarcastic. "But if I'm wounded in my next battle, it will be a fond memory of you." He cocked his head and grinned.

She straightened. "What a terrible memory to have of me."

He shrugged. "It's like dipping my hand in honeycomb. I've risked getting stung just to have a taste of sweet."

She stepped back, unsure how to react. His words made her think of poetry, the verses she had to read over the years, only this sounded so natural, real.

Still holding her tail, he crossed his arms. "That's what happens when you take something—or in this case, someone—that doesn't belong to you." He swung the end of her tail.

She reached for it, but he jerked it away.

To her shock, he pulled on it, dragging her closer.

"By touching and speaking to me, you've made it worse for yourself," she whispered, breathless and surprised he'd want her this close. Her head began swimming again.

His lips pulled into a slow smile. "Then I'll suffer the consequences."

The following day as Anna roasted meat outside the menstrual lodge with other women, a shout carried up not far from where they worked.

A man stood outside his lodge. He shouted as though he were making a grand announcement, motioning with his arms for emphasis.

Anna felt a hand on her shoulder and looked up to see Song Bird. "His daughter, Little Deer, passed from childhood to womanhood. She begin first menstruation."

Anna's face went hot.

"You watch. This great honor. She can now become mother and will add to number of tribe. To its power and importance."

The man shouted again, his voice stilling the movements of those around him. He then turned and re-entered his lodge.

"To show satisfaction, he give a horse to family of Bear Claws," Song Bird explained. "That is family of boy she one day marry."

Soon the girl, Little Deer, came out of the lodge wrapped in a blanket with her grandmother by her side. They walked toward the lake, while other older women followed.

"Today you to learn our tradition." Song Bird took Anna by the arm and urged her to follow. "A woman's time is not one of shame."

Unless you curse a warrior, Anna thought. But curious to learn more about the traditions surrounding this important event, she followed. Her mind turned back to her own first menstrual experience. She'd thought she was dying until she finally expressed her anxiety to one of her uncle's maids. Thankfully, the maid had told Anna that it was a normal occurrence for all women and taught her what she needed to know.

When Anna was older, she'd even read about this in the Bible. Somewhere in the Old Testament. Women in their time were considered unclean. Why they were considered unclean when they couldn't help it or do anything about it, Anna would never understand. Back then, the women had to leave the camp and would stay away in their own tents— much like the Cheyenne did today. It made her wonder how they came to practice such a similar custom on their own.

Life had been lonely with her uncle, especially compared to being surrounded by so many women, so many people now. Sometimes all the attention felt overwhelming.

Down by the lake in the cover of trees and bushes, the young girl unbraided her hair and the older women helped her to undress. Unashamed, she stepped down into the water and bathed herself. When she was finished, the women wrapped her in a blanket and they walked back to the menstrual lodge. The older women laughed as they painted Little Deer's whole body red. They then draped a robe over her, and she sat near the fire.

Song Bird nudged Anna. "They have this ceremony in home lodge, but I think they do this here for you."

The other women smiled, as did Little Deer.

Anna felt herself blush, touched by their thoughtfulness. How nice it would have been to have had someone care for her in this way during her transition into womanhood. But *this* experience was a new transition, and they were here for her now.

Little Deer's grandmother took a coal from the fire and put it in front of the girl. She then sprinkled sweet grass, juniper needles, and white sage on it. Little Deer bent over the coal and held her robe open so that the smoke rising from the incense feathered around her body.

Chapter 11

"Wake up." Song Bird poked Anna to get out of bed.

Anna moaned, peeled back the covers and staggered to her feet. A dim light flickered off the skinned walls. Song Bird had started a small fire, and its smoke wafted through the opening at the top of the lodge.

Four weeks had passed since Anna arrived. It required her total focus to adjust to the ways of the Cheyenne, while Beth seemed to do so without problems. Anna was used to work, but she just wasn't accustomed to physical labor. She was too much of a city girl, while Beth was familiar with living off the land, foraging for food in the outdoors, cooking over an open fire, and collecting wood and water. Still, Anna did her best.

If her calculations were right, it was the last week of June, and time was drawing near for her to report to teaching duty. She had until the beginning of August, but she needed time to get settled. When would White Eagle marry her and take her to Denver? How long must she wait?

She stretched her aching body, willing it to come alive and at the same time longing to crawl back in bed.

The sun wasn't up, and as usual she made herself ready to go fetch water from the lake. After the women collected water, they fetched wood for the fires. Beth could still strap more wood on her back than Anna. Later, she would have to search for roots, berries, and other plants in the forest, which would be used for foods and medicines.

Yawning, Anna slipped into her dress as Song Bird fiddled with something on the other side of the lodge. Anna had gotten used to sleeping in her chemise with Yellow Leaf around, and her strict sense of propriety seemed to be waning. She couldn't be sure if that was good or not.

"Take dress off," Song Bird said.

Anna looked at her questioningly.

Song Bird pulled out a garment from behind her back. "I make dress for you. It is gift." She smiled and held up a pair of moccasins. "Take off boots."

Anna admired the beautiful fringes along the buckskin sleeves and skirt as Song Bird helped her slip into the dress, a longer version of what the other women wore. Song Bird was likely being sensitive to her modesty. It revealed much of her arms with fringes above the elbow. Jagged patterns were cut along the hem of the skirt, and more fringes lined the seam. A slit ran up the center to the back of her knees, and the bodice, sewn with sinew, gathered below her bosom. The dress hugged her body, and her hair hung in all directions around it.

She took off her boots and slipped her feet with reverence into the moccasin skins. They felt soft and flexible on her stiff feet. What a relief to be out of those boots. Everything was beautiful.

"Thank you," Anna said, her voice hitching. She didn't deserve such a nice gift, and because she would leave one day, guilt pricked her conscience because of Song Bird's kindness.

"You wel—welcome," Song Bird said. She smiled and brushed her fingers through Anna's hair and began to braid it. It gave Anna a warm feeling all over, as if she were Song Bird's daughter. No one ever combed her hair before, other than her nanny—and White Eagle that day by the river. She'd definitely wear her hair clip again today.

The new dress gave her freedom of movement, not to mention a cool and airy feeling, though it did feel a bit strange without so many layers. First thing she would do was clean her traveling dress and mend its tears. She had to look presentable when she arrived in Denver City—if she ever got there.

Anna had seen very little of White Eagle in the past week; the last time she saw him was the day she cursed him. Her cheeks still flamed just thinking about it. Song Bird said he was patrolling the area for a black bear. It was frightening to think of all the wild animals that roamed these parts. Thankfully, she had grown accustomed to the howls of the coyotes.

Song Bird finished twisting her hair into one long braid, and Anna used the clasp that White Eagle had made for her and bound it together.

When she and Song Bird joined the other women for their early morning stroll to the lake, she noticed that Beth wore a dress similar to hers. They both exchanged giggles.

"It feels wonderful not to be wearing that clunky old dress," Beth said.

Anna laughed at her description, but it was so true, she couldn't help but agree.

"From now on, I'm going to call you by your Cheyenne name, Walks Alone. I hope you don't mind."

"I don't mind." Anna forced a smile. Really she minded very much, but it wasn't like she had any choice. It was what everyone else around here called her. "Are you happy with your name?"

Beth's face lit up with a bright smile; she was so beautiful. "I adore it. It sounds so pretty in Cheyenne. Don't you think?"

Anna nodded. Since she didn't like her own name, she thought Beth wouldn't like hers either. Perhaps Anna didn't like her name because it had a season of truth to it? Half her life she'd been alone. And despite being surrounded by so many people and new friends, loneliness still nipped at her heels.

"I want you to meet my new friend." Beth pulled a young woman next to her. "Anna, this is Laughs Like A River." Beth hugged the woman to her side. "Doesn't she have a beautiful name?"

"Oh, yes. Very beautiful." Anna smiled at the young woman who smiled in return. Her buckskin dress spilled over one shoulder, and she wore a necklace made of pipes separated by colorful stones.

"When sun come up, water is dead," Song Bird said, grabbing their attention, her English improving. "Women get water before sunrise. Living water is better and good for spirit." She was always teaching Anna the ways of the Cheyenne. She said this every morning during their trek to the lake, since it was Cheyenne tradition to fill their kettles before the sun rose in the sky. They believed the water came to life at night.

Song Bird and Laughs Like A River walked on ahead, and Beth pulled Anna aside. "I learned more about Running Cloud," she said as they made their way toward the water. "He used to fight in the Indian wars and go on raids with an Indian called Black Bear and killed settlers. He's a murderer, Anna, or at least he was. They say after the battle at Summit Springs, he stopped. I think he wants to marry me so that the whites will leave this village alone. With a white woman married to the war chief, the white men are less likely to attack. Or so he thinks. "

"Oh, Beth." Anna stopped walking. Her friend would marry a murderer. And what might Anna be doomed to marry? "Did White Eagle raid with Running Cloud and the others?"

"I don't know. From what I can understand, he definitely fought against the Union soldiers."

Anna nodded, recalling his descriptions of the battles when he showed her his ledger.

"The language is so frustrating at times," Beth said, changing the subject. "I try to follow what they're saying, but then they lose me completely. I feel like a child all over again, just trying to learn to speak and carry on a normal conversation. I've managed to collect only this much information over the past four weeks since we've arrived."

Anna stopped walking. "You've managed to collect 'only this much information'? My goodness, Beth. You're doing so well adjusting to their culture. I'm grateful when I'm able to find the appropriate root or berry, or strap as much wood on my back as you, let alone speak and understand the language." She sighed. "I've picked up quite a few words and phrases, but after a while, I feel so overwhelmed that I get lost, and their words sound like noise." They began walking again.

"You're blessed to live with Song Bird. At least she speaks English."

"That's probably why I haven't learned the language as well as you, but she doesn't give me much information. She becomes withdrawn and sad, so I try not to ask too many questions. Though she did say I make White Eagle happy, that he smiles again. Can you imagine that? When does she see White Eagle anyway? I hardly ever see him— unless I'm making a fool of myself." She sighed and decided to change the subject before questions could be asked. "Several of the Indians can speak a little English. I wonder how they've picked up the language?"

"From what I understand, White Eagle's taught them."

"Well, he does speak proper English. I wonder how he learned it so well? He must have picked it up from traders."

They reached the water and filled their kettles.

"I don't know why I bother trying to learn the language when I won't be staying anyway." Anna set the kettle down then picked up the other one and filled it with water. "When are they going to get on with this wedding? I hardly see White Eagle, and when I do, I've been too distracted to even ask. Do you see much of Running Cloud?"

"No, not at all." Beth faced her. "I'm worried."

"What about?"

"What do you think will happen when Running Cloud learns I can't have children?"

Anna didn't know what to say about that. She wished she could ease her worry by saying that love would cover such things, but even that was questionable in this case. Was Running Cloud capable of love?

Beth was a woman of faith, so it was difficult to see her feeling vulnerable. How could Anna offer her any comfort, especially in such a desperate situation? "Pray about it," she finally said, surprised by her words. Not that prayer ever did her any good. *Sorry Lord, but it's true.*

Beth's eyes lit up. "Yes, of course." She shook her head as if to ask why she hadn't thought of that herself.

Anna picked up her kettles. Would prayer really do Beth any good? The ache in Anna's shoulders from hauling wood yesterday gave her a way to escape the conversation. "I wish I could collect enough wood to last a week. My shoulders still ache."

"Mine used to hurt too. You'll get used to it."

Anna set her kettles down and rubbed her shoulders. "You're right. Before you know it, I'll be carrying more wood than you." She cast Beth a smug grin.

"You're smaller than me, Anna. You shouldn't expect to carry as much as me."

"Well, it can't hurt to hope." Anna picked up her kettles, and they headed toward the village.

"You're doing well to fit in. Besides, are you forgetting you'll be leaving here as soon as the wedding is over?"

Anna's foot stumbled. As a matter of fact, she had—just for the moment. She'd never see Beth again, her first and best friend. She'd never see White Eagle. How happy would she be without them? She'd survived for years without any friends. But given a choice . . .

Thoughts of Denver City flooded her mind, all the waiting, the time, the preparation. Home.

Denver City. That is where we belong.

She could still hear her father's words on the ship. "Of course, I'll be leaving," she said, her lack of enthusiasm surprising her. "But it doesn't mean I can't try to carry as much as you." She forced a smile.

Beth frowned. "I wish you weren't leaving, Anna. You're my closest friend."

"You're mine too." Anna looked down at the ground as she stepped through the brush along the trees. "But you have Laughs Like A River—she'll make a fine friend," she said, unable to deny the tinge of jealousy rippling over her heart.

Anna watched Beth walk, so sure-footed in her new moccasins as if she'd worn them all her life. In the same way Beth wore her new shoes, she wore her new life. As though she belonged in this world. Or the world itself was made for her. How did she do it? How did she manage to wear this new world so comfortably?

"What makes you so happy? So content?" Anna asked.

Smiling, Beth looked over at Anna and then her face became serious. "I don't know." She shrugged. "I guess it was my experience with Al."

"Pardon?"

Beth laughed. "Sounds strange, I know. But during that time I learned to trust in

God. I had no choice because I had no one. No family. Nothing. And I'll trust in Him again in this situation. Thanks to your reminder." She winked at Anna. Her face appeared thoughtful again. "I think the Lord wants us to take bad situations and learn from them, to lean on Him and trust that He'll take care of us." She motioned to the world around her, the kettles weighing down her arms. "He's here with us now."

The trouble with Beth's words was Anna *didn't* trust God. Not to take care of her, anyway. He'd allowed her to be abused for six long years. She wanted to be near her father, near someone who protected her, and she believed she'd find a part of her father in Denver City. "I just want to go home. I feel as though I've been trying to get home ever since I touched American soil, and it's constantly out of reach. Contentment—home—is waiting for me in Denver City."

"You won't find happiness in a city or in better circumstances. People will be people wherever you go."

How could she have found contentment living with her uncle? "Maybe I don't know how to be content."

"Contentment comes from knowing the Lord is with you. Knowing He works all things out for good. And knowing this life is temporary. There's something better waiting for us." Beth stopped walking, set her kettles down and looked Anna in the eyes. "I don't know what it is, but there's something unique about White Eagle. Something different. He watches you, Anna. He watches you closely. I believe God has brought you here for a reason." Beth reached over to touch Anna's arm. "God is here with you. You don't have to leave."

The backs of Anna's eyes burned with unshed tears as Beth picked up her kettles and they resumed walking. But God wasn't with her, otherwise He'd rescue her. God had left her to fend for herself. And she didn't understand why.

"I think you find contentment, even joy, by growing from bad experiences." Beth smiled, completely unaware of Anna's inner struggle. "We need to let those bad times draw us closer to the Lord. It's a choice." Again, Beth stopped. "With the Lord, you're never alone. With Him, you're always home."

With a smile and a spring in her step, Beth resumed walking again, and Anna followed beside her, almost glad for the silence. Ever since her father died she'd been alone. And that's why she had to get to Denver. Besides, how could one always be home with the Lord? It didn't make any sense.

Home was Denver City.

Other women caught the girls' attention with their chatter. She and Beth turned toward the village as the sun came up over the horizon. It lit the sky like gold. It was then that she saw the men coming toward the water to bathe.

Anna's heart skipped when she saw White Eagle watching her. Her cheeks warmed at the thought of how little clothing she had on. Her chemise covered her more than this dress. Yet he ought to be used to seeing women dressed this way since these were his people. She took a deep breath and tried to focus her mind on other things, like when she could leave.

Speaking of leaving, now was as good a time as any to have a talk with her husband-to-be. Careful not to drop her kettles, she walked straight up to White Eagle. Her stomach did a flip as she came near his towering form. He sure could look intimidating. But she shook it off. She wasn't going to let it affect her. She wanted to go home.

The other men continued on their way as she set her kettles down to speak to her Indian "beau."

"When will you take me to Denver City? It's been several weeks, and I'm afraid if I wait much longer, I won't have work by the time I get there. They won't wait for me forever, you know." She hadn't meant to sound so saucy, but it took too much effort to be polite. After all, he had kept her here long enough, and if no marriage was to take place then what were they waiting for?

His eyes narrowed. "Since you were a gift, it's my duty to marry you. And I'll do it in my own time."

His words cut like a knife. He sounded so cold. Granted, she may have deserved it, but his response hammered home that she was his captive, not a guest, for goodness sake. As if that wasn't bad enough, she was his gift, as though she were a horse or something. And even worse, he was marrying her out of obligation. Yet why should any of that matter? It wasn't like she didn't know this already.

Flustered, she picked up her kettles, turned on her moccasined heels and marched back to the village, wishing she could bury her face in her hands.

The sun's rays shot across the sky, causing the mountain near the lake to light up in brilliance and reflect in the rippling waters as the men made their way to bathe.

"Your woman wears your skins," Running Cloud said as he and White Eagle came to the water.

"So does yours."

"It's a shame we haven't had time to court the women since our return," Running Cloud said.

White Eagle glanced at his friend. Were those his words? Did Running Cloud actually find himself attracted to his wife-to-be?

There was no doubt White Eagle felt attracted to Walks Alone. Seeing her in that buckskin dress made him glad he suggested Song Bird make one for her.

He dove head first into the water, needing to cool off.

Scouting the area for Black Bear these past few weeks had kept him from the village. He would be coming soon, and they needed to be ready. Until now, there were no signs or tracks, but Black Bear was sly. He wouldn't make himself easy to find.

When White Eagle had spoken to Song Bird the night before, he was pleased to hear how well Walks Alone was getting along. As a matter of fact, he was quite surprised. He'd been certain she wouldn't fit in, being high bred and from the East; he imagined she would refuse to do most of the chores.

But Song Bird had another story to tell—Walks Alone actually made efforts to learn his people's tongue. He had also caught a glimpse of her the other day, walking through the woods with Runs With Wind, and she'd been laughing. He liked the way her freckles danced over her nose when she laughed, and the way that upturned slope crinkled when she became annoyed. And that funny little accent she developed every time she became nervous. She couldn't be from New York. Where was she really from?

She was definitely not a typical Easterner. She was special, and she worked hard. That was his Walks Alone. His woman.

His thoughts jerked him back to reality. Walks Alone was not his woman, nor would she ever be. He swam away from the men so he could be alone. While the Cheyenne wedding would mean nothing to her, it meant something to him. How was he to pull this off? There was no way to fake his own wedding, turning it into a farce. And yet, there was one way she could be his forever. He shook the thoughts from his mind. It wouldn't be right. He promised not to touch her and to take her back.

The Cheyenne wedding would be of no value to her, therefore giving her the freedom to marry someone else if she wished. That thought sent a painful shudder through his system. Maybe he should break his promise and not take her to Denver City. If he kept her here long enough, she'd eventually come to accept their marriage. If she accepted their marriage, they wouldn't have to leave. He'd have a family, children to call his own.

More importantly, he'd have her.

Days later, Anna lumbered behind Beth as they made their way back to the village with various plant roots which would be used for medicine, smoking, and eating. Anna's hands were covered with calluses. Thank goodness the blisters were finally gone. It made it much easier to use her root pick. Song Bird said that spring was usually the season to dig up roots on the plains, but here in the mountains, they'd found a surplus of what they needed. Summer was the time to pick berries. Since roots were becoming more difficult to find in these hot months, they would pick more berries.

Just as the village came into view, war cries carried through the trees. The light hairs on Anna's arms and neck stood on end. She spotted several men dodging trees and racing toward them from all sides.

The women shouted and rushed together. Two women quickly moved away from the rest, and with their picks, drew one large circle around all of them, while others quickly gathered armloads of sticks and pinecones.

Anna and Beth gaped at each other.

"Stand in circle for protection," Laughs Like A River said in Cheyenne, dropping several sticks and cones over the line.

Anna glanced at Beth. "Protection from what? The men won't harm their own women, will they?"

Laughs Like A River cast them a knowing smile and hurried into the circle with the rest of the women.

Several of the men carried fabricated shields made of willow twigs, and they rode old, lazy, or ugly horses. The women quickly laid down their roots and pelted the men with pinecones, sticks, and bark as they drew near.

"Only the men who have counted coup are allowed inside the circle. That means they touched an enemy, but let him live," Laughs Like A River said. Anna was amazed at how much Cheyenne she understood, but was still utterly confused by what was taking place.

The men surrounded them, and the women's shouts and the men's war cries continued. Laughs Like A River motioned for Anna to lay down her roots. She was supposed to pelt off any brave who tried to take them. The braves went for the women's roots, and some men were pelted so vigorously that they backed away, holding up their humorous shields.

One brave showed particular interest in Laughs Like A River. He crossed over the line and into the circle, attempting to steal her roots. She giggled, while at the same time holding him off with sticks and pinecones. Another woman turned her nose up at Spotted Owl and pelted him without mercy until he retreated and feigned defeat by falling off his horse and playing dead. Some of the women laughed at the scene, but continued their pelting at the other men.

White Eagle was nowhere to be seen, while Running Cloud had already captured most of the other women's findings.

Anna gingerly tossed pinecones over the line of the circle but spent more time watching as the women, laughing and shrieking, taunted the war-painted braves. Some men were quick on their feet, others galloped around the circle on their old, painted horses, making faces and shouting war cries, hair and feathers dancing around them, but making no effort to enter the circle.

It was all a game.

Anna giggled.

Beth had apparently caught on, for when Anna looked her way, she saw Running Cloud in front of her trying to steal her roots. He captured them and shouted. Beth laughed out loud, putting a hand to her chest, her cheeks pink. Anna had never seen Beth laugh so freely before. But Beth quieted her laughter as Running Cloud stood in front of her, gazing into her face. Slowly, almost with hesitation, he reached toward her, and brushed his fingers along her cheek, studying her as if seeing her for the first time.

Pangs of jealousy swept through Anna, and she wondered what happened to White Eagle. Her gaze darted in every direction amongst the trees, trying to spot him, but he was nowhere to be seen.

It was too late anyway. The game was over. The men gradually disappeared with their roots, and the women carried everything back to the village, talking and giggling amongst themselves. Anna took up what was left of her roots and shuffled behind the others.

"White Eagle looks for Black Bear," Laughs Like A River said.

Anna nodded, but disappointment still plagued her. Why should it matter anyway? She was leaving, and they would never see each other again. But somehow that thought made her feel empty inside.

What nonsense. She had survived this long all alone; she could certainly survive the rest of her life without White Eagle at her side, especially as his captive.

Anna stretched her weary back and brushed her filthy hands off on her skirt as she and the women came down toward the village from collecting roots. This time they sat down together and laid their roots out in front of them, but no line was drawn. Some shouted war cries, and one waved a blanket toward the village. Anna set her roots in front of her, wondering why she should even bother. It'd been three days since they began playing these games—the women had apparently stopped when Anna and Beth had first joined them, but now that everyone was comfortable, they began again—and White Eagle never showed.

In this game, since the women weren't surprised by the men but had initiated it themselves, only men who had been wounded in war or who'd had his horse shot from under him during war were permitted to take the roots.

Anna sat down near her roots, humming a tune to herself to keep her mind distracted from the others and their obvious pleasure. She still tossed small sticks and cones just to act as though she were playing the game, though her lack of enthusiasm was obvious.

Just then, a dark hand snatched the roots in front of her. She looked up.

White Eagle knelt before her. "You make this game easy," he said, grinning.

Anna's lips tugged into an uncontrollable smile, and she jumped to her feet.

He held up her roots, along with several others he'd caught, for her and the other women to see. She noticed the other women nodding their approval, so she held out the roots that were hidden behind her back and waved them before him. He stepped toward her, and she stepped back.

Odd how quickly she came to like this game. She held the roots out to him.

He reached for them, but she jerked them away and held them behind her, daring him to grab them.

His arm moved around her, but she turned so he couldn't get them. He chuckled, his smile sending a warm tingle down her spine. He seemed hesitant, as though he feared touching her, but she egged him on.

"Take them, I dare you." She giggled, surprised by her own boldness.

He straightened, crossed his arms and raised a brow. His smile vanished, and she was certain she'd insulted him by her impropriety. Would a wild Indian think her improper?

"What's wrong?" She dropped her hands at her sides, prepared for a scolding.

He snatched the roots.

"You cheater!"

"I don't cheat." He grinned.

"You're a tease," she said, relieved he didn't rebuke her, and she reached out to poke him in the arm.

He snatched her wrist, put it to his lips and kissed the soft skin near her palm. Flames of heat coursed down to her elbow and all the way to her toes. He tugged her to him and purred in her ear. "*I'm* a tease?"

Suddenly she couldn't breathe, couldn't move.

"Thank you for the roots, Anna." Grinning, he released her. Raising the roots over his head, he shouted a victory cry and strode toward one of the hills to eat them.

Anna studied her wrist, thinking of that kiss, feeling it. This must be what it was like to be branded.

She walked next to Beth, her legs wobbly. If it weren't for the nervous pounding of her heart and the weakness in her knees, she might have skipped as they headed back toward the village.

Chapter

The day of the wedding finally arrived.

Anna trembled as she thought about the coming events. She trusted in White Eagle's promise and tried to set her mind on Denver City. But now that she was faced with the actual event, she couldn't help but believe they'd truly be married. How could he get rid of her if they were married? Why was he willing to deny their marriage? She could understand a white person not accepting it, but *him*? It made no sense. Maybe deep down inside he didn't want a white woman for a wife? Maybe he was simply doing this for Running Cloud like he said. If he had any affection for her, wouldn't he want to keep her?

What was she doing? She had to stop this wedding. But if she tried to leave, Running Cloud might kill her. Something inside her ached. She couldn't deny this marriage, despite the things he told her about the white man never accepting a Cheyenne wedding. If he set her free in Denver, she'd never be free. She'd never be able to remarry.

Lord, what am I to do?

She was getting *married*. She'd be his wife. A real *wife*. It all seemed unreal. A part of her felt giddy at the idea of being White Eagle's wife. He was so handsome. But marriage had to be more than that. More than whether someone was attractive or not. She had such limited experience. Really, she knew very little of what a good marriage required.

Song Bird had braided her hair, and now helped her slip into a new dress, its skin soft and smooth to the touch. Layers of fringe trimmed the skirt, and painted quills wove in and around its entirety. It was much more elaborate than the first dress given to her.

She felt beautiful, and yet her attire would have made her uncle faint. He would have thought her a savage. She smiled to herself. She had more Indian dresses than civilized ones. If only her uncle and his arrogant high-class friends could see her now.

Song Bird led her to the opening of the lodge where a horse waited outside. The men stood around the camp, watching the scene with their arms crossed, while several women helped her onto the horse. Silence hung on the air with no singing and no words spoken; such was the tradition of a Cheyenne wedding. The women led her through the village toward White Eagle's lodge, and the sounds of the horse's hooves echoed through the camp.

Upon arrival, she remained on the horse, while the women spread one of White Eagle's large blankets before his door. They then helped Anna off the horse, not allowing her to touch the ground, and set her on the blanket.

She reclined, and the women picked her up in it. After carrying her into the far side of White Eagle's lodge, they gently set her down. Where was White Eagle? The women left, and other women came in to undress her.

Her cheeks warmed as the women removed her clothes. Thank goodness Song Bird had explained what would happen on this special day, otherwise at this point she might have panicked. Not that she didn't feel like panicking anyway.

The women then had her kneel for the next part of the ritual. In silence, they smeared paint on her cheeks and arms. Her skin tickled under their feather-light touches as they painted designs on her white skin. Her heart pounded in her chest. Soon the ritual would be over, and she would have to face the groom.

They then unfolded a long, white wedding dress. It cascaded to her ankles with fringes at the hem. When she stood, its wrap-around skirt made a slight train, with fringes folding over the inner skirt to her waist. Blue and green painted eagles and flowers, highlighted with yellow painted quills, splashed from the hem up to her knees. They met silver, blue, and green diamond-shaped patterns and white horsehair, which flowed down the sides of the skirt just below her hips.

The bodice had two layers. The bottom layer, sewn with sinew, gathered at the neck and hugged against her waist in one solid color. Its long, wide-cut sleeves broke out in small fringes at her wrists. The top layer draped over her like a cloak. Long fringes spilled down her back and over her shoulders along its hem. Small quills reflected blue, green and silver, creating numerous diamond shapes.

She carefully spun around, watching the layers of fringe twirl around her. It took her breath away. Giggling, the women slipped beaded bracelets onto her wrists and a necklace of shells around her neck.

Beth was likely having the same experience on the other side of the village. She hoped all was well with her friend and felt almost giddy about showing Beth her new wedding gown and jewelry.

The women exited as soon as they were finished, leaving her to sit on the blanket awaiting White Eagle's arrival. His lodge differed little from Song Bird's and Yellow Leaf's home. Feathers and cloth with quilled designs hung from the walls and stakes. White Eagle's shield hung from another stake. A long tail of feathers dangled from its large, round shape. She imagined the war stories it could tell.

At that moment White Eagle's large form shadowed the opening of the lodge.

Her gaze traced his long form, up his arms and shoulders, to his face. He smiled.

"Are we married now?" she asked, suddenly short of breath.

"Yes."

The cold hard truth slammed into her. "That was it? What about vows?" She didn't even get the chance to say, "I do," let alone, "I don't." Not that she would have had the courage to refuse him anyway. Anna thought Song Bird had just left out those details. After all, those things were common knowledge. *Oh, Lord. I'm a married woman now. What do I do?* "I didn't even get a ring," she whispered, tears threatening.

His mouth opened as if he might speak, but he suddenly closed it. "This is a Cheyenne wedding. Running Cloud and Yellow Leaf already gave their consent, and that's enough." He strode to her, wearing buckskin leggings with a loincloth draped over the front and back, and a buckskin shirt. Fringes dangled from the edges of his clothing and over his shoulders where quills were sewn into pretty patterns; the same patterns she had on her new dress. She couldn't deny that he looked handsome.

"Will you take me home now?" Her voice choked. She desperately wished she were back in Song Bird's lodge. At least she felt at home and safe there and not defenseless like now. Suddenly she didn't trust White Eagle.

He knelt next to her, his closeness making her take in a sharp breath.

"I'll take you to Denver when I'm ready." He propped an elbow on his knee, and fiddled with the fringes on her dress, his fingers snagging her attention.

"Tell me about yourself," he said. "Why did you come so far all alone? Didn't you have anyone to take care of you?" His voice was warm and soothing, and his unusual accent swelled through the lodge on a baritone wave of comfort. His eyes gazed into hers, and she could see that he was sincere.

"There was someone."

"Who?"

"My uncle." She traced a trembling finger along the smooth quills on her dress.

"I thought you didn't have any family?"

"I don't," she said, hugging her knees to her chest. She hated to think she was related to such a man. "After my father and I arrived from Holland—"

"You're from Holland?" His eyes brightened.

She nodded.

"So, you're a Dutch girl." He chuckled. "You sailed across the ocean on a ship." He nodded as though intrigued. "I knew you weren't from New York. How old were you?"

"Ten."

"That explains the accent." He studied the air. "I've never seen the ocean before," he murmured as though in deep thought. "I imagine it looks like the open plains. And the rolling hills are like the waves."

"Yes," she said. "I couldn't have described it better."

"And its color . . ." His gaze flickered to hers. "What color is it?"

"Mostly gray, but there are parts that look like the lake, really like . . ." her cheeks warmed, "like the color of your eyes."

"My father used to tell me about the giant fish." His brows furrowed. "What were they called?"

"Whales?"

"Yes. That's it."

For a long time he was quiet, his gaze never leaving hers. "So, what happened after you arrived from Holland?"

She stared off at the skinned wall as her mind went back to those days, those days filled with big dreams, only to be snatched away in a breath. "My father died. He had a bad cough during the journey, but as soon as we arrived in New York, it got worse. They say it was pneumonia. Once he was gone, I had to live with my uncle. He was my mother's brother. I'd never met him before."

"You must have been scared."

"Yes." She stared down at her hands.

He leaned down, trying to meet her gaze. "Did your uncle hurt you?"

She searched his face, the concern evident in his eyes. She nodded.

"Did he . . . touch you?" Anger darkened his features.

"No." She shook her head. "He just—he beat me."

"Why?"

No one had ever asked her so many questions before. He seemed genuinely interested and concerned. Did he truly care?

"He had a temper." She didn't dare tell him that she was a disappointment to him and that he just didn't want her. She stared down at the blanket, tracing the geometrical shapes with her finger. Suppose White Eagle became disappointed in her too? Suppose later, he wouldn't want her either?

But he didn't. He was going to take her to Denver. She didn't know whether to be happy or sad.

Fringes from his sleeve dangled across his thigh as his arm rested on his knee.

She looked up at his face.

The muscles in his jaw pulsed, and he seemed to contemplate all she'd just shared. Maybe he did care?

Their eyes met, and he half smiled.

Anna returned the half smile. Why had she come so far from the East? Why did she and her father come all the way from Holland? To find a new home, to find freedom—yet she'd found neither.

"When will you take me home?" she whispered, testing him. Would he still take her there even though they were married? Even though all along he'd said he would?

"We'll leave after two sunrises."

She wasn't sure how to feel about his answer. Yes, she wanted to go to Denver City more desperately than ever. But that meant losing him.

He leaned back on his elbows, stretching out his long legs. "So, what made you decide to come all this way, to the West?"

She took a deep, fortifying breath. "My father made sure I received a good education." Thank goodness for conversation to distract them. She would try to make this one last. "I needed work, but didn't have any experience, and my uncle rarely let me out of the house. In fact, my tutor was forced to come to the house to give me lessons. Since my father had already paid for my education, it was the school's legal obligation to make sure I received one. My uncle tried to fight them and get the money, but he lost. When I learned that there was a need for teachers in the West, I decided this was an opportunity to find freedom." She grinned. "I also wanted the adventure."

He chuckled. "You got your adventure, all right."

"Yes, I suppose I did." She giggled and felt herself relax.

"Two more nights, and I'll take you to Denver City. Can you wait that long?"

"Really?" She could hardly believe it. Her dream would finally be realized.

"Yes," he said, half smiling.

"Then I can wait." She sighed. "I hope I'll still have work when I get there." She bit her bottom lip. What would she do if she lost her job?

"I'm sure you will," he said. "You traveled far. They're used to delays."

Because he seemed so certain, she didn't question him. She held on to all the hope she could, but wondered how an Indian could have knowledge of such things. What did it matter? White Eagle was special. Compared to the others, he was rather—civilized.

"Tonight Woman Of Sorrow will dine with Running Cloud's sisters. We will go to Yellow Leaf and Song Bird's lodge. Song Bird will have a meal waiting for us. Then later the entire village will celebrate the two weddings." He stood. "I'll show you where you'll sleep."

He helped her to her feet, his hand warm and large around her own, and led her to one side of the lodge.

"I made a bed here for you, and I'll sleep on the other side. A husband and wife aren't supposed to have physical contact until ten days after the wedding. So you don't have to worry that I'll touch you for at least ten days."

Anna gasped and glanced up at him. "But I'll be gone before then."

"Yes." His face hardened, the planes becoming more prominent. "You'll be gone." White Eagle's eyes narrowed. "My people believe we're married. It would be disgraceful and offensive to them if you slept in any other lodge. You can hang blankets from the stakes for privacy if you want, but during the day, I want them down."

She listened in silence. He was actually keeping his promise. Relief poured over her, and freedom sprang anew in her heart. Freedom from her uncle had been brief. Next thing she knew, she'd been kidnapped by Indians, losing her independence all over again. But now her captor would set her free.

Willingly.

She stared down at her wedding dress. Sadness mingled with joy.

———⸻———

That evening a great celebration took place in honor of the newlyweds. Anna noticed Beth's bright smile, indicating her joy, but when Anna took her hand, she felt it tremble.

"I'm so nervous. What if he beats me?" Beth whispered below the laughter and singing of the celebration.

Anna, in all her ignorance, wasn't sure what words might comfort Beth. Thank goodness she didn't have to worry about such things.

"Why would he hurt you?"

"Al was always cruel. If Running Cloud treats me worse, I couldn't bear it. He's a savage, after all. How gentle could he be?"

"Use this waiting period to get to know him, to let him get to know you. I think that's the idea of it anyway. You can tell him about your fears and maybe he'll understand."

Beth nodded, worry still reflecting from her face. "He seemed genuinely interested when we talked today about my life before coming here. We had quite a time trying to understand each other. We finally resorted to drawing pictures on the ground." She giggled, staring at the campfire in front of her.

The dancing and singing of the Indians captured their attention. Feathers, horsehair, and other unusual ornaments waved from robes and clothing. She stared at the performers in the glow of the firelight.

White Eagle grabbed her hands and pulled her to her feet. He spun her around and laughed.

She giggled. "What are you doing?"

"Dance with me!" His eyes sparkled.

"But I don't know how."

"Follow me."

He held her hand and led her around the fire. He raised a knee then placed his foot back on the ground, again and again as he showed her the steps.

She pulled her focus from his moccasins and looked up at his handsome face.

He grinned, and a warm comfort she'd never known before filled her heart. He continued staring at her, making her pulse race at the sight of his hair and feathers. She was in another world, a world in which she didn't belong, and yet it seemed to draw her in, enticing her.

That night, Anna sat cross-legged on thick buffalo robes in White Eagle's lodge. White Eagle sat in front of her and dipped his finger into a small turtle skin of red paint. She watched the firelight dance on his arm as he reached over her. One by one, he carefully painted slashes on the sides of her forehead. Each time he reached over her, she held her breath as though she were about to go underwater.

"Each line counts for one coup," White Eagle murmured.

"What's a coup?" Anna asked. She'd heard that word several times, but had never understood its meaning.

"When a brave fights in war, he carries a 'coup stick.' The idea is to strike an enemy without killing him, and without getting killed himself. It's an act of great courage. Each time a brave does that, it's counted as a coup. The more you have, the braver you are."

She thought how contradictory it was that she felt so safe and secure before him, while he boasted in paint about his feats as a warrior——feats against her own people. She watched as he dipped his finger and reached over her again. The firelight reflecting off the red paint made her think of blood. Those same fingers, those same large hands had killed men. And yet, he sat before her, a warrior whose hands could crush her, and treated her as if she were a delicate flower.

"Do all couples do this on their wedding night?" she asked, her voice catching.

White Eagle slowly painted another stripe with his finger, his touch warm and gentle, despite the roughness of his hands. "Oh, only the upper class and on special occasions like this."

"Are we upper class?" she asked, surprised at the thought. Did Indians have "classes" like civilized folk?

"Yep." White Eagle, studying her forehead, dipped his finger into the paint again. "The chief adopted you." He gave her an amused look. "I think that's as high class as you can get, don't you?"

Anna's gaze followed White Eagle's hand as he reached over her. Having lost count, she wondered how many stripes were already up there and what her forehead must look like.

"You're going to run out of room," she said, looking up at his serious face and realizing she'd complimented him on his bravery.

He grinned.

That boyish smile never failed to stun her.

Paint dripped from his finger onto her cheek.

"Oh, sorry," White Eagle whispered and grabbed a cloth. He dabbed the paint away, and then his hand stilled. Holding her in his gaze, he leaned closer and drew her chin up, his eyes intense and drinking her in.

"Wife," he said in Cheyenne, his tone low and husky. White Eagle's lips hovered near hers.

Again, that sense of going underwater enveloped her.

She held her breath.

Gently, their lips touched.

Her first kiss. Her first wonderful, delightful, magnificent kiss.

Chapter 13

"Oh, it was marvelous," Beth said the following morning as she knelt next to Anna by the lake. "I never realized a man could be so kind. We talked for hours, even if most of it was with our hands and drawing in the dirt." She giggled. "I can't believe he's my *husband*."

Jealousy pinched Anna's nerves. Her wedding was nothing but a farce in White Eagle's mind. Really, she reminded herself, that was all she wanted. Anyway, that kiss would sustain her for a lifetime. She couldn't expect more kisses since she didn't belong here. Besides, she was truly happy for Beth. Her life with Running Cloud would be good. It made Anna feel better about leaving.

"When we awoke this morning there were wedding gifts left outside our lodge."

"Really? For us too! Song Bird made a lovely blanket for us. It has the same geometrical designs woven on it as on our wedding clothes. It's beautiful." Anna bent back over her dress, making a few final repairs before she was to leave in the morning. "I wonder which gifts White Eagle will allow me to take to Denver?"

Beth took the seam of Anna's dress in her hands and continued working. "I'll miss you," she said, her tone quieting.

"I'll miss you too. I wish there was a way I could come visit, or you could come to Denver City." Anna peered over the lake to her left, admiring the pines and the hills. "I have to admit. I'll miss this place. It's so beautiful here."

The needle slipped from her hand, and she leaned down to pick it up. When she straightened, she noticed an arrow protruding from the ground in front of her.

Indian war cries pierced her ears. In the distance dust flew in the air and White Eagle and Running Cloud galloped toward them. War paint covered their faces and horses. Feathers waved behind them. It looked like they were aiming their rifles at Anna and Beth. Had the men changed their minds and decided to kill them both?

Something punched Anna in the right shoulder. After a moment it burned like fire.

Beth dropped the dress, stood with horror in her eyes, and screamed.

Anna looked down at her pained shoulder. An arrow pierced her through. It had come from behind, and blood had splattered onto her newly cleaned dress—her blood. She stood. She couldn't take her eyes off the arrow and sucked in panicked breaths.

White Eagle and Running Cloud charged toward her and Beth; their rifles fired with loud explosions.

Beth screamed.

The hills behind White Eagle rippled like water as his feathers and black hair caught the wind. His eyes were aflame and a deep frown, like none she'd ever seen, etched on his face. If she hadn't known the man, she might have fainted. His fierce gaze connected with hers as he leaped from his horse.

"Back to village!" Running Cloud shouted amidst Beth's screams.

Anna's ears rang. She felt faint. "Am I going to die?" she asked as White Eagle lifted her into his arms.

He hurried with her to the village as Beth ran, wailing behind them.

Anna's shoulder burned like fire, and it hurt to move. She couldn't even cling to his neck.

"No, you're not going to die," he said. "Not if I can help it." His voice was low and came from deep within his throat. "Get the healer!" he shouted at Beth.

Beth ran to get the medicine man.

White Eagle rushed Anna into his lodge and set her down on his bed. "Don't move."

She heard a crack and felt a quick jerk of the arrow. It sent stings of pain through her shoulder. "What'd you do?"

"I broke off its end so we can pull it out."

Her mouth went dry. The pain throbbed and sent waves of nausea through her body. He whipped out his dagger and quickly cut through her buckskin dress, exposing her shoulder. He examined the wound, and without warning, he pulled out the arrow. She gasped as blood poured over her skin. Did a hole really go right through her body?

Firmly, he pressed thick wads of cloth on both sides of her wound, clamping her shoulder between his strong hands. "You're going to be just fine, Anna," he said as he rested his cheek against hers. "You'll be just fine." He kept repeating the words, and something in his tone made her wonder if he meant what he said or if he was just trying to convince himself.

A wave of dizziness swept over her. A hole pierced her body. She shivered and suddenly felt cold. Her hands became clammy. "I don't feel very well," she said, her cheek still pressed against his rough jaw. Her tongue felt thick, and her speech sounded slurred. Her ears buzzed. Dark clouds filled her vision then blackness consumed her.

Anna fell limp in White Eagle's arms. Her soft cheek pressed against his, and his throat tightened.

"Don't die, Anna." The words were a mere whisper, but he felt like he'd shouted them. He feared the worst. What if the bleeding didn't stop? Suppose infection set in?

The medicine man came into the lodge with his wife and Beth close behind. He and his wife knelt over Anna, laying out their medicines, and when the bleeding slowed, they encouraged White Eagle to release her.

White Eagle stood near the door flap and watched. The loss of his father had been painful, but for some reason it hadn't been nearly as painful as when his mother had died. He knew it wasn't because he loved one more than the other. It was the memory of holding his mother's lifeless body that made her death hurt so much. Sometimes he could still smell her, and that was partly why he'd avoided women. But now Anna shared the scent of a Cheyenne woman. The fragrance of sweet grass and sage had swept over him as he carried her to his lodge, and the same pain, the same grief consumed him.

He had sworn in his heart to protect her, but like with the baby at Sand Creek, he had failed.

Back then Chivington and his soldiers were the threat, now it was his own friend. Black Bear's arrow had hit her. Anger swallowed his grief. It no longer mattered that Black Bear was Running Cloud's brother.

Torment boiled in his veins as he looked at Anna's limp body. Blood matted in her hair. Her small form lay helpless with her hands lifeless at her sides, small hands like his mother's. The room shuddered with violent heat, and a red cloud of anger colored his vision. He would avenge his wife.

He stormed out of the lodge.

Today, Black Bear would die.

White Eagle dismounted. He pulled the horse's reins as he wound his way through the woods. Images of Anna's body mingled with images of his mother's lifeless one. His mother had been a small woman, much like Anna. Anna's blood, bright red on her shoulder, brought back memories of the blood he saw on his mother. Only his mother's wound had been in her back from the shots of a rifle. He tried to shake the memories from his mind as he searched for Black Bear. But the memories wouldn't go away.

Jean-Marc couldn't find her; he'd been looking for her. The burned-down lodges had surrounded him. He'd felt lost in the carnage. But desperation forced him to take each step, to not give up. There was a chance she might still be alive.

So he kept going, kept searching.

He'd plodded through the village and called for her. "*Nahko'e!*" His ragged voice nearly gave way to his repressed wails.

She didn't answer.

A silver chain, half buried in the dirt, had caught his eye. He picked it up and drew it over his hand. A turquoise sparrow fell onto his palm. His mother's necklace. His heart beat in his ears as his gaze darted from one body to another.

There she lay, face down, her braids strewn over her blood-soaked dress. He stumbled over to her and dropped to his knees. With quivering hands, he turned her over. From under her, a young child screamed, her brown eyes large and frightened. The little girl clung to his neck.

"*Me'eševôtse*, my baby!" a woman's voice shrieked from behind. The woman stumbled over to Jean-Marc and snatched the child from him. "Runs With Wind!" She hugged the little girl to her chest and ran away, wailing.

He turned back to his mother. Her eyes, once warm and brown, stared past him, lifeless and gray. A braid had fallen across her ashen cheek, and wrapped around it was the colorful leather band she always wore. He moved the long strips of leather from her placid face.

"Mother?"

No answer.

His throat tightened. He brushed his bloodstained knuckles against her cold cheek, and his lips began to tremble.

"*Nahko'e!*" An anguished wail ripped from his throat. He hugged his mother, her arms dangling at her sides. Rocking back and forth, he cried, taking in her familiar scent of sweet grass and sage, hoping beyond reason that she would awaken, embrace him, tell him all would be well. His whole body shook as he sobbed. "*Nahko'eehe.*"

"They're coming back!" someone shouted in the distance.

Jean-Marc glanced up and saw chief Black Kettle struggling to lift his wounded wife over his shoulder. He stopped long enough to notice Jean-Marc and motioned for him to follow.

Jean-Marc kissed his mother and gently laid her on the ground. He untied the leather band from her braid, clenched it in his fist, and ran with Black Kettle to safety.

White Eagle saw no signs of the enemy. He had chased Black Bear a few miles from the village, and Running Cloud still hadn't joined him. Had he been so lost in his own thoughts that he hadn't paid proper attention? Where could they be? The eerie silence cloaked around him like a thick buffalo robe.

Shots cracked and echoed over the mountain. They came from the direction of the village. More shots fired. White Eagle's heart went to his throat.

Anna.

White Eagle galloped into the circle of the village where he spotted Running Cloud and the sole female warrior, Beaver Claws, waiting with their rifles at their sides. He jerked so hard on the reins that his horse rose on his hind legs.

"Where is he?" White Eagle shouted.

"Black Bear is gone," Beaver Claws said, anger evident on her face.

"We lost him." Running Cloud motioned toward the trees. "He won't stop until Woman Of Sorrow, you, and Walks Alone are dead."

"He's gone mad! Fighting against his own!" His horse danced in agitation, and White Eagle's mind heated with rage. "He'd destroy his own people? He's gone too far!"

Running Cloud straightened.

White Eagle watched his friend, noticing a change that he couldn't explain. A calm, meaningful realization reflected from his gaze, and his eyes locked on White Eagle's.

"He is ruled by anger."

The words were said with an authority that startled White Eagle. As if they carried a warning that was meant for him and not Black Bear.

White Eagle tightened his grip on his reins. "It's not safe here. I have to go to Crystal Springs. I'm taking Walks Alone with me."

The wind rustled a feather over Running Cloud's shoulder and his horse's head bobbed. "She'll endanger our village with the knowledge she has of us."

"She'll keep quiet. Besides, she's *mine* now." White Eagle wheeled his horse and galloped away.

Chapter 14

Anna's eyes fluttered opened, sleep still weighing down her limbs. Had she been sleeping for days? The fire from the center of the lodge lit up the walls, casting long shadows about the room. It must have been night. Her body felt like lead weights held it down. When she struggled to sit up, pain shot through her shoulder, neck, and arm.

"Be still." White Eagle's voice came to her ear. He put a damp cloth on her head. "You're not well."

"You're alive." She tried to lift her arms, but she couldn't move. "Is the fight over?" Obviously the fight was over, White Eagle and Running Cloud had survived, but she excused herself with delirium.

"Lie back down, love. You need to rest."

The lodge spun, and a chill came over her. When she pulled on the blankets, her shoulder pinched in pain.

"Lie still. Your wound is healing, and you have a fever." He pulled the blankets over her body and tucked her in.

A sense of warmth and comfort swept through her. The danger was gone. She was safe. He was safe. She nestled in closer and rested, listening to the sounds of his humming and his breathing. In and out, until his breath became like the wind. It carried her up into a mass of comforting clouds. The clouds folded around her, circling her like a blanket, and their scent was White Eagle.

But the cloudy blanket tightened around her, nearly suffocating her. She pushed herself free. The cloud pulled away and became a billowy cave, forming a long tunnel.

Wicked laughter echoed across the sky. Anna turned and saw Uncle Horace and his dark eyes closing in on her. He brandished a long, sharp ring.

Anna turned to run, but her feet sank into the cloud. She trudged to the light, knowing her father and their new home were on the other side.

Breathless, she glanced in Uncle Horace's direction. He hovered behind her, his cold smile chilling her to the bone. She tried to run faster, but her feet sank deeper. With his dagger-like ring, he punched her in the shoulder.

Anna cried out, the pain overwhelming. Her uncle laughed as he grabbed her chin. "No one could love you. Your father didn't love you. You were too much for him. You killed him. That's why he sent you to live with me!"

His hands were on her face, in her hair. She fought him.

"Wake up!" White Eagle's voice came from her uncle's lips.

She opened her eyes, struggling against a solid shadow.

"Anna, it's me," White Eagle said.

Where was she? She searched the darkness.

"You had a nightmare." White Eagle's voice came close to her ear. She was in his lodge. It was only a dream. But the pain in her shoulder was real. She wept.

White Eagle held her in his arms, where she felt small and safe, and whispered words of comfort. She didn't understand his words. He wasn't speaking English or Cheyenne, but he spoke in soothing tones. "Pray to your God, Anna. He will comfort you."

Pray? Where'd White Eagle get such a notion? "God doesn't answer prayers." She cried. "Not mine, anyway."

White Eagle's hug tightened.

Sun pervaded the room, and Anna slowly eased up in bed. She took a drink of tea the medicine man had left at her side. It felt cool and refreshing to her lips. Her shoulder throbbed, but her body didn't ache anymore, which told her she'd get well.

She glanced around the lodge. She lay in White Eagle's bed, his blankets and skins draped over and around her. Then she saw a book. Her mother's Bible. Had it fallen out of her carpetbag? She couldn't remember. It must have. Since White Eagle couldn't read, who else would have been reading it? Guilt seized her. She hadn't read her mother's Bible since she left Uncle Horace's. How could she be so thoughtless, so wicked? And yet, so much had happened since the day she left. Still, that was no excuse. However, getting kidnapped by Indians seemed like a fine excuse. Although, if she heeded Beth's words then she should have been drawing closer to God during this difficult time.

White Eagle entered the lodge and came to her bedside. He knelt down next to her. "How do you feel?"

"Much better, thank you." Her voice was hoarse and her limbs weak.

"You look better," he said and brushed his large hand through her hair.

She didn't pull away from his touch. He had shown her such care and devotion, she couldn't imagine telling him to stay away. He was the first person, other than her father, who ever took care of her.

Moving closer, he took her hand in his. He opened his fist, revealing a silver ring with a turquoise stone in the shape of a sparrow. His gaze held hers as he slipped the ring onto her finger.

"I knew it'd fit," he said.

"It's beautiful."

"Now you have a ring." He grinned.

She swallowed hard. He repeated her own flippant words from the day of their wedding. "I'm so ashamed. I don't deserve a ring. We're not even really married." At least *he* didn't think they were. She didn't understand him at all.

He cupped her cheek in his hand. "You deserve much more than a ring."

She didn't know what to make of his words, so she just smiled. She liked the ring and was glad she would have something to take to Denver City as a reminder of her experience with him and his people. Whether it'd been good or bad, it was a memory she would always cherish. And he was her husband after all, so wasn't a ring appropriate?

It'd certainly ensure no other man would come near her.

"Tell me something." White Eagle spoke with such seriousness that Anna felt she could tell him anything. "What prayers didn't your God answer?"

Anna's careless words from that night jolted through her. Perhaps White Eagle wanted to know more about her God? If so, she needed to make a good impression. But how could she make up for accusing God of not answering her prayers? Then the answer hit her.

She looked down at her hands, at the beautiful ring he'd given her. "He did answer my prayers. He simply said, 'no.'"

"'No' to what?"

She took in a deep breath. "No to setting me free from my uncle and sparing me of his abuse."

White Eagle furrowed his brows and studied her. "But he did answer your prayers."

Anna shook her head, not understanding.

"You're free from him now. He's not beating you anymore." He shrugged. "So He did answer you, just not as quickly as you'd hoped."

White Eagle's words sent a cold realization of truth over her. She gasped as she searched his face.

He simply smiled and nodded.

Tears sprang to her eyes. "You're right," she whispered, questions suddenly bombarding her from all sides. "But . . ."

"What?"

"I did it myself. I sewed in secret and earned my own money so I could leave."

"No." He shook his head. "*Ma'heo'o* made it possible."

Anna pondered his words. God opened and closed doors whenever He wished. He could have kept her from earning enough money to leave.

But she had been so scared, hiding in closets, under her bed. Anything to get away from her terrifying uncle. She clenched her fists as she stifled the anger that rose within her, knowing full well this wasn't an appropriate question for a heathen. Where was God all those years? Why didn't He rescue her sooner? And why was she here at this village married to a man who would never be hers, a man who didn't even want her, a man who didn't love her like a husband ought to love his wife, when she could be in Denver City? Didn't God realize how important Denver was to her?

"Why did He take so long?" she asked.

White Eagle's eyes clouded with . . . was it guilt? "Maybe this life isn't about you."

"What?" His words were like a slap in the face. "How can you say that?" Her anger began to rear its ugly head. "This is *my* life, and from the time I've been with Uncle Horace it's been awful, a nightmare!" She shook with pain. Nobody ever loved her but her father. And now her own husband didn't want her. "What did I do to deserve this?" Silently she referred also to her kidnapping, to Black Bear's arrow, and to her marriage. A marriage she would be bound to for life. A life of loneliness and misery.

"Maybe you're here for someone else." White Eagle said, his tone hinting at something deeper, something she didn't understand.

But she was too angry to ask. Too hurt to discuss it any further.

———⌬———

Two weeks passed before Anna was finally free to bathe in the lake. Her wound was closed, and she longed to dip in the cool waters.

Her whole being trembled as she neared the place where she'd been shot. The other women walked ahead to where trees and shrubs hovered slightly over the lake's edge. She followed and watched as they stripped out of their dresses and got into the water. She purposely wore her chemise under her dress. Even with only women around, she wasn't comfortable stripping down to nothing in broad daylight.

The other women giggled as she slowly eased into the water wearing her chemise. She shrugged off their amusement and joined in the chuckles. The cold water sent shivers all over her body, but it felt refreshing against her skin and numbed her aches. She swam around the women, but her movements brought pain to her shoulder, so she floated on her back.

Beth and the other women played in the water, splashing and teasing one another.

Anna kept her distance and worked her way to deeper waters, away from the excitement. She just wanted to soak up the quiet and coolness. She had no desire to use more energy than necessary.

Several minutes had passed when Beth called to her. "Anna, we're finished. It's time to get out."

"Go without me," she said, still floating on her back and staring up into the clouds. She hadn't felt this alive in a long time.

"You shouldn't be alone, Anna. I'll send White Eagle after you if you don't come now."

Anna ignored the warning, wanting to revel in the coolness of the water as her hair floated all around her. She stared up at the clouds and watched the different shapes. They were so white and fluffy, and if she imagined real hard, she might be able to reach up and touch one. The warm air feathered against her cool cheeks, the blue sky hovered over her like a warm blanket, and the sounds of birds singing in the trees echoed around the lake.

The voices of the other women faded as they returned to the village, and just then a snap of fear chilled her from head to toe.

She was alone.

Alone at the lake where she'd nearly lost her life. Her breath caught in her throat, and she sank under the water. She came up for air, treaded, and she looked toward shore. Shocks of pain stabbed her shoulder. The water suddenly felt colder, and she shivered.

No one was there. The women had left her, including Beth. How could they do that to her? And yet, they did say they were leaving, and she'd refused to go. But she didn't realize how frightened she'd become once all alone.

Her heart pounded in her chest, and her shoulder throbbed. She had gotten too far from shore and was now too weak to swim toward shallow water. The only way she could get there was to float on her back as she had been doing the whole time. But she didn't want to turn on her back, for fear someone or something might try to attack her.

Just then, she spotted White Eagle jogging to the lake's shore.

"Help me!" she cried just before she sank under. The water was clear. Had it been murky she might have become even more frightened. What if something or someone was in the water waiting for her? Her shoulder pained her too much to keep treading. She broke the surface and sucked in air, only to go under again.

White Eagle's hands clamped around her waist, and he forced her above water.

She gulped in air and clung to him. Her hands trembled on his shoulders, wet strands of hair streaming over her eyes. "I don't want to be alone, not here."

"You're safe. No one's going to hurt you." He kissed her and nearly took both of them back under. A warmth of comfort swelled through her system.

He broke away, gripping her about the waist and treading to stay afloat.

"I can swim now, if you just stay with me."

He nodded and stayed right next to her, giving her a push every once in a while as she floated on her back toward shore. If she wasn't so cold from the water, she might have blushed from that surprising kiss, not to mention from her silly predicament.

"Forgive me. I shouldn't have come out so far, and I should have gone with the others. I didn't realize I would become so scared." Thoughts of her old adventurous spirit came to mind. She gave a half-hearted chuckle. "I've come this far from the East all by myself, you'd think I'd have courage enough to go for a swim." She shivered. "I'm sorry for being so foolish."

When they reached shallow water, he put his arm around her waist and helped her toward dry land. Thank goodness she had her chemise on. But her whole body stiffened when she looked down at the fabric clinging to her every curve and leaving little to the imagination. Would she never learn? Well, this was better than having nothing on at all. Still, she hugged her arms around herself.

"You're the bravest white woman I know," he said.

She looked up into his warm eyes. He gave her a look that told her she had a friend. One who understood what was in her heart. She didn't have to be strong around him, and he would still care about her.

She avoided his gaze. If he cared about her, why didn't he want her?

"Will we leave for Denver City soon?" she practically choked out the words, wondering if he'd changed his mind, but at the same time hoping he didn't. It was almost as though she no longer wanted to go, but how could that be? It was her dream and the only place that offered her what she wanted and needed. Or was it? How could she doubt something that had always been so certain?

"Not until you're better." His gaze flickered over her body.

Aware of her appearance all over again, she hugged herself tighter.

"It's a hard trip, and you need to be strong."

She didn't like his answer, though she knew he was right.

He snatched her dress from a rock and draped it over her. He then turned toward the village.

Weariness came over her as they made their way back, and her limbs felt like boulders. He must have noticed for he lifted her into his arms. She didn't fight it and reveled in the comfort of his strength.

It should only take a couple more days to heal, then they would be on their way— she hoped. But right now, since she felt so exhausted, as soon as she got out of her wet clothes, she would take a nap.

Several days passed before Anna was able to get around without growing weary. She helped with light chores and managed to carry one kettle to and from the lake early in the morning. Though she felt better, her shoulder was still bruised, and White Eagle insisted she wasn't yet ready for the hard journey to Denver City.

Her hopes were dashed. She knew no job would be waiting for her when she finally got there.

The baby's body lay still on the cold earth. Blood colored the snow beneath him.

Jean-Marc fumbled to reset his bow and arrow, swallowing, but his throat became dry.

He'd never forgive himself.

He aimed at the man who killed the child. He let the arrow fly; it went through the man's neck. The soldier drooped and fell.

Out of the corner of his eye, Jean-Marc spotted Running Cloud and Black Bear sneaking across the bank. Their war cries pierced his ears as they shot the other two soldiers.

Jean-Marc stumbled down the bank. He dared not look at the toddler's body as he swiped away his tears.

He should have saved that baby's life.

He had failed.

He grabbed the reins of the fallen soldier's mount and climbed on. Cracks like thunder came from the other side of the village, but on this side no other soldiers could be seen.

He had to find his mother.

He charged into the village as Black Bear and Running Cloud's war cries followed behind. Black Kettle's American flag waved in the smoke. Below it hung the white flag that signified peace, a promise that the village would not be harmed. But at the base of the pole lay the dead bodies of women, elderly men, and children. Moans and cries carried through the air from those who still suffered from their wounds.

Jean -Marc urged his mount toward the fighters and readied his arrow. He spotted two braves kneeling in the distance, aiming their arrows at the soldiers, fighting to defend the village. Smoke burned his eyes as he galloped between smoldering lodges. Tears blurred his vision as he took aim at a blue coat. The arrow missed.

Running Cloud's cry caught his attention. Jean-Marc swiveled around and saw him fall from his horse. Running Cloud rolled on the ground, his body curling in obvious pain. A soldier hurried to stand over him and fumbled with his rifle. Black Bear was nowhere to be seen.

Jean-Marc grabbed the tomahawk from his belt, wheeled his horse, and galloped toward the soldier. He swung his leg over the saddle, leaped from the beast and landed on the soldier's back. He sliced the man's throat, and the rifle fired.

They plummeted, twirling to the ground. The man's weight slammed onto Jean-Marc, forcing the wind out of his lungs. He shoved the heavy, bleeding soldier off his body and gulped in air. The pressure in his chest made it almost impossible to breathe, but as he held his breath, he climbed to his feet.

Another soldier lunged at him with a saber.

Jean-Marc spun as pain sliced across his ribcage.

He cried out, but his lungs were like stone, and silence met the air. He dropped to his knees and grasped the wound, realizing that the sword only tore the surface of his flesh.

The man swung back his weapon for the final blow.

In one fluid movement, Jean-Marc threw his tomahawk at the man's chest.

The soldier stepped back, dropping his saber, and collapsed to the ground.

Jean-Marc's hands trembled, and his chest and lungs burned like fire. He staggered to his feet as the sounds of gunshots faded. He searched for another threat. There was none. He spotted Running Cloud climbing to his knees—alive.

The pressure in Jean-Marc's chest diminished, and he sucked in air. Smoke filled his lungs, strangling him, and the stench of death filled his nostrils.

His mother.

He stumbled toward his family's lodge, gasping for air, but became disoriented by the fallen homes and burnt-out lodges. He looked behind him and from side to side. Dead bodies of people he knew lay wasting on the ground.

Through blurred vision, he scanned the markings on the lodges that were left standing. Recognizing them, he trudged his way through the carnage toward home. It was still intact with the buffalo skin stretched into a point high above him.

He pulled away the skin flap and peered inside, trembling with the thoughts of what he might find. A small fire flickered, casting light about the wide room, warming the place. His books, stacked in a pile on his bed, showed no signs of an attack, and the blankets were folded where his mother had slept. Then he saw his grandmother sitting next to her own bed, slumped over a pool of blood.

"Grandmother?" His voice came from deep within his throat.

Silence.

He crept across the room and knelt in front of her. Slowly, he reached out and placed his fingers beneath her chin; her silver braid brushed against his arm as he raised her head.

She was gone.

He'd never seen a dead person before, not someone who'd been murdered. She looked like she was sleeping sitting up, as she so often did. To find her this way almost seemed natural. But the fact that she sat in her own blood, and the fact that she wasn't really asleep, made this whole nightmare stand still.

The reality he once knew no longer existed. And this new reality had yet to completely unfold.

He scanned the lodge again. His mother, nowhere to be seen.

He forced himself to leave and ducked under the lodge's flap. His nose burned as he held back tears.

His grandmother. Gone.

He refused to cry. He plodded through the village and called for his mother. He barely realized that he'd stepped over a body as he tried not to look at the small child who had been thrown onto the stakes above a lodge.

He glanced from side to side to avoid another threat, but the danger was gone, the battle was over.

Silence. And the sounds of death carried on the air.

"White Eagle," a soft voice called. He turned to the voice, but saw no one. No soldiers. Just lodges and blood. He glanced over his shoulder and spotted his grandmother. She sat outside a lodge, someone else's lodge, his lodge, the lodge he owned in the mountains. What was she doing there? She was alive. He hurried to her.

"White Eagle," his grandmother said, but it wasn't her voice. He knelt before her and she placed her palm on his cheek. "Wake up," she said. He touched her hand, but it wasn't hers. It was too soft, too small. "You're having a nightmare." This time his grandmother's lips didn't move. Where was the voice? "White Eagle, wake up." The soft voice reverberated through his mind.

White Eagle's eyes opened. The hint of a yellow braid draped over Anna's shoulder, her hand on his cheek, his hand over hers. He pushed up on his elbow.

"You had a bad dream," she said, stroking his cheek. Her scent of sweet grass and sage wafted over him.

The scent of a woman.

"It was no dream." His throat tightened as he stood.

She moved back. "Do you want to talk about it?"

"No." He ducked from the lodge. His words came out stronger than he'd intended, and she'd probably think he was angry. But he had to get away. He had to get away from that scent, from the memories.

From her.

Chapter 15

A few weeks later, Anna walked hand in hand with Runs With Wind toward the lake. She made herself come here as often as possible in order to face her fear. As a child, she'd never feared the water, but this water caused a certain dread to turn in her stomach. She knew it was foolish. And that's why she forced herself to come to the very spot she'd nearly lost her life. Runs With Wind, seeming to sense her uneasiness, leaned her chin against Anna's arm.

Children laughed and played around them, as if nothing terrible had ever happened in this place.

"*Me'êševôtse!*" A woman's voice shrieked, echoing off the hills and lake.

Anna turned to see a woman running amongst the children along the shore, searching frantically. The woman stopped and screamed, pointing in shock at the water.

"*Me'êševôtse!*" the woman cried out again.

Anna understood the word to mean *my baby*. She looked out at the lake, and a ways from shore she saw bubbles forming on the surface.

"Get the doctor!" Anna shouted to Runs With Wind as she ran into the water, fixing her gaze on the bubbles. She sucked in air and dove just before she reached them. A cliff dropped beneath the surface. The child must have fallen off. She scanned the blue haze as she swam toward the bottom.

Nothing. Nothing but weeds. She pushed them away and kicked through them, searching for the bubbles. A bubble floated up from behind a thick weed. She swam to it, and tangled in a plant was a child, no more than two years old. Her lungs hurt, and she fought the desire to swim up for air, but she had to get the baby first. If she went up, she might not find him again. Letting out a little air to ease the tension in her lungs, she swam down, forcing herself toward him. She clawed the water, reaching for the child's arm. Her fingers clamped around him, she tore the branches from his body and kicked upward.

Breaking the surface, she gasped for air. She held the baby's head above water as she turned on her back toward shore. When she touched ground, she got to her feet as quickly as possible. Taking the baby under her arm, she held him upside down against her hip, smacking her hand firmly on his back as she made her way toward land. Once on shore, she turned the child over her knee and hit him again on his back.

He choked. Water spewed from his mouth, and he cried.

With trembling hands, she held him up as he wailed before her. "You're going to be all right," she cried, shivers of relief pouring over her. The baby gasped for air, and she hugged him, brushing her fingers through his wet, matted hair. His mother rushed to her side and snatched the baby from her arms.

"*Nea'eše!* Thank you!" the woman said in Cheyenne, repeating the words over and over again. "You saved him." The child clung to his mother, crying on her shoulder. Tears filled the woman's eyes, and Anna reached out to touch the shivering boy.

"He's safe now," she said in broken Cheyenne.

Voices and people swarmed around them. She hadn't noticed that anyone else was near. The medicine man led the woman and her child away from the group, and Runs With Wind hugged Anna. It was then that she became aware of the throbbing in her shoulder. She rubbed her hand over the ache.

After expressions of appreciation, Anna and Runs With Wind moved from the small crowd. She stopped when she saw White Eagle standing away from the people. Runs With Wind ran up to him, shouting. The words came too fast for Anna to understand. She caught a few, something like "save" and "child, save child's life."

White Eagle nudged his chin toward the lake. "You saved the child?"

Anna shivered, water still dripping from her hair and dress. "With the Lord's help, yes. I suppose I did," she said, wondering how she knew what to do. Memories of her childhood waded across her mind. Most Dutch people learned to swim at an early age. The threat of floods from an overflowing dike was a constant concern, so they taught their children how to swim, how to save someone who might be drowning. All those lessons from her father had engraved themselves into her mind. She didn't even have to think when she went after that baby.

White Eagle stepped toward her and brushed his knuckles over her cheek. "You all right?"

She nodded.

"Good," he said, staring at her, his jaw ticking. He then turned and walked away. He seemed tense, for he squeezed his hands into fists at his sides and kept shaking them out.

Runs With Wind cast her a questioning look. Anna shrugged, and a small pain shot through her shoulder.

———⚬≻≺⚬———

It had been almost four months since the day Anna left New York. Her shoulder was still bruised and puffy, but no longer painful to move. The wound had healed nicely, although she could see that the marks would likely scar, but she wasn't worried about it since her shoulder would always be covered, unless she wore her Cheyenne clothing. But she wouldn't have to worry about that.

Her lovely traveling dress had been ruined, stained with her blood, so Beth had offered the use of her own dress since she would have no need for it. Anna sat at the opening of White Eagle's lodge and repaired the tears. She yanked the needle too hard, breaking what little thread she had left.

In the distance near the yellow and red aspen trees, the men spent a great deal of time in the sweat lodge. It was an interesting structure: a short, rounded-off tipi, made of buffalo skin, resembling a very large beetle without legs. She had helped the other women heat up rocks after they'd carried them up to the lodge. Apparently the men would go in, smoke a long pipe together and sweat out all the evil from their bodies. It was some sort of purification ritual. She watched closely, wondering if White Eagle would ever join them. She'd never seen him enter. Where could he be?

When she finally finished with the repairs on Beth's dress, she went into the lodge to make her things ready for her trip, whenever they would leave. It couldn't be much longer. She hung Beth's dress from one of the stakes and noticed her Bible on White Eagle's bed. How'd it get there? It must have fallen out when she set her carpetbag there. She placed it back in her carpetbag and knelt by her bed to fold her Indian dresses so they would be easy to pack. She planned to speak to White Eagle today about their eventual departure.

It was time to leave, whether he thought so or not. She'd healed enough, and she'd been patient. What he was waiting for, she didn't know. When she finished sorting through the rest of her things, she decided to help the women with their chores. She ducked through the opening of the lodge and tied back the flap. As she turned, she noticed White Eagle with a frown, striding toward her.

She opened her mouth to ask, yet again, when they would leave.

"I'm going hunting," he said. He strode past her and entered the lodge to pack.

Anna followed him inside. "When will you take me to Denver?"

"We'll talk about it when I get back," he said, taking up his rifle, bow and quiver. "I'll be back tomorrow." He headed for the door flap.

She wrung her hands, sensing White Eagle's moodiness, but not wanting to wait yet another day to hear his answer. "But I've waited so long already."

He turned on her, eyes blazing. "I'm tired of hearing about that city!"

His anger sent a painful tremor from her head to her toes.

"We'll go when I'm ready," he said between clenched teeth. With that, he marched away.

Stunned into silence, Anna watched him go.

The following day, Anna wore her civilized clothes, not necessarily as a statement of defiance to White Eagle, but because they reminded her of who she really was, where she really belonged, and right now, her own clothes were her only form of comfort.

While the men were hunting, Anna collected wood with Beth. Laughs Like A River wasn't around, and the other women ignored them, but one in particular kept eyeing them suspiciously. Anna had seen this woman before, though she'd never paid her any mind. One thing was certain, the woman rarely smiled and never had anything to say to her and Beth.

Anna dragged a thin log over to her rope to bind the wood together and dropped it next to the others. She straightened to rub her aching back, keeping an eye on the woman, who was obviously keeping an eye on them.

Beth knelt next to Anna and began binding her wood together. Anna watched, irritated that Beth was already finished and could carry so much more than she could.

From the corner of her eye, Anna saw the suspicious woman straighten and stride over to them. As the woman neared, she raised a root pick high in the air over Beth.

"Bet!" Anna leapt forward and grabbed the woman's wrist. Beth scurried out from under them, and the force from the woman's blow made Anna's arms buckle. She let the woman bring it down, but guided it into the ground. The woman reached to yank the pick back up, but Anna stomped on it and the woman's hand. The woman gasped, but to Anna's surprise she didn't cry out.

"Nay!" Anna said, her heart in her throat. Then remembering the word in Cheyenne, she repeated, "*Hova'âhane!*"

The other women came to stand around them. Anna eased her foot off the root picker, watching the woman's hands to see if she'd go for it again. "Don't hurt my friend," Anna shouted, her limbs trembling.

"She white. No belong here," the woman said in broken English. "*You* no belong here." The woman pointed at Anna.

"And your braves kidnapped us!" Anna's anger flared, especially when realizing she could be in Denver right now rather than defending their lives. "Do you think we *chose* to be here?" Anna stepped toward the woman. The trees seemed to shudder from her rage. "Don't ever hurt my friend! She's your war chief's wife, and if you ever lay a hand on her, he'll kill you!" She shouted everything in English, too angry and upset to think of the right words, but the woman who'd threatened Beth seemed to understand their meaning. The thought that poor Beth would be stuck here made Anna realize the urgency of the matter that she make it clear they not hurt her best friend. Her eyes narrowed in on each woman standing around them, making her point clear.

The woman said something in Cheyenne that Anna didn't understand, but one thing was certain by the look in her eye, it wasn't meant to make peace. Anna took another step toward her, and the woman straightened.

"If you want to hurt one of us, then hurt me," Anna said, trembling. "Let what you do to me be a sign to chief Yellow Leaf and our husbands that you don't approve of us. But after that, you promise to leave us alone."

The woman's nails slashed across Anna's cheek. Shocked from the blow, Anna stood her ground, straining to keep her hand from grasping her burning cheek. She wouldn't give this woman the pleasure of knowing she was hurt, just like she'd learned long ago not to give her uncle that pleasure. The woman shouted something she didn't understand and slapped Anna. She then seized Anna's throat.

The other women watched as Anna tried to pry open the woman's fingers. She spotted some of them holding Beth back. The trees swayed. She clutched the woman's wrists, but she wouldn't let go. She clawed her way down the woman's arm, but she still kept her grip fastened around Anna's neck.

Desperate, she kicked the woman, grateful she'd worn her boots. The woman released her, and Anna side-kicked her in the gut. The woman buckled over. Anna gasped in air and rubbed her throbbing neck. The woman also struggled for breath. They both stared at each other. Anna didn't dare look away.

The woman pointed a quivering finger at Anna's cheek. "This sign." She then turned, plodded with a heavy slouch, took up her pick, and walked away.

Relief flooded Anna's eyes, but she covered them with a quivering hand. She wouldn't give any of them the pleasure of seeing her tears. Suddenly, Beth was beside her. Beth grabbed her arm and pulled her aside. Anna stumbled into her.

She leaned on her friend as Beth led her back to their woodpiles. "Are you all right?" Beth finally asked, once the rest of the women dispersed.

"I think so," Anna said, unable to control the quake in her voice.

"Let me take you back to the village."

"No. Dat's . . . *that's* what they want. That's what she wants. We can't let them scare us, Bet. It's important."

"How do you know?"

Anna could say it was how she dealt with her uncle, but she didn't want to get into that. Besides, she remembered some of the Indians in her book being impressed with an enemy's show of bravery, forget the fact that they'd killed him anyway. "I read it somewhere," she finally said, not mentioning it was fiction.

<hr />

It was late afternoon when Anna saw White Eagle and the other men return from their hunt. Behind White Eagle's horse, the travois was weighed down by a dead animal. The women, as usual, ran up to take care of the beasts. This time Anna stayed behind wringing her hands.

White Eagle strode toward her with the carcass of a bear on his travois. Pride showed on his weary face. He had done well in his hunt, and a good wife ought to reward him with praise.

It made what she wanted to say more difficult.

"What happened?" he said as he came up to her, his gaze locked onto her cheek. "How—?"

"I want you to take me to Denver City tomorrow, or I'll . . ." She squared her shoulders. "I will walk there myself!"

He stopped and frowned.

She wondered if he'd expected her to greet him the way the other wives had greeted their husbands, praising them for the job well done. She should have at least said something about the bear he'd killed. It was quite amazing, really.

Other men and women untied the travois from his horse. They frowned at her, but at this point, she didn't care what anyone thought. She didn't belong here, just like that woman said.

"You are my wife." He towered over her. "You belong with me."

Anna stepped back. Why would he say that? Did their wedding mean something to him after all? The thought that he might actually believe they were married caused her heart to flutter. If only for a moment. Yes, she was desperate to get to Denver City, but did he really want her? She clung to the sudden hope that welled inside her. "I thought our marriage wasn't real?"

His eyes flickered to her ring, and he swallowed. "Of course it isn't." He turned away.

Anna's heart sunk. "Then take me home." She choked out the words, angry and disappointed.

He faced her, and his gaze raked over her. "A cat," he said between clenched teeth, looking her up and down with an accusing glare. "You purr and flick your tail under my nose to tempt me."

Anna gasped. "I did no such thing!" She clenched her hands into fists. "I'm no temptress," she said, barely able to control her tears. "You're the one who brought me here. I didn't ask to come!" She trembled, thinking of her recent battle in the woods, of his promise to take her to Denver. "You're not a man of your word."

He came inches from her face. "If that's true, I'd have taken you by now. And I don't mean to Denver City."

Fear and anger paralyzed her.

He walked on.

Her throat clotted, and she wondered if she could still speak. "Please." She followed after him, half running to keep up with his long strides, her voice barely passing the knot in her throat. His back was to her and a feather dangled from his hair, his broad shoulders towering over her even in their slumped, tired state. "I mean it. I'll go alone."

He stopped and turned, and she nearly collided with his chest.

"Walks Alone," he said, his jaw ticking.

She bristled, wondering why he suddenly called her by her Cheyenne name.

He strode away. "The name suits you."

She clenched her jaw. No words for a proper response came. She wanted to cry, to stomp and scream.

"We leave tomorrow." He tossed the words over his shoulder.

Chapter 16

"Anna, before you go, I have to share something." Beth pulled her aside from the others crowded around the horses that were packed and ready to go.

"What is it?" Anna asked, sensing something very important had happened. She hoped it wasn't something terrible, like another encounter with the woman in the woods, which would obligate her to stay.

Tears welled in Beth's eyes. Her cheeks bloomed with color, and a smile turned up her lips. "I'm with child."

Anna stared in stunned silence. She couldn't believe her ears.

Beth simply smiled.

"How can that be?"

"It just is." Beth shrugged.

Anna's heart soared with delight. She took Beth by her arms and they jumped up and down, giggling. They both laughed and cried. "You're so blessed. I simply don't know what to say. Does Running Cloud know?"

Beth nodded. "He's so careful with me." She giggled. "Almost too careful."

Anna laughed and hugged her. "I am so happy for you!"

"And he knows all about that wicked woman who tried to attack us. You can leave without worry. He'll protect me. Besides, he says she won't harm me because of your act of bravery. She respects you, even if she doesn't like you, and that means she won't harm me." Beth brushed a dark curl from her face. "I hope you'll be happy."

Anna sighed with relief. Beth would be safe. "Thank you." Only Denver City could make Anna happy.

She felt a tug on her clothes and looked down to see Runs With Wind.

"Oh! I have something for you." Anna knelt down next to the little girl and handed Runs With Wind a lock of her hair. The little girl's face looked puzzled, but she finally smiled and hugged Anna around the neck.

Song Bird came to the women with a worried face, holding out the folded clothes Anna had earlier refused to pack. "You wear these."

Anna looked at the clothes as Song Bird continued to hold them out to her. Reluctantly, Anna took them. "Thank you." She'd lost track of how many times Song Bird had tried to coax her into wearing the improper man-like clothing. "I'll pack it on the horse," she said, hoping to have reached a compromise.

Song Bird nodded and turned away.

White Eagle let Song Bird take him by the arm and pull him aside. He gazed into the woman's eyes, wondering why they were round with concern.

"Walks Alone is afraid," Song Bird said in Cheyenne. "But she is strong. She saved Beth's life. Return to us soon. Be proud and not ashamed. She's the only woman brave enough to fight our female warrior. She wears the mark of Beaver Claws."

He looked at Anna's scratched cheek. He assumed she'd caught herself on a tree branch. Now he understood. Now he understood everything.

"I've been thinking." Running Cloud's voice carried to them. "About what happened between Beaver Claws and Walks Alone in the woods." He sauntered up to White Eagle's horse. "She doesn't have the courage to touch prairie turtles, but she has the courage to fight Beaver Claws?" He chuckled and patted the horse. "Walks Alone is a brave woman."

White Eagle forced a frown, despite the pride he felt. But now he also felt shame. Shame with himself for not protecting her, for not being aware of what happened.

"Beaver Claws said she was a brave fighter. News of their fight has fanned through the village like a prairie fire," Running Cloud said, laughter in his voice, and a glimmer in his eyes that told White Eagle he knew of his ignorance.

"A prairie fire that never reached my lodge," White Eagle finally said. "Husbands are always the last to know." He nodded his appreciation to them both.

After saying goodbye, he turned to his horse. Never had he been more pleased, knowing his woman, his Walks Alone, was the only woman to ever stand up to one of the few female warriors, Beaver Claws. And to his amusement and pleasure, by doing just that, she'd managed to gain the woman's respect. No, she likely still didn't like Walks Alone, or Woman Of Sorrow for that matter, but she respected them, both of them.

And now that everyone in his village respected her, he was taking her away, taking her to a place he could never belong, taking her to a place that hated him and his people. All he had to do was break his word, but it'd be wrong. Just as his father always said, his yes must be yes, and his no must be no. Besides, she didn't believe in their marriage and would never be truly happy until she made it to Denver City.

Misery consumed him.

⸻ ❧ ⸻

When they set out for Denver City, White Eagle had given Anna her own horse to ride. She missed riding with him on horseback, missed the comfort and warmth of his nearness. Now the distance between them had grown, and not just because they didn't share a horse.

Still, she couldn't help but think she should enjoy this trip much more than the first. After all, she was finally going home. But by the end of the day, she became worried. White Eagle had hardly spoken to her the entire journey. She'd tried to be pleasant, only to receive a gruff, blank stare in return.

In the distance, a white billowy cloud rolled over a red, yellow, and green mountaintop. It made her think of cream spilling into tea, swirling into brightly colored teacups. She never realized trees could be so colorful. It was as if God had taken a paintbrush to the entire mountainside, stroking in autumn shades, contrasting them with the green pines, white clouds, and blue sky.

"Isn't it beautiful?" she said.

White Eagle said nothing and kept his back to her.

"Please talk to me," she said. "You've hardly said a word all day."

Silence filled the air, and she might as well have been talking to the trees. Feathers and leather waved in his raven hair as she stared at his back. The fringes on his shirt shifted below his shoulders, but he otherwise remained still and silent as a rock.

When she caught a glimpse of his profile, he wore a blank expression, and it ate at her that he refused to talk. She knew she'd made him angry, but she'd hoped that by now he'd be over it. After all, it'd been the plan from the beginning that he'd take her home. What was the point in putting it off?

A cloud cast its shadow over the side of a mountain when they made their way through evergreens, only emphasizing the gloom she sensed from White Eagle. Leaves fell helplessly to the ground, and Anna couldn't help but empathize with their predicament. It was as if, like the dying leaf, she were falling, drifting away from the only one she'd ever be able to call her husband. And all he could do was ignore her, just like the horses ignored the leaves, crunching them under their hooves. As the day wore on, more dark clouds rolled in, and lightning streaks filled the sky. Just over a clearing, rain cried over the land in the distance. Despite her misery, it was a beautiful sight.

"We need to take cover," White Eagle said, finally breaking the silence.

"It's nice to know you still have a voice."

He shot her a dark look, and she shivered. Still, it was better than no words at all. At least he knew she was alive.

He turned to lead them through a thick patch of trees just as trickles of rain began to fall. She ducked under protective branches, dodging the pellets of rain, until they came to a rocky slope. It came together with another slope and formed a covered crevice between the two.

Thunder cracked across the sky. The winds picked up, and the rain quickened its pace. White Eagle dismounted and reached to help Anna down from her horse. A sudden shower of water rushed over them as she slid between his arms to the ground. It was as though somebody had dumped a horse trough of cold water over her.

"Get in the cave," he said as he gathered their belongings from the horses. He tossed the rolled blankets into the cavern then turned to collect the rest of their things.

Thunder exploded in her ears, and lightning flashed. One of the horses bucked and charged. White Eagle grabbed for the animal, but the horse got away and galloped through the trees.

She sprang out of the shelter to help, only to receive another wild blast of wind and rain. "What do we do now?"

White Eagle pointed her back in the cave. "Stay there!" He grabbed hold of the remaining horse's reins, guided it toward the cave's mouth, and handed Anna her carpetbag and other belongings.

"Wait here," he said. He mounted and whisked away between the trees.

She scrutinized the cave. It was fairly deep and offered enough protection from the elements, though shadows cloaked the back, making it too dark for comfort. She spread a blanket on the ground away from the back and shivered. The light would soon fade, and the cool evening air already chilled her to the bone. She perched atop a damp blanket, pulled another around her, and waited.

Rain pellets clapped the ground so hard she could barely hear herself breathe. She searched the trees, hoping for any movement or sign of White Eagle as she huddled with her knees pulled up to her chin. The sun faded in the dark sky, taking her courage with it. Loneliness seeped off the cave's walls, crawled over the ground, and wrapped its icy fingers around her. What if he never returned? What if something happened to him? She wouldn't know where or how to find him. Then what would she do? What if a wild animal came for her while he was gone? What if . . .

White Eagle's form appeared in the opening of the cave.

She jumped up and ran to him. "Did you find the horse?" she asked, touching his arm. He was soaking wet and cold.

"No." He walked past her and began stripping out of his shirt.

"What can I do to help?" she asked, shivering from his chilled tone but relieved that he'd returned safely.

"Look for dry branches. There should be a stack of them in the back. We need a fire."

She searched the cave in the dim light, following along the cold stone wall. It was difficult to see, so she crouched down and searched with stiff hands. Every so often flashes of lightning from outside lit up the cave just enough for her to catch a glimpse of their surroundings. Three rolls of buffalo skins lay near the far wall.

"Look in the back," White Eagle said.

She crept farther toward the back of the cave. What if she found a rodent? Or even worse, a snake? She focused her mind on White Eagle and his need to get warm. Finally, her hands brushed against a stack of branches.

"Here, I found some." She carried several branches to the center of the cave, and White Eagle arranged them on the ground. She backed away to collect more.

Soon his fire horn had made a fire and smoke filled the air. Flames ate at the branches and glowed before them, casting shadows on the walls and illuminating White Eagle's bare chest as he squatted before the fire in his leggings.

Her eyes took on a will of their own. What might it be like to touch him? Her gaze fluttered to his face.

He watched her.

Cheeks flaming, she turned away. Holding the blanket tightly around her, she settled on the ground against the hard wall.

"Stay near the fire. It won't last long. We should build up heat between us."

"How do we do that?"

He stood. "Bring your blanket and come here."

The downpour echoed throughout the cave between the cracks of thunder as she shuffled over to him. A flash of lightning lit them up and then vanished.

"Are you warmed up yet?" she asked, practically shouting over the rain, worried that he might become sick from the cold.

"Not yet." He took her by the elbow. "You need to get out of those wet clothes."

She stopped.

"You'll get sick."

She hadn't realized just how wet she was. Even her blanket was wet. When she moved to get her buttonhook from her carpetbag, a bloodcurdling scream filled the air. A chill coursed up her spine. "What was that?" Another scream ripped through the forest, like the sound of a terrified woman, and Anna nearly joined in.

White Eagle cupped her face in his hands. "It's a cougar. You're safe."

"A cougar?"

Another shrill carried through the trees.

"And what was that?" she asked.

"That was the horse."

She clung to him, and he held her close.

"I have to get him," he said.

"Please, don't leave me."

He looked toward the sound then back at her. He lunged toward his leather satchel and yanked out a revolver. "Do you know how to use one of these?"

"No." She shook her head, staring at the large gun.

He held it in front of her. "First you cock the hammer like this, and aim." With one hand, he cocked it and aimed at the wall of the cave. "Then you pull the trigger." Instead of pulling the trigger, he released the hammer and handed her the heavy gun. He moved away and grabbed his rifle. "Stay here, and stay by the fire."

"But—"

"Do as I say and you'll be safe!" He gave her such a fierce look, she didn't dare argue. "Stay by the fire," he said again, his voiced calmed. He stepped toward her again, and his look softened. "Remember what I said about the coyotes?"

She nodded, recalling his words that they were safe as long as they stayed by the fire.

He lightly brushed her cheek and then left, disappearing between the trees.

She stood holding the heavy revolver in her quivering hands. It felt cold to the touch, and ever so dangerous. She examined its smooth octagonal barrel and brushed her fingers over an engraving on the cylinder where a scene depicted battling naval vessels.

After settling back on the ground, she shivered as the creepy walls closed in around her again. Two loud blasts shot through the air and she jumped. Was that White Eagle's rifle, or was it thunder? She couldn't be sure. After more lonely minutes passed, she finally saw White Eagle's shadow moving through the pines as he led the limping horse beside him. The lightning revealed torn flesh on the horse's leg, reaching his flank.

White Eagle motioned for her to give him the revolver.

She ran up to him, blasts of water splattered against her face.

"You're not going to kill him, are you?" she shouted above the rain.

"I have to. He's suffering." Steam came from the horse's nostrils and his flanks twitched and trembled.

"But can't we—" A huge piece of flesh hung from the animal's side, and she froze at the sight.

Reluctantly, she handed White Eagle the revolver and stepped back. He spoke words of comfort to the horse and took him a distance away from where she stood, disappearing with the animal behind the trees.

Back in the cave, Anna trembled near the fire, watching the dark forest.

The explosion of the revolver echoed over the mountaintops and between the trees, sounding not much different than the cracks of thunder above them. Then all went silent, except for the pattering of rain on the ground. She tried to swallow the knot that filled her throat, but it grew, threatening to explode in wails. The thunder rolled and shook, rattling her ribcage. Suppose whatever got the horse would get him? She shivered at the thought as water dripped from her clothes to the floor. She wrapped her arms around herself to ward off the cold, praying for his safety.

Finally, with drooped shoulders, White Eagle returned to the cave. She threw herself at him. "You're safe!" What had attacked the horse? Was it really a cougar? She was too frightened to ask. She didn't want to know. All that mattered was that White Eagle was safe. He didn't tremble and seemed calm and unafraid. He didn't seem worried about the dangers outside, so she shouldn't either.

Still, she clung to him, hoping his calmness might rub off on her.

He pulled her close and stroked her hair. Her tears blended in with the rain on his bare chest as she held onto him, unable to control her quivering. He warmed her despite the cold water dripping from his body.

"You're cold," he said, breaking the silence. The downpour outside steadied, but thunder and occasional flashes of lightning quaked through the woods.

Yes, she was cold, but she didn't care. She just hoped he'd never let her go. Never allow her to live without him.

"You have to get out of these clothes." He stepped away, studying her with concern pulling on his features. He then went to the back of the cave, unrolled a buffalo skin, and held it up like a wall before her and the fire. "I won't look."

Wet material clung to her skin, and when shivers prickled up and down her back, her teeth began to chatter.

"You need to take it off." He motioned to her with his chin.

"But I don't have anything else to wear. All my clothes are wet." The blankets were also wet.

"Why didn't you wear the clothes Song Bird gave you?" He let the buffalo skin fall and picked up her bundle.

"They were leggings. It's improper."

"Wear them tomorrow." He shook them out and laid them on a boulder protruding from the wall. "You wouldn't be so cold if you'd worn them."

She nodded, too chilled and tired to argue.

He came back and held up the robe, turning his face to the ground.

Anna crept between the robe and the fire and quickly got out of her wet clothes. She then moved into the robe, and he wrapped it around her.

He went to the back of the cave, grabbed another buffalo skin and spread it out next to the fire. They knelt down, and he gently held her away. "Your hair needs to dry," he said as he unbraided her strands and draped each damp mass over the robe.

Perched between him and the fire, she shivered as he wrapped part of the buffalo skin around his shoulders and then around her, enclosing her in his warmth.

Despite the buffalo skin covering her, she'd never felt so exposed. How dreadful. She shivered, partly from the cold but also from a spark of desire as heat radiated from them both. He was her husband after all, so she didn't need to worry. Yet he planned on letting her go. She imagined what it'd be like if he kept her as his wife. She'd be his. And they would have children. He would have a family again, and so would she. But all of that was a dream. None of it was real.

The crackle and warmth of the fire filled the small cave. She watched as tiny sparks soared up and fell back down, their small glow dying next to the fire. White Eagle rested his chin on her head as they both stared into the dancing flames.

"Why didn't you tell me?" White Eagle whispered.

"Tell you what?"

"About Beaver Claws."

"I—I don't know."

"Don't ever keep anything like that from me again," he said, his voice rough.

Anna wondered if there ever would be an "again."

For a long time, neither spoke. All was silent except for the storm thundering just outside. His warmth consumed her. Would they ever share such a moment again? The thought of losing him, the thought of never having him in her life was like watching those tiny sparks die, slowly losing their light. How could she say goodbye to her husband? Nobody had showed her affection the way he had, other than her father. The way he cared for her after the arrow, the way he pointed out how God had indeed answered her prayer.

Her gaze dropped down to his fist as it clasped the buffalo skin together. She always liked looking at his hands. Cautiously, she slid her fingers over his knuckles. She took one of his hands in hers and turned it over in her palm, admiring its strength. How could one hand be so powerful, and yet so gentle? She pressed each of her fingers against his, finger to finger, palm to palm. Her fingers, long and white—his, large and rough.

Their fingers intertwined and their wrists came together. Easing away, she peered up into his serious face. The light of the fire danced against the contours of his rugged jaw, reflecting in his eyes as he stared at the flames. He looked down at her with a dark want of desire.

"I can't fight it," he said, his voice ragged. "No matter where I go, you are there. You're all around me, Anna." He hissed as he leaned in closer. "The wind whispers your name. In the forests your voice rustles in the leaves; your image beats in my blood." His breath brushed against her cheek, and he kissed her. "And then your scent carries over to me at night and haunts my dreams." He dragged in a breath. "I want you so much it hurts." His throaty voice confirmed his pain. "I can't stop needing you, Anna. I am your husband, and I want you. Please. Don't deny me." He tightened his grip on her hand, his heat melting away her doubts.

Tears streamed down her cheeks. "I thought you didn't want me," she said, her voice choking.

He lifted her chin, searching her face and forcing her to meet his gaze. "Why would you think that?"

"You said our marriage wasn't real."

A light came to his eyes. "I only said what I thought you wanted to hear."

"I don't want to lose you," she whispered, but wanted to shout the words, thrilling in the fact that he did want her, that he never wanted to let her go.

He captured her hand and kissed the tips of her fingers. "You'll never lose me."

She marveled at his words, barely able to believe they were real. "Please, tell me again what you said. About my name in the wind and the trees."

A flash of lightning lit up the urgency in his face. "I'll tell you. Without words."

A clap of thunder exploded in the distance and slowly rolled away. The storm finally faded, as did her innocence.

Chapter 17

The following morning White Eagle awoke with Anna curled next to him. He propped on an elbow and admired her golden hair streaming around her face. She reminded him of the morning sun with its golden rays lancing over the plains.

With the tip of his finger, he traced over each freckle sprinkled across her nose. Her lashes lay against her rosy cheeks that had been alarmingly pale the night before. Now she rested peacefully with a contented smile. And her lips that had been blue from the cold were now full and tempting. Unwilling to fight the urge, he leaned down and tasted their sweetness.

She sighed, and her eyes fluttered open.

He smiled and feathered his fingers down her slender throat, brushing away a wild strand of hair.

"Morning Sun," he said. "That will be your name."

She moved against him and rested her head on his arm, gazing up at him with those forest green eyes. "It's a beautiful name."

Finally, she was his. All that he'd been longing for had suddenly come true. Despite the pain, he'd been ready to set her free, to give her the freedom she'd so desperately wanted, and now, all at once, she'd given herself to him. Like a dove set free and ready to take flight, she'd flown right back to him.

"I love you," she said.

His heart quickened. Her voice, soft and melodious, touched the depths of his soul. He brushed her cheek with his knuckles, wanting to speak the same soft-spoken words she had uttered to him, but a knot lodged in his throat.

"Don't you love me?" she asked.

"Yes," he managed to choke out. He did love her. He loved her so much it hurt.

She pushed up on an elbow, her eyes clouded with worry.

"More than words can say," he said, amused by her doubt. He lifted her chin and kissed her, lovingly, tenderly. "You are mine, now and forever. I'll take care of you." He kissed her again. "We'll go back to my village and have our own family."

"Back to your village?" Her hand rested against his chest, panic in her eyes. "But you're supposed to take me home."

"You're my wife. Home is with me."

She sat bolt upright, covering herself with the buffalo skin. "But you promised—"

"There's nothing for you there. You belong with me now."

"But you gave me your word." She stood and grabbed her clothes.

"How can you still expect me to take you to Denver?" He jumped to his feet and snatched his clothes.

"We can stop in a town before we reach Denver City and pick up some normal shirts and trousers." She waved her hand. "Dress you up like a gentleman."

Normal shirts and trousers? Sparks of anger flamed. He already had normal clothes. Gentleman? Did she have any clue what a true gentleman was? Had he not been a gentleman, he would have made her his long ago. Besides, was she naïve enough to think their marriage would be accepted by the white men?

"What could possibly be in Denver City?" he finally asked, exasperated by the conversation they were having.

"My freedom." She faced him and whispered, "Home."

"*Home* is with *me!*"

Flustered, she straightened in the short buckskin dress. "You promised to take me there." Then she turned and quickly slipped into her leggings. "I should have known." Her voice trembled. "You kidnapped me. Why would you have told me the truth?"

White Eagle strode toward her.

She stepped back, her eyes wide. He stilled his movements and sucked in a deep breath. He didn't want to frighten her, but now his blood boiled.

"I never lied to you," he said, forcing his tone to a simmering calm. "I told you I'd take you to Denver City when I thought our marriage didn't mean anything to you. That's why we're here!"

She swallowed visibly. "Our marriage was real from the moment you forced it on me. And whether you thought I thought it was real or not, you still promised to take me to Denver City."

"There is nothing for you there." Saying the name of the city that took his family and now threatened to take his wife made him want to spit fire. "No work, no family, nothing!"

"You gave me your word." Her chest heaved. "And now you're going to break it?"

Had she lost her mind? He turned and paced the cave. He ought to just throw her over his shoulder and carry her all the way back to his village. She was his now, whether she liked it or not. What was it about Denver that drew her so much? She'd never even been there before. And now, after all that city had done to him, having initiated the massacre on his people, his new bride—who claimed to love him—expected him to take her there?

"The white man is like a snake. He has no honor and devours the young of his brother." The words exploded from his mouth.

"You hate white people?" Her voice was small. "How can you possibly love me?"

He cupped her face in his hands. "I only *hate* Denver."

She studied him, looking at his eyes and then his mouth. Would she give in? "'Hate' is such a strong word," she whispered.

Growling, he dropped his fists at his sides.

"I just want—I just need to go there. For years—before I ever left New York," short quick breaths escaped her lips, "I planned to start a new life for myself—in Denver City. Please. Just let us go there, that's all I'm asking, and ten—*then* I'll go back with you to your village."

"You want to go to Denver to gain your freedom, but you've already lost it. You won't be free to do what you please if we went there. You are mine now."

Her cheeks turned bright red, and she crossed her arms.

She had said she loved him. She had said she would go back to his village. And he had promised. He ought to give her what she wanted. No matter how much it hurt, he ought to do this for her. His stomach knotted at the thought of going back to that hateful city, especially now that he really didn't have to. He raked his hand through his hair and gazed into her wide eyes.

Wonder played through his mind as he realized her ignorance. She actually believed they, as a married couple, could go to Denver without any persecution from the palefaces. The Cheyenne were more open to mixed marriages than the white man ever would be.

But what was he thinking? He wasn't going back there. Ever!

"We're not going. That's final." He began to pack up their things, anything to distract himself from the small whimpers coming from the other side of the cave.

To his relief, she began packing. It didn't take long before she had her carpetbag and packages together.

He went out to get the horse ready, anything to get out of earshot of her whimpering. As he untied the animal, Anna marched passed him. She marched through the trees, shoulders straight and chin high. The determination in her stride amused him.

But where was she going? Did she need to relieve herself? Why would she need her carpetbag and package of dresses? Last time she took off with her bag she'd tried to escape.

She disappeared between the trees.

Blowing out a breath, he dropped the horse's reins. "What are you doing?"

"I'm going to Denver City," she snapped.

"Anna, get back here!" he shouted in the most firm tone he could muster, his voice echoing through the trees.

But she didn't come.

"Don't make me drag you back with me."

Quiet.

"I'll do it. Get back here, *now!*" He pointed to the spot in front of him.

And waited.

When she still didn't come, he retied the horse and strode after her. "Women." He grumbled. No wonder he'd avoided them for so long. She was already hidden between the trees, so he tracked the broken branches and footprints and found the path she'd taken.

"You're already heading in the wrong direction, Morning Sun. You'll never make it." He stomped through the trees.

No answer.

He stopped and listened for her. A few branches stirred ahead. He marched in that direction. When he got his hands on her there was no telling what he'd do.

When he caught a glimpse of her hair, he picked up his pace.

She glanced over her shoulder and ran.

It reminded him of hunting in his youth, but this prey wouldn't escape. After dodging branches and ignoring her frightened pants and cries, he locked his arms around her waist.

She dropped her carpetbag and packages, flailing her fists. "Let go of me! I'm going to Denver wit or wit—*wit*hout you!"

"You're not going anywhere *wit*hout me, my love." He growled in her ear and felt her bristle.

"Let me go!"

He released her.

She turned to face him, eyes blazing with fury. She lunged at him, fists clenched and teeth barred, but she straightened and stomped her foot. Bending down, she gathered up her things.

He forced a frown, trying not to laugh at her wild behavior.

Pressing her belongings to her chest, she marched away—in the wrong direction.

"Wrong direction again, Morning Sun," he said, arms folded.

She kept on walking, so he went after her again, this time impatience ready to boil over.

He swung her up in his arms, carpetbag and all. Grateful she and her things were light, he strode back with her toward the cave.

"Nay!" She shrieked and kicked the air.

Had she gone mad?

When he spotted a thick bed of pine needles, he bent and dropped her in them.

The needles hugged around her body, and she stared up at him, eyes wide and mouth open.

"Who's in Denver City?" He hissed and knelt over her. If she was willing to go without him, he wondered if there was someone waiting for her.

She blinked.

With one arm resting over his knee, he waited for a response.

She shoved herself up on an elbow, and he pushed her back down, her hair framing her beautiful face. She blinked again, her lips parted.

He continued to hover over her. "Explain yourself."

Moisture welled in her eyes. "My father."

He shook his head. "I thought he was—?"

"He is," she whispered. "It was his dream."

Studying her, he took a long deep breath to control his elevated pulse.

"Before he'd ever met my mother, he'd traveled to the West, all the way to Denver City," she said, breathless. "It was his dream to settle there, but he had obligations to his parents. On his way back to Holland, he stayed in New York for several months where he met my mother. They fell in love, got married, and she went back to Holland with him. That's where I was born; she died giving birth to me."

With each deep breath, her chest rose and fell. She swallowed and continued.

"After her death, he decided it was best to stay with family; all he had were his parents, and I was all he had left of my mother. But after my grandparents died, he couldn't stop talking about the West. That's when he decided to leave Holland. To finally fulfill his dream."

Tears trickled over her face and into her hair as she relayed the story to him. And now he understood. But one thing bothered him. Not once did she ever mention what she wanted.

"Do you have dreams of your own?" He touched her soft golden stands streaming in the cushioned bed of needles. "What are your dreams, Morning Sun?"

"This is my dream." She furrowed her brows. "I just have to go there. Please. Then I'll go back with you to your village," she said in one long breath. "I promise."

His anger cooled, and he brushed a lock of hair from her cheek. For a long time, he gazed into her desperate eyes, wondering what she expected to find there, how long she expected to stay.

"I'll take you," he finally said. "But . . ." he held her gaze and tried not to clench his teeth, "we're not staying."

To his surprise, she wrapped her arms around his neck. "Tank—*th*ank you." Tears streamed down her cheeks as she kissed him all over his face.

The joy in her eyes made this gift worth the pain. He wouldn't have to stay long anyway.

Chapter

The sun cast columns of light between the trees surrounding them, and the horse's hooves crunching pinecones echoed off the surrounding woods as they made their way toward Denver City. Anna wore the buckskin leggings Song Bird had given her, and the slit cut dress made it possible to straddle the horse, which was very awkward.

"Are you uncomfortable?" he asked.

"Yes."

He lifted her leg so she sat sideways. She cuddled up against him, resting her cheek on his chest. She would always be his. Just like the biblical words, she and White Eagle had become one flesh, and now she understood its meaning. The innocence she'd lost made her recall a young maidservant who'd worked briefly for her uncle. He'd promised to marry her, and she'd given herself to him. Shortly thereafter, he'd dismissed the poor girl. Anna would never forget the devastation in the girl's eyes when she'd left that day. Now she understood the valuable gift the girl had given.

What if in the end White Eagle decided he didn't want her? What if he changed his mind, like her uncle? She'd practically forced him to say he loved her. What if he suddenly decided that their marriage meant nothing?

She took a deep breath, trying not to worry. He was taking her to Denver City, despite the fact that he clearly didn't want to go there. That ought to tell her he loved her. She took comfort in that thought. At last, she was going home. Her dreams would finally come true, and then she would be ready to begin new ones.

In Denver she'd no longer be his captive, just his wife. Once there, she would be free. If not literally, then in her mind and in her heart.

Her city of dreams, of dreams come true.

Home.

A cluster of birds flurried to the sky.

She glanced up at White Eagle. He reined in and tensed his grip. "Shhhh. Don't say a word." His breath came hot against her ear.

She froze.

He pointed between the trees.

As she followed his finger, she spotted fur, then whiskers, and the eyes of what looked like a cat watching them.

White Eagle slowly dismounted. "Stay on the horse," he said.

He moved away and grabbed his tomahawk in one hand. Why didn't he just get his rifle and shoot the creature? Fear gripped her like hands around her throat. She wanted to scream, but she couldn't. Even the horse stood frozen, as if he also knew danger was near.

White Eagle moved like a cat, turning his tomahawk as he distanced himself from her. She wished he'd stay near and not leave her so alone. He was just a few feet away, but at that moment it felt like miles. And worse, what if the cat got him? Hurt him?

With a loud hiss, White Eagle sprang from the ground as if he would pounce on the animal. The cat scurried away into the woods.

He strode back to the horse and tucked away his tomahawk.

"Why didn't you kill it?" she asked.

"No need." He shrugged. "Mountain lions only attack if you're alone. If it's outnumbered, it usually won't go in for the kill." He mounted the horse and took her in his arms. "He must have thought we'd make a mighty fine meal." He growled against her neck.

She jumped, clutching his arm.

He chuckled.

"That's not funny," she said, finding it impossible to repress a smile.

That evening, they came upon a small log house where lights glowed from the windows. White Eagle helped her dismount, and she followed him as he led the horse into a small barn.

"Where are we?" she whispered. He had been so quiet, she felt like she was breaking some unknown rule by speaking.

"Mountain Jack's. We'll stay with him for the night."

"Is there a town nearby?" She was certain she'd heard distant town noises just before coming upon Jack's place.

"Crystal Springs." He took her carpetbag and other belongings and strode toward the house. White Eagle opened the creaking door, allowing her to go in first as he followed behind. Wooden flooring and leather filled her senses.

"Jack, you here?"

"You bet your moccasins I'm here," a rickety voice called from a room on the far side of the cabin. "Where else would I be? 'Bout time you got back. Joe's been lookin' for you." An old man with bull legs and a frazzled beard came in from a back room.

He stopped and stared at Anna.

Two scars ran down the side of the old man's face. "Well, well." The old man's smile revealed a few missing teeth.

"We need a place to stay for the night," White Eagle said.

"Well now, this here lady is more than welcome." He rubbed his beard and chuckled. "A white Indian. Never seen one like you before." He motioned with his chin toward White Eagle. "You sure know how to pick 'em."

"She's from the East."

"We're going to Denver," Anna said cheerfully.

"Denver City?" The old man straightened and his eyes narrowed. "How long has it been since you moseyed on down that way?" He eyed White Eagle and shook his head, rubbing his beard. "Not since . . . well . . . . And now you're takin' a lady there? Hmm, not so sure that's a good idea, if you ask me." The old man lowered his chin and raised his brows in a suggestive manner.

"Nobody asked you." White Eagle frowned.

Anna forced her gaze on the room around her, trying to ignore the tension rising between the two men and hoping this man Jack didn't change White Eagle's mind about going to Denver. The stone fireplace held a warm and inviting fire. She stepped onto a bear rug to get near the flames so she could warm her hands. Before the fireplace was a chair, and next to it an oil lamp sat on a table. Against the wall, a closed cupboard likely stored pots, pans, and dishes. Opposite the chair and cupboard, near the door, stood a small dining table with another lamp. The house definitely needed a woman's touch. Nothing hung on the walls except animal heads. One bear, a deer, and a . . .

"What kind of animal is that?" she asked, pointing at one of the trophies.

The old man's face lit with pride.

"You asked the wrong question," White Eagle said as he set her things on the nearby table. He seemed to relax. She sensed he felt at home in these new surroundings, despite the moment of tension that passed between him and Jack. Strange that a white man would befriend an Indian. But Mountain Jack couldn't be considered typical. Certainly not compared to anyone she'd ever met.

"That there is a puma," the old man said, pointing at the bust. "He's the one that gave me these here scars." He touched the side of his face. "Nearly blinded me, the ol' devil. But I got him!" He slammed his fist into his palm so quick and loud it made Anna jump. "He wanted me for dinner, but I cut him open with this here knife." He held up a dagger that hung below the animal trophy; it was the longest, sharpest looking knife she had ever seen. In her hands it would have been more like a short sword. "That's how's I got my name. Mountain Lion Jack is what they call me, 'cause I killed me a mountain lion practically with my bare hands."

"Mountain Jack, this is Anna," White Eagle stepped forward, "my wife."

Jack's mouth fell open. "Well, I'll be," Jack said. "It's a privilege to be making your acquaintances, ma'am." He then glanced sharply at White Eagle. "How'd you manage that? A fine lady from the East turned Indian. What'd you do, kidnap the pretty thing and force her to marry you?" He chuckled at his joke and scratched his head. "I never thought you'd get married, boy. Must have been that blonde hair. You Indians sure have a thing for blondes. Did I ever tell you what happened to that there gal—"

"It's been a long trip." White Eagle put his hand on the old man's shoulder. "I think we ought to let the lady rest."

Jack glanced over at Anna. He cleared his throat and gave short, quick nods. He then looked around him as if he were lost.

"Pardon me, ma'am." He shuffled past her into a room near the front door. "Come on this way."

She followed Mountain Jack.

An oak nightstand stood next to a small, brass bed in the little room. Rather fancy for a poor old man living in a small cabin. The bed nestled under the window to her left. No pictures hung on the walls, and on the right sat a matching oak dresser.

"You can sleep here. This is where Jean-Marc usually sleeps." Mountain Jack rolled his eyes. "When he's here. It'll be good for him to sleep on the floor. I won't be givin' up my bed though. No-sir-ee. It's in the room there on the other side of the house. I'm gettin' too old for floors, let me tell you." He rested his hands on his lower back and cackled.

She hadn't noticed anyone else in the cabin, and was curious to know who Jean-Marc might be. "Oh, I can't take someone else's bed." Really, the small bed looked inviting, and every muscle in her body screamed for rest. How wonderful it'd be to bury her face in the soft pillow. How long had it been since she slept in a real bed? "I can sleep on the floor," she said, still trying to be thoughtful to the owner of the bed. "I did so last night, I can do it again."

"Oh no, ma'am." Jack shook his head. "I can't be makin' a beautiful woman sleep on my dirty old floor. You rest here comfortable-like. If you need anythin', you just give a holler." He sauntered through the door. "Jean-Marc, hope you like the floor. It's mighty hard compared to a bed of pine needles."

White Eagle came in to the room, carrying her carpetbag and the bundle of belongings. "I won't be sleeping on the floor." He put her things down, set a small lantern on the dresser and faced her. "And neither will you."

"Did he call you Jean-Marc?" she whispered. "Why? Are you . . . ? I thought . . ." White Eagle straightened.

"Why didn't you tell me you had a name? A real name. I mean, a civilized—"

"You never asked." He shrugged.

"There's no way I could have known to ask something like that. How many people have two names?"

"You do." He crossed his arms in that typical male stance of his.

"But that's because . . ." She clenched her fists. "That name was forced on me. How'd you get yours?"

No answer came but Jack's humming in the back room and the crickets outside. Her gaze fell on White Eagle's black hair. Feathers and that colorful leather band tumbled over his broad shoulders. The light from the oil lamp reflected off his tinted skin and the motif on his fringed shirt, leggings and moccasins.

No doubt, Cheyenne blood ran in his veins.

She locked onto his blue-green gaze.

Everything about him was Indian, savage.

Everything . . . but the eyes.

She didn't recall the other Indians having such bright eyes. The differences flooded through her mind. His eyes, his white name, he spoke English better than any of the others. She never realized it could mean he wasn't full-blooded Indian. How could she have been so naïve?

"Why didn't you tell me this sooner? Like when you kidnapped me. Didn't it ever occur to you to say, 'Hey, I'm half-white, so I'm not going to kill you?'" She glared at him. "Why didn't you tell me that in the beginning? It would have saved me a lot of worry, let alone fear."

"How many Indians have pale eyes? How could you not know I was half-white? Anybody in their right mind would have known."

"I had never seen an Indian in my life! How could I have known?" She paced. "You should have told me," she said between clenched teeth.

His face darkened, and he strode toward her.

She stepped back.

"Having white blood in my veins would not have changed things for you. I'm still Cheyenne, and being half-white shouldn't matter." He said the word "white" with a sneer, as if he had a bad taste in his mouth from saying it.

She trembled but held her ground. "It does matter," she said in a harsh whisper.

"Why?" His jaw pulsed.

"Well, for one . . ." Her voice quivered and answers fled. What could she say? Her brain still processed the fact that he wasn't what she thought. He was a stranger. She was married to a perfect stranger. "I wouldn't have been as frightened."

"What makes you think you would have been any safer with white men than with my brothers?"

She recalled Running Cloud's threats. "Because I'm not one of you!" She jabbed her finger at his hard chest then took a few steps back from his immovable stance. "I'm not a savage."

His eyes became like ice, narrowing in on her, and his face hardened.

She swallowed. The last time she saw such a fierce look, he shot Black Bear.

"Suppose I was all white." He stepped toward her. "Or let's suppose I was a white man looking for a good time. Looking to steal and *take*." The whites of his teeth flashed as he closed the short distance between them.

She stopped against the bed.

He moved inches from her face. "Suppose all I wanted was *you*." The heat of his breath feathered her cheeks.

She tried to step back, but her legs caught against the bed.

He bent over her. "To take you by force."

"White Eagle—Jean-Marc, you're scaring me."

"Good," he said. "Suppose I just wanted one thing . . ." His gaze raked down her front. "And took it!"

She slapped him.

A red mark formed on his cheek, but he didn't move. It was as if she didn't slap him at all, and the only proof was the mark on his face and the echo still hanging in the room. "For a woman with schooling, you sure are naïve." He hissed between clenched teeth. "A man's greed is what's dangerous, Morning Sun. Not his race." He straightened and turned from her. "Goodnight." He strode from the room and slammed the door behind him.

Tears flooded her eyes as she dropped on the bed.

How dreadful. She buried her face in the blankets and wept. What had she done? How could White Eagle be so cruel? Come to think of it, even if he and Running Cloud had been white, she would have thought they were Indians just the same. All the raids she'd read about in the papers had frightened her, nothing more.

Trembling, she glanced down at her ring. The silver reflected the light from the lantern as she touched the turquoise sparrow. She shouldn't have slapped him. White

Eagle wasn't Uncle Horace. He wouldn't have harmed her. She should apologize and try to explain herself, but look where her first explanation had gotten her. Somehow they had to work this out. She'd talk to him in the morning, give him time to cool off. And give herself time to calm down.

During the night, Anna awoke to voices and a light coming from under her door.

She heard what must have been a fist slamming on a table. "I can't go now," White Eagle said in a harsh whisper. "I gave Anna my word."

She jumped out of bed, whipped on the robe she'd received from Song Bird, and put her ear to the door. What could possibly be taking place that would keep White Eagle from taking her to Denver now?

"If you don't go, we won't get this chance again." An unrecognizable voice carried from the other room. "They still don't trust me. They believe I'm just an acquaintance of yours. But you've won their trust. They'll let you ride with them this time, I'm sure of it. But it won't happen if you don't go now. They're waiting for you in town. I've drug 'em all over these mountains looking for you. Where in this green earth have you been? I've known you to disappear, but never for this long."

The voices became muffled. Anna decided it was rude to eavesdrop, so she opened the door.

Three men sat at the table before her. Mountain Lion Jack, the other had his back to her and his shoulders slumped, while White Eagle sat opposite Jack and looked at her from beneath his long hair.

"Forgive me if I'm interrupting." She pulled the robe closer around her body.

White Eagle frowned.

The unknown man barely glanced over his shoulder and tipped his hat.

"Anna, this is Mr. Joe Morgan," White Eagle said.

"Nice to meet you," she said.

She turned to White Eagle. "Are we still going to Denver City?"

"Something's come up." He stood. "I have to leave tonight."

She felt like stomping her feet. "For how long?"

"I don't know."

"Then I'll take the stage. Surely one goes to Denver City from here." Then she could experience the city on her own, have a taste of independence.

Of freedom.

"No," he said, his voice firm.

Taking a deep breath, she straightened.

"Wait here until I come for you."

"How long will I have to wait?" she whispered.

"I don't know. Just do as I say. You'll be in good hands with Mountain Jack. He'll take care of you. When I get back, I'll take you to Denver City."

She looked at Jack.

He winked and nodded. "I'll keep you company, ma'am. I have enough stories to entertain you for a lifetime."

Mountain Jack wasn't lying when he said he had a lot of stories to tell, and they were all about himself, mostly about fights he'd had with people or animals.

Anna thought she'd heard it all when yet another one would come to his mind.

Mountain Jack was away at the mine most of the day, and during that time, she seethed in the silence within the log walls. She kept herself busy by giving the place a good scrub. Sometimes she'd imagine that the floor was White Eagle, and she'd scrub its wooden surface that much harder.

How dare he abandon her and make her a burden to this old man? When the floors had been scrubbed, not to mention pounded, she came up with new ways to redecorate. In the evening when Jack would return from working at the mine, she'd make sure she had a nice warm supper ready. Every time he saw a meal waiting for him, his whole face beamed. "I've died and gone to heaven," he would say.

But Anna thought she'd die in the Rocky Mountains, having been forgotten by White Eagle—or Jean—whatever-his-name. Three weeks. And she hadn't seen hide nor hair of the man, and Jack wouldn't tell her where he had gone or when he'd return.

That kind of information wasn't appropriate for a decent young lady like herself, he would say, which just made her all the more curious, but he wouldn't budge. Worst of all, anytime she asked about White Eagle and who he really was, he said that was for Jean-Marc to tell.

Often, she sat outside the cabin door watching and waiting for White Eagle's arrival, but he never came. Maybe he'd changed his mind about their marriage? She wouldn't be surprised if that were the case, considering the magnitude of their last quarrel. Maybe he had dumped her off with this old man just so he could escape and not be tied down with a wife? Maybe he married her just to please Running Cloud and now he wanted to get rid of her?

Oh, what had she done? Why did Running Cloud force this marriage on them? Maybe her uncle was right. Maybe she wasn't worthy of anyone's love. Maybe she hadn't adjusted to Cheyenne life as well as she should have and now she was an embarrassment to White Eagle.

She stood to go back into the lonely cabin. A wave of dizziness came over her. She gripped the doorjamb. She'd stood too fast. Or perhaps she'd been locked away in this place for too long? She was developing an extreme case of cabin fever. She'd married a man who abandoned her, who didn't even want her, a man with a mysterious past, a man she didn't even know. Her stomach gave way to a sick sensation. What was she to do?

"My partner, Franck Charvet, was more the social type," Jack said one evening during supper. She had heard the stories from the time Jack had arrived in Colorado to when he and his partner finally found gold. "When we struck it rich, he built himself a nice place in the city, even built himself a hotel. I stayed here to watch the mine. A lot of thieves in these here parts." He chuckled. "I just ain't the social type. I'd much rather live on my mountain and enjoy the wilderness. I don't like havin' too many people around me much. I don't mind being around those miners though. They're good, hardworkin' men."

Speaking of being around people. "May I go to town?" she asked.

"What would you want to go to town for?"

Anna tried not to raise her voice. "I've been here day in and day out all alone in this cabin for the last four weeks. I haven't complained once. It would be nice to see some new faces for a change. Not that I don't enjoy yours. You're wonderful company with your stories and all." She noticed her speech sounding like his. She had to get out of this place. "I'd just like to pick up a few magazines and have a look around." *And get back to civilization.*

"Well, I don't see anything wrong in that," he said. "Before I leave for the mine tomorrow, I'll drop you off in town first thing."

The next day, wearing Beth's dress, Anna arrived in Crystal Springs. A lake on the town's edge reflected sunlight off the cool morning waters. The waves rippled, making it shimmer like diamonds. She understood how the town derived its name. Nestled beneath a towering mountain colored in reds, yellows, and greens, several shops lined the main, dirt street.

She hurried along the boarded walk and brushed past other early morning shoppers. Her ears tingled when she heard women speaking English, and her feet froze in place when she caught site of the beautiful dresses in the shop windows. But what made her mouth fall open was the large sign hanging next to the post office, announcing that the next stagecoach would leave for Denver City the following week.

She stared at the sign for a long time. It was just white paint slapped on a board, ready to be painted over and reused. But the words "Denver City" had never looked more beautiful. Inviting. She swallowed, but her throat became dry. White Eagle's words of warning her not to leave echoed through her mind. She wouldn't do it. She was a married woman and ought to wait for her husband to return—if he ever returned. What if he never returned?

No, she would trust him.

It was as though her feet had become lead weights; it took enormous effort to turn around. When she gazed absently into a window displaying a nice traveling dress, she could still see the sign reflecting in the glass, as if it were waving to her. She breathed deeply, straightened, and marched into the store.

After a day of shopping in town, avoiding the sign, and a fairly pleasant conversation with Jack that evening, she lay in bed wide-awake, staring at the log ceiling. She hadn't fallen into temptation; she hadn't given in. White Eagle would be pleased.

She curled on her side. But what if she never got a chance to tell him? What if he really had left her? After all, just like her uncle had done to so many, he could easily walk away, and the last time she saw White Eagle, he seemed angry enough to do just that.

Later that week as she changed the bedding, she thought about how easy it would be to get a ticket. Denver City was so close. All she had to do was just go down there and buy one. Simple as that! Later she scrubbed the floors, drawing signs of Denver City onto the polished surface. If in reality she couldn't buy a ticket, it wouldn't hurt to *imagine* buying one—imagine standing at the counter and saying, "One ticket to Denver City, please," just like she'd done when she'd escaped her uncle in New York. Didn't she feel as trapped now as she had then? Hmm. No. Instead of being abused, she was trapped without the man she loved.

Anna scrubbed the floor harder, erasing the Denver sign she'd drawn on the wood. She scrubbed more vigorously until her hands became raw, so raw she could scrub no more. Tears welled in her eyes and she pounded the floor with her rag, and then she wept.

By the end of the week she'd lost track of how many times she'd cleaned the windows. They were more fun and actually made the game easier when she talked to each pane, pretending she stood at the ticket counter. But that never seemed to ease her tortured mind.

The stage was gone, and White Eagle still hadn't come.

One day Jack stayed home, and Anna had a feeling he stayed to keep her company. He told her story after story and seemed to be at a loss for something to do. To fight off the autumn chill, and to have something to keep her busy, Anna offered to clean the bear rug. The exertion would keep her warm, despite the light snowfall from the night before. So she carried it outside and slung it over a strong tree branch, while Jack kept himself busy piling a stack of wood next to the house.

Anna beat the rug. "Where did White Eagle, I mean, Jean-Marc go? Why can't you tell me?"

"That kind of information just ain't appropriate for a decent young lady like yourself," Jack said, giving his typical answer.

"But every time you say that, it makes me more curious."

"You need to save all them questions for Jean-Marc."

Anna beat the rug harder. "For a man with so many stories, you sure know how to keep secrets."

"Well, let me tell you about the time I uncovered a secret treasure well-hidden in these mountains for a good number of years—"

Anna glared at Jack and then gave the rug a solid whack.

A couple nights later, Anna found herself kneeling behind a tree, vomiting. When she finished, she wiped her mouth and held her churning stomach. He'd left her. She knew it. He was never coming back.

"Where are you?" she cried into the darkness. She leaned on the tree, her fingers pressing against the rough bark. It brought to mind White Eagle's words, when he said her voice rustled in the leaves, that her laughter lifted their branches. She peeled away a piece of the bark. Were those just pretty words? Pretty words like her uncle used to whisper to his woman of the week? Tears flooded her eyes.

Her quiet cries carried on the night air and over to Jack where Anna noticed him waiting for her on the porch. He stood, chewing on his toothpick, watching her as she'd wept quietly into her hands. Finally, he shook his head and threw down the toothpick. Ashamed of her tears, Anna dried her eyes as he turned to go inside.

The next day, Jack dropped Anna off in town again. When she came to the shops the sign to Denver City was up again, and it seemed to shout like a trumpet from down the street. It was much brighter, the white letters that much bolder. She ignored White Eagle's order that she wait for him—as if he'd come—and took a deliberate step toward the sign. Then she took another, and another, until she found herself at the counter.

A man behind wire-rimmed spectacles glanced up. "May I help you, ma'am?"

"One ticket to Denver City, please," she heard herself say. She'd practiced this while cleaning the windows so many times that the words came easily.

Back at the cabin, she stashed the ticket under her pillow, as if that would change the fact that she'd actually bought it. She paced the room, squeezing her hands together until her knuckles turned white.

In the morning she would finally be on her way home.

What had she done? Had she lost her mind? But where was White Eagle? She stared at the pillow; it was as though she could see right through it to what lay beneath.

Well, now that she'd spent the money, she may as well go through with it.

During supper she would convince Jack to let her go to town the following morning alone. Once in town she would leave a note at the post office for Jack, explaining her absence. Then she'd leave his horse at the livery stable and send White Eagle and Mountain Jack word as soon as she was settled in Denver. If White Eagle still wanted her, he could come for her. If he no longer loved her, this could be her way of setting him free.

Setting him free. Yes. He'd be free, but she'd be enslaved forever.

The plan was ready. Finally, her long awaited dream would be realized. If only she could feel happier about accomplishing it.

That evening, Anna set out supper, wondering how she could casually broach the subject of Jack taking her to town without arousing suspicion. By the way Jack watched her as she set his plate and cup on the table, she had an uneasy feeling he could see right through to her guilt. Would he try to stop her? She wrung her hands together and turned to collect the food from the stove. Despite her worries, her step felt light. She was going to Denver City, even if Jack knew what she was up to. But one thing bothered her. She'd have to go alone. The last time she made a journey alone, she was kidnapped by Indians. She set her plate on the table. What more could possibly happen to her when the worst already had?

Jack ran his hand over his beard as she joined him at the table. He shifted in his seat.

Anna scooted up her chair, its legs scraping against the wooden floor in the silent cabin. Now. Now was the time to ask him. She opened her mouth to speak.

"Seven weeks," Jack said, tucking his napkin into his shirt and shaking his head.

"Seven weeks and no word is just too da—gosh darn long." He cleared his throat. "So what do you say me and you take us a trip to Denver City? Maybe find out where that good-for-nothin' husband of yours is."

Stunned into silence, Anna gaped at Jack. "I—" He'd take her? He'd actually take her? Why didn't she think to ask him? He'd take her! He wouldn't try to stop her. He would escort her to Denver City. The place her father always spoke about. Home. She put trembling fingers over her mouth as tears welled in her eyes. What could she say? She opened her mouth to speak, to tell him about the ticket, to thank him, to . . . but nothing came out. All she could do was cry. She buried her head in her apron and wept.

Jack shifted in his chair, clearly uncomfortable. "Umm, well, we don't have to go if you don't want—"

"No!" Anna's desperate gaze met his. "I mean, yes!" Anna's stomach swirled. "Yes! Let's do!" She leaned closer. "Please, I want to go."

Jack watched her, confusion clouding his eyes. "Why do women have to cry?" he mumbled to himself, scratching his head. "Why can't they just be happy and that be the end of it?" He sighed and dropped his gaze to the table. He then remembered his food and dug in.

Anna laughed.

Chapter 19

Anna felt like a caged bird set free all over again as the stagecoach rumbled down the road. She gripped the window ledge to keep from falling off the thinly cushioned seat. Riding in a stagecoach was a lot less pleasant than riding White Eagle's horse. Especially in his arms. She shook the thoughts from her mind and glanced down at the ring he had given her.

She wondered if he'd gone on to Denver without her and if that was why Jack had suggested they go. Or maybe he could see the imprints she left of "Denver City" still in the windows? Perhaps she and Jack should have waited, though the fact that she'd likely be in Denver City in just two more hours thrilled her. They had already stopped for lunch, and just clearing the hills, they neared some trees. She glanced at Jack next to her. He grinned in return.

The coach jerked and jarred her backside. She smiled at the other passengers sitting across the small seat. One man dressed in a top hat and a black frock coat said he was a banker. The man next to him, his assistant, wore less extravagant attire. Even they gripped the window ledges to keep their balance.

She took a deep breath and glanced out the window as the trees grew dense. She smoothed her skirt, a deeper green than the first dress she had made back in New York. She also bought herself a new hat with green ribbons and plumes, and this time with a brim large enough to protect her from the sun.

Her money pouch was well-hidden under her dress, and she'd spent several hours re-sewing her mother's jewels into her bodice. She hadn't bothered buying any other dresses. Thankfully this one fit as well as it did, even though it didn't hug her waist as snug as she liked. More dresses would have been too cumbersome with traveling, and she planned on making some when she arrived in Denver.

Jack cleared his throat. "Did I tell you all the story about them there bear cubs—"

"Yes! Twice now," the banker's assistant said.

"Sun sure is bright," the banker said, peering out the window. "Looks like it's going to be a mild winter."

"How much longer to Denver?" the assistant asked, grumbling.

"I'd say about two hours. Two *long* hours," Jack said, eyeing the assistant with obvious contempt beneath his bushy brows.

Anna stifled a chuckle.

"Last time I was on this run, my ears were ringing from gunshots." By the way Jack's eyes narrowed at the man across from him, Anna had a feeling he was trying to put some fear into him. "Lost my closest friend that day." Sadness reflected from Jack's gaze as he looked out the window. "He wanted to find his son. Had ourselves an Indian scout to help, but it was all a waste."

Anna had heard enough of Jack's stories to know this one was different. By the way his eyes searched out the window, she had a feeling he was looking for something, or someone.

Jack began his story, but rather than sitting on the seat as an outsider listening in on his latest tale, Anna found herself being pulled in, pulled in as if Jack had taken her hand and forced her down a path of danger and peril. He tugged her along like an ocean's wave, back and forth, until finally, he sucked her in to the depths of the dark story of his friend and partner's death, Franck Charvet, and how he'd been shot on this very road. Murdered by thieves.

The carriage jerked, bringing Anna out of the seat and out of the horrible story. She came back down with a thud just as gunshots and shouts exploded outside. Men, with faces half-covered, fired revolvers in the air and raced furiously on all sides of the stage.

"Not again!" Jack said with an incredible whine. "Every time I set foot in this bla— worthless carriage those da—" Jack glanced at Anna. "For cryin' in the bucket, I don't even get the pleasure of a good cuss word!"

Jack rose from his seat, pulling out his revolver. He motioned Anna to the floor.

"Get down and don't get up till I say."

Anna sank to the floor with the banker and his assistant, shocked at the change in Jack. He went from being a gentle old man to a fierce cowboy who knew what he was about. From the dangerous look in his eyes, she could see how he might have killed that puma with his bare hands.

Shots fired again outside.

Would their fate have the same dreadful conclusion as Jack's story? She had been kidnapped by Indians and was now about to be robbed. Unbelievable. Would she ever get to Denver City?

She watched as Jack braced himself against the seat, ready to fire. He poked his head out the window.

Anna's gaze darted to each passenger. They looked as frightened as she felt. The coach came to a sudden stop, and she skidded along the narrow floor, crashing into the couch.

Jack ducked in from the window and put his revolver back in its holster. He bent to help Anna up. "You all right?"

Anna nodded. She didn't trust herself to speak. From the window, she saw the driver hit the ground and roll away in the dirt.

"Get out of the coach!" a bandit shouted, swinging open the door.

Bile rose in her throat. Her arms and legs trembled as she climbed out with Jack's help. Terror coursed through her veins for the second time since her journey had begun. Would these men kidnap her too? Or did a worse fate await her?

The bandits were dressed like cowboys. They wore wide-brimmed hats, leather chaps, and boots with spurs. But what made her shudder were their guns pointing at her, Jack, and the other passengers.

"Toss that pistol over here, old-timer," one of the bandits said. "Nice and calm-like."

"It ain't no pistol." Jack raised his hands and then eased his revolver out of its holster with two fingers and slid the gun in the bandit's direction.

"Whoooooeeee!" another bandit shouted. "Look what we have here." He urged his horse next to Anna.

Her mind seethed with rage. She'd nearly made it home and these brutes had stopped her. But her anger was tempered by fear as White Eagle's last words flashed through her mind. He'd deliberately frightened her in that small room, but she'd still been safe. And now, she couldn't help but wonder if his words might be prophetic as well. She closed her eyes, wishing desperately that she and Jack had stayed at his place.

Two other members of the gang came into view. Their horses danced and pawed the ground. There were three bandits in all, while a fourth stood on top of the coach throwing down luggage.

One of the men dismounted and strode up to her, spurs jangling. She stepped back. Even White Eagle, when he kidnapped her, hadn't looked as cold and calculating as this man. He spit tobacco juice at her feet. Half of it dripped from his red bandanna. He tipped the brim of his hat up on his forehead, and from the crease of dirt covering his brow, it looked like he hadn't bathed in weeks. He seized her arm and yanked her against him.

"Nice and soft." He snarled. "You're a pretty little thing. Let's say you and me get acquainted." He jerked her by the arm and dragged her away from the group.

Anna looked to Jack for help, but he didn't move. "Anna, girl! Just scream nice and loud! You do that, *Anna*!" Jack shouted as he glanced to the top of the carriage.

"Shut up, old man, or I'll shoot your mouth right off your already sawed-up face," one of the other bandits said, then laughed and looked to the top of the coach. "Johnny, you get all them bags?"

Anna's heart went to her throat as the bandit dragged her around to the other side of the carriage. She tripped over his boot and tried to regain her balance. He yanked her up, still holding her arm in a vise-like grip. After he shoved his revolver into its holster, he grabbed both her arms and violently pushed her in the direction he intended.

She fell on all fours but climbed quickly to her feet and ran.

He seized her around the waist.

"Don't be difficult. I might have to hurt you," he whispered hotly against her cheek and laughed as he shoved her on the ground.

She slid on her stomach, tasting dirt.

He rolled her over, pinned her arms above her head, and dropped on top of her, crushing her. "Don't worry, pretty thing. I'll be gentle," he said, breathless.

"Stop!" She screamed, but it came out as a stifled cry. "Please! Don't!" She pushed against him, but he was too strong.

The man pulled up her skirt. "Whoa! What's this?"

She felt him tugging on her money pouch.

Lord, help me!

Without warning, his weight lifted from her. Another man tossed him over the road like a sack of potatoes.

"This one's mine!" the man said. Legs braced apart in black chaps, boots, and shiny spurs, the man quick-drew his revolver and aimed it at the man who'd just attacked her.

"What's going on?" another one of the bandits shouted, lumbering from around the coach and unhitching the horses.

Anna pushed up onto her elbows and tried to crawl away backwards, but her feet tangled in her skirt. Now there were three of them. What was she to do?

"Johnny's trying to take my woman!"

"She's mine," Johnny said, his tone low as he cocked his gun. A black bandanna covered his face, and a hat similar to the other bandits shadowed his eyes. Dark hair pulled into a ponytail dangled over his broad shoulders and black vest.

"Aaahhh, Billy. Let him have her, this being his first big heist and all."

Red-faced Billy climbed to his feet and stormed to the other side of the stagecoach, slapping his hat angrily against his leg.

"Don't take too long," the other said with a grin, then spit and turned to unhitch the rest of the horses.

Anna continued to inch backwards.

The one called Johnny turned and glared down at her, his eyes like shards of glass ready to pierce her through. Before she could back away any farther, he dropped on top of her, held her down with one arm, while the other moved under her skirt. She screamed and tried to push him off.

Then the familiar blue-green of his eyes snagged her attention. "White Eagle?" she said, breathless.

He forced his hand over her mouth. "Quiet," he said in a deep growl. "You should be at Mountain Jack's. What are you doing here?" he asked between clenched teeth. It was a question not meant to be answered, the anger in his eyes evident. His weight pressed her into the rocks and dirt as she felt him tug on her money belt then cut it away. "This ought to keep you out of trouble."

She pushed against him, shocked that he was actually going to rob her. "You're nothing but a thief," she said, stunned and still processing the fact in her mind. "What are you doing with these men?" How'd he go from a band of raiding Indians to a band of thieving cowboys?

He pulled her to her feet and yanked her to him. "What'd you do? Convince Jack to take you to that city?" He practically threw her from him and turned to leave.

Anger and hurt nearly broke through in wails. "Aren't you forgetting someting?" she shouted at his back. Her nose burned as she held her tears at bay.

He turned to face her, eyes narrowed under his black hat.

She threw her wedding ring at him. It hit him in the chest and dropped to the ground. When he knelt down to pick it up, she noticed her carpetbag strewn all over the road behind him, her parents' pictures lying broken in the road.

Her anger boiled over. This man was nothing but a thorn in her side. And to think, they were married. Tears welled in her eyes and she wanted to scream with rage. Instead, she kicked the dirt as he rose to stand.

"You *dief!*" she cried. "And look what you've done. My pictures are ruined!"

He strode toward her, determination in his stride.

Every part of her trembled, and she stepped back as he neared. "I don't even know who you are anymore. I never knew you!"

"Be quiet." His gaze bored into hers.

"I'll never forgive you for *tis* White, Jean, whatever your name—"

Quick as lightning, he raised a hand. Blackness enveloped her.

Jean-Marc caught Anna in his arms before she hit the ground. She had every right to be angry. But it could have cost them both their lives had he not silenced her.

He laid her gently on the ground.

Thankfully, he knew just how to hit a man in order to render him unconscious. Black Kettle, Cheyenne chief, had taught him most everything he knew. Jean-Marc just never dreamed he'd have to use that technique on a woman—the woman he loved.

What was she doing here? Had she planned on leaving him? But if so, would she enlist Mountain Jack's help? Pain sliced through him.

Still, he ached at the thought of hurting her. "Forgive me, Morning Sun," he whispered, despite the fact that she couldn't hear him.

His face went cold as he looked upon her still form and his hands trembled. He hoped and prayed he hadn't struck her too hard. He reminded himself that he had done it for her safety, and his. He hated leaving her, but she was just a couple of hours from Denver City, and he knew Jack would take care of her. He rose and headed toward the other side of the coach, but a part of him remained with Anna.

Billy saw Jean-Marc coming and made a move for her. Jean-Marc checked him up. "She's in her time. You don't want that."

"Yuck! No way!" Tom, Billy's older brother shouted. "Let's ride."

Tom mounted up with the stage horses ready to go. The boys and Jean-Marc followed, and they galloped away.

"Miss Anna? Wake up, girl."

Anna felt someone patting her lightly on the cheeks.

Slowly, she opened her eyes. Jack and his scraggly beard hovered over her. Her head throbbed.

"You all right?" Jack asked.

The horror of what just happened swept through her mind. She sat up and held a hand to her head to keep the dizziness from taking over.

"Are you hurt?" he asked.

Her hat hung lopsided over her head, and some of the pins had fallen out of her hair. When she noticed the dirt covering her dress and a tear in its seam, she wept.

He helped her to her feet.

"Now, now," Jack said, patting her shoulder. "Please, don't cry."

She cried, not because she was hurt, but because she was furious. How dare White Eagle hit her! He was a thief! When in the world had he become a thief? How long had he been doing this? What was she to do?

In a daze she pulled free of Jack, wiped her nose on her sleeve, and marched toward her carpetbag. She stood over her belongings. Her carpetbag lay empty and tossed aside, Cheyenne clothing sprawled out in the dirt, and her broken pictures reflected the pain in her heart. The frames were damaged, but thankfully the pictures themselves were unharmed. She stooped to gather the frames and cradled the pictures of her parents in her arms as she collected her other belongings.

She gathered her Cheyenne dresses, including her lovely wedding dress, folded them neatly and wrapped them in their packaging. Who was this man she married? She sniffed and wiped the tears from her eyes.

Jack and the men tried to help her, while the driver ranted and raved about losing his horses. "Confounded bandits!" he shouted and kicked the dirt.

"They took the horses?" she asked Jack.

"'Fraid so."

She wanted to cry harder, furious that she would have to walk. Now it would take them twice as long to get to Denver City. Thank goodness she didn't pack a trunk. Otherwise she'd have to leave it behind. With a deep sigh, she snatched up her carpetbag.

The banker handed her the torn package of dresses, once again bound securely with the leather strap.

"Thank you," she said, sniffing. She turned on her heels and marched down the road.

Jack caught up to her. "Where are you going?"

"Denver," she snapped. "And don't try to stop me."

Jack tried to reach for her things, but she pulled away and hugged the packages. He dropped his hands at his sides as they continued to march along.

"Kind of like a fly bangin' against a windowpane," Jack said, breaking the silence. "You see what you want but can't get to it."

Anna glanced over at Jack and saw compassion in his eyes. His gaze swept over her packages and he held out his hands to help. Reluctantly, she gave in and handed him her belongings.

Jack motioned with his chin to the carriage. "Miss Anna, that, those there—"

Anna held up her hand and stopped. She was in no mood to hear it. Besides, the humiliation of it all was too much. How much had Jack witnessed? Had he seen what that man did to her, attempted to do to her? Had he seen White Eagle? She couldn't bear to think about it.

Jack shrugged.

She continued in silence, her boots kicking up dust as she walked.

Lord, did You see what happened? What could have happened? She wanted to lift her hands and cry out, "Why?"

And what about Jack? How must he be feeling? She cast a side-glance in his direction and swallowed. "I'm sorry that you lost your friend."

He looked at her, surprise in his eyes, and he nodded.

After that, she focused only on the road and on her destination.

Hours later, a couple in a wagon heading for Denver offered them a ride. Anna and the others climbed in, worn out from the robbery and long walk. Anna rode in silence as the others told the couple what happened.

Later as the wagon crossed the wooden bridge over the Platte River and the boxed buildings of Denver City came into view, no sparks flew. No bolts of excitement and no great feeling of accomplishment assailed her.

Instead, numbness swamped her veins as they rumbled onto the first street. Buildings perched on both sides of the wide dirt road, dogs barked in the streets, and before one shop, barrels and boxes stood outside ready to be loaded onto a wagon. An ox hitched to a wagon lay in the dirt, enjoying the shade of the building; she would never have witnessed such a beast on the streets of Amsterdam, except at a farmers market perhaps.

"Thank you for the ride," she said to the friendly couple who had brought them this far. Jack helped her down from the wagon.

"Anytime, ma'am," the man said, tipping his hat, and they rode away.

Cowboys lumbered around in their chaps, boots, and spurs, striding by with their bowed legs. None looked as vicious as the ones who'd just robbed her. Other men looked like the gentlemen she was used to seeing in New York, wearing neat trousers and vests. Three Union soldiers tipped their hats as they strode by. Noise carried up from the street, while horse-drawn carriages trotted along, kicking up dust.

What was she going to do? All thanks to White Eagle, she had no money and no job. Unbelievable. He was a complete stranger. And finally, she'd made it to Denver, but her thoughts were in too much turmoil to enjoy the city's splendor. She walked down the wooden sidewalk in a daze.

Jack took her by the arm. "We need to find the marshal and report what's happened."

In Marshal Dell's office, Anna shared her version of the events. She told him everything, from the trip out of Cheyenne to the robbery. Though she glossed over some of the more lurid details, such as the wedding and that she had gone unwillingly with the Indians. As much as she hated White Eagle, she didn't want to get the others in trouble. For all she knew, he wasn't really an Indian at all.

As she told her story, the marshal's brown eyes sparkled, and his red mustache twitched over his lip as though it might be hiding a smile. He seemed to be amused by her tale, though he never smiled—not that she could see anyway.

Still, his whole demeanor bothered her.

"It's a good thing you went willingly," he placed emphasis on that last word as if he didn't believe her, "with those good Indians, Miss van Stralen." He shifted in his seat. "We found the settlers between Cheyenne and Denver; they were all dead." He shook his head and frowned, looking at his folded hands. "Never made it to Denver City. It's a sad, sad shame."

Dead? Her mouth fell open. Suppose she had remained with the settlers? She would be dead too.

He glanced at her. "You get used to hearing about Indian raids when you live out West, ma'am." He raised his brows and nodded toward her. "You're a lucky woman."

The blood drained from her face. She could have been killed. "They murdered the children too?" She swallowed hard. White Eagle had unwittingly saved her life.

The marshal nodded then stood and escorted her out of his office to the street where Jack waited.

"I wanna talk to you," the marshal said to Jack.

Jack disappeared inside, leaving Anna waiting on the platform.

Visions of what must have happened to the settlers kept playing through her mind. Kept playing over and over again until she couldn't see anything around her.

Later, Jack stepped outside of the marshal's office. He ambled right up to Anna, gaily smashing his hat on his head. For a man who'd just been robbed, he seemed in awfully high spirits. "Well, that's taken care of."

"Joe, round up the men!" the marshal shouted from inside.

A man flew out the door and down the street. Anna watched him go. Where had she seen him before? Something about the way his shoulders slumped seemed familiar, but she couldn't place him. Besides, she didn't recognize his face at all.

"What are we going to do?" she said to Jack. "We have no money, no place to stay. Nothing."

Jack offered Anna his arm. "You just follow me, Miss Anna. We're gonna take advantage of Jean-Marc's pocketbook." With a chuckle, Jack escorted Anna down the boardwalk.

Anna frowned. What pocketbook? Perhaps he had one as a result of thievery.

The streets bustled with life, mostly with men hurrying home, mothers pulling their children along, and some stopping before windows to admire goods.

The shop windows displayed ready-made dresses and fabric. If they hadn't been closed, Anna would have gone in and bought something. Then she remembered she was penniless, robbed by the man she loved.

Jack stopped in front of a beautiful six-story building.

The Grand Palace Hotel towered over her with windows stretching along the sidewalk in both directions. A porter took her carpetbag and other items as he escorted Anna and Jack inside. The lobby took her breath away. Crimson curtains draped from tall, arched windows, and thick red carpet lined a grand staircase in the center of the great room.

Jack motioned for Anna to wait as he crossed the lobby to a dignified man behind the check-in desk. She couldn't imagine how they would be able to afford such a fancy place.

"Jack? What are you doing here?" the man behind the desk said with a thick French accent. He greeted Jack heartily. Jack spoke in hushed tones while Anna admired the tapestries and sashes draped from the ceiling.

Finally, Jack and the dignified man walked up to her. Two men couldn't have been more opposite, with Jack's rough mountain-man appearance, and the other's suave demeanor.

"This is Hervé Dubway," Jack said introducing Anna to the tall elegant man.

The man cast Jack a sharp look. "*Dubois,*" he said. "The name is Hervé Dubois." Mr. Dubois raised Anna's hand to his lips and bowed gallantly. "*Bonsoir.* Pleased to make your acquaintance, Madame Charvet."

"Why, thank you." She had never been treated with such charming respect. "But the name is Anna van Stralen."

Both Jack and Mr. Dubois exchange glances.

"Hervé can show you to your room and you can—uh, you can take a nice hot bath. How's that sound?" Jack said.

"But we can't stay here," Anna said, pulling Jack aside, then in a low whisper added, "We don't have any money."

Jack grinned and patted Anna on the arm, escorting her through the lobby. "You don't worry your pretty little head about that."

"We are obliged to have you stay with us for as long as necessary," Mr. Dubois said.

"What do you mean, 'obliged?'"

"Jean-Marc will be covering all expenses. It is the least we can do to reimburse you for what he's done."

"I don't understand? How can White—Jean-Marc afford this? He's a thief."

"Hmm, *oui*, madame, I suppose he is. That is why he must reimburse you for your loss. Jean-Marc is officially the owner of this hotel, and I manage it while he is away. It is a minor expense to have you stay with us, madame."

White Eagle owned a hotel? Why didn't he tell her? Yet, why didn't he tell her he was half-white, a thief, and who knew what else—what more might she discover?

"Do you also know Jean-Marc as White Eagle?"

Mr. Dubois nodded. "*Bien sûr.*"

"Then if Jean-Marc owns this hotel, why is he out robbing carriages? He obviously has plenty of money." Her voice rose with those last words. Was it normal to be a part-time thief and part-time hotel owner, not to mention a part-time Indian? No wonder Colorado wasn't yet a state.

"I am not at liberty to give out that kind of information, madame. You will have to speak with Jean-Marc himself."

Anna shot Jack a pointed glare. "Where have I heard *that* before?"

Mr. Dubois and Jack continued to escort her into a hall. They each had an arm, as if they feared she might run away. Something she certainly felt like doing. And she probably would if she had money.

"*Voici*, Madame Charvet. Your room. If you need anything you won't have to go far." Mr. Dubois held the door open and motioned her in.

"Thank you." She went into her room then stopped and pivoted before Mr. Dubois could close the door. "Please stop calling me Madame Charvet." She looked at Jack. "I assume that's White Eagle's surname?"

Jack nodded.

"Seeing as how I know so little about *Mr. Charvet*, I'd rather you just call me Anna."

Hervé and Jack exchanged concerned glances.

"*Oui*, madam—er, I mean, Miss Anna."

Anna closed the door on them. She envisioned White Eagle standing before her in his bandits' clothes. Her only desire was to way-lay him just like he'd done her.

An hour later, Anna sank into a porcelain tub. The steam and warm water enveloped her, and her body finally began to relax. The moment she had been waiting for. She just hadn't expected it to be so luxurious. Here she sat in a magnificent hotel, one very much the equal to any she'd find in New York City and never be able to afford. On top of that, Mr. Dubois had treated her like a queen, bringing food to her room, among other necessities. She didn't deserve such treatment—she ought to get robbed more often.

The events of the day turned over in her mind. She never even had a chance to use her fake jewelry to mislead the thieves. No. Instead, they took all her money.

And it was White Eagle who had done it. Who was he anyway?

A sick sensation turned in the pit of her stomach. She had loved him. But one thing was certain, she wanted nothing to do with anyone who was like Uncle Horace.

Still, something wasn't right about all of this. It made no sense. The stories she had heard about White Eagle from the Indians had to be true; they couldn't all be liars. White Eagle was indeed Indian. But was there anything else she knew about the man, other than he was Indian, white, a thief, and also a hotel owner? His being half-white explained his associations with Mountain Jack and those thieves. But if he was part white, then why did he hate the idea of coming to Denver City? And why did he dislike white people if he was one of them?

Shaking her head in frustration, a sudden wave of nausea came over her. She'd just spent several months of her life with a man she knew nothing about.

Despite the warm water, she shivered. She loved him; or thought she did. Worst of all, she'd given herself to him. To a complete stranger! What had she been thinking? She'd thought they were married. Were they even really married? Her nose burned from tears as she thought about the tenderness White Eagle had displayed when she'd been wounded, when he rescued her from the water, his words about her God. Had it all been a farce? How could anyone pretend such feelings?

Tears streamed down her cheeks. She wanted answers. She wanted to understand. Why had he left her? Why had he hit her? Why had he robbed her? Who was he?

Here she sat, finally in Denver City, and it didn't matter anymore. She had worked so hard to get here, fought with everything she had, and what did she have to show for it? A broken heart—and no money.

What was she going to do? She really didn't want to sell her mother's jewels. And she couldn't stay in this luxurious hotel forever. Especially since it was owned by White Eagle. It made her feel trapped all over again. Would she ever be free? Would she ever not be somebody's captive? But if she left, where would she stay? How would she buy food? Without her mother's jewels, she had absolutely nothing. And the last thing she would be able to buy was a new dress.

All she had ever wanted was a decent dress, ever since her uncle had burned the ones her father had given her so long ago. One at a time, all her lovely gowns disintegrated in the fireplace.

Her eyes welled with tears all over again. She shouldn't be so silly. She had a beautiful Cheyenne wedding gown, and a nice traveling dress. Of course, the wedding gown would look out of place in civilization. She'd just have to wear her traveling clothes.

It was time to think sensibly and quit crying over dresses. Or was that really what she was weeping about? White Eagle's face flashed through her mind: his boyish grin; his passionate, blue-green eyes; his laughter when he discovered her fear of snakes.

She'd experienced enough adventure to last a lifetime. Her thoughts turned to when he had said those same words on the day of their wedding.

Their wedding. She was married to a kidnapper and a thief. Her stomach turned, and she thought she might be ill.

Lord, help me. What should I do?

Chapter 20

"'Just like a woman not to be dependable,' indeed." Anna said in a huff as she left the board of education office.

Jack had been waiting for her outside and joined her as she marched down the walkway. "What'd they say?"

"They revoked my position."

"Did you tell them what happened?"

"No, I couldn't."

Jack nodded with understanding as he escorted her down the street.

Of course she couldn't tell the education board what had delayed her. She didn't want to give those poor Indians a bad reputation, or a worse one than what they already had.

How she wanted to strangle that man in the education office. How dare he look down on her because she was a woman. Yet who didn't look down on women? Even Jack didn't think she was strong enough to handle the truth about White Eagle. It seemed all she had worked so hard for had vanished. It all went up into a puff of smoke the day White Eagle abducted her.

She took a calming breath. She'd secretly hoped they would offer her another teaching position, but even that wasn't an option. If the railroad hadn't been completed, they'd still be desperate for teachers and she'd probably have a job, but now that people swarmed to Denver City, all the positions were taken. Really, they had every right not to consider her dependable, especially since she wasn't willing to explain her delay.

It was time to move on. And that did not involve living under White Eagle's rule in his fancy hotel. She would find work again. She'd make her plans just like she did when she was back in New York. Anger boiled towards White Eagle. She wouldn't be in this fix if it weren't for him. Then her thoughts knocked her upside the head. She wouldn't be *alive* had it not been for him. Was he aware that he saved her life? Those poor children. Why didn't he save them too? She leaned against the wall of a shop to steady herself, trying to erase the thoughts from her mind. She had to move on, and she couldn't afford to start crying if she were to find a job.

Jack watched her closely, as he always did. She gave him a waning smile to keep him from worrying. She couldn't tell him about her plans. He might put an end to them.

No time like the present. She lifted her chin. "I feel like shopping," she said with forced enthusiasm. Guilt pricked her conscience for deceiving Jack, but at the same time, wasn't he keeping secrets? He plodded along, obviously not enthused about the idea of going on a shopping spree. Still, she headed down the street into the nearest store.

"I'll just wait here," Jack said, leaning against the shop wall.

Anna nodded and entered the store. Dry goods were piled high on tables, and they drew her attention to the calico fabrics. How she would love to make a dress in those lovely patterns.

"May I help you?" a young woman asked, standing behind a long counter.

"Yes, I'm looking for work. Would you happen to need an extra clerk in your shop?"

"We're a family business, so I'm afraid we're not hiring."

"Thank you for your time." Anna breathed deeply. This was only her first try. There were several more shops left.

A familiar Indian headdress caught her eye as she turned to leave.

She stopped.

Pieces of jewelry and a long pipe, resembling what she saw at the Cheyenne village, rested on a small shelf.

The woman came to her. "Do you like these?" She picked up a small gold earring, the same size Anna remembered the young children wearing. "Beautiful, isn't it?"

Anna's gaze then fell on three scalps hanging just below the shelf. She went cold, and her heart froze. She stepped back. Someone she knew could have been hanging there on display.

"Ma'am? Are you well?" the woman asked, setting down the child's gold earring and stepping toward her.

Anna waved her hand to keep the woman from coming too close.

The short, shiny hair on one of the scalps also could have belonged to a child. Runs With Wind flashed through her mind. All the times they shared, playing in the fields and crushing berries. White Eagle and his mother had saved her life, but had she not been spared, it could have been Runs With Wind's hair and earrings hanging on display.

Gray Feather. What if some of these things, the hair, the earrings belonged to Gray Feather? Yellow Leaf and Song Bird's only daughter. Anna's insides turned. Speech failed her. She couldn't move. It was as though someone had kicked her in the stomach. Where did the Indian pieces come from? She didn't dare ask.

"I must say," Anna choked on the words. "I am rather shocked by the display of Indian scalps you have in your store." She took in a deep breath to steady herself and squared her shoulders. "I can't imagine hanging up a white man's scalp and selling it, let alone that of a child." She met the woman's gaze having laid emphasis on those last few words.

"Just where are you from?" The woman pursed her lips.

"Holland." Anna never liked saying she was from New York since she was never supposed to have ended up living there. She forced her chin high, despite the nausea curdling in her stomach.

"Have you never heard of the atrocities committed by the Red Man on settlers?"

"Of course I have." Not to mention that she could have become another statistic. "I've also heard of the atrocities committed by white men against the Indians."

"Those savages have been a threat to settlers for years." The woman turned and went into a back room then came out with a box and set it on the counter.

She took out three photos and laid them one by one on the countertop, raised her brow, and motioned toward the pictures.

Anna walked up to the counter.

The photos displayed dead bodies of a white family.

"This," the woman said as she pointed at one photo, "is Nathan Ward Hungate. And this," she said again as she pointed at the other two pictures, "is his wife and two children. Those savages murdered them in cold blood."

Anna stepped back from the pictures. Indians may have killed that family, but not the Indians she knew. Yet hadn't Running Cloud taken part in murdering settlers?

"This is supposed to make what Chivington's men did at Sand Creek acceptable?" Anna's voice trembled.

The woman shifted her stance and deliberately put the photos back in the box. "At least we don't have to fear them anymore. Now they know if anything like this happens again, they will pay dearly for it."

"How?" Anna asked, breathless. "By slaughtering women and children?" She pointed to the shorthaired scalp. "Do you realize this was taken from a child? Even that earring had belonged to a child. A young child. Probably no more than three or four." The room spun as she said the words.

"Nits make lice." The woman lifted her nose in the air.

"What?" Anna gasped. "What is that supposed to mean?"

"Those little maggots will grow up to be one of them. A *savage*." She said the word with so much disgust, Anna thought the woman might spit.

How could anyone be so cold? Anna knew about the Sand Creek Massacre, but to hear it firsthand from someone who justified the killings made her reel with shock. She stepped back, staring at the woman. Likely her own age, with pretty blonde hair pulled up in a bun. But her beauty somehow faded behind the hate.

The woman turned to put the box back on its shelf in the storage room. "If you're not going to purchase anything, I suggest you leave."

Mortified, Anna turned to leave and slammed the door behind her.

Jack straightened. "Didn't find anything, huh?"

Anna cleared her throat, trying to regain her dignity. "We're just window-shopping today," she said, wondering how he expected her to buy anything when she was broke.

No wonder White Eagle didn't want to come to Denver City. She shouldn't have pressured him into bringing her here. Now she may never see him again. Why would he come to this awful place for her?

"Miss Anna, maybe this 'window-shopping,' as you call it, is a bit too much. You look tired."

"I'm not tired," Anna said a little too quickly as she straightened and started walking again. She could see by Jack's expression that he was bored. "Why don't you go on back to the hotel and I'll meet you there?"

Jack furrowed his brows. "You know the way back?"

"Of course." Anna nodded. "I can see you're not having any fun, and I'm going to be window-shopping for several hours yet." She placed emphasis on those last words.

Jack frowned then shifted his stance. "Well, maybe you're right." He shoved his hands deep into his pockets. "I'll just meet you back at the hotel."

"Wonderful," Anna said, a little too enthusiastically.

Jack tilted his head and narrowed his eyes. "Back at the hotel," he said emphasizing each word.

"Yes. Later." She couldn't help but feel trapped all over again by the way he spoke to her. What did he think? She was going to run away?

Jack pivoted and ambled down the boardwalk.

As Anna crossed the street, the woman's hateful words and the Indian earrings and scalps tormented her thoughts. She tried shaking them away by focusing on the streets of Denver. This was her place, her home. She swelled with pride thinking how she had finally made it to Denver City. Yet had it not been for White Eagle's intervention, she wouldn't be here at all. She swallowed back her short-lived pride. Besides, was this really the place she wanted to call home? Did she want to remain in a place where they sold human parts for profit?

But she'd dreamed of coming here for six long years. And she'd finally made it. She shouldn't let a few bad apples take away her joy. Yet those bad apples weren't just bad, they were rotten, rotten to the core. And their rot could bleed out, infecting all the other apples in the basket.

She found herself at a furniture warehouse. With her education, she could easily handle secretarial skills.

But they weren't hiring women.

Continuing to look for work, she went from one shop to another. Thank goodness she saw no more displays of Indian scalps, but no one wanted her. Still determination and desperation spurred her on.

As she walked down the street, the mountain range rose against the horizon in the far distance. It was strange to think she'd just spent the last several months up there in the wild. Yet she had survived. In fact, she had more than survived; she'd discovered a whole new world hidden out there in its depths. She smiled to herself, feeling like she'd had the privilege of taking part in a big secret, which indeed she had.

After several more rejections, she rounded the corner and found herself near the hotel. Denver City was a big place. She wouldn't lose heart. She still had several more streets that weren't covered, but by now the heat made her tired, and her stomach growled.

As she came closer to the hotel, she spotted a shop with a sign reading, "Peterson's Tailoring." One last try. Besides, she had plenty of sewing experience. When she walked into the store, an older lady sat behind a wide table at the far back of the well-kept shop.

"What can I do for you?" the woman asked, not looking up from her sewing.

"I'm looking for work. I was wondering if you might be hiring?"

The woman looked up. "You got any experience?"

"Plenty. I sewed for three years back in New York City."

"New York, huh? That's a long ways from Denver City." The woman, a small lady with a friendly face, stood from her worktable and walked up to Anna. "As a matter of fact, I am hiring, but I won't need you for another two weeks yet."

Anna didn't know whether to leap for joy or cry.

"My assistant, Barbara, is getting married and she'll be leaving. She lives upstairs. Will you need a place to stay too? I'll have a room to rent."

Anna couldn't believe her ears. She felt as though she'd stumbled upon gold. "Yes, I'll need a place to stay."

"Wonderful. If you prove your worth then you can stay here. The rent is taken out of your pay and we can decide what the appropriate amount will be." She put her hand out and smiled. "I'm Irene Peterson."

Anna introduced herself.

"It's hard to find good help these days." Mrs. Peterson motioned to a chair and grabbed some material from a nearby table. "Sit down, sit down."

Anna gratefully took a seat, only then realizing how tired she felt. Her body and limbs felt heavy and the room swayed.

"Oh dear, you look tired. Shall I fetch you some tea?"

"That won't be necessary," Anna said, spotting the fruit bowl behind Mrs. Peterson and thinking how juicy those red apples might be.

"Show me what you can do with that sleeve."

Anna took the fabric and studied the pattern. She recognized what needed to be done and started sewing.

"So, what brings you to Denver City?"

"Work."

"Not a man, huh?"

Anna giggled. "No, not a man." For some reason, she felt like she'd just told a lie.

"My husband died a couple of years back," Mrs. Peterson said, pulling out a chair from one of the sewing tables. "Since then, I've had to run the shop all by myself. Business is faring well, and since the Pacific Railroad has been completed from Cheyenne, I'm getting more business. Sometimes I do odd jobs, such as curtain repairs for the hotel. Franck Charvet was a good friend of my husband. It's a shame they're both gone now." She gave a warm pensive smile. "It will be nice to have a young lady like yourself working here." Her eyes brightened. "I'll enjoy the company."

"I'm a hard worker, ma'am," Anna said, pulling the needle through the fabric.

"Why are you in need of work, dear? Don't you have family?"

"My parents died when I was young." Anna glanced up from her work, feeling like it'd been a long time since she'd had a dignified conversation with a civilized person. Mrs. Peterson gave off a motherly air, something Anna missed. It brought Song Bird to mind and the way she'd taken care of Anna. Song Bird combed her hair, made dresses for her, and taught her things—just like a mother would teach her own child. White Eagle was right, both Song Bird and Yellow Leaf had adopted her as their own. Recalling them gave her the same pang she used to get after her father died. What would she do if she never saw them again? Finding work seemed to make things more final, more sure.

She forced her thoughts back to the conversation at hand. "I had a teaching position offered to me, but . . ." She stiffened in her chair—she had said too much. "Well, you see—"

"What happened, dear?" Mrs. Peterson cocked her head, her brows knitted with concern. "We may have just met, but something tells me that you are not the type to lose a job through any fault of your own."

Curious how the woman would react to the truth, Anna said, "I was kidnapped by Indians, ma'am."

"Oh my." Mrs. Peterson touched her mouth. She then immediately took hold of Anna's hand. "You poor child. And how did you fare? Were you harmed?"

"They were good people," Anna said, recalling all her experiences, though Black Bear and Beaver Claws were a different story.

Mrs. Peterson sighed with visible relief. "Still, you must have been quite frightened. I'm sure I would have died of fright." She squeezed Anna's hand.

"Actually, in the beginning, I was terrified. I even tried to escape, but they recaptured me," Anna said, resuming with her sewing.

"And still they didn't hurt you?"

"No." It was the first time she received such a show of sympathy for her abduction. It surprised her. Of course, she had shared the same story with the marshal, but his reaction had been more of a smug, "I told you so," while Mrs. Peterson seemed genuinely concerned. But more importantly, no hate surfaced in the woman's eyes.

"They must have been a decent group of Indians, I must say." The woman cleared her throat. "Except for the fact that they kidnapped you, of course." She patted Anna's lap.

Testing the woman, Anna added, "Most Indians are quite decent. I'm sure they would never have begun raiding white settlers and kidnapping women, had we kept the treaties we'd made with them." Would Mrs. Peterson respond similarly to that hateful woman? She could be risking her new job, but at this point, she'd resigned herself to its loss. She could never work with someone who hated Indians.

"You're right, dear." Mrs. Peterson sighed. "And I'm relieved to know you see things that way, despite what's happened to you." She shook her head. "And to think, that dreadful massacre had been led by one proclaiming to be a man of God. The name John M. Chivington will always make my stomach turn." She scooted in closer. "But let me advise you to take care with your words. There are still plenty in Denver City who support what Chivington and his men did. Some, like Silas Soule, who've spoken out against what happened, have been murdered right here in the streets." She shook her head. "Mr. Soule's poor wife. They'd just gotten married. One morning Mr. Soule walked out the door, and a man shot him."

Anna's heart lurched.

"It's been a blessing to have the former governor, Mr. Evans, make it possible for all the railroads to run to and from Denver City." Mrs. Peterson's gaze darted to the windows, as if to see if any listeners might be lurking outdoors. "But his deed toward those trusting Indians at Sand Creek was dastardly."

Anna hadn't realized she'd been holding her breath until she sighed long with relief.

"It's a shame Mr. Peterson isn't still around. He would have enjoyed meeting you. He was a friend of the Red Man."

"Friends?" Anna's stomach flip-flopped. She still couldn't believe her ears and all this woman shared.

"Yes, indeed. The wife of his closest friend was Cheyenne."

Anna froze. "It was a group of Cheyenne that kidnapped me."

Mrs. Peterson blinked. "Oh, forgive me, dear. Perhaps we should change the subject?"

"That's not necessary." Anna moved to the edge of her seat. "I'm curious how your husband came to befriend the Cheyenne." A wave of dizziness swept over her, and she took hold of the nearby table to hold herself steady.

"My heavens, are you well?"

Anna put her hand to her head. "I'm afraid I'm just hungry, is all. I better be going." She stood to leave, showing the sewn sleeve to Mrs. Peterson.

"Well, here. Have some fruit." Mrs. Peterson handed her an apple then studied the sleeve.

Anna took it gratefully, her mouth watering. She liked Mrs. Peterson. Thank goodness she hadn't been hateful like that last woman. In fact, it turned out to be more than what she'd dared hope for. If only she could start work right away. She wanted to know more about Mr. Peterson and his relationship with the Cheyenne, but there would be time for that later.

"This is fine work. Very fine." Mrs. Peterson looked up from the sleeve. "You're an answer to prayers. You're hired."

Anna smiled, thrilled beyond belief.

"You're welcome to come by again before you have to start working. Barbara isn't around much after hours with all her wedding plans. Right now she's having lunch with her fiancé."

"Thank you, I'd like that." Both ladies stepped out the door. "I'm looking forward to working for you." Anna meant it. She wanted to stay and chat, but she had to get back to the hotel before Jack started worrying.

"The pleasure is all mine, dear. You probably won't last long as my employee. I'm sure some gentleman will snatch you up in no time."

Anna giggled from embarrassment. "I don't think you have to worry about that." The only man she wanted, or didn't want, was a thief. She waved good-bye, and biting into her juicy apple, she headed down the street.

Lord? Did you do that? Did you find me this wonderful job? Maybe He hadn't deserted her after all.

As she neared the hotel she came upon a wig store. An idea struck.

With hair now down to the middle of her back and money in her hand, Anna remembered the ready-made dresses she saw in the shop windows when she'd first arrived and headed in that direction.

She had sold her hair.

It used to fall to her knees and now came to the middle of her back. It'd been quite startling to see all those long strands being cut away. But at least now she could buy herself some dresses.

Her hat sat comfortably perched atop her head where the sides of her hair had been pulled up into a ribbon. The rest hung over her shoulders and down her back, making her feel like a schoolgirl. As soon as she got to the hotel, she would pin it back up. At this length, her natural curls had taken more form.

The fancy shop bore a sign that read Mode de Paris. When she entered, two women glanced over at her, their lips pinched in unison and their noses went up a notch higher. Strong perfume hung on the air.

Ignoring them, Anna admired the beautiful silk and crinoline gowns. All of them had elegant bustles, larger than any she had ever worn before, with lovely ribbons, ruffles, and embroidered edging on them. They were very much like the dresses she would have found in New York City—much like the dresses her father used to buy for her.

"Are you lost?" one of the women asked, frowning.

"As you can see, I'm in need of a dress." Anna smiled, hoping to win the woman's good affections, but the lady continued to scowl.

"Are you sure you can afford the gowns in this store? We usually only sell to—well, to upper-class citizens."

Anna glanced at one of the price tags and nearly lost her breath. She forced a smile as if nothing was wrong.

"If you're looking for dresses that are ready-made, perhaps you should try the shop on Blake Street. It's much more to your liking," the woman said as her scrutinizing gaze raked Anna from head to foot.

Despite the fact that Anna couldn't afford the clothes, she faced the woman and held her chin high. "Do you want customers or not? Obviously, with this kind of attitude, you're not interested in selling anything." She glared down her nose at their smug grins. "Do you happen to know Mr. Jean-Marc Charvet?" She didn't wait for an answer. "He is the owner of the Grand Palace Hotel. Yes, the one just down the street from here." She marched toward the door then turned back to face them. "He just happens to be my *husband*."

The woman's mouth gaped open, while the other's eyes widened in apologetic surprise.

A silent sigh of relief escaped Anna. Thank goodness, they didn't know him as a thief. Although, from the reactions she'd gotten already, maybe it wouldn't even matter. With that, she opened the door and without looking back, she said in the most haughty tone she could muster, "Good day, ladies."

She strode down the walkway feeling mighty pleased. She had put them in their place, all right. Forget the fact that she wouldn't have been able to buy one dress, let alone two or three. She headed back for the hotel to find out how to get to Blake Street.

The following day, Anna, wearing her new dress, pranced into the hotel lobby. Her dress was pale blue and cut at the neckline with a splash of lace for modesty. Its bustle was larger than the one on her traveling dress, and its sleeves came just below her elbows with a fan of lacy fringe. For the first time since her wedding day, she felt pretty.

She had managed to buy two more dresses, a cloak, and a nightgown. They weren't as lovely as what she'd seen in the expensive shop, but they were serviceable. And best of all, they were ready-made—despite the fact that she stayed up half the night shortening the hems and sleeves.

"Good morning, Mr. Dubois."

"*Bonjour*! You look lovely this morning, madame—Miss Anna."

"Why thank you," she said. "I'm going for a walk, Mr. Dubois. It's time I familiarized myself with this city." She glanced around the lobby. "Is Jack around?"

"He went to the marshal's office to inquire about Jean-Marc."

"Oh. Well, I'll go alone then. Jack would be bored anyway."

"Will you return for lunch?"

"Will that be a problem?" She leaned toward the desk and lowered her voice. "I mean, the expenses—"

"Most certainly not. It's the least we can do. Don't you forget that."

"Well, then yes," she said, smiling. "I plan to take full advantage of White Eag—Jean-Marc's pocketbook." She winked, and Mr. Dubois chuckled.

When she stepped out the door, she went the opposite direction of the Mode de Paris shop. She didn't want them to see her in a dress from Blake Street.

Despite the light snowfall from last night, it was a lovely, warm day. The sparse amount of trees bore few leaves, but the sky remained clear. The sun shone bright and shimmered off her light blue dress.

She felt like dancing through the wide streets, and she might have skipped through them if there wasn't so much mud from the recent snow. They weren't anything like the cobblestone streets of Amsterdam. The buildings were also wider, more box shaped, and not as close together. With the blue sky opening above her, she had a feeling of wide open spaces, even though she was surrounded by buildings in such a large town.

She wasn't sure what she had expected when she'd arrived here, but an air of being far away from anything homey swept over her. Nothing was familiar in Denver City, except for the Mode de Paris shop. Those ladies were probably even from New York, considering the dresses they sold. And anything or anyone from New York didn't sit well with her since it was the place she'd hoped to escape. As for companionship, she didn't know anyone; there was no Beth, no Laughs Like A River, and no Runs With Wind to laugh and talk with. No one to show her new dress to. However, she could stroll by Mrs. Peterson's. If she wasn't too busy, maybe she'd like to have tea together. She turned in that direction.

Denver City would be her new home, and she would be happy to adjust herself to her new environment, assuming White Eagle wouldn't come for her.

What if she never saw him again? What would she do? Yes, she'd made plans to stay in Denver City, but the thought of being without White Eagle gave her stomach an unsettling start. She was his wife, after all. They should be together. After she rounded a corner, she stopped in front of a store and took a deep breath. This was silliness. Who would want to be married to a thief anyway? Let alone a perfect stranger.

"It's *her*, Mother." A familiar voice came from down the walkway. "The woman I told you about."

Anna turned and saw the clerk from the store that had the Indian scalps and horrid pictures of the Hungate family. The young woman stood with an older lady. They had just come out of the dry goods store, the same one she'd been to just the day before.

"I'll have you know—" the young woman marched up to Anna with the other woman in tow, "that my father fought at Sand Creek. It was a victory for Denver City and for all the civilized folk in the surrounding area. I'm proud of my father's accomplishments, and I will continue to show off his trophies to any and all who come to our store."

Anna stepped back and tried to focus on the red-faced woman in front of her, aware that people had stopped to stare.

"Indian lover!" The woman spat.

Anna watched as spit trailed down the small, fake pearled buttons on the front of her bodice. Her new dress. In fact, her favorite dress. She clenched her fists and wanted to tear the woman's foul-mouthed lips off.

But she took a deep breath and tried to calm herself.

From experience, Anna had learned that the best way to deal with someone so unreasonable was to remain calm. Forget the fact that for the first time in her life she really wanted to hurt someone—not counting White Eagle.

"For a lady, you sure know how to spit." Anna took a deep breath. "But you're not a lady, are you?" She stepped back, turned, and walked away.

"You'd better watch your back, hussy!" The woman shouted behind her. "We don't take too kindly to Indian lovers in this town!"

Anna kept on walking, her cheeks flaming with heat. She was curious if someone would really try to hurt her—more curious than afraid, surprisingly. Out of the corner of her eye, she spotted onlookers stopping and staring at her as she strode by. Feigning dignity, she nodded and kept on walking.

After several days of boredom, Mr. Dubois offered to take Anna to the theater. She was thrilled, since she'd never been to one before, so as he helped her out of the carriage, her stomach fluttered violently.

With the suave and elegance that suited Mr. Dubois, he held the door of the theater open for her. As she went in, the beauty of the lobby took her breath away. Colorful dresses painted the floor, while bright chandeliers hung low from the high ceiling.

A porter took their coats, and Mr. Dubois offered her his arm.

They were the most underdressed couple present. Other men wore top hats, and women wore dresses with enormous bustles and large plumes sprouting from their heads—not to mention expensive jewelry dangling from their necks and wrists.

"Do not fret," Mr. Dubois said, smiling down at her. "You are the most beautiful one here, madame."

"Why, thank you, Mr. Dubois." She returned a smile, knowing full well he wasn't wearing his finest so she wouldn't look out of place.

He held his arm out to her. "Shall we?" He escorted her through the lobby to the stairs as she soaked up all the details of the moment.

The production of *MacBeth* was marvelous. She smiled up at Mr. Dubois as they applauded the performers, delighted that he'd given her this experience. He reminded her of her father and how he would have done something like this for her when he was still alive.

Later, he escorted her back down the stairs and through the crowded lobby. "I will fetch the carriage," Mr. Dubois said as he nodded to Anna.

She waited by the door, admiring the chandeliers as they reflected off the women's beautiful gowns. It brought to mind the flames scorching her own lovely gowns when her uncle had thrown them in his fireplace. She hadn't worn anything as beautiful since then.

A woman caught her eye. The woman smiled and came up to her. "Why, Mrs. Charvet, how nice it is to see you."

Anna cringed. It was one of the women from that fancy dress shop. Of course, the woman's dress and hat outdid Anna's. The woman smiled as if they were good friends.

"Is Mr. Charvet back in Denver? You know, it's shameful he never announced his engagement, let alone his marriage." She clucked. "He hasn't been around in ages. Honestly, I've never even met him, though Franck Charvet was a good man. Before his death, few people even knew of his son's existence." She leaned in, a glint in her eyes. "I've heard him called more a phantom than a real person. He's only known by name, and no one has ever seen his face. I suppose he doubts whether he can take on the hotel and run things as well as his father had. The son is a half-breed, you know."

"He's part Cheyenne, to be exact." Anna's blood boiled hot. "Really, it's quite rude of you to assume he is incapable of handling his father's affairs. The hotel has run smoothly for this long, hasn't it?" She tried to look down her nose, just like the woman did to her, but it was difficult when she was forced to arch her neck to meet the woman's gaze. The room spun angrily as she tried to keep her focus on the sharp-tongued shrew. Anna really knew nothing about running hotels and even wondered how much White Eagle had to do with its success thus far, but it didn't matter; as long as she put this woman in her place, she'd be satisfied.

"Well, I wasn't assuming he couldn't run his father's hotel. I'm sure he, even being a savage, is quite capable."

"Are you ready?" Mr. Dubois announced, coming up next to Anna and gazing sharply at the woman.

Anna took his arm.

"Oh my, I thought you had come with Mr. Charvet. I take it," the woman raised a suggestive brow, "he isn't in town."

"Mr. Dubois is a friend." Anna turned with him to leave, but she couldn't help but notice the woman's knowing expression.

Once outside, she glanced back to see if the woman was still watching them, and to her horror, the woman chattered to another and pointed in Anna and Mr. Dubois' direction.

How dreadful.

They climbed into the carriage and headed back to her hotel. Funny. Inside the theater she'd felt like she was back in New York City, serving her uncle's snippety clients, and had now just stepped out of the big modern city into a backwoods town.

She missed the mountains. She glanced over at Mr. Dubois, wishing White Eagle was sitting next to her, thief or not.

Back at the hotel Anna relayed all the sparkling details about the theater to Jack. He listened with a smile in his eyes. Of course, she left out the details about that wicked woman who accosted her in the lobby. Despite her glee, a cold sensation and dizziness swept over her.

"Well, it's getting late, and I think I better go to my room," she finally said, thinking maybe she was tired and needed rest.

When she stood, the room spun, and she braced herself on the table.

"Miss Anna? You all right?" Jack leaped to his feet and came to her side.

The dizziness subsided and she straightened. "Just tired is all," she said. If White Eagle hadn't robbed her, she could see a doctor. She'd spent everything she earned at the wig shop on new clothes.

She turned to leave, but the room tilted.

"Miss Anna, are you feeling well?" Mr. Dubois came up and took her by the elbow. "You look pale."

"I'm fine." She immediately regretted her sharp reply. "Thank you for your concern, Mr. Dubois, Jack." She gave them both a reassuring smile. Mr. Dubois and Jack had been very kind to her ever since she'd arrived, always looking out for her from a distance. It wasn't like they were the ones who had robbed her and left her stranded.

They escorted her to her room, and once inside, she closed the door and went to the basin. She filled it with fresh water and washed her face. After combing her hair, she slipped into her nightgown then picked up the broken frames of her parents' photos on the bureau.

Loneliness engulfed her. She set the pictures down and plopped on the bed, glancing around the empty room. A sick wave of heat poured over her, and she broke out into a cold sweat. Her stomach turned. She leaped up from the bed and ran to the basin, just in time to empty her insides. When finished, she patted her mouth with a clean towel. The queasiness didn't go away, and her body trembled.

Perhaps it was something she ate? Yet hadn't she been feeling this way ever since she'd been at Mountain Jack's cabin? She had brushed off the other incidents of nausea as a sign of distress. Why now? Nothing terrible or shocking had happened. She grabbed the sides of the basin as another retch seized her.

After cleaning up she peered out into the hall and caught a glimpse of Mr. Dubois walking through the lobby.

She waved him down.

Thankfully, he spotted her. When he came, she hid halfway behind the door.

"Hello, Mr. Dubois," her voice cracked. "I'm sorry to bother you, but could you send a maid to bring me a clean basin with some fresh water and towels?"

"You're not well, are you? Perhaps you should see a *docteur?*"

"Well, truthfully——" Another turn of her stomach made her swing back to the basin, but nothing happened.

"I will send for a chambermaid and fresh water." He closed the door.

Thankfully, nothing more came up. She slumped on the bed when a slight knock tapped at the door. She stood to open it, and the room swam.

A chambermaid came in with fresh water, a clean basin, and some towels.

"Oh dear, miss. You don't look so well." The petite maid set down the fresh pitcher of water. She turned to Anna. "Get down under them covers and let me take care of you."

"Oh, you don't have to take care of me." The room still swam, and Anna would have loved to crawl out of her body.

"You just do as I say and get into bed." The woman bustled about, pulling down the bedding and fluffing up her pillow.

"Thank you," Anna said, feeling weak. "I just hate to be any trouble."

"You're no trouble at all, miss. I'm happy to help."

As much as she hated to admit it, she missed White Eagle and wished he were here to comfort her. But at the same time, how could she want him? Her stomach swam again, and cold dizziness swept over her. She had to see a doctor.

Whatever she'd caught at Jack's simply wouldn't go away.

Chapter 21

A shadow crept through Denver City. Only the saloon showed signs of life as Jean-Marc's shadow stretched down the lonely streets of the slumbering town. The shadow of a man riding his horse in a welcome cloak of darkness.

He came upon the *Rocky Mountain News* building, the newspaper that had helped stir so much hate against his people. Torching the place entered his mind, but he rode on.

When he neared his father's house, he stopped before it and leaned against the saddle horn. He pushed back his hat and took in the old place. He'd last seen his father in this boarded-up house six years ago. He could still hear his father's voice.

"They were not Union troops!" Franck Charvet had slammed his fist down on the table, speaking in French. "They were volunteers and did not represent the Union's wishes. They'll be punished for what they've done."

He turned to face Jean-Marc, his eyes clouded with sorrow. "We just buried your mother and your grandmother. I won't bury you." His voice was ragged.

"I've given my word, Father. I have to fight." Jean-Marc had remained with his father long enough. And the latest parade in Denver City's streets, honoring Chivington and his men as they brandished their trophies of private parts from the recent raid on his village, had made him physically ill. "The Cheyenne from the North and the South have already retreated to the Dog Soldiers' village. I will join them."

"*Non*! You will not. I forbid it."

"Father, please." Jean-Marc sank onto a chair next to the mahogany desk. He had never deliberately gone against his father's wishes.

Franck stared out the window. His jaw clenched, a sign he was deeply distressed. The light from the window showed the gray in his dark hair and mustache. His posture slumped, no longer the self-assured stance of the successful businessman he was known to be, but that of a tired, anxious father.

The rattling of a carriage and the shouts of its driver on the street broke the long silence.

"I understand your need to fight. If I were you, I'd want to do the same." His father expelled a long breath. "All I want is what's best for you. You've done so well. You've mastered the English language even better than I. It's been good that I brought you to town whenever I needed to conduct business." He pressed his fingers against his temples. "If only I had taken you and your mother with me this last time. *Ma chérie* would still be alive." His eyes glistened.

Before his mother's death, Jean-Marc had never seen his father cry. His nose burned, and he swallowed back tears. "You can't blame yourself, Father. There was no way you could know this would happen. We were all promised safety."

Franck sighed heavily and stared at the ceiling, making evident the deep lines etched on his once handsome face. "Thank You, God, for sparing my son." Again, he rubbed his temples, and then as if an idea struck him, he faced Jean-Marc. "You must realize the asset you can be to the whites and to the Cheyenne. You have your feet in two worlds, and you can help them understand the other's culture. This, my son, is a great blessing."

Jean-Marc understood his father's meaning, but he also knew the anger and hurt that filled the hearts of the Cheyenne. The same anger and hurt filled his own heart, and it was more than he could bear. He had to do something. He had to avenge the deaths of his friends and family. He couldn't just sit around in Denver City while his Cheyenne brothers fought for their people, for their very existence.

"Why don't you go stay with Jack? The mountain air will do you good, not to mention getting away from Denver for a while."

"Why do you want me to leave, Father? You don't want me to go be with my people, but you don't want me here either. Are you afraid of what the palefaces will do to me?"

Silence.

"All the more reason why I should fight." Jean-Marc clenched his fists. "The whites need to learn that the Cheyenne and other tribes are people just like them. They need a taste of what's been done to us."

His father's eyes blazed and his face reddened. He raised a trembling finger. "You will not murder the innocent!"

Jean-Marc sprang to his feet. "They murdered our innocent!" The memory of his grandmother sitting in her own blood, his mother's dull eyes staring past him, and the small child's blood painting the snow flashed through his mind. "They are savages, and I will fight. Black Kettle and the other chiefs trusted the words of the palefaces, and they betrayed that trust. I've given my word. I must abide by the promise I made to my people."

His father straightened and eyed Jean-Marc. "You are a Christian, boy. What you're about to do is wrong."

It was like he tossed cold water in Jean-Marc's face, and he sucked in air. His baptism, just a year ago in the Platte River, swept through his thoughts. The happy memories and his father's proud smile burned like hot coals in his soul. But he forced it from his mind and replaced it with Chivington's self-righteous preaching in the streets. He saw the man puffing up his barrel chest, wagging his tongue at the crowd.

"*Christians* slaughtered my people." Jean-Marc's hollow voice carried off the walls.

His father stepped back, his face pale. He stared at Jean-Marc as if he didn't know him anymore and then turned and paced the floor, mumbling and rubbing his temples.

Jean-Marc gazed at his feet. He couldn't bear to watch his father's torment. But he knew his father couldn't argue with his words, since it was Chivington, a former minister, who led the attack on his tribe.

A minister.

Jean-Marc hadn't even thought of it before. Men who called themselves *Christians* killed his people.

And yet he called himself a Christian. Believers in the One Great Spirit weren't supposed to slaughter villages—were they? Why would God let this happen? Where was *Ma'heo'o?* Where was God?

Finally, his father stopped pacing. He dropped his hands at his sides, as though too weary to continue, and stared at him.

Jean-Marc met his blue-green gaze.

"You are a child of the Most High God." His voice trembled. "Whether you're Cheyenne or white, you answer to *Him*. Don't you forget that."

Jean-Marc took a deep shuddering breath and refocused on the boarded-up windows. His father's words were like a branding iron on his soul. They haunted him everywhere he went, with everything he did.

He had promised to return to Denver City. He just didn't realize it wouldn't be in his father's lifetime.

All because of those Batland Boys.

Normally, the brothers would have robbed the stage while it was still in the mountains and not so close to Denver City. The brothers had been testing Jean-Marc's dedication to their gang. Had Anna given him away, it would have been over, and the last two years of winning their trust would have been for nothing.

When Jean-Marc had seen Billy's filthy hands on her, his Morning Sun, it had taken all his strength to keep from killing the swine right there on the spot. After all, that was the way of the Cheyenne, to kill a man who forced himself on his woman. But had he killed Billy, not only would Anna have been left to their mercy because they surely would have killed him, he would have lost his chance at catching their oldest brother, Rick.

Rick, their leader, had waited for them at their hideout. The brothers had stolen the coach's horses, and that meant the death penalty. And Rick was already wanted, dead or alive, for the murder of Jean-Marc's father.

Jean-Marc's hunger for justice was finally satisfied.

It'd been almost two years since his father died, but it still felt like yesterday.

A senseless death.

Jean-Marc hadn't been back to Denver City since the massacre. Few people knew about Franck Charvet's son, which made it possible for him to go after the Batland Boys. Between fighting the battles with the Cheyenne against the Union soldiers, reestablishing their village, and chasing down the dogs that killed his father, it had been a complicated two years—an agonizing two years. But finally justice was served.

The marshal was pleased. The stagecoach robbery had been reported to him in Denver, which was the signal to Deputy Joe Morgan that it was time to make their move. It had been Jean-Marc's job to inform the authorities in the nearest town as to the location of the Batland Boys' hideout, which he'd already informed Joe was near Leadville. After the robbery was reported, Joe had headed out a team to Leadville, and they finally caught those maggots.

But why did Jean-Marc still feel so empty?

And now, here he was in Denver City. For Anna.

Why hadn't she listened to him and remained at Mountain Jack's? Anger shot through his veins. He didn't know what he'd do once he got his hands on the stubborn woman. The marshal had said she was at the hotel. Hervé and Jack would have taken care of her. Besides Mountain Jack, Hervé was the only one—and now the marshal and his deputy— who knew Jean-Marc by both names.

What a life. He'd have to do a lot of explaining in order to make Anna understand.

He'd been hiding from his responsibilities in Denver City. Perhaps now was the time to return and run his father's business affairs?

Was he insane?

Yet if he stayed in Denver City, Anna would be happy. If she still wanted him. Would she ever forgive him?

If not now, she would later. Whether she liked it or not, she belonged to him.

He urged the horse to move on. He'd stay at the hotel tonight.

Denver City had changed. More buildings had sprung up on all corners, and old vacant lots had been filled. As he neared Sixteenth Street, he recalled the vendors selling body parts of his people.

After arguing with his father, Jean-Marc had left his house for the Grand Palace Hotel to talk with Hervé, an old friend who came from France with his father many years ago. Hervé had spent many hours with Jean-Marc, teaching him English and helping him with his education.

On that day when Jean-Marc had planned to leave, he took this same path. As he had neared Sixteenth Street on foot, he had seen a vendor across from the hotel, standing behind a long table. Clusters of people had gathered in front of him.

"Get your red-skin souvenirs here!" the man had shouted. He held up a scalp of hair.

Jean-Marc had stood behind the crowd, reliving the nightmare in his mind. Dare he go closer? As always when he came to town with his father, he wore the clothing of the white man, but his skin shone darker than those around him, and his mother's woven, leather strap bound his hair behind the ear. Still, in his hat, white shirt, vest, and heavy boots, he became an anonymous member of the crowd.

But why should that matter? Especially now?

He was Cheyenne.

Yes, he was also white, but he would never be like them.

"And this here, ladies and gents, is a real Indian bone. Notice how small it is. Taken from a child. That little savage won't grow up to harm your baby, ma'am." The vendor winked, motioning toward a woman with a pram. "Nits make lice."

The racial slur stung him, a slur that made it acceptable to murder innocent children. Visions of the small child he had failed to save stormed through his mind. Jean-Marc looked at his hands. Useless hands. Couldn't even save that baby. He closed his eyes. The child. The blood. Death. All because he'd failed.

He broke through the crowd and marched to the table filled with Indian scalps. Bones of children and adults had been polished until they shone. Some were made into elaborate necklaces, while others lay bare. Moccasins, earrings, pipes, and other ornaments of his people lay on display for the shoppers.

A silver ring with a turquoise sparrow caught his eye. With trembling fingers, he slowly picked up the cold silver and turned it over in his palm. His mother's ring, given to her by his father.

He clutched the ring in his fist. His blood raged. "May God avenge my people!" he cried out in Cheyenne. With one stroke of his arm, he shoved the wares off the table.

Women screamed.

"A savage. He's a savage!" a man shouted.

Another cursed. "Your scalp ought to be up there too!"

Jean-Marc whirled toward the crowd, his jaw clenched.

Silence fell. Onlookers stepped back with opened mouths and shocked faces.

"Is he white or is he Injun?" someone murmured.

Jean-Marc's gaze darted from one person to the other. Women looked on with fear, while men scrutinized him with curiosity.

"He has the eyes of us whites, but his skin is that of a savage," a man said.

"*Savage*," Jean-Marc's voice came from deep within his throat, "is murdering innocent women and children and putting their bones on display!" It was awkward speaking English, and his accent was thick, but the words were spoken without hesitation. "This ring belonged to my mother. Who you killed!" He shook his fist in the air as tears blurred his vision. "Free Sparrow was her name." He pointed at the woman with the pram. "How would you like your baby's dead body sold as a souvenir?"

The woman gasped and flung her arms over the pram as if to protect her baby. "He threatened my child." Her wild eyes searched the crowd. "That savage threatened my baby!"

Shouts arose all around him.

The crowd turned on Jean-Marc.

"Get him!" someone shouted.

"He's going to kill her baby!" someone else cried. "Kill him!"

Jean-Marc stepped back. An opening formed between two men off to the side. He lunged through the space, but one grabbed his arm. He twisted free and stumbled into the muddy street. Footsteps closed in, and people shouted behind. A carriage rumbled toward him. He spun out of its way and staggered through the slushy mud but regained his balance and bolted to the hotel.

He burst into the lobby and almost collided with Hervé's lanky form meeting him eye to eye. "They're after me!"

"Lock the doors!" Hervé shouted to the porter, who jumped at the command. The man did as he was told just as the crowd thundered toward them.

Out of breath, Jean-Marc pointed to the pursuing crowd. "They think I threatened that woman's child," he said in French. "Maybe it came out that way because of my English. They'll hang me in the street like they did the others."

Hervé turned to another employee. "Go through the back and get the marshal. He'll put a stop to this. Franck Charvet is a respectable man, and so is his son. Marshal Dell will do right by them."

Jean-Marc backed away toward the stairs at the other end of the lobby. He watched as the mob banged on the doors and windows with angry force. No wonder his father wanted him to leave town.

Glass cracked and doors rattled on their hinges. If they broke through, Jean-Marc would fight.

He stood firm and reached for his tomahawk. It was gone! He patted his thighs. Of course it wasn't there. He wasn't wearing his normal clothes. He clenched his fists, recalling all the war moves chief Black Kettle had taught him.

The marshal moved between the crowd. He shouted, waving his hands over the men and women, trying to calm them.

The people dropped back. Jean-Marc inched closer to the doors and peered through the broken glass.

"That's him!" One man pointed. "He threatened this woman's child!"

The marshal braced his legs wide apart and cleared his coattail from the Navy Colt at his hip. "That's Franck Charvet's son. He wouldn't have threatened her baby. Now, go on home, all of you, and take those souvenirs away from here." The marshal waved the people away. "Get on home."

After a lot of arguing, the crowd eventually broke up, and Marshal Dell was admitted into the hotel.

Jean-Marc backed away toward the stairs.

The door closed behind the marshal, and the gold star pinned to his vest shimmered, reminding Jean-Marc of his authority.

From below the rim of his hat, Marshal Dell's eyes scanned the room until they fell on Jean-Marc. With his Colt still resting in its holster and his spurs jangling across the creaking wooden floor, he strode toward him. The marshal took his hat in his hand and gave one quick nod.

Jean-Marc stood with his feet planted to the floor and awaited his arrest.

Marshal Dell waved his hat toward the door. "They're just a bunch of ignoramuses." His thick red mustache dangled over his top lip. With bowed head, he raised his eyes to Jean-Marc. "I'm sorry for what happened to your mother and grandmother, and to the rest of your people."

Jean-Marc swallowed hard, clutching his mother's ring in his fist. Was he just trying to make his arrest easier by using consoling words?

"I want you to know, I don't support what Chivington and his men did to your village. He calls himself a man of God, but after what he encouraged those soldiers to do . . ." The marshal cleared his throat. "If the same thing happened to me, I'd kill them all where they stood."

Jean-Marc fixed his gaze on Marshal Dell, an old friend of his father's. He longed to trust his words, but still, he doubted. Too many hangings had taken place.

"But you're a decent fella. I know your father, and I know he taught you what's right. What those people did out there on the streets, it ain't right." He shook his head. "No, it's downright sinful. But I can't stop them. Governor Evans is above me, and he, along with most of the town, supports what Chivington's men did out there by Big Sandy. I can only do my best to keep the peace until this madness blows over."

Jean-Marc didn't know how to respond, so he kept quiet. A long silence passed between them as his fingers squeezed the ring over and over again in his fist. *Ma'heo'o* had obviously left these people, left this city. Jean-Marc would leave too and find Him elsewhere.

"I'm saying this for your own good, son." The marshal shifted on his feet. "I think it'd be best if you left town."

"I plan to, sir." There was no way he would hide out at Mountain Jack's as his father had suggested. The mad citizens of Denver City fueled Jean-Marc's anger for vengeance. He would join the renegades.

The marshal placed his hat back on his head. "I think the sooner you leave the better. I'll escort you back to your father's house. And my deputy will escort you out of town."

After saying goodbye to his father and promising one day to return, Jean-Marc left Denver City. He never looked back.

Until now.

What in the world was he doing here? Had he gone completely mad? Perhaps. He'd gone mad for a woman. A woman who loved a place he despised.

And now, she probably despised him. He wouldn't be surprised if she refused to go back with him to his village now. Likely, she thought him no better than Uncle Horace for what he'd done. He turned that fateful moment over in his mind, like he'd done every day since the incident. There had been no other way to hush her up.

With amazing calm, he tied his horse outside the hotel. Right now, he needed sleep; he'd ridden all day and through the night.

A porter held the door for him.

"Take care of my horse," he said to the man as he went into the building.

The man raised his brow.

Jean-Marc stopped and stared him down, not in the mood for an argument.

The man nodded quickly and stepped out to take the horse to the livery stable.

"Where's Hervé staying these days?" Jean-Marc called over his shoulder before the door closed.

"Who wants to know?"

"Your boss." Jean-Marc cast a weary glance at him. He knew the fellow was just doing his job, but he was too tired to appreciate his caution.

"Sir? Mr. Charvet?"

"Yes."

The porter's eyes widened as he looked Jean-Marc over for the first time. He straightened and thrust his chest out. "Room 114, sir."

Jean-Marc tipped his hat. "Take good care of my horse. I rode him hard."

"Yes, sir. I'll do that, sir." The man quickly disappeared.

Jean-Marc trudged up the stairs, his jangling spurs and large boots making his feet feel twice their weight and size. He missed his light, comfortable moccasins. When he made his way down the quiet hall to room 114, he noticed a light coming from under the door. He hadn't wanted to wake him, but anxious to see his old friend, he was glad to know he was awake. He knocked. Why would he be up at such a late hour anyway?

"Who's there?" A familiar, muffled voice came from the other side of the door.

"It's Jean-Marc."

He heard brisk footsteps and the door swung open. There stood his father's old friend and confidant.

"*Oh la vache!*" Hervé spoke in French, his father's native tongue, and it made Jean-Marc feel at home. A familiar pang of longing wrenched in his gut. He opened his mouth to speak, but Hervé grabbed him by the shoulders, dragged him into the room then held him at arm's length.

"I thought I'd never see you again. I had hope when Miss Anna arrived, but never dared dream you'd show your face in this town again." Hervé's eyes welled with tears and Jean-Marc's throat hurt all over again. "It's good to see you, son."

"It's good to see you." Jean-Marc nearly choked on the words. Hervé's hair had gone gray and a few more wrinkles covered his face, but he still looked good. He hadn't seen Hervé since the day he'd left Denver City.

"How are you doing? It's been so long. Too long. Jack talked to the marshal. You managed to help capture those Batland Boys."

Jean-Marc nodded.

"They murdered and robbed a lot of people in these parts. Denver City will be grateful."

"I don't care about Denver."

"What's brought you back? Why are you here?"

A silence fell between them.

"It's Miss Anna, isn't it?" Hervé's eyes twinkled.

Not wanting to explain himself, Jean-Marc asked, "What are you doing up so late? I didn't expect you to be awake."

"It's Miss Anna. She's been sick since she arrived. Some kind of stomach flu."

"What?" Jean-Marc went cold. "Did you have the doctor look at her?"

Hervé's brows furrowed. "*Oui*, but it was his apprentice. I'm sure she'll get over it soon."

"It could be something serious."

"I've had one of the chambermaids take care of her. By now, she ought to be resting. It's not as bad as it sounds. She'll be up and around tomorrow, like she always is."

"I want to see her." The thought of being this close to Anna made his heart race. He had to see her. To see if she was well, to see her face before the hurt and anger showed in her eyes.

Hervé stepped back. "Jean-Marc, you may own this hotel, but it doesn't give you the right to sneak into a decent lady's room."

"She's my wife. Now take me to her."

Hervé gaped in silence then ran a hand through his hair. "So it's true. Why didn't you send word?"

"There was no way I could from the Batland Boys' hideout. If I tried to send anything, I would have been found out. Besides, Jack knew. She's been well cared for?"

"*Bien sûr!* The marshal told me she'd been robbed." He cleared his throat. "By you."

Jean-Marc breathed deeply. "I'll explain later, but you already know the circumstances. It was all a farce." He moved toward the door. "Now, are you going to take me to my wife or not?"

"The town gossips are in an uproar that your wife is having an affair," Hervé said as he led Jean-Marc down the hall.

Jean-Marc stopped. White-hot jealousy pounded his temples. "An affair? *Avec qui?*" The walls seemed to shake. When he got his hands on this man, he'd kill him.

"Shh," Hervé put his finger to his mouth. "It's nothing like that. The man is *moi*. A couple nights ago, I took her to the theater, and people started talking. I assure you, she has no interest in me," he said with a twinkle in his eye.

Jean-Marc resumed his step. Right now all that mattered was to see that she was safe. He'd worried about her to the point of feeling sick. Finally, he could see her. Even if she hated him, he would at least know she was well.

Hervé handed Jean-Marc an oil lamp and key and then stayed in the hallway as Jean-Marc crept into her room. The lamp cast long shadows over the walls and small bed. He recognized her sleeping form under the covers, and the lamp lit up the braid draped over her shoulder like a rope of gold. While still long, the braid was shorter than when he last saw her. She'd cut her hair. Why would she do such a thing?

He knelt next to the bed, careful to keep the lamp at a distance so as not to awaken her. Her lashes rested against her snow-white cheeks. She'd lost her coloring from the sun. Her lips, pressed together, still looked as tempting and beautiful as when he'd first kissed them. How he ached to take her in his arms. Instead, he brushed his knuckles lightly across her cheek.

She stirred.

His hand froze and he held his breath, but she continued sleeping.

Finally, he stood and crept from the room. She was safe. All was well, and now he'd find a doctor to rid her of this illness.

How would he win her trust again? Would she ever forgive him?

Chapter 22

Anna pranced into the lobby. Today she'd start her new job.

"Where is everyone?" Anna asked Mr. Dubois as she glanced around the empty lobby.

"Why don't you go see for yourself?" He smiled a mischievous grin. "You'll find them all in front of the marshal's office. It's a grand celebration." He bent down behind the counter and pulled out a *Rocky Mountain News* and a *Denver Post*. "And take some of these."

Beneath lightly falling flakes, Anna read an article from the *Denver Post* as she headed toward the marshal's office.

> BATLAND BOYS HUNG IN LEADVILLE!
> Despite local partisanship, Jean-Marc Charvet will arrive in Denver City to a hero's welcome after infiltrating and capturing the stagecoach bandits, who not only terrorized Denver citizens, but also murdered his father, an upstanding citizen, Franck Charvet.

Anna stopped and read the words again. He wasn't a thief. He was a hero.

The day of the robbery flashed through her mind. He'd saved her from nearly being ravaged. He'd kept telling her to be quiet, and when she wouldn't—he'd silenced her the only way he could. She'd believed he was a thief. And no better than Uncle Horace. Shame swept through her.

A woman brushed by, snapping Anna out of her thoughts. It had stopped snowing, and along the street a large crowd gathered in front of several booths. Her hands and feet became cold in her thin gloves and boots. Still, she eased her way through the mass of people and alongside a booth where women passed out fliers advocating their right to vote.

"Women have been given the right to vote in Cheyenne, Wyoming! We should have that right too!" a woman shouted.

Outside the office the marshal stood on a makeshift platform and shouted to the crowd. "And now, you can hear the story from my fine deputy, Joe Morgan."

The crowd cheered and applauded.

As Anna entered the crowd before the marshal's platform, she spotted the woman from the dry good's store standing in front of her. The woman held her mother's arm, and both dabbed their eyes.

Anna stopped, hoping they wouldn't see her.

Deputy Morgan's voice droned over the crowd as he shared with the audience all the atrocities the Batland Boys had done to several Denver families.

"Those animals that killed Daddy have finally gotten what they deserved," the young woman said. "They also killed poor Mr. Charvet's father."

Anna spotted White Eagle standing next to the platform. She knew White Eagle's father had died, but always thought it'd been in an Indian battle. It hadn't occurred to her that because he was white he had died some other way, especially this way. Of course, now it all made sense.

"That's him," the woman said to her mother.

"Who?" The older woman craned her neck.

"That's Mr. Charvet." The young woman pointed toward the platform. "Oh, he's handsome," she said as if surprised.

Anna stood on tiptoe to see over the crowd. Between several shoulders, heads, hats, and bonnets she spotted White Eagle's long form walking up to the platform. His spurs jangled, and he wore his bandit's clothes and cowboy hat, reminding her of the last moments they had together. The shocking discovery of his being a thief. What a fool she'd been.

The crowd cheered and clapped as Anna threaded her way between the people to get a closer look.

The marshal shook White Eagle's hand. "Won't you say a few words for us, Mr. Charvet?" he shouted above the crowd.

As she squeezed by one last person and came a few feet from the platform, the crowd quieted. She froze when White Eagle's gaze met hers. He didn't smile, and appeared rather serious considering he was being honored as the town hero.

"I came to Denver City for one reason." He kept his eyes locked with hers. "One reason alone." With that, he tipped his hat then turned, nodded to the marshal and stepped down from the platform.

The crowd cheered and roared. Several people clamored toward him.

"Thank you, Mr. Charvet!" a woman's voice carried above the crowd. Anna saw that it was the mean woman's mother who had shouted. "Those boys robbed and killed my James."

"My father's death has been avenged, all because of you!" the younger woman shouted.

Anna cringed. If only White Eagle knew what that woman's father had done to his people. Anna gritted her teeth as she watched the woman dab her eyes, crying out praises to White Eagle.

The sun broke between the clouds as he tipped his hat and tried to maneuver away from the people, but they wouldn't let him pass.

Anna marched up to the young woman, clutching the newspapers to her chest to keep from shaking. "You hypocrite." She glared at the woman before her, surprised by her sudden burst of courage.

The woman stepped back, not recognizing Anna. Finally, her eyes widened. "You."

"Yes, *me*," Anna said, full of fury. "And that man whom you honor today is one of the people you think would be better off dead."

"Obviously more white blood flows through Mr. Charvet's veins than that of his savage mother."

Anna clenched her fists around the newspapers. She had a mind to spit on the woman like she'd done to her, but decided against it. Besides, she wasn't sure her aim would be of much benefit. People bumped around them and shouted, clamoring toward White Eagle.

"He may have avenged your father, but who will avenge his mother, who *your* father killed?" Song Bird, Yellow Leaf, and all those she loved flashed through her mind.

The woman stared Anna down, her eyes narrowed. They stood nose to nose, and suddenly Anna saw past the anger, past the trembling in her own body, and into the eyes of a woman, a frightened woman. Not that she was afraid of Anna, but afraid of the unknown. And Indians, whether Cheyenne or from another tribe, were unknown, and strange, different.

"Heathens." The woman nudged her chin at Anna. "You dare stand here and defend heathens?"

Anna stepped back, unsure how to respond and unprepared for any kind of theological debate. She blurted out the first words that came to mind. "People! They are *people.*" Anna emphasized the word, realizing the significance of what she said. "They are God's creation, and we should love them, not murder them and their children. Their scalps are not trophies to be won." Anna swallowed. "You call yourself a Christian by calling them heathens, but if I were them, I would want nothing to do with the Christian faith. We are their murderers. We are destroying their race. Instead, we should try to win them over to Christ. And we can only do that by our love, *His* love, not by our hate."

The woman made no response.

Anna turned and walked away, stunned by the words that just left her mouth. Where had they come from? She trembled, fighting back tears. And who was she to talk about God? She'd been angry for so many years, and yet God used White Eagle to reveal her answered prayers. All that time with White Eagle's tribe could have been used for good. Not once did she teach any of them her faith. What little she had. She determined right then to grow. To grow in her faith and in her relationship with God. But how? How was she to do that?

God, please help me to do better.

Aimlessly, she followed the crowd as White Eagle started walking, ignoring the women who shouted their appreciation and reached out to touch him. It was as though no one existed as he strode down the walkway back toward the hotel.

Anna followed, and after walking a few blocks, the crowd dispersed. She thought about his hurt. The pain of being so alone in the world, the pain of losing both his parents. She wouldn't even know where to begin to teach him about her faith, and she couldn't help but think that it would be an impossible task. Besides, who was *she* to teach anyone anything?

He took off his hat and batted it against his leg, shaking off the snow. She spotted his leather band just before he placed the hat back on his head as he strode on toward the hotel. His strides were long and confident, like those of his Cheyenne brothers. Yet buried beneath his regal exterior beat a hurting heart.

He had risked his life to avenge his father. She thought of Mountain Jack, how he had told her story after story about his partner. If only she had known then that his partner had been White Eagle's father. Now she'd do anything to remember the details of every story she'd heard.

A couple passed by as Anna came upon an open carriage. "Miss van Stralen, is that you?"

She turned to see a young gentleman with a black handlebar mustache just stepping down from a carriage. The man she'd met on the train those many months ago. He tipped his hat.

"The name's Steven Kane. Remember me?"

"Of course, yes, I remember you." She smiled. How could she forget. He was the one who had encouraged her to get off near Julesburg. She imagined how different her life would have been had she taken his advice.

"I see you made it here all right."

"Sure did," she said, half smiling. "I'm finally home." It felt good to say the word "home." Though it didn't carry with it that satisfying feeling she'd long expected to have.

She then noticed two older gentlemen in the carriage with him. They nodded and smiled.

"This is Mr. John Evans." Mr. Kane motioned toward the smaller man nearest him.

"Evans? That name sounds familiar."

Bright-eyed Mr. Evans grinned. "I used to be the governor of Colorado, ma'am."

"Oh! But that's not all. You helped create the Union Pacific rail line from Cheyenne to Denver City. I read all about you."

"I see you're well informed. Where are you from?" Mr. Evans asked.

"Holland."

"My, that's quite a distance." He smiled.

Mr. Kane motioned toward the stern-faced, barrel-chested gentleman next to him. "Allow me to introduce retired Colonel John M. Chivington. He's visiting from Nebraska."

The familiar name sent a cold chill down Anna's spine. "Chivington?" Her voice quivered.

The man nodded, giving a faint smile beneath his neatly trimmed beard.

"Are you the man . . ." How could she say it? The world spun around her. ". . . who led the attack at Sand Creek six years ago?"

"That I am." The man smiled with pride.

"It was a mighty fine victory," Mr. Evans said. "Mr. Chivington here and his men received a hero's welcome."

"Wiped out about five hundred of them red-skins," Chivington added.

The entire world stopped spinning and focused itself on this one, hateful man in front of her, and her mind exploded. "You call killing women and children a victory? I thought you were a man of God. A minister!" She straightened, gripping her newspapers.

"Nits make lice." Mr. Chivington scowled.

"And where is that in the Bible?" Anna asked, caught in the grip of emotion and surprised at her own reaction. "Let me guess. Chivington, Chapter One, Verse 666."

"Miss van Stralen!" Mr. Kane's voice erupted between them.

Anna faced Mr. Kane. "Good day, Mr. Kane!" She turned to leave.

Mr. Kane grabbed her wrist. The newspapers scattered at her feet.

"How dare you." He snarled between clenched teeth.

"Let go of me!" Her voice trembled as she fought his painful grasp.

***

"Take your hands off my wife." Jean-Marc's voice was low. He'd watched the scene unfold from a distance.

The man loosened his grip.

Jean-Marc grabbed him by the collar and slammed him against the carriage.

Anna jumped back, staring in dumbfounded disbelief. Seeing she was unharmed, he turned his furious gaze back on the man in front of him.

"Mr. Charvet—I—" Mr. Kane babbled.

"Touch my wife again and lose a hand." Jean-Marc brandished his dagger, noticing the fear in the man's eyes. This was nothing new to him. He'd killed countless men, watching the fear on their faces as they died. But he wasn't that person anymore, so he released him.

The man slumped to the ground. Then quickly scrambled to his feet, and as he attempted to step into the carriage his foot slipped.

"Coloradans don't take kindly to Indian lovers, ma'am. You better watch yourself." Chivington's voice leaped out of the carriage, knocking the wind out of Jean-Marc.

He looked up to see his greatest enemy. Chivington tipped his hat as the other man found his seat.

Jean-Marc threw his dagger. It protruded from the couch next to Chivington.

Chivington stared at the dagger, slowly seeming to realize what'd just happened, then his eyes widened. He stood and drew his gun.

Jean-Marc quick-drew his Colt. With a loud crack, the pistol flew out of Chivington's hand.

None of the men in the carriage made a move for his weapon.

Jean-Marc stood, his gun drawn and smoking.

Movement on the streets stopped and people watched closely as a chilling silence settled on the air.

Chivington.

The butcher. The murderer of Jean-Marc's people stood before him. His mother. His grandmother. He cocked the hammer on the revolver and straightened his arm. His one true enemy, finally in his sights.

Liquid fire seared his blood as he drew in one long breath. He aimed the Colt right at the monster's forehead, his gaze unwavering.

Now.

It was time. Time to avenge his family. Hand steady, his finger tightened on the trigger.

"White Eagle," Anna's soft voice carried over his shoulder.

His finger froze, a heartbeat away from killing the monster.

"Please," she whispered. "Let *Ma'heo'o* have His vengeance."

He wanted this for himself. God could have His vengeance any day. This moment, right now, belonged to Jean-Marc. His entire body ached for this moment. Nothing mattered, not even getting hanged in the streets; his family would finally be avenged.

Silence hung on the air like a suffocating cloak.

"Driver." Jean-Marc's voice cut through the stillness like a knife. "Leave, before I kill someone." It felt like he'd shouted the words, but they came out deadly calm.

The carriage pulled away and tore down the street, leaving dust in its wake.

Jean-Marc stood frozen, Colt still poised, his arms and legs still braced. His mind buzzed, barely registering the fact that he'd let the swine go. The sounds of footsteps and the sight of people on the streets came to life as if he were gradually waking from a dream.

His vision came into focus, and he saw himself standing there, his revolver aimed at the dry goods store across the street. The tension in his body slowly began to melt like snow dissolving on the plains.

He let the Colt drop to his side and released the hammer.

He'd let him go.

Anna's voice echoed in his mind. She'd been talking to those men. She'd been talking to Chivington.

He turned on her.

She stepped back.

Why was she speaking to his worst enemy? To the murderer of his family. He seized her arm and led her into the shadows between the buildings.

"What were you doing with those men?" His voice came out harsher than he intended. He studied her expression, searching.

Her eyes filled with guilt and fear. "I didn't know who they were." Her voice quivered.

"You knew exactly who they were!"

"I knew one of them from my trip to Colorado, but I didn't know who the others were until now." She practically choked out the words.

He stood over her, unsure how to respond. Finally, he hissed through his clenched teeth and walked away, leaving her alone.

Chapter 23

Still shaking from White Eagle's fury, Anna stopped outside of Mrs. Peterson's shop. Today was supposed to be a good day, her first day of work. She took a deep breath, forced a smile, and went in.

Mrs. Peterson stood from her worktable. "Why, Anna, it's you! I've been on pins and needles awaiting your arrival." She laughed and motioned around her. "Literally!"

"And I've been anxious to start." Anna swallowed back her emotions. "I can begin now, if you'd like."

"You're in a hurry, aren't you?" Mrs. Peterson smiled, but then a look of concern washed over her face as she stepped closer. "You're so pale." She took her by the hand. "What's happened, dear? Do you want to talk about it?"

Anna tried to swallow the knot in her throat. Not trusting herself to speak, she shook her head.

"Come, I'll show you to your room."

Touched by Mrs. Peterson's concern, she slowly followed her up the stairs, past a parlor on the right, and to the last door on the left. Mrs. Peterson took out a key, unlocked the door, and held it open.

"You get yourself settled, dear. There's no need for you to start today. Just get some rest. Tomorrow will be a new day." She smiled and squeezed Anna's hand. "When you're ready to talk, I'm here." She patted her on the shoulder then turned and closed the door.

Anna dropped on the bed. Emptiness was all she felt.

She looked around her new room. Not too big, not too small, with a single bed, bureau, a wardrobe where she could hang her dresses, and just enough room for her to have a tub brought in for a bath.

Only problem was, she'd left all of her things at the hotel, and there was no way she'd show her face there now. She'd come directly from her confrontation with White Eagle.

Tears burned behind her eyes.

Though she was finally free, a certain emptiness and void filled her heart.

Was this the dream she'd hoped to obtain for her father? Was this really the home she'd longed to have for these six years?

Swallowing her unshed tears, she thought of the things she had left behind. Her favorite book, *The Last of the Mohicans*, the only connection she had to her father, and one of the few physical pieces from her life with him—when everything was good. The book had reopened the dream and sparked her interest again in going west, in finding adventure and freedom.

Her father's dream had come true. "I'm here, Papa. I made it."

Finally, his dream was realized.

"But what are my dreams?" she whispered to herself. That day in the woods with White Eagle came to her mind when he'd asked her that very question.

She glanced down at her empty hands and thought of how often she'd pretended to be Cora and Alice in her book. She would escape into their world, only as a means of escaping her own. They'd been kidnapped by Indians, and how ironic that she had become just like them in many ways.

White Eagle, his village, and the friends and relationships she'd made passed through her mind. An old familiar ache came to her gut, the kind she used to feel shortly after her father died. She'd always thought it meant she was homesick. But that couldn't be. She was home now. Truly home.

Loneliness permeated the room. Emptiness surrounded her. If only she could talk to her papa. Maybe he could straighten her life out.

Lord? Will You fix this mess I'm in?

Then she remembered her photographs. She bit her lip. That meant she'd have to go back. She also had to get her dresses. Maybe she could send for them? The thought sent a chilling dread down her spine.

There was nothing she could do about it.

Right now, she'd wash her face and get to work. She had to focus, and she wanted to do her best and show Mrs. Peterson that she'd hired a good worker.

Jean-Marc took a long drag from his pipe as he sat in front of the hearth. Unbelievable. He'd actually let the monster get away. How would Running Cloud, Yellow Leaf, any of his loved ones react? Would they think he failed?

Just like that day on the banks when he couldn't save the child, when he couldn't save his own mother. He'd watched helplessly as the soldiers came back to desecrate their bodies, had watched as they left cheering in the distance, waving trophies from their hats and rifles.

That night, Jean-Marc, Running Cloud, and Black Bear had helped carry back the wounded; few were found alive, and he dared not return to his mother or grandmother, fearing what he might find.

Jean-Marc, reeling in shock, staggered with some of the younger men into one of the trenches.

"I will fight!" Black Bear shouted. He crouched next to Running Cloud and slammed his fist in the dirt-covered snow. Moonlight flashed in his eyes. "I and others will go to the Dog Soldiers' village. Who will join me?"

"I'll go with you," Running Cloud said, eyes red and swollen. He too had lost his mother. One of his little sisters had been seriously wounded, while the other two had survived. They'd managed to escape.

"We will also fight," others called out.

Jean-Marc remained silent, clutching the necklace and the leather band he'd taken from his mother's hair—all he had left of her. He still waited for his father's arrival. Would he have heard what happened? Or would his father suffer the same shock he had just suffered?

"I will fight," Jean-Marc finally said.

"You will fight against your father's people?" Running Cloud asked.

"I won't murder the innocent, but I will fight the soldiers."

"They murdered our innocent!" Black Bear said. "Now they must suffer the same loss. They're savages."

"And I won't become like them," Jean-Marc said, his gaze set on Black Bear. Had Black Bear no grief, no anguish for what just happened?

"Jean-Marc saved my life." Running Cloud's voice hung in the air. Everyone stilled as their gazes rested on him. "He's a brave warrior. A soldier knocked me from my horse and stood over me with his rifle. Jean-Marc flew through the air like an eagle, and he took the soldier down." Running Cloud cleared his throat. "For now on, his name is White Eagle."

Jean-Marc's heart swelled. He would be fully accepted by the Cheyenne, and would now be called a brave. But in an instant his pride vanished with the finality of what had taken place. He had killed men and watched their blood soak into the ground and snow. He looked at his murderous hands. In one day, he had gone from boyhood to manhood, and he wasn't sure he liked the man he'd become.

Again, Jean-Marc looked down at his hands. His pipe in front him, a steady stream of smoke drifting into his face as he sat before the hearth in what he'd always consider his father's hotel.

"I *did* become like them." His voice penetrated the air.

The realization made him shudder. Angry, he tossed his pipe into the flames. He groaned and rubbed his temples as he watched the pipe burn—a gift given to him by Black Bear. He tried to retrieve it, but it was too late, the flames were too hot. Black Bear was right. He'd never fully be Cheyenne. Whether he liked it or not, white man's blood flowed through his veins. But it no longer mattered. None of it mattered. The Lord didn't look at the color of a man's skin or his race. He looked at a man's heart. Jean-Marc had only Him to answer to, and he knew his bloodlust shamed God.

His gaze fell on Anna's Bible sitting on the shelf not far from him. He'd kept her Bible without her knowing and wondered if she even missed it. She was obviously a believer, but he never heard her pray or saw her reading *Ma'heo'o's* words.

Yet, how often had *he* prayed? It'd been six long years.

Too long.

"*Ma'heo'o?*" Jean-Marc felt like he'd shouted His name, but the cry came out as a mere whisper and sounded hollow in the large room. It felt strange to call out to Him after so long. Would He even hear his cries? His soul grasped through the dark void that threatened to strangle him, reaching for the One he'd pushed away for so many years.

He'd always associated Christianity with what Chivington did, but now he knew just how wrong he'd been.

"A *true* Christian would not murder people. I know that now."

Jean-Marc shook his head at the simple revelation. Just because a person called himself a man of God did not mean he met with God's approval. And Jean-Marc hadn't met with God's approval any more than Chivington had. That thought made him shudder, putting himself in the same ranks as his worst enemy. But it was true. He was a murderer. And so was Chivington. Both of them would have to answer to God for what they've done.

After reading Anna's Bible, he came to realize one thing. God granted everyone free will. God wanted people to come to Him because they wanted to, not because they had to. It was no different than when he kidnapped Anna. He wanted her to love him of her own will, not because he forced her—which he did, and now he had to make up for that.

And he would.

Jean-Marc was never able to give himself over to the Cheyenne spirits when he knew in his heart *Ma'heo'o* was a jealous God. It'd be like him or Anna having an affair. He'd never forget the pain when he discovered Anna speaking to his worst enemy. If that pain was anywhere close to what God felt when man worshipped other gods, then Jean-Marc was relieved he never brought himself to do that. Nonetheless, because of his lust for vengeance, he'd turned his back on *Ma'heo'o.* After he'd been washed by His Son's blood, he'd turned away. Now he was alone.

Loneliness suffocated him as he stared helplessly into the empty room, into the flames where his pipe lay melting, too late to rescue it from the fire—melting and dissolving, just like the Cheyenne people.

Just like his past.

"Father, I have sinned. I'm sorry . . . ." He caught his breath. Would God forgive him? "I'm sorry that I hurt You. You are not Chivington. It's not about the Cheyenne or the white man. It's about You and me, and I made a mistake. I chose the wrong path."

He took a shuddering breath, fighting the knot that swelled in his throat. "I know my lips have not praised You and my tongue has not sung to You." He ran his hands through his hair, desperate for his Lord, his Savior. "Please, hear my cry. Please let me live." He shook his head and swallowed back tears. "Forgive me, Father. Please forgive me."

He lifted his hands, his useless hands, and held them up, palms spread, in front of him, the fire in the hearth blurring in the background through his tears. "I put Chivington and all my enemies into Your hands. Vengeance belongs to You. Only Your hands can help me now. Mine have failed."

Anna worked diligently, and Mrs. Peterson said she was a faster and a more precise seamstress than her former employee.

However, Anna began to worry. It had been the longest two days she'd ever experienced, and she hadn't heard a whisper from White Eagle.

She had let Mr. Dubois know where she was, and he'd sent someone by with her things the same day she'd arrived. But her photographs weren't amongst them, and she still hadn't mustered up the courage to go pick them up. She set aside her sewing and stared out the window. It was nearly closing time.

"Would you be a dear and take these curtains to the Grand Palace Hotel for me?" Mrs. Peterson asked as she held out the folded, packaged material.

Anna's heart lurched, but she didn't dare say no. "Yes, ma'am."

Mrs. Peterson set the package on the table, turned, and busied herself with another project. "This needs to be done before tomorrow, and I'm nearly finished." She peered over the rim of her glasses. "I'll get it done much faster if you could run those curtains over for me."

Anna pulled on her cloak and gathered the package in her arms. The streets were unusually quiet with a light fall of snow carrying on a soft wind. But fear made her chest tighten, almost making it difficult to breathe as she headed for the hotel, praying the whole way there that she wouldn't have to see White Eagle.

"Please don't let him be there," she whispered under her breath. "Please don't make me see him." She could hardly breathe just thinking about the hate he must have for her. The anger in his eyes, the anger and hurt she saw there just a few days ago plagued her thoughts day and night.

Once in the hotel, she was relieved to find only the porter standing in the lobby. She quickly dropped the curtains on the counter and turned to leave.

"Morning Sun." A cold chill sputtered down her spine.

She peered over her shoulder and saw White Eagle standing at the top of the stairs, eyes narrowed. She knew by his frown that she should leave. Quickly, she pushed through the doors.

"Anna!" he shouted after her as the doors closed.

Hurrying down the walkway, the doors burst open behind her. Startled, she glanced over her shoulder and saw White Eagle taking long, determined strides in her direction. He caught up to her and took her by the arm.

"Why are you running from me?" he asked, concern reflected in his eyes as they swept over her.

The weariness in his eyes and face caused all the pent-up guilt from the last two days to rush to the surface. She was the cause, the cause for all his grief.

"Oh, White Eagle, forgive me for making you come to Denver City. This is an awful place! There's so much hate!" Stepping back, she buried her face in her trembling hands. "I'm sorry I made you come here."

"You didn't make me do anything." He inched toward her.

"I should have done something," she said. "Those men—what they're thinking is wrong. I should do something."

"You can't change them." He reached out and ran his fingers down her cheek. "I just realized," he said with a slight chuckle, "the only person you can change is yourself." He motioned toward her with his chin. "*Ma'heo'o* will raise His bow and quiver to the men who have so much hate. It's not for me to take that from Him." He took a deep breath. "I can't change the tracks my moccasins have left behind. I have to look to the open plains where new tracks can be made."

Anna listened as he spoke his poetry, and a new light sparkled in his eyes. Something about him was different, lighter, as though he no longer carried a heavy load.

"I've finally made peace with *Ma'heo'o*. And I've come to take you with me. We're going home."

"Home?" She stepped back. She was home. Wasn't she? Well, either way, she wasn't ready to leave.

"How could you still want me after what I've done? I carried on a conversation with the murderers of your family!" She feigned dignity and straightened, but immediately betrayed her feelings when she choked on tears.

"Aaahhh, Morning Sun. Don't cry. Why would you want me after I kidnapped you? Forced you into marriage? After I robbed you?" He brushed her cheek with his knuckles. His fingers threaded around her neck. He dragged her to him. "After I hurt you?"

She hadn't expected that kind of an answer.

Gazing into her face, he breathed deeply. "There's more to life than revenge. I could have killed him. But I didn't, because of you. Because of *Ma'heo'o*. He brought you to me." He closed his eyes and sighed. "I'm not angry, not anymore. Men like Chivington should be pitied. He has a lot to answer for."

"I don't know what to say," she said, as his lips came dangerously close to hers.

"Forgive me," he whispered.

"But I'm the one who needs to be forgiven."

"You have a good heart, Morning Sun. Now be quiet and kiss me." He pressed his lips against hers, gently, tenderly.

"Take that demonstrative behavior indoors," a woman said with disgust as she swished past.

Anna pulled away, breathless and suddenly conscious of the people walking by. "We're making a scene."

"We've already made a scene." He kept his hold on her.

She stared into his hot, possessive gaze. Despite longing to be in his embrace, she hadn't found what she was looking for. What happened to her dream? Whatever happened to "home"?

"I need time," she whispered.

His eyes flashed, and he tightened his grip.

"Free will," he whispered the words as he stared at her. An understanding reflected in his gaze. "*Ma'heo'o,* how do you stand it?"

She knew he wasn't talking to her, but she remained captive in his grip, puzzled by his meaning.

Slowly, he released her. "Go. Fly away to your dream, Morning Sun. I'll be waiting."

Chapter 24

That evening, Anna was alone folding an unfinished garment when a knock sounded through the shop. She peered out the curtain to see a doctor standing outside. She unlocked the door and opened it.

"Good evening, ma'am. I'm sorry to bother you." He stepped in and removed his hat.

"Oh, you're no bother at all."

"I'm looking for a Mrs. Anna Charvet."

"Yes, that's me."

The doctor cleared his throat. "Well, the doctor over there in Cherry Creek took sick, so I've been mighty busy taking care of his patients. That's why I didn't have a chance to come by sooner. But now he's fine, and I can get back to my own patients." He pointed with his thumb at the door. "I looked for you at the hotel, and they said I could find you here."

"Please, sit down," she said.

The doctor took a seat. "There are a few questions that my apprentice didn't think to ask."

She raised her brow, wondering what they could be.

He asked his questions, and though they were quite personal, she answered him honestly, especially if it meant they'd provide answers to her illness. She also slowly realized where he might be leading. "What is it, doctor?" Anna's cheeks flamed, thinking she might already know the answer, but had to be sure.

"You're with child."

"A whole week," Anna muttered as she hung her dress in the wardrobe. How much longer could she stand to keep this secret from White Eagle? This was the longest week she'd ever experienced in her life.

Thankfully, the sick sensations hadn't bothered her today. The doctor had said nausea was normal for someone with child.

With child! How could that be? Well, she knew how. She remembered asking Beth questions and how Beth had laughed at her naivety, but she had answered. Anna just didn't realize it could happen from the first time ever being with her husband. She knew very little about such matters. She should have guessed since she had been quite late for her menstrual cycle, but really, it never occurred to her. She just assumed it had to do with the ailments she suffered. How right she had been.

She slipped into her nightdress and caught a glimpse of herself in the full-length mirror. Turning to the side, she pressed her gown against her body. Just a tiny paunch, only noticeable to herself and invisible to others.

She shuffled over to the basin and splashed water on her face. She had to tell White Eagle. But if she did, that meant he'd take her away. She'd have to say goodbye to Denver. And she still hadn't found what she came for. Maybe she'd never find it.

What are your dreams, Anna?

White Eagle's words echoed in her mind.

What were her dreams anyway? She thought it was Denver. But now she doubted.

After drying her face, she climbed into bed. As she leaned over to put out the lantern, she remembered her parents' photographs. Why hadn't White Eagle returned them? He knew how important they were to her. She should ask him tomorrow where they were. But if she went to him tomorrow, she'd have to tell him about the baby. No, she couldn't go to him tomorrow. At least not until she'd found what she was looking for.

The next morning she woke up weak and tired. After getting dressed and ready for work, she hurried from her room down the hall.

"What's the rush?" Mrs. Peterson called.

Anna stepped back and peered into the small kitchen that boasted a nice wood-burning stove and small table set for breakfast near the far window. "I'm going down to work," she said.

"It's Saturday, dear. My husband decided long ago that we would close the shop on Saturdays, and I've been very happy with that rule." She flashed a big grin. "So, you don't have to work today."

"Oh." Now what would she do? Work was the only thing that kept her mind off of White Eagle. "Well, I can work some more."

"Anna, I admire your enthusiasm, but you're working yourself to death." Mrs. Peterson dried her hands on her apron. "Look at yourself. You've got circles under your eyes. It's time for you to take a day off. You've earned it. Besides, I have wonderful news! Mr. Dubois has arranged for a party tonight in celebration of Jean-Marc's heroism." She stepped closer as if imparting a secret. "From what I've heard from Mr. Dubois, it was like pulling teeth, trying to get Mr. Charvet to agree to the party." Mrs. Peterson giggled.

The last thing Anna needed was to go to some party, especially if White Eagle would be there. "I don't have anything to wear." That would be a good excuse not to attend.

"Oh, yes you do." Mrs. Peterson removed her apron, her eyes light and merry. "There's something for you downstairs." She winked.

Anna followed Mrs. Peterson downstairs to the shop. A garment bag hung from one of the high hooks. Mrs. Peterson opened the bag and pulled out a mass of royal blue silk. Pearled buttons lined the back of the dress, and a sheer string of white lace barely showed itself above the collar. Its cuffs and hem were embroidered with dark blue flowers. It was the most beautiful gown Anna had ever seen.

"This is for you, my dear. You'll be the most beautiful woman there."

Anna's breath caught in her throat. This dress was for her? How could Mrs. Peterson afford such a thing? It was just as lovely as those gowns she'd seen in the Mode de Paris shop. "I've never owned anything so beautiful in my life."

"Well, now you do." Mrs. Peterson smiled.

"Thank you." The words barely made it past her lips.

"Oh, don't thank me, dear." She winked and turned to go upstairs. "We have a big evening awaiting us. Now come, let's enjoy today and later we can make ourselves ready. I have a bustle you can wear. It will fit perfectly with this dress. Grab that hat box—it goes with your gown."

Fancy dresses and ballroom dancing filled Anna's mind. Finally, she would have the opportunity to take part in an elegant party, wearing her own beautiful gown. Anytime her uncle wished to impress new clients, all she'd ever been allowed to do was serve at such functions.

She could almost bring herself to skip up the stairs, but she stopped short when she realized she would have to see White Eagle.

A dread turned in the pit of her stomach. How could she hide this secret to his face?

With all the fuss over getting ready for the party, Anna and Mrs. Peterson were late by the time they arrived at the hotel. The porter welcomed them into the empty lobby, and they shook off the cold as they handed him their cloaks. The sun had been out all day, but the cold evening air went right through Anna's thin gloves and boots.

As the porter escorted them up the stairs, her heart fluttered with every step she took. Would White Eagle be there yet? Would he be happy to see her? It seemed like forever since they'd last spoken.

They neared the top of the stairs, and she held her breath. Her dress fit perfectly, and her hair hung in ringlets over her shoulders and down her back, hopefully all still in place. She felt like a princess going to her first ball.

When the doors opened, bright colors swirling under the beautiful chandeliers spilled in front of them. Dancers turned and glided across the floor, and their gowns reflected in the polished wood. A group of musicians performed at one end of the grand ballroom, and sashes draped from one high window to the other on all sides. Mr. Dubois, in his fashionable frock, whisked Mrs. Peterson away. Her laughter filled the air, as the music, talk, and perfumed scents rushed over Anna.

Holding her breath, she crept into the room, feeling like she didn't belong. Never had she been in a room so grand, not even when serving at one of her uncle's parties. Her gaze darted from one guest to the other, her vision almost blurring in the mass of people. But finally she found White Eagle.

Their eyes met, and her heart leaped in her chest. She moved back near the wall.

He held a glass and watched her, strikingly handsome with his polished shoes, nicely fitted trousers, and dark blue frock coat. His black hair, brought into submission and bound at his neck, brought to mind his savagery. Their first meeting swam through her mind when she'd seen him standing on the bank with feathers and painted face. Now there he stood like a new penny, clean and shiny, all prim in civilized attire.

He set his glass down on a nearby table decked with various foods. With his gaze trained on hers, he strode toward her.

As he neared, her heart quickened. She recalled the last party they'd attended at his village. He'd danced, and she'd watched him move to the rhythm of the drums. His moccasins and clothes had flourished in the moonlight, but now, his sure stride was smooth and gentleman-like.

"May I have this dance?" He took her hand in his and kissed her fingers. His gentle touch burned hot when she spotted her wedding ring pushed down on his pinkie.

The ring. She'd completely forgotten about the ring. To think, she threw it at him.

She nodded, unable to speak. His very presence made every part of her go weak, including her tongue.

He placed her hand on his elbow and led her amongst the dancing guests.

"It's been a long time since I've danced," she said. "I'm sure I've forgotten how."

"I'll keep it simple," he said. "I'm not very good at it myself."

He whisked her across the floor, and the other guests watched them. Mrs. Peterson flashed a smile and winked.

He grinned and nodded then gazed at Anna. "You look beautiful, *tsevestoemose*." As always, he said the word in Cheyenne.

"I know what you're calling me, White Eagle. *Wife*."

"Aaahhh, to hear you say it just confirms that I'm right." He grinned. "After this week, I began to wonder."

Those blue-green eyes she'd longed to see. She had no idea how much she had missed him until now. Excitement and intrigue radiated from his presence.

"What do you mean?" she said, trying to force her mind back to the conversation.

"Word has it that my new wife is having an affair with a certain Hervé Dubois."

She felt the blood drain from her face. "That woman from the dress shop. She's nothing but a slanderer," she said, more to herself than to him.

"And what have you been telling the women at the dress shop?" He arched his brow.

"Noting." She swallowed.

"Noting?"

"No*th*ing."

"Hmm. There's a lot of gossip going around for someone who has supposedly said no*th*ing."

"She was being rude." Anna stared at his silk shirt, avoiding his gaze. "I wanted to buy a new dress and she scoffed at me, practically kicked me out of her 'high-class' store. She was quite insulting." She recalled all the cruel things the woman had said, especially about him. "She's not a kind woman at all."

"And you thought if you told them you were my wife that they would treat you better?"

"I—well, yes." She looked up at him again.

He smiled. "Well, I didn't hear the gossip from the woman at the fancy dress shop." He placed emphasis on the word "fancy" as though he were amused. "I heard it from

Hervé who had heard it from some woman at a cafe."

The heat in the room became so great Anna wished for a fan. Amazing how fast gossip traveled in such a large town.

His boyish grin made Anna smile. Oh, how she missed him. "So, where have you been?"

He arched a brow. "You've missed me?"

"Well, I . . ." She dropped her gaze to his silk shirt again.

"You said you needed time."

Time. Yes, she did say that. But all she could do during that so-called time was think of him.

"I simply gave you what you wanted. And it wasn't easy," he added in a low tone.

They spun on the dance floor. He'd been respectful of her wishes.

When he relaxed his hold, she eased away and noticed his eyes graze over her. "The dress suits you," he said. "Blue is definitely your color. I chose well."

"What do you mean? Mrs. Peterson gave me this dress."

"I doubt she said that."

"Well, no, actually she didn't, but I just assumed—"

"You assume much, Morning Sun. The gown is my gift."

Her gaze fell on the colors of his silk tie and the deep blue flowers embroidered on his vest and noticed how perfectly they matched her dress. "Thank you. Really, you shouldn't have."

"It's my pleasure. There are a lot more where that came from. Come home to me and you can have all the gowns you want."

Arguing with him now would be useless, so she would change the subject. Besides, how could she explain that she still hadn't found what she was looking for?

"I've been meaning to speak with you," she said, clearing her throat, "about those Batland Boys." She took a deep breath, still trying to bring her mind to the subject at hand.

He frowned.

"I know you're not a thief, and I know you did what you had to do to save my life. Forgive me for ever thinking the worst," she said. "I read what you did in the newspapers. It said that one of those men killed your father." She kept her voice low. "You rode with them for the marshal just so you could capture those horrible men. And they were the ones that robbed the stagecoach I was on."

He nodded.

"I could have gotten you killed. I had no idea . . . . Why didn't you tell me what was going on while we were still at Mountain Jack's?"

His faced darkened. "Why did you leave Jack's place?"

She blinked, hoping to mask her guilt. "It was Jack's idea."

"Hmm."

Seeing in his expression that he didn't believe her, she realized he knew the truth and that she'd planned on leaving on her own. "You were gone so long, I thought you'd abandoned me."

"I had no choice." He frowned. "I told you to wait. I thought white women were supposed to obey their husbands."

His words burned. She pulled away, but he held onto her. "I liked you better as a savage," she said.

White Eagle's eyes flashed. "If I was savage," he whispered, his voice tense and cutting the air between them, "we wouldn't be here right now, all dressed up in these fine clothes." He flicked the lace at her collar.

Anna stepped back, but he pulled her close.

"Do you even know what that means?" His body tensed. "*Savage?*" He bent closer, moving inches from her face. "Savage is murdering innocent women and children. Savage is cutting a baby out of his mother's womb."

She gasped, her hand going to her abdomen. "Please. I never meant—"

"*That* is savage." His jaw pulsed, obviously working to contain his anger. "Mind your words."

They continued dancing, and she followed in numbed silence. She knew he referred to Sand Creek. She hadn't thought about her words hurting him, not that deeply. After all, everyone used those words. But that didn't make them right. Shame swept through her.

"Forgive me," she whispered.

"You have a good heart, Morning Sun."

"Then why did you say those things?" As if she were to blame for what happened. She had no idea women were cut open. She looked away from him. His words were enough to give her nightmares as horrifying images flashed through her mind. She'd longed to peer into his thoughts, to understand him. Finally, he'd opened a window for her to look inside and she didn't like what she saw.

"You need to respect my people."

"I do." She loved Song Bird and Runs With Wind. They were family to her, the only family she knew, and she missed them dearly. More importantly, she loved him. "I want you. I just need time," she said, her throat tightening, still unsure what she'd expected to find. This was home. She was supposed to feel like she'd come home. But where was that satisfaction, that contentment she'd been so desperate to find?

"No." White Eagle stopped and looked down at her, his gaze filled with remorse. "You don't want me."

Stunned by his words, she stepped back. Though he hadn't shouted them, his words reverberated in her mind. She couldn't dance anymore. He led her near the door where few people stood.

She studied his face. She saw hurt. Pain.

Was she the cause of his suffering? But how could she be? She hadn't done those horrible things to his people. Uneasy, she moved toward the banister near the stairs.

He just stood there, watching.

She backed away carefully, nearing the first step, refusing to take her eyes off him.

All of his words echoed in her mind. Savage, babies being ripped from their mother's womb, respect for his culture, his people, and it was *she* who didn't want *him*.

Her foot slipped, and she lost her balance. Her hands reached for the wooden rail.

White Eagle caught her by the arm and swung her up to the platform. "Are you hurt?" he asked, his eyes wide with concern.

She shook her head, thinking of what might have happened to their baby had she fallen. To think, he had no idea he'd just saved not only her, but his child. She had to tell him. She opened her mouth to speak.

"I have something for you." White Eagle smiled and led Anna down the stairs to the hotel lobby.

A wrapped package sat on a table, and next to a chair was a pair of furry boots.

He plucked up the boots. "For you."

She rubbed her hand along the soft fur. Its leather ties fell between her fingers. They would come as high as her knees.

"It's rabbit, but the insides are layered with buffalo skin for extra warmth."

He then pulled something from the chair. A muff to match the boots.

"Oh, White Eagle, they're beautiful." Finally, her feet and hands wouldn't freeze in this cold weather.

Before she could thank him, he held out a package. She set the boots and muff down and took the gift, wondering what it could be.

As she opened it, she saw the familiar faces of her father and mother looking back at her. They were placed in a double, hand carved frame. The carvings bore the same flowered patterns as the hair clip he'd made for her those many months ago. They were beautiful.

"You made this." She brushed her fingers along the carved designs. "The dress, the boots and muff all came from you, and now my pictures . . ." He'd been thinking of her all this time.

He lifted her chin. "I'm sorry for breaking your pictures. I know how much they meant to you." He brushed his thumb over her cheek.

"They mean so much more to me now." Her voice was a mere whisper. "Thank you."

He then lifted something from off the seat of the chair. It was her mother's Bible.

"How did you—where did you—?"

"You never missed it." He frowned.

Guilt consumed her as she took the book into her hands. "You've been reading it." All those times she found her Bible outside of her carpetbag, it had been him. He'd been reading it.

"There's a story about a man and a big fish. It made me think of you." His gaze softened with amusement.

"How so?"

"He ran away."

She frowned, not sure she wanted to hear what he had to say. "Where is Jack?" she asked, changing the subject.

"He went home."

"Without saying goodbye?"

White Eagle shrugged. "That's Jack." He moved closer to her. "As I was saying,

Jonah thought he could run away from God," White Eagle said. "He thought he could hide from *Ma'heo'o*. But even after the big fish swallowed him, *Ma'heo'o* was there." White Eagle continued to stare at her, but suddenly the amusement in his eyes vanished and they narrowed as if at that very moment he realized something. "*Ma'heo'o* heard Jonah's cries from the belly of a fish. As stubborn as he was, Jonah was never alone." White Eagle watched her, as if searching deep inside her, then he whispered, "I think when he ran away, he must have forgotten what *Ma'heo'o* was like, forgotten that He'd always be there—no matter where Jonah went—waiting for him to return." She sensed he said those words not just to her, but also to himself.

Anna gazed wonderingly at White Eagle. Here she thought she'd married a heathen, and now he was teaching her, helping her to understand her own faith.

"How do you do it?"

"Do what?" He straightened.

"I pray and pray. I want to be close to God too."

White Eagle's brows furrowed. "Read His word. No relationship can survive on a one-sided conversation."

Anna opened her mouth to speak, but then she closed it. Slowly, she nodded. "Of course." She hugged her Bible.

"'Draw near to Him and He'll draw near to you.' That's what He says." He took her hand in his. "I want you to wear this." He placed the wedding ring back on her finger, and his large hands lingered over hers.

Words wouldn't come. Even if she wished to speak, she knew she couldn't. Tears threatened to fall as she gazed up into his loving eyes. Only God could turn this horrible situation into something right. And that's exactly what He'd done.

White Eagle gently cupped her face in his callused hands. He bent down, and she stood on her toes to meet him. His lips touched hers, softly, tenderly.

The room spun from his gentle kiss.

He then held her away and gazed down at her. "I will wait as long as it takes. But know this." His jaw ticked. "You are mine."

Chapter 25

Later that week, Anna worked late with Mrs. Peterson on a large sewing project, trying to keep her mind off of what a horrible person she was. She'd pricked her fingers three times already, and it was all she could do to keep from getting blood on the fabric.

Maybe White Eagle's words were true? Maybe she wanted Denver more than him?

What happened? She felt lost. Not like she'd come home at all. Something had to happen, and soon. How much longer could she put off telling White Eagle about their baby?

"You know," Mrs. Peterson said, watching Anna from the other side of the shop as she worked. "I was reading the Scriptures and came across the story of Jesus when he walked on the water." Mrs. Peterson let her hands rest on the fabric, and Anna stopped what she was doing. "Well, Peter wanted to walk on the water to meet Jesus, and he did. But when he saw the wind, he got scared and began to sink.

"It occurred to me that Peter started sinking when he took his focus off Jesus. He allowed the wind to frighten him." She took a deep breath, still gazing at Anna over her spectacles. "I think the wind can be compared to the worries of the world. The trials we face. We start sinking when we lose our focus."

Mrs. Peterson's started working on her project again as her words turned over in Anna's mind. Anna had lost focus all right. She'd been so desperate to get away from her uncle, so focused on his abuse, she'd completely lost focus on God. And now that she'd reached Denver City, she was in a fog.

Anna sighed. "I lost focus a long time ago."

"What makes you say that?"

Anna put down her sewing. "I've been angry at God," she whispered, finally voicing what bothered her the most. Her worst fear. She couldn't help but wonder if her anger ignited God's anger. And if He'd ever be able to forgive her.

Mrs. Peterson set aside her sewing.

"I blamed Him for what happened. Not because He caused it. It's just that I knew He could have stopped it. I knew he could take me away from there if He wanted to."

Mrs. Peterson lifted a questioning brow.

Anna told about her uncle, all the abuse and terrifying nights. She then told about the kidnapping and then before she could stop herself, she told about her marriage to White Eagle and the baby. Before she knew it, she'd told her everything, including her anger with God and her desperation to get to Denver City.

By the time she'd finished, the shock on Mrs. Peterson's face told Anna she'd said too much. But Anna, in her misery, no longer cared. It no longer mattered that she'd overwhelmed her boss with her story. That she might lose her one and only job. Nothing mattered other than being with White Eagle.

"Anna, girl," Mrs. Peterson leaned forward in her chair, concern reflecting from her eyes. "I'm not going to pretend to have all the answers. I can't tell you why you had to go through what you went through with your uncle. But what I do know is we're all living under the curse of the garden."

Anna nodded, completely familiar with the story of Adam and Eve and that she and everybody else in the world were sinners.

"I'm not saying you did something to deserve your uncle's abuse. What he did was wrong, evil." She shook her head in disgust. "And sometimes, the innocent suffer because of another person's bad choices. What we need to do is grow from those experiences. Use them to make ourselves stronger. To help others."

Where had Anna heard those words before? Beth. Beth had said the same exact thing.

"Trials can either build character and faith, or they can break us down and destroy our faith. It's our choice."

Mrs. Peterson came closer and knelt before Anna, taking her hands in her own. Her gentle touch brought Anna so much comfort, tears welled in her eyes. "You became a Christian at such a young age when your father was still alive, you had so little time to grow and learn from him. But now is the time." She squeezed Anna's hands. "God is with you, child. And your anger is not too much for Him to handle. He understands."

Tears streamed down Anna's cheeks. God still loved her despite her anger? He understood her? The thought seemed too good to be true.

Then White Eagle came to her mind. How she'd hurt him.

"But what about White Eagle? I've kept the knowledge of our baby from him. How can he forgive me for that?"

Mrs. Peterson "humphed," then straightened. "Well, that's another story. His father would never have stood for this." Mrs. Peterson shook her head.

"What should I do?"

"Get some rest." Mrs. Peterson patted Anna's hand. "You go lie down and rest, child. Right now you look like a withered leaf. You can talk to Jean-Marc and tell him about the baby in the morning."

"Do you think he'll be angry?" Anna asked, thinking of how she'd kept this secret despite his kindness and all the gifts he'd given her.

"If anything, I think he'll be thrilled. Still, it's better for you to go to him in the morning, when you're well rested." She pinched her lips. "As if he has any right to be angry after what he put you through." Mrs. Peterson took a deep breath and stood. "I think a hot bath would be good for you right now. Why don't I fill up the tub?"

In no time Anna found herself soaking in a small tub in her room. The water's warmth engulfed her. She laid her head back with her hair dangling over the edge of the tub to keep it dry, realizing how right Mrs. Peterson had been. Anna used this quiet time to talk with God. She didn't hold anything back. She told him how she felt about the situation with her uncle, thanked Him for finally getting her out of that situation, and asked Him to forgive her for being angry and blaming Him. After her talk with the Lord, a peace came over her that she hadn't felt since she'd first become a Christian. It was a wonderful feeling, and so freeing. Finally, she was free. Free from captivity.

And that's when she realized it was Satan that had kept her in bondage, not her uncle.

Not White Eagle.

First thing in the morning, Anna would go to White Eagle and tell him about the baby.

⸺◦᚜᚜᚜◦⸺

"How dare you do this to someone so innocent, so young, so naïve!" Mrs. Peterson paced. "I certainly hope your love is sincere after all this!" She faced Jean-Marc, eyes blazing.

Jean-Marc stared in disbelief at the red-faced Mrs. Peterson as she ranted before him in his study.

"To hear you kidnapped that poor girl and *forced* her into marriage. Anna has been nothing but confused and upset from the moment she came to work for me. I expect you to do something about this!"

Mrs. Peterson wrung her hands together and paced. "Anna shouldn't be so upset. It's not good for her and the baby. If your father knew you'd turned to kidnapping an innocent woman, forcing her into marriage and leaving her with child—I'd hate to know what he'd do if he were still alive. He's probably turning in his grave as we speak!"

"Wha . . . what?" Jean-Marc's heart flip-flopped. He stood on wobbly legs. Was he going to be a father? But Anna had never said anything. Why hadn't she told him? Maybe he hadn't heard Mrs. Peterson right. But if he had, that meant Anna had been expecting all this time, and she'd never told him. How long had she known?

"What do you mean 'what?'" Mrs. Peterson pointed at his chest. "Tomorrow, you will march right over there and apologize like you should have done from the beginning."

Why had the truth been withheld from him? Mrs. Peterson, who had no business rummaging in his affairs, knew more than he did. He bent over her. "Did you say she is with child?" His voice was low.

Mrs. Peterson stepped back, her eyes widened. "Well, I . . ." She put her hand to her chest. "Did I say that?"

"You did." Jean-Marc spoke with a light-hearted tone he didn't feel. "And she told you, but she hasn't told me." He strode toward the door. "How long has she known?"

Mrs. Peterson held up her hands to stop him. "I'm not sure how long, but it wasn't my intention to tell you."

Jean-Marc opened the door.

"Don't do anything rash. She'll come to you tomorrow, I'm certain of it."

"She'll come to me now." Jean-Marc marched down the hall toward the lobby. Forget giving her time. Time to chase after invisible dreams. Her time was up. As for free will, she just lost it. She was his wife and carrying his child. He would claim her now, whether she liked it or not. She would come back to his village by force. He'd no longer delay what was meant to be.

"She needs rest. She was completely distraught," Mrs. Peterson called from behind.

He ignored her pleas. Nothing would stop him. He had a wife, and a child on the way.

Somewhere buried beneath his anger, his heart quickened. He would have a family. A family of his own.

After slipping into her white nightdress, Anna brushed through her hair before the full-length mirror. A good night's rest was all she needed, and then she'd go straight to White Eagle no matter the consequences. She owed him the truth.

The door swung open and slammed against the wall. In the mirror's shuddering reflection she saw White Eagle's long form fill the doorway.

"What are you doing here?" She turned to face him.

Eyes flashing, he strode toward her.

She stepped back.

"I tried to stop him, Anna. I didn't mean to tell. I'm so sorry!" Mrs. Peterson's voice came from the hall, gasping for breath. She sagged against the doorway and cast Anna an imploring look.

White Eagle grabbed her, sending hot shivers down her spine. He forced his large hand on her abdomen, covering the little knot that grew there.

"It's true." His voice rasped. "Why didn't you tell me?" His words reverberated off the walls in the little room.

"I—I—" Anna sputtered as she dropped the brush. She didn't know what to say.

He knew. How could he know? Then she glanced at Mrs. Peterson still leaning against the doorjamb, and her words finally cleared in Anna's mind. She gasped. If only she could faint. If only she could die before White Eagle could kill her.

"Leave us." He tossed the words over his shoulder.

Mrs. Peterson quietly slipped away.

A chill went down Anna's spine as she realized that without Mrs. Peterson there, she'd get the full brunt of his reaction.

"Why'd you keep this from me?"

"I was going to tell you. After . . . tomorrow." She wanted to say after she found what she was looking for, but all her former reasoning sounded silly now.

"How long have you known?"

"A . . . well, a couple days." She swallowed hard.

His eyes darkened. "At the dance? You knew then?"

She nodded, slowly lifting her chin then letting it fall. She wanted to explain herself, but the words lodged in her throat as she watched his eyes turn cobalt blue and his face harden in contained fury.

He turned and grabbed her cloak from behind the door. In one sweep he wrapped it over her shoulders. "You're coming with me, *wife*." He swung her up in his arms and carried her to the door.

Numb with shock, she clung to him as he marched with her down the stairs, out of the shop, and kicked the front door closed.

On the way to his hotel she couldn't speak, the lump in her throat had become so thick she could barely breathe.

The porter held the door open when he saw them coming.

Shame swept through her at being seen in such a state. Anna hid her face in White Eagle's neck, and immediately his wonderful leather scent assailed her. If he weren't so angry, sending ice-cold chills running through her limbs, she would have reveled in this moment in his strong arms.

He marched with her up the stairs and down the hall to his room.

Once inside, he set her down on the edge of a large bed, his eyes blazing. His dark hair flowed down his broad back as he turned to slam the door. He then paced from one end of the room to the other.

She waited, quivering hands folded, in silence.

He panted, drawing her attention to the powerful chest beneath his white cotton shirt. His black leather vest hung open, and his belt buckle shimmered at his waist.

He reminded her of a panther, waiting impatiently for its meal. She'd read about one once, and now she wished she'd kept her nose out of all those books. Obviously, he wasn't finished with her yet, and she wondered how much would be left of her once he was through chewing her to bits.

Eyes narrowed, he faced her. "I've let you have Denver City. I've let you have your freedom. Well now it's *gone*, whether you like it or not." He spoke so quickly his accent became more pronounced, and that's when she realized, all this time she'd heard that unusual accent, it had been French.

The fierceness in his stance and dark gaze kept her from uttering a word.

"And don't think I want you now just because you're carrying my child. I know how you think, Morning Sun. And I want it to stop, right now. No more doubts, no more fears." His eyes flashed. "My love for you is like a torch," he said between clenched teeth. "A torch that burns so strong it can't be put out." He bent over her, inches from her face. "It *consumes* me."

A sharp, almost painful tingle shivered from her hairline down her spine.

"You will come back to my village." He straightened. "And *you will be my wife!*"

His words were like a fierce wind. What could she say, how should she respond? She agreed plenty with what he said, but she continued to quake as the speech she'd prepared moments before vanished from memory. She wanted to make things right. To tell him she'd been wrong for running from him, for keeping the knowledge of their baby from him.

"I'll go back with you, White Eagle," she whispered, still reeling from the thunder of his words. "And I'm not going back because you're making me," she said, her voice breaking past her tight throat. "I refuse to be your captive. I'm going back of my own free will . . . because . . . I love you."

He straightened to his full height, lifting his chin in that arrogant Cheyenne tilt she'd come to know so well.

Her gaze dipped from his belt buckle all the way down to his feet, where she had expected to see boots, but in their place were moccasins. No matter what, he would always be Indian, and that thought made her love him even more. The long silence filled the room like a thick fog. Awaiting his response felt like she had to hold her breath for an endless amount of time. She averted her gaze from his feet and stared down at the bearskin rug.

Taking a deep breath, she dared to meet his gaze again. "I should never have planned to leave Jack's on my own, or kept the knowledge of our baby from you. Please, forgive me," she whispered, tears threatening.

He knelt in front of her and seized her shoulders.

She stiffened, preparing herself for a shaking, but he dropped his head and wept.

Stunned by his silent reaction, she clung to him. The power of his emotion swept over her like a wave, the storm of his pain melting into her. She clung to him, stroked him, as tears burned a path down her cheeks.

He truly loved her. She wanted to revel in it, to wrap herself up in it. He'd loved her enough to set her free, despite how much it tortured him. And now, the depth of his love pierced her through.

She'd never doubt him again.

More tears trickled down her cheeks as she kissed his head. She ran her fingers through his hair and toyed with the leather band he always wore behind his ear. Sweeping through his long raven strands, she watched it shine against her white skin.

This was her man, her wild man. And she loved him.

Eyes shimmering and hot, he peered up at her, a hint of a smile touching his lips. "Morning Sun," his voice caught as she ran her fingers over his jaw. "You brought me face to face with my worst enemy."

Her hand stilled.

"I don't mean you, or Chivington, or Denver City for that matter. I mean . . . myself." He took a deep breath, his eyes still intense. "'Walks Alone' should have been my name." He shook his head. "It's as if all these years I've been wandering the plains at night, lost and alone, until your light showed me the way. *Ma'heo'o* brought you to me. You are my morning sun." He kissed her forehead then brushed her eyelids with his trembling fingers. "I thought God was far away from me."

He leaned in closer to her, brushing his knuckles over her cheek. "I'm sorry for what your uncle did. I'm sorry you had to suffer so much. But God's timing was perfect when he brought us together."

"Brought us together?"

"Yes." White Eagle smiled. "There was a reason you left your uncle when you did."

A reason for all that waiting? All Anna knew was that God hadn't answered her prayers soon enough.

"Don't you see? God used you to help me find Him again."

God used her? Beth's words from that day in the woods flooded into her mind. She'd said that God was using Anna to His glory. That there was a reason Anna was there. But in all practicality, Anna hadn't done anything. She didn't reveal her faith to his people, or to him.

"I'm sorry for the pain I've caused. I'm so sorry I hurt you," he whispered.

Their fingers intertwined, her fingers spread wide between his thick ones, and slowly he kissed her.

Dare she believe? Dare she hope? Could God have truly used her? As weak as her faith was, God found a way to use her to help White Eagle. It seemed unreal. But all things were possible with God. So maybe there was a reason God took so long to answer her prayers.

God knew exactly what He was doing. And He used . . . He used White Eagle to help her. To help her understand. To show her that God works all things out for good.

Chapter

"Morning Sun." The voice belonging to the man she loved carried through Anna's dreams. Her neck tingled and her eyes fluttered opened to find White Eagle nuzzling her. She was in his lodge, their lodge, surrounded by buffalo skins and a warm fire burning in its center. Three months had passed since they'd left Denver City, and they were nearing the end of winter in the Rocky Mountains.

"Good morning," he said, his hair brushing over her cheeks. He gazed down at her, eyes glimmering and bringing to mind the clear lake outside the village. She hoped her baby would inherit their blue-green color and his dark lashes—like turquoise set against black velvet.

She lazily twirled a yellow lock of hair between her fingers and held it next to his. "What color hair do you think our baby will have?" she asked, and brushed the dark and light strands over his cheek.

Backing away from her, he chuckled. "I have something for you." He lifted a small chain from beside the bed. A necklace. It matched her wedding ring. "This used to belong to my mother," he said, draping the necklace around her neck. "I want you to have it."

She pushed up on her elbow and looked down at the necklace. She held her ring next to it. Both had a turquoise stone the shape of a sparrow—like his mother's name. "You mean, from the very beginning you had given me something dear to you?"

"You were as much my wife then as you are now." He brushed his knuckles over her cheek. "Rest now. I'll collect the wood."

Touched that he gave her something so valuable, she nodded. "Promise me you'll be back."

"Promise me you won't leave before I get back." He smiled.

"I promise," she said, a grin tugging on her lips.

White Eagle gazed into her eyes. "From the moment I first saw you, I wanted you."

Anna feathered her fingers along White Eagle's jawline. "I'm glad you took me."

"I'd do it again." The determination in his gaze sent shivers down her spine.

Late in the afternoon, Anna twisted her yellow braid as she read her mother's Bible. Caught up in the words, she soaked in the knowledge and closeness of God.

After an hour, she set her Bible down, and the words she just read turned over in her mind. God wanted her to cast all her cares on Him because He cared for her? How amazing was that? She leaned over her swollen belly and picked up some sinew to repair White Eagle's summer moccasins. She ought to share what she just read with Beth. Life at the village was good. She and Beth had so much fun sharing their pregnancies together and learning all the customs of pregnant women and new mothers. Beth had always been an encouragement to Anna. Maybe now, Anna could be an encouragement to her.

She chuckled. Beth probably already knew this verse.

Knowing that God was there with Anna during that difficult time with her uncle reminded her of Jonah. Like White Eagle said, Jonah prayed to God from the depths of the ocean and from inside a fish of all places. To think, God cared enough to listen, even after Jonah ran from Him, even after he'd disobeyed God. And because of Jesus' sacrifice, nothing could keep her from God. Nothing.

Yes, she'd cast all her cares on Him, because He did care. For now on, she would trust in Him.

———◦〰〰〰◦———

Smoke streamed into the crisp air through the top of each lodge. The scent of elk meat wafted over White Eagle as he made his way home. He couldn't wait to be with his Morning Sun.

Anna.

It hardly seemed real that he had a wife and a child on the way. He'd finally have a family.

Shouts and war cries carried on the air. White Eagle turned to see Running Cloud galloping toward him.

"It's Black Bear!" he shouted. Running Cloud reined in. "Do what you must to end this war." He tossed White Eagle a shield and galloped to where gunshots thundered through the air.

White Eagle ran to get his horse. He knew that was Running Cloud's way of giving him permission to kill Black Bear, his only brother.

Mounted, White Eagle arrived amongst the fighting warriors. He had hoped Black Bear had given up, but he had apparently been collecting his own group of braves to come back and fight. Yellow Leaf stood at a distance, waving a blanket. White Eagle blocked a flying arrow with his shield and urged his horse away from the fighters.

Yellow Leaf held the blanket up to him. "This belonged to Running Cloud and Black Bear's mother. I'm too old to fight, but maybe if Black Bear sees this, his heart will soften toward you and his brother."

White Eagle snatched up the blanket and tossed Yellow Leaf a quick nod. It seemed a strange idea. He doubted it would ease the rage in Black Bear. But out of respect for Yellow Leaf, he would try. He wrapped the blanket over his free arm so that it could easily be seen.

"Where's Morning Sun?" he asked Yellow Leaf before wheeling away.

Yellow Leaf shrugged. "In your lodge."

White Eagle cringed. If Black Bear's braves knew she belonged to White Eagle, they'd know where to find her. He had to get to her.

War cries pierced his ears as he neared the battle in the middle of the village. Black Bear's twenty braves against their seventy didn't have a chance, and yet Black Bear kept fighting, hoping to win over more braves from the village to his side. White Eagle's gaze darted from one lodge to the other. Running Cloud's lodge was the only one in flames and White Eagle's was too far away to be seen; he prayed Anna was safe. He dodged another arrow and raced toward the sounds of exploding rifles.

He spotted Running Cloud and Black Bear mounted on their horses and face to face in combat. Their rifles lay on the ground, and they each swung tomahawks. Black Bear wore the headdress of buffalo horns, and red paint covered his face, typical for Black Bear. Black stripes raged down the sides of his face, accentuating the rage in his heart. He threw his tomahawk at Running Cloud and missed. One of Black Bear's warriors raced past the two brothers and tossed a lit torch. Black Bear snatched it out of the air and waved the torch at his brother. All Black Bear had to do was take out Running Cloud and White Eagle, and the other warriors would submit in defeat.

White Eagle dodged the swing of another warrior's tomahawk then grabbed his dagger. He threw it at the warrior. The man fell back, his buffalo headdress toppling as he dropped to the ground.

White Eagle set his heels in his horse's flanks. He charged between Running Cloud and Black Bear. He held the shield between him and the torch. At the same time, he waved the blanket in hopes that Black Bear would spot its colors and patterns and recognize them as his mother's.

White Eagle turned and shouted, "Black Bear! I come in peace." He waved the blanket. "We're all brothers. Let's end this war between us!"

Black Bear's eyes narrowed when he saw the blanket, but quickly he glared at White Eagle. "Yellow Hair must belong to you!"

White Eagle's horse danced in agitation from the tension that radiated from his hot body.

"You never wanted our kind. You are more white than Cheyenne. No white man, or woman, will survive in this village when I am war chief."

Black Bear jerked on the reins, turned, and raced toward White Eagle's lodge. In a cold sweat, White Eagle galloped after him as they approached his home.

Black Bear waved the torch at the lodge. "Today, your woman will die!" He threw the fire.

"No!" White Eagle tossed the blanket and scooped the flaming torch from the air. He snapped it back and released it as he raced past his old friend.

The blanket wrapped around Black Bear, and the flames engulfed him. His horse bucked, throwing him down on his back. Screaming, he wrestled with the cover of flames. The fire burned, sending sick wails and shouts from the thick, smoldering mass.

White Eagle dismounted, unsure how to rescue his friend.

Running Cloud appeared at his side and armed his bow. The arrow flew, and the wails ceased. His face fell, torn in anguish, as he stared at his brother's burning, lifeless form. Slowly, his gaze lifted to White Eagle.

They stared at each other in silence as tendrils of smoke drifted before them.

"His anger destroyed him, not you," Running Cloud finally said, his voice solemn. He stared again at his brother. Finally, he grabbed the reins of Black Bear's horse, let out a whooping cry and raced after the other fighters to reveal the death of their leader.

White Eagle dropped to his knees on the cold hard ground. "Forgive me, Lord." The smoke carried up to his nostrils, threatening to choke him.

⌾

Anna wasn't in White Eagle's lodge.

He desperately searched the entire village for her. He also couldn't find Runs With Wind, Beth, or Song Bird. His search brought back forbidden memories. "God, please don't let this happen again." Finally, he headed toward the trees where several women and children had escaped to safety. But no Morning Sun.

A silver chain, lying in the dirt and snow, caught his eye.

He trudged over to it and knelt down to pick it up. As he drew it over his hand, a turquoise sparrow fell into his palm. His mother's necklace; Anna's necklace. Memories and the pain of Sand Creek jolted through his gut, the burning lodges, the moaning sounds of death, the blood in the snow.

He glanced around. Black Bear's men were gone. A certain dread turned in the pit of his stomach. He squeezed the necklace in his fist.

⌾

Anna had been sewing in the lodge when she remembered her pouch of fake jewels. She'd wanted to surprise Runs With Wind with them, and she'd thought that moment would be a perfect opportunity to give them to her.

She'd put on the thick rabbit boots with buffalo lining that White Eagle had made. After tying her jewel pouch to her waist, she'd slipped on her buffalo cloak and muff and headed outside.

Anna had hurried along, anxious to surprise Runs With Wind, when shouts and gunfire carried into the air from the other side of the village.

Song Bird came around a lodge and stopped. She turned to the awful sounds. "Black Bear!" She faced Anna and pointed to the trees in the distance. "Run!"

Anna ran toward the trees, but with each step she took the gunshots grew louder. She scurried between lodges, and other villagers ran as well.

"Cover your hair!" someone shouted in Cheyenne as she ran by. She had no idea who said those words. If Black Bear saw her blonde hair, he'd try to kill her. She tugged on her hood as she left the lodges behind, but it fell right back off. She jerked on it again, but the hood kept snagging on her necklace. Several women and children ran ahead of her, and she followed their tracks toward the trees. She spotted Beth and Laughs Like A River. Beth faced Anna, and her eyes widened and she screamed.

Horse hooves closed in on Anna's heels. There was no way she could catch up to the others. Her chest hurt from the cold, and her legs became heavy under the weight of her swollen belly. Suddenly, Anna was grabbed under her arms and her feet left the ground. The man dragged her onto his horse. The rider's grip tightened around her, and she couldn't see his face. For a moment, she thought it was White Eagle, until she didn't recognize the scars on his arms, scars that were made into deliberate shapes. She glanced up and saw the painted face of a man who wore a buffalo headdress, a man she didn't recognize.

The horse tore into the trees, passing Beth, Laughs Like A River, and others. Anna struggled.

"Be still, or die!" the man shouted in Cheyenne.

Anna stilled, fearing she might fall off the horse and hurt the baby. Instead, she sent up a silent prayer.

The woods grew dark, and blackness cloaked the trees. Anna squirmed to break free of her captor's grasp, but the heavy buffalo skin made moving impossible.

He urged the horse up a hill, and they raced to higher ground where the snow became less deep. Finally, he tightened the reins, and the horse kept a slow, heavy breathing pace, steam carrying up from his body.

They came to a bare patch of ground where the horse could tread easily. There, the man reined in and, without warning, yanked her down with him. She stumbled, and her footing caught in the thick cloak, pulling her to the ground.

He shoved her back, dropped on top of her and wrestled with her cloak.

She tried to scream, but he forced his hand over her mouth.

His silence terrified her.

The exhausted horse spooked and disappeared into the darkness. Something had to be very wrong since it was desperate for rest but still took to the trees.

She tried to warn the man, but he kept his hand pressed against her mouth.

A low growl and a screeching cry filled the wilderness as the man flew off her. The outline of a large cat landed on top of him.

The man's shrieks carried up through the trees.

Filled with terror, Anna froze, studying the dark trees and the movement of fur beside her. Dare she move? Suppose the lion turned on her?

White Eagle's words played in her mind. Since the horse spooked, and the man had been right on top of her, it must have thought they were one animal.

Anna knew she had to get out of there. But how? She thought back to White Eagle, how he jumped at that cat, scaring it away. She just couldn't act scared—but she couldn't act foolish, either. Somehow she had to make herself big, intimidating. Before she could talk herself out of it, she scrambled to her feet, screamed, and waved her arms.

The cat hissed, and jumped back, cowering to the ground, but not taking its glowing eyes off her. Scared to death the cat might spring, she screamed harder and waved her cloak more vigorously.

The cat crouched down, watching her, and slowly inched back.

What else should she do? She'd hoped it'd run away like the cat had done with White Eagle. Quickly, she whipped off her cloak and waved it over her head. This way she looked much larger, like a giant beast. It backed away growling.

The man moaned, and the animal's gaze darted to him and then to her. It fled into the trees.

Relieved, she dropped to her knees at the man's bleeding side.

His trembling hand reached up for her, so she crawled closer. He seized her by the neck. Grabbing his wrist, she reared up on her feet and kicked him in his side. He released his grasp, and she fell back. Even with him half dead she wasn't safe. She crawled to her feet, looking around for another threat.

A chill shuddered over her spine, so she grabbed her cloak and whipped it back on.

The man groaned. His revolver caught her eye, obviously taken from a white man.

Slowly, she crouched down and reached for it. He caught her wrist in a steel-like grip, his bloody fingers biting her skin. She couldn't break away and reached for the Navy Colt, freeing it of its holster. Screaming, she pounded his arm with the revolver. He loosened his grasp, and she scrambled out of reach, her wrist throbbing in pain.

White Eagle's explanations of how to work the revolver flashed through her mind. She cocked the gun, aimed it at an angle in the sky, and fired one shot. The trees shuddered from the blast, and snow floated to the ground.

At least the shot would help frighten the cat, but she had to find the horse. There was no way she'd get out of the woods on foot in the deep trenches of snow.

She scrambled to where the horse had been, looking for tracks in the dim light of the moon. Spotting some, she hurried in that direction, holding the revolver up, ready to shoot anything or anyone that dared approach.

Her feet sank deeper as she came to an incline, making her all the more grateful for the knee-high boots. Thankfully her feet stayed warm, though her hands and fingers became stiff in the biting cold. She had no idea what became of her muff.

The horse whinnied.

She wheeled to the sound, and he spooked, only to become caught by his tethers in a nearby tree. Speaking softly and hoping to calm the animal, she trudged to the beast. She watched for the cat, but he wasn't anywhere that she could see. She stood on a high rock, pulled herself onto the horse's back, and yanked on his tethers.

Once he was free, she forced her heels into the animal, but before she came in contact with his flanks, he galloped through the woods.

The revolver flew out of her hand, and she nearly lost her grip on the reins as the horse flew between the trees. She imagined running into a low branch and getting knocked off and left for dead or buried alive in a snow bank, so she leaned down toward the animal's neck, grasping its mane.

He galloped faster.

They ran until the horse foamed and spit. Regaining control, she finally reined the animal in.

Its breath filled the cold air with mist, and the eerie silence engulfed her. They moved between the trees, and dark shadows cast by the moon's light spilled onto the white snow. All was quiet but the horse's hooves and his heavy breathing as they trudged through the white powder between the thick trunks.

Thankfully, the light of the moon illuminated bright patches on the path before them. A chill tingled from her neck to her spine, and she urged the animal forward, having no idea which way to go.

What had become of the village? What had become of Beth and White Eagle? What would become of her?

Chapter 27

The woods thickened, and blackness engulfed Anna. She could barely see her hand before her face and wondered how the horse knew where to go. She had to find an opening through the trees so she could at least be guided by the moon's light.

The cold made her shiver. Now she was more than grateful for the buffalo cloak, not to mention the boots. By the high, weary steps of the horse, she could tell the snow was deep.

An owl hooted in the distance, sending a cold chill down her spine. They had to get out of these dense woods, but she had no sense of direction and just urged the horse forward.

After what seemed like hours, she spotted a blue, misty glow through an opening in the trees. She steered the horse toward it, thankful for the riding experience she'd gained with White Eagle.

Low branches brushed along her shoulders and caught in her hair. She tore free and pulled the hood of her furry cloak over her head. Silence hung on the night air. Every so often the sound of a branch above would crack under the weight of snow, while the smell of pine intoxicated her senses.

Finally the horse came to an opening in the trees, and the field before her stretched out like a quilt with glowing patchworks of white. The horse found better footing and picked up his pace.

Exhaustion threatened to overcome her, and she knew the horse was tired, but fear kept her holding on tightly. What if she stopped to rest and a wild animal attacked her or the horse?

White Eagle was glad he had brought his fire horn. When he'd found Beth and Laughs Like A River, they told him in what direction the warrior had taken Anna. They'd described the brave as having a black slash of paint through his buffalo headdress. White Eagle and Running Cloud had formed a search party and broken off in several directions.

Now alone, White Eagle held the lit torch over the ground and spotted bloodied clothes, the clothes of a Cheyenne warrior with a buffalo headdress, a headdress with a slash of black paint. An ice-cold chill cut through his veins as he listened to the night sounds. Nothing, other than the hooting of an owl, but that was a good sign. It meant danger was no longer near.

He dismounted and examined the body. One of Black Bear's braves. But where was Anna?

A mass of tracks led away from the body: tracks of a horse, a cougar heading in the opposite direction, and—his heart thundered in his chest—and of boots. Anna's boots. She must have escaped. He mounted his horse and followed the remaining tracks. They led to the single tracks of a horse, and it had been galloping. He kept his eyes open for any signs that she might have fallen.

"Anna!" he called, his voice sounding hollow as it carried off the trees.

<hr/>

Anna ran the horse as far as she dared. He panted, and his coat was soaked. For as long as possible, she stayed in well-lit areas, but before she knew it, they came to a patch of dark woods. Afraid she might run the horse to death, she slowed his pace. If she stopped to let the animal rest, would he freeze under his wet coat? She knew so little about horses and felt sorry for the animal.

The rushing of a river sounded in the distance. As they drew near, the beast went from a lope to a trot. He must have been thirsty, so she kept the reins loose, allowing the horse to go at his own pace.

The moonlight glowed on the snow in the trees, and she couldn't help but wonder at its untouched beauty. She also hoped that if they followed the river, they might eventually come to a town, or maybe the village.

As they neared the edge of the woods, the sounds of the river became louder. The horse's body suddenly dipped forward. He whinnied and bucked his head, but they kept falling and sliding down a steep incline. Fear seized her when her feet touched the ground. In desperation, she reached for a better grip on the reins, but they slid faster, knocking her backward off the saddle and against the horse's rear. He might somersault, so she rolled off to the side and reached for a bush, a rock, anything to keep from falling. Her fingers clamped the branches of a small tree, and she jerked to a stop, but to her dismay the horse kept falling, faster and faster, squealing and whinnying the whole way down. Just as she'd thought, she saw his form somersault, and he hit the bottom of the incline on the banks of a small river.

Anna froze, hanging on to the shrub. The rocks and cold seeped through her thick cloak as she listened to the silence. Only the rushing sounds of the river below and her own breathing filled her ears. She had to see to the horse, so she secured her feet on a rock and, careful not to trip over her buffalo cloak, worked her way down the hill.

The horse lay on his side, breathing so hard it brought to mind a locomotive as it slowed on the tracks. She ran her hands along the wet beast, feeling for wounds. When she couldn't find any, she tugged on his reins and tried to pull him to his feet, but he wouldn't budge.

The animal whinnied.

She knelt by his side and searched again for any wounds.

His body twitched as the moisture dampened her palms and cloak.

What had she done? She'd killed the horse. She wiped away her tears and rested her cheek against the horse's head.

"I'm so sorry. So sorry," she said as she petted his nose.

His breathing labored, and the moon lit the outline of his weary face.

As long as she heard his breathing, she stayed there. It brought to mind the day in the hall when she waited to see her father, to hear that he was dying. The ticking of the clock brought her closer and closer to that fateful moment of her father's death. And now she waited as each breath brought the horse, and possibly even her, closer to death. She kept rubbing the horse's wet nose and neck, reassuring him with calm words, just like she remembered White Eagle doing the day he had to put down his horse. The animal's breathing slowed, and became slower, until finally it stopped.

Tears choked her, and she hugged the animal. There was nothing more she could do.

When the salty smell of the horse permeated her cloak, she pushed herself up. She had to leave him behind.

She couldn't stay there, she had to find help, so she tucked her hands under her arms and decided to head down river, hoping it might lead her to a town. But her toes were cold, despite the warm boots, and her fingers were stiff. She'd never felt so alone. She'd always had White Eagle to take care of her in the wilderness, but now he wasn't there. What was she to do? With the horse gone, the loneliness suffocated her. With each step she took, loneliness closed in. What if the river didn't lead to a town? What if she never found the village? What if a wild animal came and attacked her?

With the Lord, you're never alone. Beth's words carried through Anna's mind.

"Lord, help me. Please help me," Anna whispered into the darkness. "I realize Your timing isn't always mine, but I'm sure You'd agree that a quick rescue would be beneficial in this case."

The riverbank narrowed, and she found herself facing a small cliff protruding over the water. She'd have to climb the bank to get around. Shadows lurked in all directions, and at this point, they were everywhere. One might move, and another might jump out at her. Her hand flew to her mouth. She had to calm down. Her imagination would get the better of her before the elements or animals would. With heavy legs, she climbed over the rocky edge, dragging herself over its rough slope. At one point her foot slipped, but she secured it against the trunk of a small tree. She rested there until she could catch her breath, holding on with cold, numb hands. Taking a deep breath, she pulled herself upwards.

With one last pull, she finally reached the top. Her limbs felt heavy, and her abdomen tightened. She rested there for a while, waiting for the pain to go away and worrying that she'd strained herself too much. The sounds of the river filled the darkness. The rushing water was the only sign of life and calmed her nerves. She decided to continue her journey along the river. With renewed strength, she pushed up and hugged herself, trying to hold in the warmth and keep it from escaping.

After what felt like hours of trudging through pine and lumber, her legs wobbled from exhaustion. She had to rest. She remembered how White Eagle would gather pine needles in a pile for her to sleep on. Funny how something like a bed of pine needles sounded so inviting right now.

At the base of a large tree, she used a thick stick and dug through the snow. The exercise of shoveling warmed her arms after being so stiff. Beneath the snow's cold crust lay a thick layer of needles. She pushed the snow away with her boots. Exhausted, she curled up into her cloak on the cold, soft bed.

She must have slept a while because when she awoke her arm was sore, though it was still dark. She shifted her weight and just began to doze off when a vague sweet odor filled the air. What was it? She listened. The crackling of branches under the weight of the snow was all she could hear. Every so often, small gusts of wind blew through the pines and took the smell with it.

Hopelessness swallowed her as she thought of her circumstances, alone and lost in the wilderness. How would she survive? There was no hope of being saved. At least when she left her uncle's house, she could see the ray of hope and run to it. But now, there was no ray. There was no hope. She would freeze out here. She would die.

If only she were at the village or in White Eagle's arms. She'd be safe, comforted, happy.

But now she was alone.

Completely alone.

But no.

She wasn't alone. God was with her.

Anna realized the danger she now faced, but a calmness replaced that strangling sense of fear. Tears flowed steadily down her cheeks as her thoughts drifted to the scriptures she'd recently read.

She had never been alone throughout all of this, just like White Eagle had taught her about Jonah and the fish, how God had been with Jonah even in the depths of the sea. Had she been as blind to God's love as she'd been to White Eagle's? Running from God in search of a dream, only to finally realize it was to Him she needed to run?

She wouldn't give up. Somehow God would find a way to work this all out for good. She drew on the strength of the Lord and put her trust in Him. No matter what happened, He was with her. He never promised there wouldn't be problems, but she didn't have to face them alone.

Soon the smell faded, and she began to drift off to younger days back in Amsterdam when she'd curl up on her papa's lap. She'd rest against his chest and listen to the sounds of his breathing, just like now, the sounds of the wind whispering through the pines, swaying and rocking, taking the cold with it—as though she'd curled up on God's lap.

Daylight broke, and an unusual light flickered against Anna's closed lids. She opened her eyes and the strong sun reflected off something shiny. She stretched her aching body and pushed up from her surprisingly warm bed of needles. As the glare came into focus, she spotted her pouch of paste jewelry lying open next to her. She'd completely forgotten about them. Anna slipped the stone back into the pouch and began tying it shut when the smell from the night assailed her, the edge of sweetness turned sour. The stench was enough to make her stomach roil. She got to her feet and followed the direction of the horrific odor. It led to the other side of the tree.

On the ground lay the half-eaten carcass of a deer.

Anna stumbled back, tripping over her thick cloak. Her gaze darted in every direction, looking for the creature that left his meal behind. Not wanting to be there when it returned, she scrambled to her feet and ran as fast as she could, praying for speed.

She raced along the river and past the bluff, trying not to stumble. Her stomach growled from hunger, but stopping wasn't an option. She had to get as far away from the dead animal as possible. The shallow depths of snow made it easy to run as she hurried along the edge of the river, leaping over pinecones, rocks, and dead branches.

Finally when she could run no more, and she felt somewhat reassured that enough distance separated her and the carcass, she stopped to catch her breath. What in the world had killed that deer? What kind of animal would do such a thing? Thinking about it made the small hairs on her arms and neck stand on end.

She imagined a wild animal, a mountain lion, coming after her. There was no way she could outrun the beast. Tears filled her eyes, and she fought the urge to scream. Instead, her stomach growled audibly, screaming for her. The sound was so funny, she almost laughed. And the desire to laugh brought her mind to attention.

God was with her. Therefore, no need to panic.

Taking in a deep, reassuring breath, she kicked a stone and continued her trek along the water, wishing she had food. If only she had an arrow, maybe she could catch a fish like White Eagle had done. But then, how would she start a fire? White Eagle always had that handy fire horn strapped over his shoulder. She could just eat the fish raw. She remembered doing that in Amsterdam as a girl when the fishermen returned from sea, although without salt, they wouldn't be as tasty. For that matter, she could just turn back and eat the raw deer. Of course, that was out of the question.

White Eagle. Where was he now? Surely he knew she was missing, assuming he wasn't wounded in the last attack. He had to be well. He had to be alive. The thought made her shudder. It didn't seem possible. They were married. She carried his child. He was definitely alive. She felt it in her heart. But what if she was wrong? She shook the thought from her mind. She prayed he'd find her——she prayed he was all right.

After several hours of following the river along a high bank, she came to a section where the river broadened. Much of the snow was melting, and streams of water ran under the crusts of snow and ice. She followed the river around a bend and was met with a large body of water. The river that was supposed to provide hope, her only guide to civilization, had turned into a swamp. Patches of snow and ice floated along its surface and near the muddy banks, and dead shrubs and pines protruded from its depths.

Dizziness overwhelmed her, and with each step she took, the ground seemed to move. Now what would she do? Her stomach hurt from hunger, her legs felt like boulders, and her belly grew heavier by the moment. Thankfully the sun had been strong, helping to keep her warm. Her toes and hands were no longer stiff from cold, and she even grew hot enough to take off the buffalo cloak.

With no river to follow there was little chance of coming to a town or village. Her empty stomach clenched at the terrifying thought of spending another lonely night in the woods, and she hugged the cloak against her pounding chest.

God was with her, she reminded herself, and she began talking to Him.

Wanting to avoid the slush, she hiked up the bank where she found the snow had melted. A cool breeze swept over her, but not cold enough to be buried again under her buffalo cloak. She would have frozen to death last night had she not had that skin.

After about an hour, she came to a familiar patch of trees, and she wondered if she'd been walking in circles. She walked on, but her heart sank when she found herself standing in her own tracks near the swamp again. Panic snaked over her skin, leaving tingling ripples in its path.

"No!" she cried out in frustration and fear. She was trapped, stranded in the wilderness with nowhere to go. It was hopeless. White Eagle was right. She had no sense of direction. How would she ever get out? How would she survive? Even if she wasn't alone, she wasn't ready to die. "Please! Not yet, Lord." She'd read that He wouldn't give her more than she could handle. Well, now she realized He meant that in the spiritual sense and not the physical. She could die out here. But she'd remain faithful. Faithful to Him. She wouldn't give in to fear and doubt.

Then an idea struck her. She opened the small pouch containing the paste jewelry. If she'd just drop them one by one, she wouldn't walk in circles again.

Poor Runs With Wind would never get her pretty jewelry. She slipped a ring onto a bare branch as she trudged through the sparse forest where the snow had melted into the pine-covered ground. Farther along and feeling certain she was finally going straight, she hung a necklace from another branch.

It wasn't until much later that something caught her eye. A small plant sprouted in the sunlight, just as green and perky as could be. And she recognized it. For the life of her, she couldn't recall its name, but she knew its leaf. She'd dug up several roots of that very plant in the woods with Laughs Like A River and Beth. And it was good for eating.

She flew to the spot, dropped to her knees and dug into the surprisingly soft ground. It was completely alone, with no others like it, basking in the sunlight, as though waiting all along for her to come. "Thank you, Lord!" Her fingers clawed the ground. She needed a root pick, or a stick, anything like what she'd used with the Cheyenne. A dead branch lay just a few feet away. She snatched it up and resumed digging.

White Eagle led the horse behind him through the forest. It'd been next to impossible to track anything in the pitch-black woods, and finally he had to go on foot to get a closer look. As daylight came, he spotted a break in the snow at the top of a ridge.

At the base of the bank, he found a dead horse, and White Eagle froze. He dismounted and scrambled down the ridge, sliding every time he lost his footing.

His pulse raced when he found no sign of Anna under the horse. This was one time he was thankful not to have found her. She'd obviously managed to continue on, but she could be hurt. He had to find her.

Much of the snow had melted, but he checked for more tracks and spotted the familiar boot prints in a large patch of snow farther down the small river.

He hurried back up to his horse. As he followed along the bank, he picked up a trail of tracks that led away from the river. He spotted a lump at the base of a tree and a sour stench wafted over him. He knew that smell. Definitely animal, not human. Rifle in hand, he dismounted and recognized Anna's boot tracks everywhere. He followed them to the other side of the tree. The carcass of a deer. No sign of Anna. Thank *Ma'heo'o!*

The sight sent an urgency through him like none other. He had to find her before a wild animal did. The boot prints had larger spacing between them, leading away from the tree. Perhaps the sight of the deer frightened her and she took off running. By the looks of her tracks, that appeared to be the explanation. The snow was melting. He'd better move on before he lost the trail.

By the time he reached a swamp, he dismounted and checked again for tracks while the horse drank. He spotted her boot prints heading into the forest. He remounted and hurried in that direction. He kept on, only stopping long enough to double-check the tracks.

They ran in all sorts of directions, fading away with the melting snow, but still revealing themselves in the pressed pine and broken branches. When he realized he was going in circles, he wasn't terribly surprised. She never did have a good sense of direction. If only she'd just followed the river back. At least that would have kept her from wandering aimlessly around.

He dismounted and focused on one set of tracks that left grooves in the pine beds. Something shiny from one of the trees caught his eye. Its color was out of place in the wilderness.

He took the ring between his fingers and realized it was Anna's paste jewelry. He grabbed the reins of his horse and led it in the direction of the tracks that led beneath a hanging necklace. This must have been the final direction she took, so he followed the trail of jewels.

As he followed the jewelry he wondered what she'd hoped to accomplish. He could imagine she'd use it to find her way back somewhere, but not for this. Rather than it keeping her from walking in small circles, she'd made one large arc, right back to the same river close to where he'd found the deer carcass. At least it helped him get on the right track. He felt confident that he'd soon find her.

As the sun threatened to dip behind the mountains, the rushing sounds of the river carried to his ears. He thought Anna might have gone there since she'd followed it the last time, but as he hurried, he still kept an eye out for more jewelry, plucking it off trees and shrubs.

When he reached the river, he found himself on a small ridge of boulders. Just below in the distance farther down the river and kneeling by the water was a sight that sent a shower of relief through his system.

Anna.

His Morning Sun, with her buffalo cloak cast aside and wearing her Cheyenne clothing. She rubbed her round belly.

His chest swelled with joy as he watched her by the water. But just as he was about to call out her name, movement in the trees caught his eye not far from where she stood.

A cougar crept toward her.

White Eagle froze.

Any sudden movement could make the lion spring. One strike to the back of the neck and Anna would be dead.

He stared at the cat. Nothing was real anymore. He thought the dreams had ended, but now reality slapped him in the face with a nightmare.

He forced himself to move and grabbed two arrows. His hands felt numb against the bow as he fixed his gaze on the cat.

Smoke, gunshots, bloodied snow all rushed to his mind. He could almost hear the crying of the small child on the banks of Sand Creek. He could see the baby's tears, his fingers in his mouth, his wet cheeks—the face of the baby he'd failed to save.

And now he must save his own wife and child.

He shook his head and focused on the mountain lion as it crept toward Anna. Back then his arrow had missed its mark. But this time his aim would be true. It had to be true. The cat assumed a crouched position. Its tail twitched and its ears stood upright.

White Eagle braced his legs apart and drew the bowstring tight, his muscles tense.

"God help me," he whispered.

The cat laid its ears back, ready to spring.

Like lightning, the arrows sliced through the air.

━━━━◦⫘⊃━━

Splashing water caused Anna to look up. A man. White Eagle. Racing right through the water to meet her. She straightened, crying out.

An urgent look flashed on his face as he caught her in his arms.

She clung to him. "It's you! It's really you!" She cried into his neck, hardly able to believe it was true. He was alive—safe and alive. "You found me. I can't believe you're really here."

His arms tightened around her, and she could feel his trembling as he kissed her head. "My Morning Sun, you're safe." Then, as if to make sure she wasn't harmed, he felt her neck, shoulders and arms, and caressed her abdomen. Seeing that all was well, he cupped her face in his hands and kissed her forehead, then took her in his trembling arms again. "You're safe now, *chérie*."

The sound of his voice and his wonderful accent filled her mind as the warmth of his arms enveloped her. He held her for a long time, nuzzling his face in her hair. Finally, her own trembling began to subside, and she relaxed against him.

"Will you say that again?" she whispered.

He held her away, determination darkening his eyes. "You're safe now."

All at once she giggled between tears.

"What is it?" he asked.

"It's just so good to hear those words."

It was time to head back so she turned toward shore, but he caught her and faced her in another direction.

"My cloak," she said.

He held her shoulders and kissed her. "Let me get it for you." He started toward the buffalo robe but turned and pointed away from him. "Look at that," he said.

She turned. "What?" All she saw was the mountain and water trickling from a small stream along its rocks and bushes.

He scooped her into the robe, her back still to him. "The sky. Isn't it beautiful?"

She didn't recall him pointing upward. Nestling into her cloak, she looked up at the sky. The lowering sun caused the clouds to glow pink. Yes. He was right. Beautiful. She gazed up at him.

He grinned. "This way." He guided her toward shore. "I'll take you home," he said.

His words warmed her heart. She thought of her long journey to fulfill her dream, to find home. She'd been foolish to think home could be found in a city. The strength of his arms sheltered her, and she nestled close.

"I am home."

Acknowledgments

Thank you, Lord, for allowing *Walks Alone* to be published. Thank you to the WhiteFire staff for seeing its value. And thank you to my Wendy flower for editing all the many rewrites on what I call "my practice novel." It was a great learning experience for both of us.

I'd also like to thank Don Vasicek for making the research for this story possible. Thank you for putting me in contact with Chief Laird Cometsevah and for being willing to teach me so much about the Sand Creek Massacre. I never would have known about it had it not been for you.

But most importantly, I'd like to thank Karsten, my wonderful husband, who not only inspired White Eagle's character, but supported me in every way while I wrote this book.

If you enjoyed *Walks Alone*, you may also enjoy these other titles from WhiteFire:

Sahdowed in Silk by Christine Lindsay

She was invisible to those who should have loved her.

"Political unrest, suspense, romance, well-developed characters, and a strong spiritual thread. What more could a reader ask for?" ~LENA NELSON DOOLEY

Dance of the Dandelion by Dina L. Sleiman

Love's quest leads her the world over.

"This richly imagined book is a passionate medieval coming-of-age tale.... It will have you turning pages eagerly." ~ LINORE ROSE BURKARD

Jewel of Persia by Roseanna M. White

How can she love the king of kings without forsaking her Lord of lord?

"This is biblical fiction at its absolute best . . . . You will love this intriguing story of tenderness and nobility, cutthroat suspense and fierce love."
~ SHARLENE MACLAREN

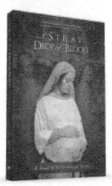

A Stray Drop of Blood by Roseanna M. White

One little drop to soil her garment.
One little drop to cleanse her soul.

"Haunts you centuries beyond the last page."
~JULIE LESSMAN